A SONG OF SIN AND SALVATION

A Song of Sin and Salvation by L.H. Blake

Ebook ISBN: 978-1-7386572-2-3

Paperback ISBN: 978-1-7386572-3-0

Cover Design by Sam Palencia (Ink and Laurel)

Editing by Britt Taylor

Proofreading by Rebecca Prokop

Formatting by Letizia Lorini

To all the girls who were told
they were to blame for the sins of boys,
and to all the boys who showed them
that's bullshit.

Playlist

Eyes of a Stranger - The Payolas
The Antichrist - Slayer
Papa Don't Preach - Madonna
D.O.A. - Van Halen
Don't You Want Me - The Human League
I Wanna Be Somebody - W.A.S.P.
Somebody's Watching Me - Rockwell
California Dreamin - The Beach Boys
Livin' on a Prayer - Bon Jovi
Damage, Inc. - Metallica
Total Eclipse of the Heart - Bonnie Tyler
Take On Me - A-ha
Mother Stands for Comfort - Kate Bush
Owner of a Lonely Heart - Yes
Just Can't Get Enough - Depeche Mode
Danger Zone - Kenny Loggins
Smooth Operator - Sade
Let's Make a Deal - Gloria Gaynor
Parental Guidance - Judas Priest
Like a Virgin - Madonna

Escape - Rupert Holmes
You Give Love a Bad Name - Bon Jovi
Girls Just Want to Have Fun - Cyndi Lauper
Part-Time Lover - Stevie Wonder
Beat It - Michael Jackson
Material Girl - Madonna
Dream On - Aerosmith
Breaking the Rules - ACDC
Your Song - Elton John
I Want to Break Free - Queen
Love is a Battlefield - Pat Benatar
The Evil That Men Do - Iron Maiden
Paranoid - Black Sabbath
Flight of Icarus - Iron Maiden
The Writing on the Wall - Iron Maiden
My Last Words - Megadeath
True Colors - Cyndi Lauper
Runaway - Bon Jovi
Sweet Dreams (Are Made of This) - Eurythmics
In Your Eyes - Peter Gabriel
Somebody to Love - Queen
Walking on Sunshine - Katrina and the Waves
A Lesson in Violence - Exodus
The Sound of Silence - Simon & Garfunkel
For Whom the Bell Tolls - Metallica
Don't Stop Believin - Journey
Hallowed Be Thy Name - Iron Maiden
Tiny Dancer - Elton John

CHAPTER 1

Eyes of a Stranger

REBECCA

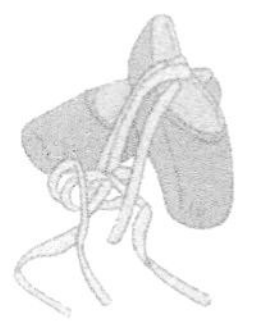

Have confidence in your leaders and submit to their authority, because they keep watch over you as those who must give an account. Do this so that their work will be a joy, not a burden, for that would be of no benefit to you.

Hebrews 13:17

I've always wanted to be like the little ballerina inside the music box. Beautiful, graceful, delicate . . . everything I've ever been told I should aspire to be. So, it never made sense to me why the music she dances to is so sad. It wasn't until I grew up that I realized it's because she's trapped, spinning endlessly in a perfect loop. Never experiencing anything outside of the pink paper walls. She's the picture of perfection to everyone looking in, but she's alone. Now, as I watch her pretty pink tulle tutu spin around and around, I wish I could set her free, because then at least one of us would be.

Today is Saturday. And while it's a wicked thing to think, it's my favorite day of the week. The only day where I have some modicum of freedom to do what I want, go where I wish, and see who I like. And while I *should* meet Mary at the mega mall to see the new *Pretty in Pink* movie, or attempt rollerskating with Amy, I'm forced to wait by the front window at nine in the morning for Eric Corbley to pick me up.

Okay . . . that sounds worse than I mean it to.

Eric Corbley is my boyfriend. Has been since I turned sixteen two years ago and my parents deemed me old enough to finally date someone. In fact, he'll one day be my husband. After college, of course. The perfect Godly union—that's what my mother said—and in the grand scheme of things, I could do a lot worse than Eric Corbley. He's handsome and comes from a good family. He's everything I could want.

I pull on the neck of my cream turtleneck shirt under my knit cardigan and tartan pinafore dress, the fabric itching my skin. Maybe I should change. This isn't a late-March dress, but my mom didn't approve of what I was wearing before and stopped me the moment I stepped into the kitchen, demanding I change and put a cardigan on as well. And, like the dutiful daughter I am, I marched my behind right back up those stairs to change. If it gets hot at the track, I might actually die of heat stroke from wearing this.

I finger the gold chain of the cross around my neck, pulling so the clasp is at the back below my hairline. I perk up a little as a vehicle turns down the road, but it's not Eric's car. In fact, it's a black van—one I've never seen before, and it's headed right for our house.

My heart rate spikes. The windshield is too dark to see through at this distance and most of the windows are blacked out. Is this the van my parents threaten me with? The one to take me away to Mercy Christian Home for Girls where who knows what awful things await. My breathing grows shallow as the van nears, my mind turning desperately over what I could have possibly done to warrant such a punishment. Did my mom find out I peeked at Jeanine Matthews's math homework before class last week? Have I forgotten to put the laundry out on the line? Have my parents somehow found out that Eric put his hands on my breasts last Tuesday?

The van turns just before it reaches my house, pulling into the neighbor's driveway. I swallow hard and sigh with relief, sending a silent prayer to thank God that I'm not being taken away. That I'm *good* and that I'm sorry for peeking at Jeanine's answers.

Another vehicle turns down the street, and I recognize the square body of Eric's Monte Carlo as it gently glides toward my house.

"Bye mom, I'll be home before dinner," I call out to where I'm sure she's sitting in front of the television watching *The Gospel Bill Show* reruns with her sewing machine.

"Did you put a sweater on?" she calls from the back of the house.

Checking my reflection in the mirror, I sigh. "Yes, Mom."

"Okay. Be good, Rebecca," I hear back.

Good. Sure. Because sitting on metal bleachers all morning watching Eric run and toss a javelin and jump over poles is exactly what a good girlfriend would do. I mean, just last night my father made sure to bring up Thessalonians 5:11, "Encourage one another and build each other up, just as in fact you are doing." So that's what I'll do—I'll encourage and cheer on Eric's accomplishments. I just wish he would do the same for me.

I pull my black leather dance bag over my shoulder and head out the door as the car pulls into the driveway. The moment I'm outside, I hear it. Loud, raucous noise blasting out of the black van that turned into the neighbor's. I glance at it as I walk down the steps of our front porch to where Eric is waiting for me.

There's someone still in the van, the shadow of their hands tapping aggressively on the steering wheel to the overly complicated drum beat as the bass vibrates my lungs. I grip the handle of the car door and wrench it open, quickly ducking inside and slamming it shut. Relief washes over me as the noise is muffled by the car door, but even Eric's car windows rattle a little.

"Who's that?" Eric asks. He hasn't even looked at me yet, he's just watching the black van intently out of his window. His light brown hair falls across his forehead and he smells like he always does—*too much cologne*.

I shrug. "No idea. They pulled in just before you did. Maybe Ms. Walton is having something delivered?"

Eric scoffs loudly and glances at me. "Delivering what? A headache?"

I grin and settle back into the seat, pulling the seat belt over my shoulder and buckling in. Eric turns to face me and smiles.

"Hey, babe." He grasps my left hand and brings it to his lips, where he plants a kiss on the top of my knuckles. His eyes linger on my modest chest for a few moments before they flick back up to my face. Somehow I don't think the cardigan is helping today, and I silently pray that looking is all he'll do. "Ready to cheer me on?"

I nod, and he drops my hand before wrapping his around my headrest so he can back out. As we pull away from my house, I glance back at my neighbor's driveway once more and pray I never do anything bad enough to be taken away in a van like that for the rest of my life.

THE TURTLENECK WAS A MISTAKE. I realize that now as sweat trickles down my temples and spine. Thankfully, I wore my hair up in a high ponytail today, but my ribs are killing me. This dress is too tight—they're always too tight, and the fabric doesn't breathe. I told my mom it only *just* fit when she made it for me, yet she insisted on taking it in anyway, assuring me it would help me lose those pesky few pounds she insists I've put on over the last few weeks. And now with the extra layer over top . . .

It doesn't help that I'm sitting. I feel like meat being stuffed into a sausage casing. I've been sitting for hours, bored out of my skull as Eric goes through his track training. I wish I remembered to bring a book, or maybe even my calculus homework. At least then I would have something to do other than fidget with the gold chain around my neck, pulling it around and around until the hook and eye clasp sit at the back of my neck again.

Though Eric made today sound like a super important practice, it's just me sitting alone. My knee bounces absently. All the while he laughs and chats animatedly with his teammates. He's only glanced over once or twice in the two hours since we've been here. Why did he even insist I come? I shake my head, stopping myself. How can I be so selfish? Wishing I were anywhere else is a sinful, self-absorbed pleasure. If it pleases God that I'm here, baking in the heat, then who am I to say otherwise.

As if God hears me, a sudden breeze ruffles the wispy hairs around my face and cools me down, making my eyelids close for a few moments as I enjoy it.

"Not falling asleep on me, are you?"

My eyes open to find Eric standing at the foot of the bleachers. He's smiling, but it's a smile I'm all too familiar with. This is his "I'm actually annoyed with you but there's people around" smile.

"No . . . no, of course not. I was just—"

"Practice is done for today," he says abruptly. "I'm just going to get showered and change then we'll go grab some lunch."

I blink, wishing I could explain that I only closed my eyes for a moment, that I watched the entire practice, that my momentary selfish thoughts were stopped in their tracks, but the words won't come. "Yeah, okay. Sure."

He nods sharply, then turns toward the open back doors of the gymnasium, disappearing inside. I huff loudly and try to cross my arms across my small chest, except the fabric won't budge. I'm stuck. Stuck being annoyed and indignant with my arms tucked down at my sides. On top of all that, the prospect of eating at a restaurant makes my palms sweat. As if I can hear her, I imagine my mother's insistence that my faithfulness to God is also determined by my self-control—particularly around food. Guess I won't be able to eat much at lunch today, either.

AFTER PUSHING some lettuce around on my plate at the diner for half an hour, wistfully staring at Eric stuffing his face with his cheeseburger and fries, he finally drops me off at the best place in the entire world—Ms. Koysh's Dance Academy. This is the main reason Saturdays are my favorite day of the week, because I'm able to go to ballet class, sometimes two in a row if I have the energy.

"What time do you want me to pick you up?" Eric asks as I climb out of the passenger side. I glance at my wristwatch, the white leather band a little loose on my wrist.

"Three fifteen is fine," I say, peering back in through the open door.

He nods. "I'm just going to head over to Jeremiah's for a bit."

My stomach clenches. "Oh."

"Don't worry, babe. I'll be back in time to pick you up."

Jeremiah is horrible. Always getting everyone into trouble—getting them involved in things we know to stay away from, like drugs and alcohol. Eric himself has fallen victim to it a few times and even though he tells me he's repented for those moments of weakness, I have a feeling they're just hollow words.

"Right . . . just be safe, okay?" I say, offering an encouraging smile.

Eric smiles back. "Of course. See you soon."

I take a step back onto the curb and shut the passenger door. Not a moment later, he's gone, like he couldn't get away from me fast enough. As usual, though, when I turn and face the black metal door of the dance studio, all thoughts of Eric fly from my mind. I'm in my happy place.

I quickly change in the studio bathroom, too self-conscious to undress in front of the other ladies in the adult class even though they must all be at least ten years older than me. Once I hit puberty and my chest grew and my hips widened, my mother found the expectations for dress in the competitive ballet classes too revealing. I was pulled out even though Ms. Koysh fought tooth and nail with my parents to keep me, saying I could wear whatever coverage they saw fit. I cried in her arms for over an hour when she told me my mother hadn't changed her mind.

So now I dance in the adult drop-in classes. Thankfully, I can still do pointe work, but it's only one day a week—and no performances. Again, I'm being selfish. Truthfully, I'm grateful for the classes I can attend even if I'm desperate for more. But . . . that's not what God wants for me. I pull on my pink ballet tights and leg warmers, then my black leotard, tying a black skirt around my hips and throwing a cropped pink sweater overtop to cover the minimal amount of cleavage God has bestowed upon me. I wrap my blonde ponytail around in a quick bun and pull a scrunchie over to keep it all in place. My feet slip comfortably into my worn leather ballet slippers, my pointe shoes in a silk drawstring bag on my shoulder, and step onto the sprung hardwood dance floor.

Where some people find comfort in their favorite home-cooked meal, I find it in the scent of the wood polish, the window cleaner, and the subtle smell of sweat and hard work that permeates the studio. I find my usual place at the first barre nearest the piano and face the mirror. The older ladies file in around me, many offering me warm smiles as we take our positions. I plié slowly to stretch out my knees before facing the barre and lifting my legs one at a time, resting my ankles against it, feeling the stretch of my hamstring muscles burn deliciously.

After a few minutes, the pianist—a kind, gray-haired gentleman with an earring named Lindsay—sits down to take his place beside me. I always found his name a bit odd for a man, but he's friendly and always offers me a peppermint at the end of each class. Ms. Koysh enters next, her salt-and-pepper hair pulled back into the most pristine bun I have ever seen in my life. Her posture is utterly regal and while every bit about her at first glance screams arrogant and pretentious, I know better.

"Good afternoon, ladies. Shall we begin with our pliés?"

TWO HOURS LATER, I'm drenched in sweat, sipping gingerly from the water fountain in the hallway. It always feels wonderful to be here. To push and stretch my body in such a graceful way. My toes are burning, but I love dancing on pointe even if my feet look like a mess the entire week afterward. There is something so beautiful about the lines of my body with these magical shoes on —it's like I can fly.

"Miss Briar, you did well today," Ms. Koysh says, appearing beside me.

I wipe the water from my chin and stand up straight to face her. "Oh, thank you. It was a wonderful class."

She grips my arm a little roughly, inspecting me. "You've gained a little weight?"

My heart plummets through the floor. "Oh . . . I—my mother—"

"I'm glad, dear. You were looking unwell the last time I saw you. Keep it on this time, yes?"

I feel my hands clench as I fight the urge to either throw my arms around her for a hug or sob at the knowledge that my lack of faith let me gain visible weight. "I—yes. I'll try."

"Your fouettés improved a lot."

I raise my eyebrows. "Really? All you did was yell at me to make them sharper and faster."

She smirks. "And you listened, didn't you, Rebecca?"

I smile, my heels bouncing with giddiness.

"I'll see you next week?" she asks, pushing back a few stray baby hairs from my sweaty forehead.

"Yes, of course. Thank you."

She pats my cheek gently, then heads back into the studio for the new class to start. There were two moments in class where I felt dizzy today, so it's probably better not to push myself with another class. Besides, I told Eric three fifteen, and it's already five after.

I slip back into my overly tight turtleneck, pinafore dress, and cardigan, leaving my hair up in a bun on top of my head before heading out front . . . to find Eric's not here. I suck on the peppermint Lindsay gave me and check my watch. Three twenty on the nose, so I wait. Five, ten, fifteen minutes. *Where is he?* I wonder, as I sit down on the curb on the side of the street. Another fifteen minutes goes by. My hands fidget as I fight back the anger threatening to bubble up in me. Of course he's late. Stupid Jeremiah. This is probably all his fault. This is exactly why our pastor discourages us from being friends with people outside of our church, Holy Grace. They just don't understand what it means to be a true believer, and they cause those of us who are to stumble on our path. I start to contemplate just how long it might take to walk home from here. Probably hours, and my muscles are already burning, my toes sore.

A horn honks, and the Monte Carlo turns the corner to pull up next to me. Eric leans across the seat to lift the lock and I pull open the door.

"You're late," I say sternly before sliding into the passenger seat.

"Sorry, things got a little crazy at Jer's," he says, turning the radio station back and forth through static.

"I told you three fifteen . . . it's almost four—"

The radio blares to life with some country song and I cringe at the noise level. It's amazing how quickly a person can go from content and relaxed to anxious and irritated.

He turns down the volume a bit. "Let's go, all right?"

"I—"

He pulls out into traffic and doesn't look my way anymore, so I swallow my annoyance and sink back, my knee bouncing against the seat.

I'd be lying if I said this was out of character for Eric, but lying is a sin. He's always been this way and I've known him since we moved here when I was eight. And while I've always tried to do the right thing and look past his shortcomings, it's especially hard today. Today he's being selfish and oblivious, and while he's never been mean or hurtful to me in any obvious way, I feel like an afterthought in his life. That is, until he pulls into the parking lot behind the video rental store and turns off the engine.

"What are we doing here?" I ask.

His hand is on my thigh a moment later, his '86 senior class ring glinting in the light. I freeze. "I thought we could just, you know . . . hang out for a bit. In private."

I blink furiously before pressing my hand to his chest. Are all the layers covering every inch of my skin still not enough to dissuade his temptation? "Eric, I don't think that's a good idea. You know I have to be home before dinner and I'm still kind of sweaty from dance class."

"I don't mind a little sweat . . ." He trails off, sliding across the bench seat toward me. His breath brushes past my cheek with the sickly sweet smell of alcohol.

My eyes widen. "Have you been drinking?"

He laughs sharply. "Just a bit."

I push harder against his chest with my hand. "I knew it was a bad idea for you to go to Jeremiah's place. Is that why you were late to pick me up? You were drinking? And now you're driving me around?"

"Becca, I'm not drunk. I'm perfectly capable of driving safely."

His hand slides down to the hem of my dress, his fingers brushing roughly along my bare skin. It feels as though every muscle in my body tightens at once, then his lips touch my neck.

"No, Eric . . . I don't want to. I'm—I'm not okay with this."

"It was okay on Tuesday," he counters.

Tuesday was such a wonderful day. I aced my history test, got extra credit on my social science paper, and Eric had been kind and doting, bringing me flowers from the corner store at lunch. But even so, when I got home, after coming face to face with the gold cross inside our front door, I nearly fell to my knees to beg for forgiveness that I had let him touch me at all.

"Yeah, well, I'm not in the mood today."

"Oh, come on, Becca," he exclaims as he pulls back, his fingers retreating mercifully from my inner thigh before he scoffs angrily. "I just . . . I want to try something," he complains.

"God sees everything, Eric," I say and turn away. I refuse to be the chewed up piece of gum that Melissa, our youth group leader, insists we'll be if we let a boy touch us before we're married. I try to cross my arms, but once again the tightness of my dress restricts me and so I just clench my fists at my sides. It's quiet for a while until I finally muster the courage to say, "Take me home, please."

Eric is silent for a minute, then he starts the engine and pulls out of the parking lot in the direction of my street. It's not a long drive but it feels like forever as the tension between us builds.

We're two blocks away now. Two blocks until I'll finally be able to breathe again.

"Listen, I'm sorry all right?" Eric says quietly.

I don't reply, fighting the urge to look over at him. He gently grabs my hand, pulling it to his mouth and kissing my fingers gently.

"Seriously, Becca, I'm sorry. About being late and . . . about earlier. You're just so beautiful it's hard to resist you."

My resolve cracks, turning away from the window to look at him. His face is anguished, like he genuinely feels bad for pushing me before. The words I've heard plenty before from Pastor Campbell come back to me. That my clothes and beauty are too much to resist, and it's my fault, not Eric's, for providing such a sinful temptation. But, short of wearing a one-piece snowsuit, how am I supposed to prevent Eric from stumbling? How much more can I do to dissuade him—how much more guilt can I feel, knowing it'll never be enough?

"Okay."

He smiles and kisses my cheek. "God really made me the best girlfriend, you know that?"

I feel the praise soak into me like a sponge. It dulls the twinge of panic at the idea that I'm not living my life for Jesus. That I'm unlovable and unworthy of the fact that God only made me for him. So instead I focus on the things he said today that make me feel good and promise myself that I'll try to do better.

He pulls down my street, just before five o'clock. As we approach my house, my heart rate spikes again as I notice the black van is still parked at the neighbor's. Thankfully, the music has stopped, but it's odd and out of place. Eric eyes it apprehensively as well as he pulls into the driveway.

"I'll see you at church tomorrow."

I nod and grab my bag before pushing myself out of the car. "Good night, Eric."

"Good night, Becca."

I walk up the stone walkway toward our porch and my stomach twists painfully with hunger as I make my way through the front door.

"Rebecca, is that you?" my mom calls.

"Yes, it's me. I'm just going to have a shower then I'll help set the table for dinner."

"Hurry up."

The pictures lining the staircase smile down at me as I trudge upstairs and open the door to my room. I place my dance bag at the foot of my bed and head into the adjoining bathroom. After turning on the shower to warm up, I tear off my sweater and pull on the zipper of my dress, the teeth practically groaning with the effort of staying closed so tightly around my body. I release a sigh as it comes off and I can finally breathe for the first time since I left dance class.

I stare at my reflection, my fingers tracing over the angry red lines on my torso where the seams of my clothes have pressed so tightly into my tender skin. My hand softly rubs over the indents and I blink back the tears that start to prickle behind my eyes. I feel like a tug of war rope—the part in the middle that splits and frays until it finally breaks after being pulled in too many directions for too long by too many powerful forces. Between my mom's constant criticisms of my body, to Ms. Koysh's encouragement to keep the weight on, to Eric's wandering hands, and the ever-present duty to show my devotion to God—it's exhausting.

The water soothes my sore muscles and toes and calms the belly pains so I can make it to dinner. Sometimes, I wish desperately that I could go somewhere near the ocean. I'd float in the water for hours, just to drift weightlessly. The ocean wouldn't care about my five extra pounds.

Stepping out, I quickly dry off and pull my hair down out of its bun to fall around my face. It's a little damp at the nape of my neck and there's a little kink to it from where the elastic held it all together, but it's suitable enough for just an evening at home with my parents. Well, maybe not for my mother, but at least for me.

I pull on a pair of underwear and stare at my mostly naked reflection, wanting to love my body. My breasts are small, my ribs visible beneath the skin and my hip bones are more prominent than I want them to be, but with nothing on I feel free. My skin doesn't feel so tight or so suffocating. I've spent whole evenings like this, in nothing apart from my underwear, doing my homework, or reading my bible, or just lying on my bed, safe in the knowledge that my parents are too busy downstairs to bother me. I feel envious of Eve in the Garden of Eden sometimes. What I would give to just be able to live in the form God made for me.

I flick my bedroom light on, then the radio, the Christian rock station playing some inspirational song as I tidy up the clothes I pulled out earlier and twirl around. I still have a few more minutes of naked bliss before I need to pull something on and help out downstairs.

A more upbeat tempo song comes on and I shimmy around my room. I grab a hairbrush from my dresser and lip sync into it like a microphone in the most dramatic way possible as I imagine myself as Amy Grant.

As I swing my hips from side to side, the hairs on the back of my neck prickle and goosebumps scatter down my arms with the uncomfortable feeling of being watched. I check that my bedroom door is closed—and it is. Then I turn toward the window. My heart rate skyrockets as I spot the figure of a boy . . . no. A young man. He's watching me from the bedroom across from my window with wild, dark eyes from under an unruly mop of dark curly hair that's almost as long as mine. There are boxes and an unmade bed behind him along with stacks and stacks of milk crates full of records and cassette tapes.

I feel my head tilt as I take him in. His hair is unlike anything I've seen before, chaotic and weird. He's wearing a black T-shirt with some sort of monster on it and words I can't quite make out from this distance. His jeans are torn at the knees and there's a tattoo of something on his hand. Our eyes finally meet and the side of his mouth pulls into a crooked kind of smile. His eyebrows lift as though waiting for me to comprehend the punch line of a joke.

His dark gaze flicks down and back up for a fraction of a second, and that's when it hits me. Other than my underwear, I am naked as the day I was born. I think my heart stops as I grab the lilac-colored curtains and try to pull them closed. Instead, the force of my tugging causes the curtain rod to pull from the wall and the curtains to fall, exposing me all over again.

Through wide eyes, I can see him try to hide his amusement and my skin flushes with a fresh wave of embarrassment. I look over to my bed, out of sight, and quickly duck under the covers. I lie there, my breathing ragged and my skin burning as if his eyes have scorched me. My hands clasp together as I mutter a whispered confession to God to forgive me.

It takes forever for my heart to calm down, my blood pulsing in my ears. I slowly creep out from under the blankets and along the wall to peek around the window frame. He's gone. I sigh heavily, my knees nearly buckling from the effort to keep me upright. I dash to my dresser and grab the first thing I see to pull on then escape into my bathroom to cover myself up, squeezing into another too-small dress.

When I exit the bathroom, I look out the window. He's still gone and I think for a moment that maybe I imagined him, but the lights are on and the boxes and milk crates and bed are all still there. I step a little closer to the window, my eyes drawn toward a vibrant poster on the wall over the bed. There's a horrible-looking demon on it, like the one that had been on his shirt and my breath catches when I see the five-pointed star. A pentagram.

My fingers grasp at the golden cross hanging from my neck. Oh no . . .

"Rebecca? What's taking you so long up there?"

My mother's commanding voice turns my attention away from the window.

"I'll be right there," I call back, my voice a little shaky.

A shadow moves in the light of the other room as though he's about to come back and I bolt out of my bedroom and down the stairs. As I set the table then spend dinner pushing the meatloaf around my plate, I can't seem to blink away those wild, dark eyes as they traveled over my bare skin. The memory of the black van and the music from this morning resurfacing out of my memory, my brain finally putting the pieces together.

The devil has moved in next door. The devil has seen me naked.

The devil has the most beautiful eyes I've ever seen.

Oh God, please forgive me.

CHAPTER 2

The Antichrist

JAMES

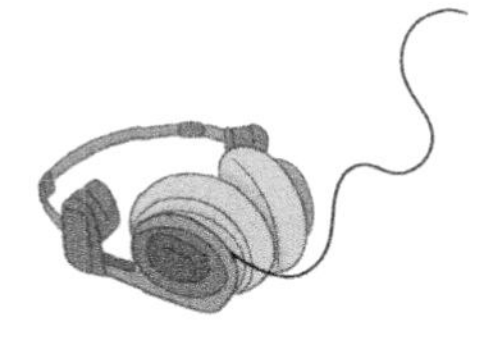

Holy shit. Maybe moving to this piece-of-shit town in the middle of Iowa won't be so bad after all.

The nearly naked blonde in the window across from me has finally noticed my gaze. In all honesty, I hadn't meant to look. It's as surprising to me as it seems to be for her to find me here, curtains wide open, strolling around wearing almost nothing without a care in the world. She watches me now like she has no idea she's almost completely exposed. For a moment I think maybe she can't see me. That maybe the sunlight has turned her window into a mirror like it does sometimes as it sets, but it can't be. Not when her eyes latch so lethally onto mine.

Perhaps she's an exhibitionist. I've met a few girls who are like that. Girls who've pulled me into a bathroom stall at a concert knowing someone could hear us getting off and be all the more turned on by it. Somehow, I don't think that's the case here. My mouth quirks into a smile, eyebrows rising to see what she'll do. She seems to remember herself because her bright eyes go wide and she turns as white as a ghost before throwing herself behind her curtains, the force of it causing the rod to fall, exposing her again. She shrieks, then disappears somewhere I can't quite see.

I choke back my laugh. Yeah, this place won't be so boring after all. I wait another minute to see if she'll peek out from around the window frame but she's gone. Chuckling again, I run my hand over my face, then head out the door to go grab a few more of my boxes from downstairs. My aunt Noreen is in the kitchen making dinner and I couldn't be more excited about a home cooked meal. I don't think I've had one in almost a year other than the boxed or microwave meals I've made myself. My mom wasn't exactly . . . well, let's just say she wasn't Betty Crocker.

My chest aches when I think about her, and I push the unpleasant emotion aside. At least for now. I squat to pick up the last few boxes that I moved from the back of my van into the living room and head back for the stairs.

"That's the last of your stuff then?"

Noreen peers around the corner of the kitchen, her hair more frizzy than normal from cooking. I'm sure people think her hair is permed but nope . . . that's all natural. I hadn't known where my curly hair came from until I met Noreen last month, after my mom died. My mom's hair had been pin straight and from what I remember of my dad, his hair had been wavy at best.

I adjust the heavy boxes in my arms. "Yeah, I think that's it."

"Right, well, take those upstairs then come back down. Dinner's almost ready."

I nod, making my way back up to the bedroom at the top of the stairs with its slanted roof and very interesting view. She's gone now. The naked girl. Her bedroom door is open, the curtains still slanted down on the one side where they had toppled as she tried to hide herself.

Setting down the boxes next to my bed, I slump down on the mattress to catch my breath. I really should quit smoking. My fingers run along the spine of a record from my collection as I glance up at the stereo system I brought with me. It'll take me an hour or so to set it up, but there's a surprising amount of space up here. Much more than Noreen made it out to be when she suggested I come live with her until graduation.

My eyes find their way back to the window. To the bedroom no more than twelve feet from my own. If there had to be an opposite room to mine, this is it. I don't know this girl, but she has ballerinas and daisies splashed all over the place. It's like a Care Bear threw up in there.

There's a music box open on her desk in front of the window with a little plastic ballerina—the kind that spins—standing upright. A handful of books line the top shelf of the white oak desk along with a white-and-gold porcelain cross.

"Shit . . ."

My eyes look around and find another cross over her door, then another on her dresser. Fucking hell, just how many crosses does one person need? I twist my mouth. She must be one of these Holy Rollers my aunt warned me about. Perfect, just perfect. I shake my head.

Oh well, she isn't really my type anyway. From what I see here, we have nothing in common. The girls I usually go for are loud and mouthy with an edge and attitude to match. Plus, I normally like girls with a bit more meat on their bones—something to grab onto. Not that I have anything against skinny girls. And even though almost all the girls I've hooked up with were darker haired, I don't have anything against blondes either. Okay, maybe I like all girls . . . especially naked ones. Especially with big, innocent eyes begging for corruption.

Fuck, the thought of bringing her over here and her touching me unfurls through my mind. What would her mom and dad think of their little angel if they caught her with her mouth wrapped around my—

"James! Come on down, it's getting cold."

I groan, my head tilting back as I adjust my hips in my jeans which have tightened considerably. When I feel safe enough to stand, I head back down the stairs to the kitchen where Noreen is sitting at her small table with two steaming plates of spaghetti and two beers.

"Uh . . . you know I'm only nineteen right?" I say, sliding into the orange vinyl kitchen chair.

She narrows her eyes at me. "Are you really going to sit there and tell me you've never had a beer, James?"

A grin spreads across my face before I grab the beer from in front of me and take a long swig.

"That's what I thought," she says, picking up her fork and digging into her spaghetti.

"This looks great, thanks," I say. I stick my fork into the pasta and twirl like my mom showed me how when I was little.

"Figured you've probably had your fill of takeout recently."

I nod. "Yeah, you could say that."

The spaghetti and tomato sauce are plain, but it's hot and cooked just for me and I doubt even a steak would taste better at this moment. We're quiet while we eat, the clinking of our forks and beer bottles on the table the only real noise.

"So," Noreen says, glancing up at me, "I've got school all sorted out for you. You'll start on Monday."

I swallow and nod, taking a particularly long drink from the bottle.

"I think it's great by the way," she says. "Continuing on, even after everything."

I shrug. "Can't really refuse a dying woman's last wish, can I?"

Noreen chuckles. "Of all the things she could wish for you to do, and she asks you to graduate high school. Sounds like Dora all right."

"She was a good mom . . . when she could be."

"There's a bar on the far side of town too that's hiring. The Shipwreck. Friend of mine owns it and told me they're looking for someone to be a runner behind the bar, bus tables and such. The clientele is probably right up your alley."

Smiling, I lean forward, my long curly hair falling over my shoulders. "Thanks, that sounds great."

"I'll draw you a map and you can go after school on Monday and check it out."

Taking another mouthful of my spaghetti, I drop my shoulders to seem casual. "What are the neighbors like?"

Noreen scoffs loudly and rolls her eyes while leaning back in her seat. "Probably no one you'd want to socialize with. Crazed fundamentalist Christians, most of them."

I press my lips together, trying to decide how best to ask about the girl from the window. I gesture over my shoulder toward the house my bedroom faces. "These people have kids?"

Noreen narrows her eyes at me. "Why do you ask?"

I shrug, trying to seem nonchalant about it. "My room faces one of the bedrooms. The amount of pink in there is going to give me a headache."

My aunt gives me a look, and for a moment I think maybe the jig is up. That she knows exactly why I'm asking about that bedroom. It passes, though, and she sighs.

"That's probably Rebecca's room. She's about your age. Careful around her," Noreen warns.

My fork nearly clatters to the table. Does she know what happened? How could she? "What do you mean?"

"These people, they're self-righteous and pretentious and think they're better than everyone else. Especially if you aren't part of their church," she says, shaking her head. "And Rebecca? She may look sweet, but she's just as righteous as the rest of them with a stick so far up her ass I'm surprised she doesn't cough toothpicks."

I choke on my beer. Covering my mouth with my hand, I cough to clear the beer from my lungs.

"Well," I say, pulling a forced grin onto my face, "they sound just delightful."

"Don't let them catch you drinking my beer. Richard Briar is a powerful man in this town with lots of friends in high places. You understand?"

Meaning, if I step out of line then Mr. Briar could make life very difficult for me.

"Got it."

After cleaning up the dishes, I head out back for a quick smoke. It's dark now and a shiver races up my spine. The night is quiet except for the odd animal scurrying through the bushes. I'm not used to it, the lack of noise is disconcerting and causing me to constantly look over my shoulder. The smoke burns my lungs, the nicotine calming my mind. I wish I had a joint. I bet the neighbors would love that. Wouldn't even know where I'd be able to get some weed in this town. I'll have to wait until Monday, see if any of the other kids at school look like they know where to score. It had been so easy back home in Detroit, but I guess this is my home now. At least for the next two and a half months.

Ten weeks. That's all that's left. Just three more credits to finish and I'll be done and free from the guilt of disappointing my dead mother. It may have taken me an extra year of high school to manage it, but I will get that diploma, then tell everyone to fuck off as I drive away to sunny San Francisco.

It isn't like I need the diploma to play music. And if my mom hadn't asked me to finish school, I'd already be out west. At this point, it doesn't even matter if I end up playing music. I just want to be involved somehow. Writing, producing, cleaning up the vomit off the stage . . .

Of course, dreaming of being a rockstar and actually becoming one are two very different things and I highly doubt many people around here will understand that dream—that drive. But I've thought about nothing outside of metal music, specifically speed metal, for the past six years, teaching myself every song I can get my hands on. It's part of the reason I still need those three credits.

I stub the cigarette out in the ashtray that Noreen has left on the back porch for me then head back inside. Taking the stairs two at a time, I pause briefly with my hand on the doorknob to my room. Will she be there? Did she tell her parents the new neighbor-boy was staring at her through the window? Probably not. The cops would've been here by now for sure. I take a deep breath and head into the bedroom.

I peer out the window and see that her curtains are closed now. Of course they are. Her dad probably fixed the rod right away and those curtains will forever remain closed. Not that I'm hoping for another show, but . . . if I had the choice between the view of a hot girl versus no girl? Yeah, my choice is pretty obvious.

I cross the room and pull out the cords for my stereo system and speakers. Yup, this will probably take an hour to get set up, but it's Saturday night and I have nothing better to do.

AN HOUR and a half later and I'm lying on my new bed, my head on the pillows and a pair of headphones blasting Iron Maiden's *Powerslave* album. I wanted to practice on my guitar for a while, but my arms feel like Jell-O after unloading and carrying boxes all day. The noise is soothing after so much quiet. Of course, I'd be in big trouble if anyone ever snuck up on me but living here, in this neighborhood—it's highly unlikely. At least here, I won't have to chain lock my door to keep shitheads from stealing my stuff.

Again, I wish I had a joint. My brain is still spinning a bit from today. I open one eye to glance out the window. There's a break in the purple curtains, the light pouring out across my bedroom floor in a sliver. A pair of eyes surrounded by blonde hair peer out at me. From this distance I'm not sure what color they are, just that they're big and bright and the most prominent feature of her face.

My heart thuds in my chest as I try to stay as still as possible. Perhaps she hasn't noticed me watching her yet. A full minute goes by, then another. I wonder what she's thinking. Is she looking for some clue as to who I am and what I'm doing here? I turn my head to face the window and she disappears, the curtains rippling and the light scattering across my floor. I sit up on the edge of my bed and pull off the headphones, brushing my hair back and away from my face. I flip off the stereo and reach over to turn off the guitar-shaped lamp my mom gave me for my twelfth birthday.

The back of my neck prickles, and I glance back through the window. She's watching me again, and this time I let her know I can see her, offering a little wave. Like a frightened deer, she backs away, pulling shut the curtains, then the light turns off.

I grin widely. Is she that sheltered or am I really that intimidating?

I laugh and lie back on the bed. Smart girl to be wary of me.

I have rules for a reason and Rebecca Briar would break them all.

CHAPTER 3

Papa Don't Preach

REBECCA

While dining with a ruler, pay attention to what is put before you. If you are a big eater, put a knife to your throat; don't desire all the delicacies, for he might be trying to trick you. Don't wear yourself out trying to get rich.
Proverbs 23:1-8

My hands tremble as we pull up to Holy Grace Evangelical Church. I've barely slept. I must have prayed a thousand times last night and still I'm worried I'll burst into flames the moment I walk through that door. Surely God knows it wasn't my fault, right? That I've lived my whole life to serve him, and even though I have moments of weakness, I would never want to face the possibility of what awaits me in the afterlife if I'm not on fire for God.

I linger a little too long on the front steps of the church, wringing my hands and bouncing my heel on the doormat.

"Rebecca, what in heaven's name are you doing?" my mother calls to me from halfway down the aisle of the church.

I take a deep breath, take a step and . . . nothing. One foot in front of the other and everything is normal. I feel like I'm ready to crumple into tears of joy and gratitude as I follow behind my parents, taking my seat with them near the front, that familiar prickling feeling on my neck making me shiver. I glance around, feeling as though all eyes are on me. That everyone knows what I've done. I may not have burst into flames when I entered, but I'm sure God knows exactly what I'm hiding.

Pastor Campbell begins the sermon, and I try so hard to pay attention. To prove I'm still devout. But somewhere along the fifth mention of "planting the seed for God" it's as if my brain switches to autopilot, going through the motions with eighteen years of practice while my thoughts begin to wander. My mind is racing, my breaths shallow. The overly tight dress my mom picked out for me doesn't help. But it's mostly because of *him*.

I don't even know his name. Who is he, exactly? My ears burn as I remember watching him through the curtains last night, not once but *twice*. And he caught me red-handed. After dinner I raced back upstairs to fix the broken curtain rod on my own. There was no way I'd let my dad see who had moved in next door with a direct view of my bedroom, or he might just move me into the basement where there are no windows at all.

I don't know why I can't shake the strange boy from my thoughts. After all, he is exactly the kind of boy that I've been warned of my whole life. From the look of him and his bedroom, he's probably a Satan worshiping evolutionist. I suppose that's why I can't get him out of my head. Here is this real-life example of the type of person I've always been taught to fear. The nightmares from my youth gurgle up out of my memory to taunt me with images of fire and brimstone and the rapture that always went hand in hand with people like him.

But he was just lying on the bed listening to music. Probably the same kind of music that rattled my brain when he'd played it in his van. His fingers tapped out a complicated rhythm on his chest for a while. My face had burned when he spotted me, then he'd waved and I felt like I would die from shame. The worst part was that this morning I looked again, like some compulsive creep. I'm not sure what's come over me—if it's fear of the unknown or just morbid curiosity, but I peered through my curtains before we left to come to church.

He was still asleep.

Lying on his stomach, his long dark hair everywhere, one arm hanging off the side of the mattress. I've never seen an arm like his before. Long and muscular and . . . very unlike Eric's. And his hands. He has big hands, with long fingers adorned with metal rings. A funny feeling swept over me as I stared at his arm, his hand, his fingers. And it terrified me. So much so that I could only sip water this morning to try and calm my stomach before being shepherded away to sit here in church and obsess over the arm of a man I've never met.

Before I even know it, everyone around me is moving, their conversations echoing off the vaulted ceiling.

"Did you see that boy at Noreen Walton's yesterday?"

"Told me he was her nephew . . . didn't even know she had a nephew."

"Well, it's not like she talks about her family much. Tragic what happened."

I freeze, my heart hammering against my ribs that are squeezed between the boning of this infernal dress. Glancing over my shoulder, I see Vivian Corbley, Eric's mother, the wife of our most dedicated church elder. She's talking to some other ladies about *him*. My ears strain as I try to pick up more of their conversation.

"Looks like a complete delinquent if you ask me. Bad for the neighborhood. Does Linda Briar know what's moved in next door to her?"

No, please don't tell my mom. As if in answer, Mrs. Corbley calls her, and I cringe.

"Linda!"

"Oh hi, Vivian, how are you?"

"Have you met your new neighbor yet?"

"Neighbor? What neighbor?"

I quickly grab one of the hymn books in front of me so I don't look like I'm eavesdropping.

"Apparently, Noreen Walton's nephew just moved in."

"Really? I didn't know she had a nephew. Is that who that black van belongs to?"

"Find out what you can, will you, Linda? Apparently he's been enrolled at the school."

A wave of nausea rolls through my stomach. Is God testing me? He's going to be at school? I thought he was older. He certainly looks older, I mean not by much, but maybe it's the hair and the clothes and those hands . . .

"Rebecca?"

The hymn book falls from my fingers to the floor as I jump to my feet. "Yes?"

"Did you see a young man over at Noreen Walton's place yesterday?"

They're all looking at me. All those eyes . . . just waiting. Do they want me to confirm this boy is everything they've ever feared? Would they accept that our brief encounter was purely accidental, or would they judge me—cast me out? Why am I so terrified if I'm sure I've done nothing wrong?

"No," I blurt out. Oh no, that's a lie. I just lied in church. I grip the cross around my neck. "I—There was a black van out front yesterday, though. Maybe it's his?"

Mrs. Corbley shakes her head. "You see? This is why we need our own school. We cannot keep subjecting our children to such depravity. It's bad enough that they interact with those worldly kids."

My mother looks at me for a long moment, her tongue

clicking before her eyes glance down at the book I dropped. "You're not going to leave that there, are you, dear?"

I take several shallow breaths. "No . . . no, of course not."

She watches my face with poorly concealed delight as I try and think of a way to bend over and grab the book without the zipper on the back of my dress popping open in front of everyone. I decide to stand over it and use my plié technique to my advantage, my fingertips grasping the leather binding. I stow it in the pocket of the pew in front of me and offer my best smile.

"Oh, that reminds me," Mrs. Corbley continues, snapping her fingers. "Rebecca, you'll be able to help out with Sunday school next weekend, won't you? I'm afraid Melissa won't be able to make it."

I feel my muscles tense. No. Not Sunday school. The sticky-fingered, crying chaos that I detest so much. But . . . I sigh. If this is what God asks of me, I'll do my best.

"Of course," I say. "I'd be happy to help."

Mrs. Corbley smiles wide and my mother's jaw twitches, but they turn toward the tea table. I close my eyes, my hand pressing against my chest where my heart is fluttering like a bird caught in a trap. My head is spinning. It's all too much. That boy—he's going to be at school and he's seen me naked. He's seen me naked and caught me watching him. He'll be there, in person, with those hands and those beautiful dark eyes. Will he try to talk to me? What if he mentions the window incident. A dizzying lightness fills my head. I might pass out.

"Becca!"

I bite my tongue. I don't have the energy for Eric right now, but here he comes, his brown hair flopping over his forehead, so I paste a patient smile on my face.

"Hey," he says a tad breathlessly, then he leans forward to kiss my cheek and I can feel where his lips are chapped.

"Hi," I respond politely, the urge to wipe my cheek a compulsion that's almost impossible to ignore.

He looks around then grabs my arm, pulling me over toward one of the tall stained-glass windows until we're standing in the shadow of the cross. When he turns, Eric's overly cheerful smile drops.

"Did you tell your parents I was at Jeremiah's yesterday?"

My eyes widen as I shake my head. "What? No. Why would I do that?"

"Because you were mad at me for being late to pick you up? Or maybe you were upset about after—"

"Eric, please, I'm not a tattletale." Closing my eyes, I recite, "You shall not spread a false report."

"Then how did they find out?"

He's panicked. Beads of sweat form on his brow and his weight shifts constantly between his feet. My mouth drops open trying to find the words to defend myself. "I have no idea how they found out but it certainly wasn't because I told anyone. Maybe you shouldn't have been there at all," I whisper harshly.

"That's not—" His lips press into a hard line and he brings a clenched fist up to his mouth. "My dad is going to kill me!" Why is he so worried? He's a boy, and his dad practically owns half the town *and* is a church elder, which means he can basically do no wrong, even if he was drinking. Unless something else happened. Are things as tense in his home as mine?

"Did something—"

"Whatever, see you at school." Brushing past me, he goes to leave.

"Wait! Are you still driving me to school in the morning?"

But he disappears through the crowd and my eyes sting from the injustice of his misplaced anger.

I LOOK up across the dinner table to find my father staring at me expectantly.

"Sorry, what was that?"

"I said, Mrs. Van Houten told me today you did very well on your math test. Nearly perfect, actually."

Something grates inside me at the way he says "nearly" perfect, but I'll take what I can get.

"Thanks."

"Anything big happening at school that we should know about?" he asks, cutting into his chicken.

Does he want me to tell him something specific? I never know with him. My parents have always encouraged me to let them know if the school is teaching us anything that Pastor Campbell would deem immoral. But at this moment, nothing comes to mind. My dad has an unreadable face when he wants to, and right now I'm not sure if he knows something I don't or if he's genuinely interested.

"I don't think so . . ."

His head tilts as he watches me. "Doesn't Eric have some big track meet coming up?"

Oh, yes, I've completely forgotten.

I swallow and nod. "Yes, I think he's going to place really well."

"Have you been praying for him?" he asks. "Perhaps we could all pray together after dinner, to ensure Eric is walking with God on the field."

Ring ring.

My eyes dart to the phone in the kitchen, the hanging spiral cord just within view, yet neither of my parents move to answer it.

"Of course," I say with a smile. Of course I've been praying for him. I've been praying for this track meet to go well for weeks. Even if he did call me a snitch today.

The phone stops ringing but the next moment something loud blares through the open window. We jump from our seats, knives and forks clattering onto the china plates. There's a ringing noise and another blaring note. Oh no . . . it's music. *His* music.

"What in heaven's name is that?" my mother asks.

I feel her look at me like I have the answer but I keep my eyes on my plate. She can always discern too much from my face and I might just confess everything to her if our eyes meet.

My father stands and walks to the window as more noise vibrates the glass. He slams it shut, looks outside for a few moments then heads for the door.

"Where are you going?" my mother calls.

He doesn't even answer, simply disappears through the door so that we're left alone together. My hand shakes as I spear a small piece of potato with my fork and lift it to my mouth.

"Rebecca," my mother says. Her gaze is fixed upon the table but there's ice in her voice. "If you are a big eater, put a knife to your throat; don't desire all the delicacies, for he might be trying to trick you."

Hearing the verses stalls my hand and even though my stomach twists painfully for the food on my plate, I set it down and push the rest of my dinner away. She smiles, then the music blaring from next door stops abruptly and there's silence.

The minutes feel like hours as I try to reconcile God's desire for my obedience and the fact that I'm so hungry I could cry. Finally, my father bursts back through the front door and I nearly choke. He looks livid.

"Absolutely unacceptable," he mutters as he takes his seat back at the table.

"Was it that boy? The nephew?" my mother asks.

"Complete degenerate . . . Rebecca?"

"Yes?" My eyes go wide as I look up. He can see it on my face, can't he? That I know there's a boy next door. That I've thought about nothing but him all day.

"You are not to go near him, do you understand?" he says sternly.

I nod sharply. "Yes, sir."

"I mean it. He talks to you, you let me know. People like him are Satan worshippers and cultists and they'll try to seduce you into a life of depravity and sin."

There's no air. I can't breathe. The guilt and shame of my own thoughts threaten to swallow me whole.

"It's more important than ever we raise that money for a school of our own," my father says. "We simply cannot allow the children of our congregation to continue in secular education."

"You're absolutely right," my mother agrees, nodding vigorously. "We should pray on it."

The three of us join hands over the table, and my dad begins reciting. My mother continues, and I mechanically voice the familiar prayer, pressing my eyes tighter each time my mind begins to wander. When it's over, I realize my appetite is gone, and I sigh with relief.

"May I be excused, please?" I ask, grateful my voice is steady.

"Of course, dear."

I take my plate to the kitchen and toss the uneaten food in the trash. I place it on the rack to dry after washing it, then dash for the stairs to shut myself inside the sanctity of my own room.

But where my bedroom used to bring me peace and comfort, that's gone too. Even behind closed curtains, I feel his presence. I wonder if he knows I'm here right now. Waiting to see if I'll attempt to spy on him again.

I catch myself taking a few tentative steps toward the window and stop. No, I won't let this man—this boy—be another thing distracting me from God. Turning to my dresser and grabbing a nightgown, I peel off the dress I've been confined to all day and although I want nothing more than to just stand here in absolutely nothing, the threat of what's next door forces me to pull on the flannel sleepshirt. Glancing at my reflection in my vanity mirror for a quick reminder that I'm actually wearing clothes, I grab both curtains and rip them open.

Sure enough he's there, and I must have startled him because he nearly topples off the edge of the bed where he's sitting. His eyes find my face immediately and they're wide . . . surprised. He's unpacked more of his things today, indicated mostly by the lack of cardboard boxes and the increase in records and cassette tapes. Just how much music does one person need? There are more posters up on the walls, and they all have the same general aesthetic as the first one. They're dark with heavy, violent graphics. One pictures an entirely naked woman and I nearly chicken out right there but power through despite the heat in my cheeks.

He's holding an electric guitar that's plugged into an amplifier. A pair of headphones—most likely the result of my father demanding he turn down his music—rests on top of his head and his hair pulled back with an elastic. He raises his eyebrows and looks at me expectantly, maybe wondering why I opened my curtains again. *Because I'm not scared of you, devil worshiper . . . that's why!* I make a show of turning my back to the window and grab my bible off my shelf before sitting down at my desk. He needs to know that I don't care that he's there. That my life hasn't changed.

What am I doing? He doesn't even know what my life was like before he came here. This is ridiculous, but now that I'm here and have made a show of trying to read, I need to actually stick with it or he'll think I'm just some silly girl. Fifteen minutes later and I'm no closer to having actually read a single page. My leg bounces nervously beneath the desk and every thirty seconds I find myself trying to sneak a glance across the divide to see what he's doing. But he just continues to play his guitar. In fact, he seems completely uninterested that I'm even here. It scratches at me, like his lack of attention after our encounter yesterday doesn't quite live up to my expectations. Did I really think he might try to lure me over with his music and Satan idolatry? Perhaps he's used to seeing naked girls. The naked woman on the poster above his bed seems to indicate that this is probably the case. My father's right. He is a degenerate.

I think about my own body. My breasts are small and my ribs stick forward too much. I'm too short and there's not much roundness to me. My face is too pointed, my cheekbones too prominent. So many of the other girls at school have that curvy feminine beauty that I desperately wish for. I bet that's what he likes too. When he saw me, maybe he thought I was disgusting. Too boyish. Too skinny. That must be why he's not looking now . . . that perhaps, coupled with the fact that I have clothes on, he's lost interest.

Well . . . good. Problem solved then.

Fidgeting with my necklace, I stand, looking over again to watch as his long fingers fly over the neck of the guitar. The arm I've thought about all day is tight and strumming the strings in a steady rhythm and a feeling like hunger creeps into my belly. His hands speed up, doing some complicated lightning fast movements over the strings, his chest rising and falling quickly. His eyes are closed and his head bobs a little to whatever sounds he's making. With a final flourish he strikes the strings then stops.

He's breathing hard and I realize that so am I, like I've just finished a two-hour dance class. Looking up, our eyes meet again. His dark eyes are bright and his mouth quirks at the side as he pulls off the headphones and stands, putting the guitar by the stereo. Turning back to me, he places one hand around his back and the other around his middle and bows. *Bows.* I stiffen where I stand and when he rises he's smiling wide as though he was performing just for me. That smile . . . that look . . . I've never had anyone look at me like that before. Like this is fun for him—like he's glad I'm watching.

My stomach clenches hard, and the uncomfortable feeling brings me back to reality. I grasp my bible tightly and back away from the window, my fingertips pulling away from the cool glass. When did I place my hand there? This can't be happening—it's dangerous and sinful. I shake my head and quickly turn to shut off the lights and with all the willpower I can muster, I keep my eyes from glancing out the window again.

Every muscle twitches and spasms as I lie in bed. And though the light from his room that spills across my bedroom floor extinguished hours ago, I can't sleep. My heart beats like a frightened mouse being cornered by a cat. Maybe that's what I am to him. Prey. I clasp my hands together and pray for what feels like the gazillionth time in the last twenty-four hours. As I stare up at the ceiling, I pray that God grants me the strength to face him tomorrow.

CHAPTER 4

D.O.A.

JAMES

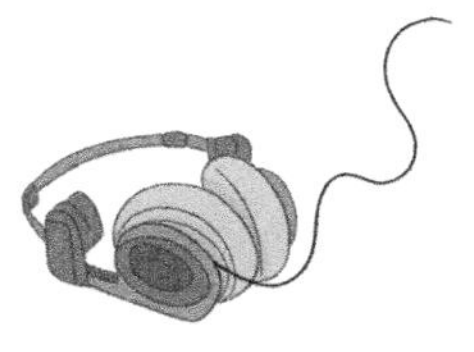

Rule #5 - Always be myself and never apologize for it.

All right. Things are starting to fall apart. I've changed my shirt three times so far trying to get ready to go to this fucking school. Three times I've picked something to wear and thought too hard about it.

"Just wear the Iron Maiden shirt with the devil on it, you know you want to," I mutter, staring at the pile of shirts on the bed.

Now, if I wear that, I know it'll piss everyone off. Normally I wouldn't give a fuck . . . but I also need to graduate so I can get the hell out of here, and I can't imagine antagonizing the teachers would be to my benefit. However, the moment I open my mouth I'll probably do that anyway. So I should just wear it—set the tone. I look over my shoulder, past my curtains and out the window, but Rebecca isn't there. Of course not. She was probably up at the crack of dawn to pray . . . or bake cookies . . . or some other revoltingly wholesome shit. Although what exactly is my plan there? Ask her which shirt to wear through the window?

"James, hurry up or you'll be late."

Noreen's voice echoes up the stairs and I groan. I toss the Metallica shirt down and grab my Van Halen world tour Raglan and pull it over my head. There's an eagle on it, that'll be cool right? Mid-westerners love eagles. After combing through my hair and fastening the chain around my neck, and another on my belt loop for my wallet, I grab my jacket and secure my bag over one shoulder. I take one last look through the window, still seeing no sign of her. "Guess I'll see you at school, neighbor . . ."

I rush down the stairs and enter the kitchen where Noreen is sitting reading the paper. She looks over the top of the pages at me and hands me a paper lunch bag. Eyes bouncing between it and her, my chest tightens.

"You made me lunch?"

I mean for it to come out like a joke, but I can't quite hide just how touched I am. She seems to have caught on too because her cheeks darken.

"Figured you need to save as much money as you can for after graduation. I drew a map for The Shipwreck and put it in there as well. Oh, and there's some toast on the counter for you too."

I clear my throat, feeling uncomfortable about all the work she's doing to take care of me. I fidget with the metal rings on my fingers. "You don't have to do all this."

She shakes her head and shrugs. "I didn't. Made too much and can't eat it all."

Something in her expression tells me that's not true.

"Right. Thanks. I'll see you later then."

"You know where you're going?"

I nod as I grab a stack of toast and head for the door. Yanking my keys off the hook and the pack of cigarettes from the counter, I push the front door open to the chilly March morning. As I walk to my van, I spot who I assume is Rebecca's mother watching me through her front window. Never one to shy away from pissing off some parents, I make a show of pulling a cigarette out of the pack and placing it between my teeth. I smirk at her as I light it and her face scrunches with distaste before she shudders indignantly and disappears.

Smiling widely, I pull myself into the van, inhaling the smoke and starting the engine, the stereo still set to blasting. Good, maybe I can wake up the whole neighborhood on my way. I look down at my chest . . . yeah, definitely should've just worn the Metallica shirt. Oh well, too late to change now.

Metal Thrashing Mad by Anthrax blares through the stereo speakers as I back out of the driveway and turn down the quiet neighborhood streets toward the school. It's not overly far away, but too far to walk, and I soon find myself behind several yellow buses queuing up. Looking around, I see a parking lot at the far end by the football field.

It seems to be mostly staff parking, but I spot a few students pulling up in newer vehicles, probably bought for them by their parents. I pull into the farthest parking space, finish my cigarette, then turn off the engine. Jumping down out of the van, the chain on my jeans heavy against my leg, I shake back my hair and head for the doors.

Fuck. It's like I stepped into a Gap commercial. The amount of pastels and collared shirts is dizzying, the neon colors blinding. And what the hell kind of flag is that? Fuck, is that a cross on it? Good grief.

Everyone is staring at me, although I'm used to that by now, and normally I don't give a fuck, but it still sets me on high alert. The most obvious threat being the group of jocks standing by the entrance. I've never run away from a fight, but it's not like getting my ass handed to me by ten football players on my first day sounds like fun, either. There's a sign pointing toward the main office, so I follow the directions to what must be the middle of the school. The halls are filling up but thankfully most students clear out of my way, backing into the lockers and whispering behind their hands.

I open the door to the office, the secretary looking up and promptly dropping her Danish on the desk when she sees me. I force a tight-lipped smile on my face and approach the desk.

"Good morning, ma'am," I say with as much charm as I can muster.

She's looking at me like she's just discovered life on another planet. I grip the edge of the chest-high counter and lean over.

"James Walton," I say. "New student. You should have a schedule for me."

She closes her mouth and blinks a few times, remembering herself, then scuttles about her desk until she retrieves a piece of paper.

"Four—four courses right? Your aunt said to enroll you in a full schedule."

I sigh. "Yup . . . Sounds about right."

She holds out the paper and I take it from her as delicately as possible. I don't fail to notice the way her eyes widen as she sees the raven tattoo on my hand. Her eyes narrow back at me with disdain as she pulls her hand back. "Bell's about to ring."

"Guess I better get going then. Enjoy your Danish," I say, flashing her another smile and heading back out into the hall.

I flip the schedule over in my hand. History first, then social science, lunch, English and geometry, exactly the same as it had been in Detroit. Glancing up at the numbers above the classroom doors I realize with annoyance that the history classroom is back the way I came. I spin around, startling a group of girls who, after recovering from nearly bumping into me, start giggling into their hands.

A bell rings loudly overhead and the halls start to clear out as people disappear behind heavy wooden doors. Where the fuck is the history room? I reach a dead end and there's no classroom here. Did I miss it? Shit, now I'm going to be late. Fucking perfect. I backtrack the way I came and spot a custodian exiting the cafeteria.

"Hey, man," I call out.

He turns and raises his eyebrows. "You lost?"

"Yeah, do you know where room one-fifty-eight is?"

"It's part of the new wing down that hall there," he says, pointing to a hallway about twenty feet away. "Didn't they give you a map?"

I shake my head. "No, but I think it might have been because the secretary was having a mild heart attack."

The man laughs. "Don't see too many kids like you around here."

"I've noticed."

"Well, if you get lost again, my office is just around there." He grins and points to a blue door down the dead-end hallway I just came from.

"Thanks man," I say, then head in the direction he pointed. The school looks drastically different down this way, but I finally see room one-fifty-eight. Wrapping my hand around the doorknob, I turn and pull. A middle-aged woman with horn-rimmed glasses turns and shrieks. That's right, shrieks when she sees me. I do my best to refrain from rolling my eyes as I step into the class, holding my schedule out to her.

"Sorry I'm late, the room was hard to find. This is history right?"

She blinks at me for a few long seconds, her mouth falling open and her eyes traveling from the top of my head to my black boots. I fold up the schedule and tuck it into my jacket pocket. Jutting my thumbs over my shoulder toward the seats, I take a tentative step forward.

"Should I just sit in the back?"

Just like the secretary, the teacher seems to finally collect herself. She coughs into her hand. "Right, yes. There's a free seat at the back. I'm Mrs. Henry and you must be Mr. Walton?"

"James."

I turn to scan the room full of wide-eyed students, and lo and behold, who is sitting in the third row, but my little window friend, Rebecca Briar. I bite the inside of my cheek to keep from grinning because she's the only one who is staring at her desk like it's the most interesting thing in existence. Mrs. Henry gestures to the back of the room.

I start to walk back making sure I go right past Rebecca's desk. Her eyes avoid me at all costs, sitting still as a statue. I wonder if she's even breathing. As I pass, I let my finger drag along her desk and hear her sharp intake of breath. Yup, definitely wasn't breathing. My tongue runs along my teeth as I try to contain my grin before sitting down at the very back. I drop my bag next to me on the floor, waiting for Mrs. Henry to resume her lesson and for everyone to stop staring at me.

"Well now, where were we?"

The class gets back to business, the eyes slowly turning back to the front of the room. As Mrs. Henry drones on and on about the Spanish/American war, my eyes are trained on the girl with the long blonde hair in the third row. Wearing a green dress with a cream turtleneck shirt underneath, her posture is so straight it makes me wonder how on earth she could be comfortable. Maybe she really does have a stick up her ass.

"Can anyone explain one of the outcomes of the Spanish–American war?"

As if she's been bursting to say something this whole time, Rebecca's hand shoots into the air.

Mrs. Henry sighs as though it is taking all of her patience not to roll her eyes. "Yes, Miss Briar?"

"Victory proved that Americans were ordained by God to

spread westward and that it was our right to claim and settle territories all the way to the Pacific."

I can't help the scoff that bursts out of my mouth. And while Mrs. Henry had opened her mouth to say something, she closes it as her eyes land on me. In fact, everyone turns to me. Everyone except Rebecca.

"Yes, well," Mrs. Henry continues, "that may be—"

"Furthermore," Rebecca continues, "it was our duty as Christian Americans to intervene. As oppressed people suffering under communism, we were able to liberate them and instill democracy."

Jesus Christ. That stick is starting to become less metaphorical now, and it's alarming at just how many people seem to be in agreement with her.

Mrs. Henry presses her lips together tightly, then smiles. "Thank you, Miss Briar."

"Ridiculous," I mutter under my breath.

I can see Rebecca stop herself from turning around, her fist clenching around her pencil. As if she's stopped breathing again, her body looks painfully rigid, all except for her knee, which has started to bounce.

Mrs. Henry hands out an assignment, the papers passing down the rows. Rebecca grips her knee tightly, her nails digging into her skin. Her head turns as she passes the papers behind her, and she steals a glance at me. I can finally see the color of her eyes and discover that they're green, like sea glass or jade.

With every minute that goes by her leg starts to bounce more and more. She's anxious, that much is clear. Is it simply because of me, or is this just a regular thing for her? How can anyone sit with their back so fucking straight for so long? I think back to last night, when she'd ripped open those purple curtains and stared at me like she needed to prove something. I feel like that's what's happening now. That she's proving to me that I don't matter to her, that she's not going to acknowledge me.

My mind wanders as I relive the memory of that night. How free she had seemed for just a few moments. So completely unlike how she is now, so rigid and stiff. I wonder what she does for fun. I shake my head as I realize her idea of fun is probably the polar opposite of mine.

"Mr. Walton?"

I turn my head toward Mrs. Henry, who's making her way over to me. After the less than desirable first impression, she seems to have collected herself now.

"May I see your schedule? Each teacher is supposed to sign off that you found the right class."

"Sure." I pull out the paper and hand it to her. My gaze flicks back to Rebecca, who's turned back to the front of the class, her pen flying over her paper.

Mrs. Henry adjusts her glasses on her nose and looks down at my schedule. "It looks like you have social science next with Mr. Adams. The room is another tricky one to find. Umm . . . Miss Briar's in that class, I'm sure she can show you the way."

Holy shit.

Rebecca spins around in her seat. "Sorry?"

"You don't mind showing Mr. Walton the way to social science, do you?"

I can practically see the gears of her mind turning. She's trying to come up with an excuse as to why she can't do that, but she's also trying to cope with the fact that a teacher asked her to do something for someone and a good girl always helps out when she can.

"I—of course, I mean . . . yes, I can do that."

Yeah, she's a good girl all right.

"Wonderful. Here you are," Mrs. Henry says as she hands me back my schedule.

Rebecca twists her lips and glares at me as if I did this on purpose, but I can't stop the grin that pulls at the side of my mouth as her cheeks turn bright pink.

I'M on my feet the moment the bell rings and making my way down the aisle toward where Rebecca is slowly putting the last of her things into her bag. She stands, and I find myself directly behind her. Fuck, she's small. Like, small enough I could toss her around without breaking a sweat. I lean down to whisper in her ear.

"Lead the way, Miss Briar."

She whips around, hair flying and eyes narrowing at me. Her mouth tightens, then after a moment she sighs and turns to head out the door. I follow along behind, observing how, just like she sits in her chair, her walking is stiff and her posture unnaturally straight. I wonder if she did pageants or something as a kid. An image of her practicing her walk with a book balanced on her head comes to mind, and I grin.

Turning down the next hallway, it's not quite as crowded, so I'm able to walk next to her.

"I'm James, by the way," I say.

She doesn't look at me but continues walking. "I know."

Man, this girl is working harder than necessary to pretend I don't exist. This should be fun.

"And you're Rebecca, right?"

I catch her eyes as they flick over to me. "That's right."

"It's nice to meet you. And I have to say, you look as good in clothes as you do without them."

Her face turns bright red, but still she continues to walk.

"I won't tell anyone, if that's what you're worried about."

She stops dead in the middle of the hall, her eyes dropping to my feet and slowly trailing up my body to the top of my head then back down to my face.

"The room you now occupy has been empty for ten years. Believe me, if I had known someone was there, that *incident* never would have happened."

My eyebrows lift at how irritated she sounds, and I smirk, knowing I'm getting to her.

"Don't worry. I don't think God will blame you for it."

She lifts her arms as if to cross them, but stops, pushing them down to her sides. "What do you know about God?"

"A lot more than you'd think."

"I highly doubt that." She spins dramatically and takes off down the hall, her blonde hair swishing along her shoulders.

I release a breathy laugh and continue after her. "I know that what you said during class is complete bullshit."

She shakes her head a little but continues on, ignoring me.

"So," I say, trying to bite back a grin, "beside being brainwashed with inaccurate recollections of historical moments, what do you do around here for fun?"

"I doubt you'd be interested."

"Why not?"

She doesn't say anything, only glances at me out of the corner of her eye.

"You know, you're not being very friendly. Doesn't the bible say to love thy neighbor?"

She stops again. "I—"

Once again she's trying to figure out what to say. It must be exhausting having to constantly filter what you really think. Because that's what she's doing. She wants to tell me off but she feels like she can't and so she chews on the inside of her cheek instead.

"Did you enjoy my performance last night?"

She blinks, seemingly caught off guard by the abrupt change in topic.

"Sorry it was a silent performance, but my neighbor's dad is a huge prick."

"My father—"

"Is an asshole? Yeah, I'm aware."

Her head shakes again. "He is not. He's a wonderful man."

I step closer to her. "And let me guess, he told you to stay away from me?"

Her face tenses and her ears turn red. Up close she's a lot more beautiful than I had originally thought. Her face has delicate features, like a china doll. A small, pink mouth, a thin nose and those green eyes that shine beneath impossibly long eyelashes. Her breathing is shallow, her chest straining under her cardigan. What I know is that Rebecca Briar is too innocent and I'd break her. She's against the rules so I take a step back and give her a quick smile, spotting the social science classroom over her shoulder.

"Don't worry, Becks, you're not my type anyway."

CHAPTER 5

Don't You Want Me

REBECCA

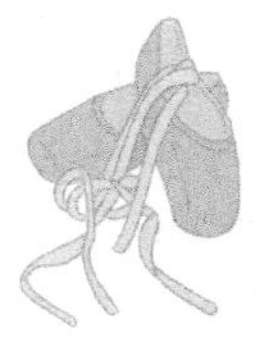

Not his type. Not. His. Type. It stings more than it should. It shouldn't matter at all! And James Walton isn't my type either, but my nails tap aggressively on the desk as I try to stop myself from screaming that at him across the room. I can feel him, sitting a few rows behind me, probably with that smug smile on his face. I've never hit anyone before, but I feel an ache in my arm, like I want to smack him.

I haven't been able to concentrate on anything Mr. Adams has said. In fact, I haven't been able to concentrate on anything since James scared the living daylights out of Mrs. Henry during first period, and as the minutes tick by like hours, I fight against what feels like every cell in my body telling me to turn back and look at him.

Mercifully, the bell finally rings for lunch, and I sprint from my seat and out into the crowded hallway. I can breathe easier out here. His presence has made the air somehow heavier, making it harder to get a full breath in. Of course this infernal dress doesn't help either. I hear the clink of the chain on his belt and quickly turn the corner. I hold my bag to my chest and squeeze myself against the wall until I see him pass by, his long curly hair swaying as he walks.

The tension in my shoulders relaxes when I'm sure he's gone and I push myself off the wall then head for the guidance office. I shouldn't be hiding. I haven't done anything wrong and while I didn't have the strength to argue with him about what I said in class, that doesn't mean he wins. Besides, listening to all that unholy rock music has probably turned his brain into mush.

Stopping in front of the guidance office, I look around. It's where I usually meet Eric before heading to lunch, but he's nowhere to be found. The muscles in my face twitch uncomfortably and I sniff loudly. Is he really that mad at me? For something I didn't even do? My toes are jittery, wiggling in my shoes with the injustice of it all, and a sudden overwhelming urge to just sit down and cry washes over me. The skirt of my dress digs into my sides and my skin feels hot and smothered.

I wish I were at home. Wish I could tear all my clothes off and just stand in the safety of my room and rid myself of this ever-present claustrophobia. I can't, though, because James will always be there. Even if the curtains are closed, I'll be able to feel him. That ominous, dangerous presence that oozes out of him like tar.

He's taller than I thought, and while I'd been so focused on his eyes and single arm before, I realize now that there is a whole lot more to enjoy when looking at him. He has a strong jaw and full lips, and even though his teasing made my blood boil, that smile of his is unbearably charming. Where Eric is handsome like someone would be in the movies or a Perry Ellis ad, James is attractive in the way that has me questioning my sanity.

No, stop it. I shouldn't be thinking about any of this. Eric is the one for me, he'll be my husband someday. Thinking about another man like this is sinful.

Besides, how can one person be so infuriating? And I've only spoken to him once. Oh no, what if I have more classes with him?

I hear a peal of laughter and turn to see Amy and Mary heading toward me, their arms linked together.

"Hey!" Amy says, waving at me. "You waiting for Eric?"

I roll my eyes. "I thought I was, but . . . I guess he has better things to do."

Mary links her arm with me and the three of us head to the cafeteria. "Are you two having a fight?"

I sigh. "No . . . more like a misunderstanding, I think."

Amy giggles. "So, a fight then. There's no shame in that. It happens."

There is shame in it, though. Amy and Mary don't understand. They're not like me. It's my God-ordained duty as a woman to follow him—to not challenge him and his male authority, even if it pains me. Even if I've been forgotten about, groped, and blamed for Eric's poor decisions with alcohol over the past few days . . . it's my duty.

"By the way," Mary says, "have you seen the new guy?"

Amy's eyes widen. "Oh my goodness, no! Have you? Apparently he has tattoos—"

"He does," Mary confirms.

"You've seen them? Do you have a class together? How old is he?" Amy asks, her rapid-fire questions leave my head spinning.

"I saw one tattoo from far away this morning before classes, not sure what it is though. Sadly, no classes with him so far. What about you, Becca?"

I shrug. "Yeah, I've seen him. He moved in next door to us."

Amy and Mary stop walking and I'm nearly pulled off my feet as they tug me backward.

"What did you say?" Amy asks, her voice pitching loudly.

My eyes flick between them. I swallow, needing to be careful with just how much I reveal. "He's living with our neighbor. I saw him move in on Saturday."

They both openly gape at me. Amy reaches forward and grasps my arm. "He's living next to you? Have you talked to him?"

Why do I feel like this is an interrogation rather than friendly curiosity? Is it because I'm hiding something—my guilty conscience keeping me constantly on edge? I clear my throat. "I only talked to him for the first time this morning. We have first and second period together."

"He's a senior?" Amy asks.

"Of course he's a senior, Amy," Mary chides. "He's a grown man."

Amy blushes and lowers her voice. "Does he really worship the devil?"

Both girls are staring at me expectantly.

"I—" I don't want to tell them I can see into his room. Don't want to admit I've been spying on him and looking at all the posters on his walls. Watching him sleep. Thinking about him in ways I know are sinful. My face heats up, and I turn to continue walking so they can't see my shame. "I don't know. My dad said he does . . ."

"I mean, your dad is a bit . . . you know . . ." Mary says from behind me.

"Crazy?" Amy finishes for her.

I close my eyes as we approach the cafeteria. "He is not! He's just making sure I'm protected and always living for God."

Amy and Mary both roll their eyes, but I'm not annoyed. They just don't understand what's at stake. At least they're not Catholic, though, or I wouldn't be allowed to hang out with them at all.

We walk through the cafeteria doors and he's there. Like a dark thunder cloud in the middle of a sunny day. I feel Amy squeeze my arm again as though trying to contain her excitement, and she whispers something I can't hear to Mary. For how different he is, I would've thought he'd choose a place to sit near the exit, a place to be on his own. Instead, he's in the middle of the room, at a table normally reserved for the archery club who, right now, are all standing with their lunch trays trying to decide whether to join him or find somewhere else to sit.

Everyone is staring at him, but he doesn't seem fazed at all as he eats a chocolate pudding cup. I have to shake my head. The absurdity of watching this man eat a pudding cup is once again making me question my reality. What exactly did I expect him to be eating? Raw meat? And besides, chocolate pudding is delicious. At least, it was years ago. It's been so long, I can hardly remember.

"Come on," Mary says, "let's go to our table."

She pulls me over toward the far wall by the windows, meaning we'll have to pass right by him. Or maybe that's been Mary's intention all along. I could kill her. His gaze lifts to look at us as we approach and my heart quickens. Will he say something? Will he try to tease me again? No, I'm not his type. Then what is his type? What if Mary is his type? Or Amy . . . or—

He looks back down at his lunch like we're not even there. I let out a short breath of relief. That's what this feeling is, right? Relief? It's certainly not annoyance. He's been like a song I can't get out of my head since the moment he moved in next door. Antagonizing me this morning only to just decide now to ignore me? I should be thanking God, but instead I'm overly hot and tense as I take my seat at our usual table with my friends.

"You'd think he has the plague or something," Amy says as she pulls a sandwich out of her bag.

"Go talk to him then," Mary teases.

Amy flushes and starts digging around in her bag again to avoid being forced to go over there.

"I wonder why he moved here," Mary ponders, her cheek resting on her hand as she stares at the back of his head. "Maybe he got kicked out of his last school for killing someone."

I roll my eyes. "Mary, that's ridiculous, he'd be in jail if that were true, not here with us."

She twists her mouth. "Well, maybe he got expelled for bringing a knife to school. He looks like the type to carry a knife. I bet he has a whole collection of them."

"Will you stop?" I say loudly. "What does it matter?"

Mary narrows her eyes at me. "What's your problem? You can't tell me you're not curious."

I won't partake in this conversation. Allowing Mary to lead me away from the right path through gossip is something I can't let happen. I've already slipped too many times today because of *him.* I open my lunch bag for something to eat and find a singular container. I pull it out and discover four apple slices—a reminder from my mother not to be anxious about what I put in my body. That God's word will provide my spirit the food it needs.

"It's sinful to gossip, Mary," I say, opening the container and pulling out a piece. "If you want to know so badly, then go ask him yourself instead of making silly guesses."

She scowls at me and for a moment I'm sure she's going to march right over there and ask him. But she just opens her lunch box and begins eating.

I've been chewing on the same piece of apple for what feels like a lifetime when wet lips press against my cheek. "Hey, babe."

Eric falls into the seat next to me.

"Oh," I say indignantly with my mouth still half full. "Hey."

"Sorry I couldn't meet up with you earlier," he says, grabbing my last apple slice from the container. "Emergency track meeting."

I watch as he chews and swallows my food, my stomach protesting angrily at being robbed of that last morsel. A few of

Eric's friends from the track team sit down around Amy and Mary, engaging them in conversation.

Lowering my voice, I lean toward Eric. "I thought you were mad at me."

He shakes his head, his mouth twisting irritably. "Yeah, about that. I know it wasn't your fault. Forgive me?"

I bite my tongue so hard I taste copper. He's made me feel like garbage the past twenty-four hours, and all of a sudden everything is okay again? I can almost hear Pastor Campbell's voice whispering in my ear that my heart will be lifted by submitting to my future husband. To let everything else go. That holding onto anger isn't Godly.

It makes my stomach churn, but I smile. "Of course."

He smiles and leans forward to kiss me on the forehead. "Will you come to our practice again after school? I'll drive you home after."

I guess we're back to normal then. "All right."

"So, Eric," Mary interrupts, "have you met Becca's new neighbor?"

Eric tilts his head and I think my heart has stopped. I'm starting to question if my friendship with Mary is really worth it.

"What are you talking about?" he asks.

She raises her eyebrows in James's direction. He looks around then his head whips back to look at me, his eyes wide. "The freak? The freak is—that's who was in the van?"

I grasp at my necklace, pulling on the chain so hard the skin on the back of my neck pinches painfully. "Yes, it is."

He narrows his eyes at me. "Why didn't you tell me?"

"I didn't know at the time."

"Dude looks like one of those Manson cultists out of California," Eric's friend Ryan says.

Mary taps the table excitedly with her finger. "Ooh, what if *that's* why he got kicked out and had to move here?"

"Wait, he was kicked out?" Eric asks.

Anger bubbles under the surface. "We don't know if he was kicked out," I mutter. I don't even know why I'm defending him. He's not my friend.

"Shh! Here he comes," Amy whispers.

I feel his eyes on me this time, hear the heavy clink of that chain on his hip. Eric's arm wraps around my shoulder in what I assume is supposed to be a protective manner but feels more possessive than anything. Like he's trying to make sure James knows that I belong to him. It's hardly necessary though because I'm not his type.

James pulls a pack of cigarettes from his pocket, shakes it and pulls one out with his teeth, grinning at us as he passes. Something strange flutters in my stomach as his dark eyes linger on mine. They flick briefly to Eric, then to Eric's arm around my shoulders, and I'm suddenly overwhelmed with the urge to throw his arm off of me, except I'm frozen in place. Our entire table is silent as he passes. He raises two fingers to his temple and salutes us, then turns and pushes out the door to the field.

"Yeah, total freak," Ryan mutters.

"I don't know, he's kind of hot," Mary says, crossing her arms over her ample chest.

I nearly choke on my water, Eric thankfully too distracted to notice.

"Mary, you can't be serious," he says incredulously. "He looks like he crawled out of a garbage heap."

She shrugs and stares wistfully over my shoulder. "I mean, yeah he's a bit rough around the edges, but I feel like I could change him. Soften him up, you know?"

"Yeah, or he could kill you and drink your blood," Ryan interjects.

Mary rolls her eyes. "Oh come on, I'm just messing with you."

Once the words have left Mary's lips, I realize she's right. James Walton is hot. And even if he's the devil incarnate, it's killing me that I'm not his type.

JAMES ISN'T in either of my afternoon classes. But even though he's not behind me, I can still feel him everywhere. Like a hot, humid day, his presence clings to me. I haven't retained anything out of either class and by the time I make my way to the bleachers behind the school to watch Eric's practice, my flushed skin is desperate for the cool breeze.

Once again, I'm alone, but at least today I have my books for school so I can get a head start on some homework. I watch as Eric runs out onto the field with the others. I guess everything is okay between us again. So why does it all feel different? He hasn't looked my way once since the practice started. I wonder if he would even notice if I left. Somehow I think he would though, and just like how he thought I'd fallen asleep on Saturday, he'd be annoyed. My stomach grumbles and even though I relished the cool breeze ten minutes ago, the sun has disappeared behind a cloud and now I'm cold, barely keeping myself from shivering. As I watch Eric toss the javelin across the field, there's an unfamiliar smell in the air. Smoke?

"So this is what you do for fun? You're right . . . I'm not interested."

I jump in my seat at the sound of his voice. I look around, but he's not there. A plume of smoke drifts out between the metal slats beside me and I peer through them. He's leaning against the metal bench from behind and looking up at me, a cigarette between his lips.

"I—what do you want?" I blurt out.

James shrugs. "Nothing. Just saw you out here and wondered what you were doing all by yourself in the cold without a jacket."

"I'm not cold," I say and as if on cue, my body shivers.

He smirks. "I'd offer you mine, I just wouldn't want to take the chance away from your boyfriend to be a gentleman."

Even through the chill, my face heats. I know it would never occur to Eric in a million years to offer me his jacket. He'd probably never even notice I was cold, yet this stranger notices? I look over the thick denim jacket covered in patches with the wool collar—it does look warm.

"You never answered my question," he says, his arms sliding down the bench toward me and pulling me out of my thoughts.

I narrow my eyes. "What question?"

"What do you do around here for fun? It can't be this, right? Sitting on metal bleachers in the cold just to be ignored by your boyfriend?"

I scoff angrily. "He's not ignoring me, he's busy," I say, gesturing to where he is on the field.

"Sure. Whatever you say."

I turn toward him in my seat. "And for your information, no, this isn't what I do for fun."

He grins at me, and my breath catches in my throat at his dazzling smile and his dark eyes which in the natural light I see are really a chocolate brown. He takes a long drag of his cigarette and blows it out into the cold air, the smoke rising in a little cloud.

"Anyway," I say through chattering teeth, "what does it matter to you?"

He tilts his head, his hair falling across his forehead pleasingly. "If you were mine, I wouldn't subject you to something so boring."

He grips the front of the metal bench and leans back. His one hand is so close to my thigh, I can feel the heat radiating from his skin. He has rings on his index and middle finger. One of a skull and the other of a rose. It's such a bizarre combination that I can't help staring, taking a moment to get an up-close look at his large hands. His long fingers and the veins that shift under the skin.

"Also," he continues, his voice dropping, "I'd never let you be cold."

My mouth is completely dry, and that fluttering sensation is back in my belly. Actually, it's somewhere lower, and I squirm in my seat. Not his type. I'm not his type. He told me that and now he's here criticizing my boyfriend and telling me he'd never let me be cold if I were with him. Please, Lord, give me strength.

"Well, I'm not your girlfriend. I'm with someone. And—" I simply can't contain myself. "I'm not your type anyway."

He laughs a little, taking a final drag on his cigarette before flicking it out through the metal bleachers and blowing the smoke up in the air. "That's right."

"Funny, it didn't seem that way when you were ogling me through the window Saturday night."

His eyes widen for a moment, then he pushes his tongue into his cheek biting back a smile. "You caught me off guard. It won't happen again."

The fluttering in my belly vanishes.

"Besides," he continues, "you didn't know I was there. You said so yourself. If you had known, it never would have happened, right?"

His gaze is intense. Waiting for me to agree with that statement. Or maybe to refute it. A challenge. And just as I'm about to say something, his eyes drop to my mouth and an entire cage of butterflies escapes inside of me.

I nod and whisper breathlessly, "That's right."

We stare at each other for a moment, then he claps his hands together loudly. It startles me, causing me to jump in my seat and set my heart pounding against my squeezed ribcage.

"Right. So glad we cleared that up," he says, backing away. "See you around, Becks."

He walks off toward the staff parking lot, and I'm left here alone and utterly frazzled, praying to keep my thoughts away from his hands and how different they might feel from Eric's.

CHAPTER 6

I Wanna Be Somebody

JAMES

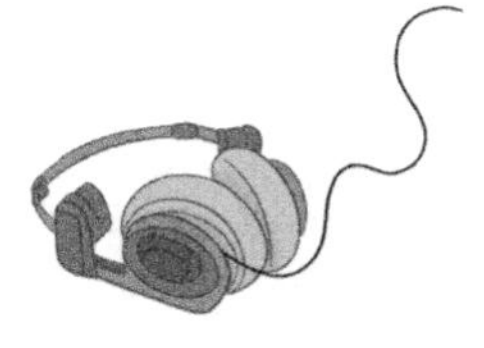

RULE #4 - NEVER RELY ON ANYONE ELSE.

What am I even doing?

I fight against the urge to look back at the fascinating blonde sitting on the bleachers. She has a boyfriend. An absolute dipshit of a boyfriend, but a boyfriend all the same. I'd gotten the very obvious hint he provided when I passed them in the cafeteria. The way he stopped one step short of pissing on her to mark his territory. Pathetic. I barely know her but one thing is certain— she's too good for him.

I make my way across the back field toward my van, the map for The Shipwreck burning a hole in my pocket. It's been hard to accept help from Noreen, so I'm desperate to find a job. I hadn't even known I had an aunt, and it wasn't until my mom's final days that she spoke of her at all. Something must have happened to cause a rift in their relationship, but I won't ask. Not when Noreen has been so kind.

My mom had been such a mess—on and off drugs most of my early childhood, which meant that I bounced around the foster care system for a while. It wasn't until I was eight that she'd been able to clean her act up and in those years, I'd learned to fend for myself. I'm not exactly proud of the things I've done to survive during that early time in my life, there's just nothing I can do now to change it. I promised myself I'd never go back to living that way. Not after enduring their violent version of God.

Even after Mom had gotten cleaned up, it didn't take long for her to get sick. The doctors told her it had probably been from the needles, or maybe one of the guys she'd been seeing, but it only took ten years for that awful disease to take her life. It didn't help that we had been so destitute and living in filth, causing the both of us to get sick all the time. I would recover fine, but Mom—eventually she just couldn't anymore.

I tried to help. Working odd jobs around the apartment complex we lived in to help pay the bills. She always refused the money, but when she had bad days, bad weeks which finally turned into months, she didn't have a choice anymore. My education obviously suffered the most. It's hard to concentrate on learning fractions or conjugating verbs when your mother's coughing up blood at home and you don't know when you'll eat next. Of course, most of my teachers didn't care, and the ones that did weren't able to do much.

I think that's why I fell in love with music. To drown out the constant horror of my life. The sirens, the yelling neighbors, and the coughing—I was never able to sleep. Then I found a record player on the side of the road, brought it home and tried to figure out how to make it work properly. A neighbor gave me Van Halen's debut album to check if I fixed it right. Amazingly enough, I had, and I listened to it all night, over and over again, the sounds of my horrible life fading away into the background. I remember ditching school the next day to go to the record store downtown with the modest money I had from fixing a water heater and buying the record for myself. There was a massive poster of Eddie Van Halen in the window, and when I saw him, I knew that was what I wanted to be.

I wanted to be like Eddie so bad. So I worked more, saved more—trading whatever I had to buy more records and dropping by the music store every day on my way home from school to practice on the guitars until they kicked me out for not buying anything. I snuck into clubs to watch local bands perform, keeping an eye on the message boards for anyone who was looking for a guitarist. A few times a "wanted" ad would go up, but I was always too young, too inexperienced, and didn't have my own guitar. I kept practicing anyway. Eventually, I'd been able to afford my own guitar, and while it wasn't anything fancy, it was mine and I could play it as much as I wanted.

I climb into my van and roll down the window before lighting up another cigarette. I can still see Rebecca sitting on the bleachers—can practically see her shivering from here.

I'd meant it as a joke, but now that I'm sitting here, I think maybe I should've offered her my jacket. Though she probably wouldn't have taken it, maybe she'd have appreciated the offer.

I'm not your girlfriend. I'm with someone. And I'm not your type anyway.

I may have imagined it, but she looked hurt. I hadn't meant to hurt her feelings when I told her she wasn't my type. If I'm honest, I'm not really sure what my goal was in saying that at all. I suppose it was partly to keep her at arm's length. The other reason was to rile her up because she looks so gorgeous when she's mad. Her green eyes flaring, nose scrunching and her cheeks burning bright pink. But I suppose telling her that was a bit cruel and not something any girl wants to hear.

I shake my head. What am I saying? I'm not trying to be her friend. I don't want to be anyone's friend. I'm here for one reason, and that's to graduate with a fucking diploma. I place the cigarette between my lips and start the engine before throwing it in reverse and heading out onto the street. The map is easy enough to follow, taking me way out to the edge of town. It's a bit rough out this way, so far from the suburbs. A few apartment buildings, a laundromat, what looks like a gym—all with the look of being just a bit run down. Neglected. Then I see it. The Shipwreck.

For not knowing much about Noreen, she seems to know *me* pretty well. This is exactly my kind of place. Not because I like dive bars, but from what I can see of the clientele at three thirty in the afternoon, I won't stand out like a sore thumb like I do at school. I pull into the lot and head for the door. There's no bouncer here now, yet there's red velvet ropes hanging by the door like they get busy enough that people would need to wait to be let in.

I push the hair out of my face and open the door. The sound of pool balls clacking and the smell of smoke and stale beer fills the air. My feet stick to the floor as I make my way across to the wide oak bar. There's a few guys sitting on the stools, a few at a table in the corner and what appear to be some bikers playing pool. They all eye me as I cross the room, but other than a quick glance at me up and down, they don't seem to care that I'm here.

It's a stark difference to how it had been at school. It was almost comical how much people had stared. All except Rebecca, although to be fair, she'd probably gotten her fill of staring at me through the window the past few days. Maybe I need to close my own curtains.

There's a man standing behind the bar with long brown hair, a long beard and an eyepatch. He looks like a pirate. The name of the bar comes to mind and I chuckle under my breath at the joke.

"Can I help you?" he asks, his voice gruff. Probably from years of smoking.

I nod a little with my chin. "Yeah, hey man. My aunt told me you were looking to hire a bar back?"

He tilts his head. "You're Noreen's nephew?"

From what I *do* know of Noreen, it seems odd she'd know the people who hang out here. But who am I to judge anything by its cover? Perhaps they're in a book club together.

"Yeah, that's right."

"Hmm . . . You ever done this kind of work before?" he asks, his one eye darting between my two.

My mouth twists and I shake my head. "No, but I'm a fast learner and willing to do almost anything for money."

He grins and sticks out his hand. "Good enough for me."

I reach forward and shake it. "Thanks."

"I'm John, by the way," he says, lifting up a piece of the counter and stepping out into the seating area. "Noreen and I went to high school together years ago."

Something wild beats in my chest. "Really? Did you know my mom?"

"What was her name?"

"Dora Walton."

He stops and shakes his head. "No, sorry, kid. I didn't even know Noreen had a sister until a few weeks ago when she came in telling me her nephew needed a job. What's your name again?"

"James. James Walton."

"Oh. You took your mom's name?"

It's not clear whether he thinks this odd, interesting or insulting. But seeing as how I need this job, I'm not about to be snarky with my answer. "Yeah. She's the one who stuck around, you know?"

John nods and leads me through the place on a quick tour. Behind the bar there's a kitchen and a massive fridge for kegs and bottles, the smell of flat, stale alcohol a strangely familiar comfort. He shows me a back door to a parking lot for staff.

"It gets busy here Thursday to Sunday, which is when I'll need you most. You can park out here. Down the stairs there's a bathroom and lockers for your stuff and storage for more cases of beer and liquor. I'm sorry to say you'll be hauling shit up and down these stairs a lot."

I shrug. "At least it'll keep me in shape."

He narrows his one eye at me. "You smoke?"

Again, I'm not sure what the right answer is, but I figure I'll be honest. "Yeah."

He nods. "Staff can smoke out the back door there. Although, you might want to keep it to a minimum with the stairs."

"Right."

"Well, that's it . . . Oh, we also have the stage over there. Fridays and Saturdays we have live bands play—"

He leads me around the corner of the bar that hadn't been fully visible when I'd first entered. John's voice trails off as I stare at the raised platform covered in amps and speakers, a metal bar with lights hanging down from above. I glance at the walls where there are posters for Judas Priest, Slayer, Dio, Iron Maiden, Slaughter . . . It goes on and on. Shit . . . Noreen really did have me pegged. This place is like paradise.

John grabs the lapel of my jacket to glance at the patches haphazardly sewn into the denim. "Seems like you'll probably fit right in here, kid. You play at all?"

I nod, my throat feeling oddly thick. "Yeah. Guitar."

"What kind do you play?"

I shrug, feeling a little self-conscious. "Just an Epiphone. I didn't have much cash and something was better than nothing."

He claps a hand on my shoulder. "Yeah, I get that."

"Do you know anyone who's looking for a guitarist?" I ask.

John points to a corkboard on the far wall. "People post on there if they're looking for anyone, but I'll keep an ear out for you kid."

I grin. "Thanks."

"Right, well, you can start on Wednesday. Be here by six. We usually do a lot of prep for the coming week on Wednesday."

"Okay, great."

He holds out his hand again. "Welcome aboard The Shipwreck."

I SPEND a few hours driving around town, getting to know the area. Besides the high school and The Shipwreck, I haven't ventured out much and I'm curious to see if there's anything worthwhile, even if I'm only going to be here for two and a half months. Unsurprisingly, Pelowna, Iowa is nothing like where I grew up. There are the well-manicured suburbs, and the gritty outer edges. The thriving downtown core and the quiet tree-lined streets. Detroit is all grit and grime and noise.

I find a music store close to the bar and I spend almost an hour trying out some of their guitars, growing particularly fond of a Gibson SG that is worth more money than I've ever had in my life. Maybe I could sell a kidney to be able to afford it. The store has a message board by the registers just like at the bar. Advertisements for piano, guitar and even vocal lessons, and a few secondhand instruments for sale. No audition notices, though. No one in need of what I can offer.

It's almost after dark when I pull into Noreen's place, my eyes automatically scanning the house next door for an unyielding blonde. No sign of her. I think about her shivering on those bleachers and wonder briefly if her shithead boyfriend had stepped up to the plate, or let her tiny body freeze all afternoon.

Stubbing out my cigarette in the ashtray of the van, I head into the house. The smell of roast chicken hits me as I walk in the door, making my mouth water.

"Hey, you're just in time," Noreen says, appearing around the door frame. "How'd it go?"

I remove my jacket and toss my bag on an empty chair in the living room. "John gave me the job."

"That's great," she says, smiling and placing a large pan on the table.

"You know, you could've warned me the guy looked like a pirate," I say, coming to stand across the counter from her.

She laughs. "Oh, I didn't even think about that. Yes, John certainly has that look doesn't he?"

"I thought briefly about calling him Captain."

"Oh dear. Well, he either would've found it hilarious or he'd make you walk the plank and you'd be somewhere floating down the river right now." She laughs and hands me a plate as she starts to scoop potatoes, chicken and carrots onto it in steaming piles.

"This looks amazing," I say quietly, "but you know I can fend for myself, right?"

"And let you deny me the opportunity to dust off my cooking skills? Don't be ridiculous."

I open my mouth to say more, to tell her I don't expect her to be my mom, or my babysitter. That I can't stand the feeling of owing anyone for their kindness. But, she points to the table sharply.

"Uh-uh. Shut up, sit down, and eat for crying out loud."

I sigh. Just like the spaghetti she made, her food is delicious and warms me all the way to my toes. We eat in silence for a few minutes before the questions start.

"How was school? Everything work out okay with your classes?" she asks.

I nod, my head bouncing around a bit as I try to make sense of the day. "It was fine. Made it to all my classes. Didn't get into any trouble, so I guess you could count that as a win."

Noreen hides a grin. "Make any friends?"

I shake my head. "Not here to make friends."

She sets her fork down next to her plate. "So, what . . . you didn't talk to anyone all day?"

I think about it for a moment. Other than the teachers, the custodian and the secretary who I was obligated to speak to, the only other person I spoke to was Rebecca. "Not really, no," I answer.

Noreen takes a deep breath. "Not everyone around here is awful. I know you have your priorities, but a few friends . . . even just one friend, could make things at least moderately entertaining for you. Even if it's simply to help you with homework to get through to the end of the school year."

The truth is, I don't really want to make friends. I don't want anything to tie me down here, and friends would do that. Noreen is the exception, but she's family. The worst thing that could happen is to make a bunch of friends which causes me to waver in my decision to go to San Francisco. Staying here forever is my worst nightmare. To appease her I say simply, "I'll think about it."

After cleaning up the dinner mess, I hop in the shower. The steam fills the room quickly, the heat opening my pores and lungs and the smell of some sort of flower invades my senses. It reminds me of my mom, and I wonder if Noreen buys the same soap as she always did. If my mom and Noreen have other similarities. I have so many unanswered questions about what might have happened between my mom and her sister, but I don't want to jeopardize how well things are going by bringing it up.

After showering, I grab a pair of boxers and sweatpants from the laundry basket Noreen has left on the bathroom counter for me. Yet another thing she has done that I feel guilty for. It's one thing for her to feed me, but to also wash my underwear? The woman is a saint. I rub a towel over my head to soak up the water from my hair. It hangs darkly around my shoulders and across my forehead. The curls are more defined when they're damp—not like I'm fussy about it. The hair serves its purpose, especially to those douchebags at school. I'd be caught dead before I cut it like them.

I head into the bedroom looking for a T-shirt, flicking on the guitar lamp on my nightstand by the bed, but there's already light spilling into the room through the window. I approach it cautiously, the curiosity to see what Rebecca's up to over there almost painful as I slowly put one foot in front of the other until I'm standing right before the glass. Goosebumps scatter over my bare chest and arms as I catch sight of her. Probably from a chill sneaking in through the old window—definitely not because of her.

She's there, though. Sitting at her desk in a flowery pajama shirt and pants, her blonde hair tucked behind her ears and the end of a pen between her teeth. To be honest, I'm surprised her curtains are open, especially after our conversation at school today and her needing to make it perfectly clear that I only caught her in that moment of undress by accident. As I watch her, I'm glad that she hasn't shut me out. I might not want friends, but an attractive acquaintance isn't off the table.

There's something so different about the way she looks now as opposed to at school, and it takes me a few moments to realize it's her posture. She's not so stiff, so straight. She's curved and soft, and while she doesn't look overly relaxed by the creases of concentration on her face, she seems more comfortable.

She pulls the pen from her mouth and turns her face toward me. Setting aside whatever she's working on, she pushes herself to her feet. For a moment, I think she'll race to close her curtains, like it's something she's forgotten to do. To prove that I'm unimportant, a nuisance. But she doesn't. She holds my gaze for what feels like forever before those jade-colored eyes travel down over my bare chest.

I've never been self-conscious, never worried too much about what anyone thought of my looks or my body, but the way

Rebecca is looking at me right now is strangely more intense than any other girl who's looked at me before. I'm like a kettle that's been flipped on, my body boiling from the inside out as her eyes drag slowly over my skin. Inch by inch, my skin prickles before her eyes land back on my face. Blood rushes to my groin as I realize with unadulterated smugness, that little miss goody-two-shoes is checking me out.

I know right there that Rebecca Briar is the perfect kind of trouble. She's a good girl who's bursting to be bad.

CHAPTER 7

Somebody's Watching Me

REBECCA

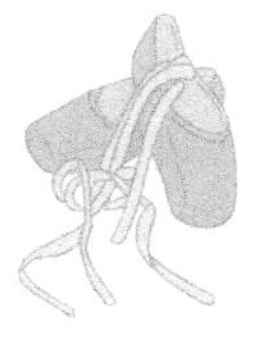

Like a gold ring in a pig's snout is a beautiful woman without discretion.
Proverbs 11:22

My heart is pounding against my ribcage, my blood pulsing in my ears, my chest, and even between my legs. James's naked torso is unlike anything I've ever seen, and it's not like I've seen much, but of what I do know, he's different. So much different than Eric when we went swimming last summer. He has tattoos of a tree and a rose on his chest, and what looks like a snake, or maybe vines, curling around his ribcage.

His body is lean, muscular, veins sliding underneath skin as he moves. A grin pulls at the side of his face and I blink, immediately ashamed of how blatantly I've been staring at him. It's so inappropriate—it's so not me. It's so sinful I'm amazed I haven't been swallowed up by the earth to spend eternity paying for it in Hell. I've never cared much about a man's physical appearance before, except for whether he accepted Jesus into his heart and maybe . . . a handsome face.

He raises one finger and steps back toward his night stand. What's he doing? I step closer to the window, my fingertips touching the cold glass as he rifles around in a drawer. Pulling a marker out, he takes the cap off with his teeth, the movement captivating, and grabs a black-and-white notebook from on top of the speaker by his bed.

He shakes his damp hair away from how it hangs in his face as he writes, then approaches the window again. As he holds up his makeshift sign so I can see, his face splits into the smuggest grin I've seen yet.

See something you like?

Something snaps, like if I was caught with my hand in the cookie jar. This is so wrong. My body shakes and my breath halts in my chest like some gigantic weight is sitting on top of it. He thinks he knows me—thinks he understands my mind—but even I don't understand it because my fingers travel to the buttons on the front of my pajama shirt.

The smug smile drains from his face as his eyes follow my fingers and before I can stop myself, I'm pulling my shirt off of me and exposing my chest to him. Again. Time seems to stand still as I let his eyes travel over my skin. James wets his lips and my skin breaks out into goosebumps, my nipples hardening painfully inside my bra. His chest flushes and I can see his breathing become rapid, and a smile grows on my face as something like triumph burns in my chest.

I turn and grab a notepad from my desk and scribble a note on it for him before holding it up.

Do you?

He blinks, mouth falling open and before I can give him a chance to respond, I grip the curtains and shut them tight.

My heart is pounding and blood rushes in my ears so loud I can't hear anything else. After tossing the note on my desk then pulling my shirt back on, I realize I'm shaking. Stumbling back toward the bed, my knees hit the edge, and I slump down to the floor. An uncomfortable prickling stings the back of my eyes, and before I can stop them, tears are falling treacherously down my cheeks. Why am I doing this? Have I been possessed? I haven't felt like myself since he pulled up in that black van, full of chaos and temptation.

I'm failing God. I am desperate for James's approval and for what? My pride? I've let him see me without a shirt on just to prove a point. I don't need to prove anything to this non-believer. I should have just ignored him. But here I am, obsessing over my own selfish needs, straying away from the herd. I'm broken and impure and disgusting. Doomed to that terrifying place that haunts my dreams.

I wipe the tears out of my eyes and rush over to grab the bible off my desk before I kneel at the side of my bed. I pray and pray and pray until my voice is hoarse. The words of John 1:9 strangely don't bring me the comfort they normally do. Is it too much this time? Is forgiveness for this too much to ask for? Will I never be worthy again?

The light of his lamp that shines against my curtains disappears and I'm bathed in darkness. The house is quiet, the sound of my erratic breaths as loud as a scream. I push myself up off my now aching knees and move back to the window. My fingers brush against the curtains, and even though we're separated by glass window panes and a twelve-foot distance, this fabric is the only thing protecting me from losing my mind.

Taking a deep breath, my fingers twitch as I back away. No.

Never again. I need to ignore him and stay vigilant. I refuse to let him turn me into an unworthy sinner. I won't be led astray again. Because that's what it is. Weakness. Not being strong enough to turn away, to close the curtains, to stop the thoughts from running wild in my head as the image of his chest and arms and hands all attached to that beautiful face and dark eyes threatens to invade every thought I have. To not devalue myself by giving in to this game of back and forth we seem to be playing. To ignore the way his smile makes my stomach flutter and remember what he told me earlier. That I'm not his type, even if his eyes tonight told me otherwise.

THERE ARE dark circles under my eyes this morning. What little sleep I was able to get was permeated by a gigantic tree and vines . . . or maybe they were snakes, the tendrils of which had wrapped themselves around my neck, my wrists, my legs, holding me so tightly I couldn't get free. And all of it was permeated by an overwhelming heat. A suffocating, sweltering heat, and I woke up sweating and in desperate need of a shower.

After my hair dries, I brush it out, pull back the front pieces and secure them with a white bow at the back of my head. I wander back into my bedroom, only to find my mom standing at the foot of my bed with a pile of fabric in her hands.

"Oh," I say with surprise, a sour taste immediately washing over my tongue.

She turns toward me, my body still wrapped in my towel. "Good morning, Rebecca. I made something for you. I thought you could wear it today. This pattern is so feminine, you'll look so lovely in it."

Dress like a girl. Act like a girl. Be feminine like a girl, but not so feminine that it makes me immodest. Seductive. It's all so complicated.

"We have Bible study after dinner tonight and I'm sure everyone would love to see you in something new."

My fingers clench in the terry cloth as I stare at her smile. The Lord is showing me the way. Delivering my mother with this dress so I can prove I am still on fire for him. That my actions last night were a momentary weakness that will never be repeated. She tilts her head and I step forward, giving her my most gracious smile. "Thanks, Mom. It's beautiful."

She blinks a few times then claps her hands together. "Well, hurry up and get dressed. Eric is waiting for you downstairs."

I nearly drop the towel. "He is?"

"Yes, something about an early study session at school, so if you want to ride with him you'll have to leave now. A Godly woman never makes a man wait." Flipping her hair over her shoulder, she gives me one more long look then heads back out into the hallway, shutting my door behind her. I let out a loud breath, quickly crossing to the bed where she's left the dress.

It's made out of a heavy cotton plaid in gray, black and red—three of my least favorite colors to wear. It has a high neck and an attached white Peter Pan collar. In any other circumstance, it might be cute. Mary would certainly look great in it, with her dark hair and natural red lips. I pick it up and hold it against me, wondering just how tight she's made this one.

But my body is the temple of the Holy Spirit, and I need to honor God with how I dress. My mother is helping me do that.

I put on a bra and a pair of underwear, then take a deep breath before pulling the dress on over my head. There's a hidden zipper at the side, which at least will make it easier for me to do up on my own. The last thing I want to do is call my mom back into my room to help zip me up and listen to her criticize me about how the zipper is struggling over the fat in my back.

The sleeves are tight against my arms and the dress hardly fits even with the zipper undone. I look up at the ceiling, trying to blink away the wetness pooling along my eyelashes. I don't want to spend the whole day with swollen eyes, so I blink the tears back, suck in a deep breath and pull at the zipper as it closes an inch at a time.

"Rebecca! Hurry up!"

Another breath in and a hard tug and the zipper closes but snags the skin over my ribs with a sharp sting. I hiss out a breath, the dress barely giving me any room to expand my lungs. Taking a quick look in the mirror, I tuck back the stray hairs behind my ears and look at myself in the dress. If it was the correct size, it would be quite pretty, but all I can see is a plaid straight jacket.

Frustration bubbles in my aching stomach, and I glance over my shoulder at the curtains remembering the cause of most of my frustration and my sinful behavior last night. I remember that I need to prove myself.

I grab my bag and head down the stairs. Eric is standing in the doorway, talking with my mother. They both look over as I descend and my mother hands out a paper bag to me.

"Here's your lunch, dear," she says, that manic grin still covering her face. "Don't forget about tonight."

I nod, realizing I won't be able to have any breakfast now that I'm being ushered out the door, but I eagerly grab the paper bag, hoping she packed me more than apple slices today. From the feel of the bag, she has.

Getting into Eric's car, I look over at the black van sitting in the driveway. It serves as a reminder—a warning. That I could be sent away. I pull my cardigan around myself as my eyes flick up toward the second story window.

I wonder if he's still asleep. What does he do in the morning? Does it take him a long time to fix his hair just right? Or does he roll out of bed looking like that? Does he—No. No, no, no. I pull on the chain around my neck again, the pinch making me wince.

"You look nice today."

I shake my head. "Sorry?"

Eric rolls his eyes. "I said, you look nice today."

I pull at the tight collar around my throat, my arms barely managing to reach further than that. I'm so restricted, like I'm in that dream and tied up in vines, completely unable to escape.

"Thank you," I manage. "You—you look nice today too."

He's wearing his usual attire—pressed jeans and a bright collared shirt under his letterman jacket.

"I hope you don't mind having an early start today," he says.

Yes, I do mind. Especially since I slept so terribly last night, couldn't eat breakfast and now my stomach is churning painfully. "It's fine."

I twist in my seat, the cut where the zipper got me throbbing with every movement of the seam over it. Closing my eyes, I try to take a deep breath. Suffering is good. I'm suffering for Jesus.

Eric turns down the street toward the school, pulls into the lot and parks at the furthest possible corner before turning off the engine. He turns in his seat to face me, his pale eyes somehow darker than normal.

"Becca . . ." he says quietly, his hand reaching out to touch my thigh.

I push his hand away, looking out the back window at the school. "I thought you had an early study session?"

"I just needed an excuse to spend some time alone with you. I feel terrible about Sunday and I've missed you."

His breath brushes past my cheek, and I catch the smell of alcohol again.

I push hard against his chest with my hand. "It's eight in the morning!"

He leans closer. "So what?"

"So—you've been drinking and now you're driving me around? You're supposed to protect me, not put me in harm's way."

"Becca, I'm not drunk."

"You always try to take things too far when you've been drinking," I say.

His hand slides down to the hem of my dress, his fingers gripping my thigh rougher than he ever has before. I'm sure it'll bruise, I think, as his lips touch my neck.

I'm frozen, partly because of this infernal dress, and partly because I'm so confused. I've dressed the way God expects, the way my mother expects, but still, he stumbles. Eric wraps his hand behind my head and pulls my face toward him, his lips brushing gracelessly over mine. Every time he kisses me, it feels awkward and cold. A kiss will only lead to him lusting after more than I can give. If Eric was following God's word, he wouldn't ask this of me. Why is everything I've been taught such a contradiction?

I'm getting light-headed. He barely stops long enough for me to take a breath, and this dress won't allow me to breathe deeply enough when he does. The sound of cars pulling into the parking lot makes me nervous that someone will see us. Then I feel his hand on my thigh again and I jump away.

"Okay, that's enough," I say breathlessly.

He groans. "Come on, Becca, we still have twenty minutes before the first bell . . ."

I shake my head, grabbing my backpack from between my feet. "No . . . this was—we shouldn't even be—"

"You think I want it like this?" he shouts.

With wide eyes, I hold my breath until he looks away. I reach down to massage the mark on my thigh and my other hand smooths down my hair, the threat of tears burning the back of my eyes. "I'm sorry," I whisper.

"All right, all right, relax, okay?" he says, opening his door and getting out, slamming it shut behind him.

I clench my fists, the nails digging into the skin of my palms, and take a few breaths to try and calm down. As I look up through the driver's side window, those dark eyes surrounded by smoke are staring back at me from inside a black van.

Why? *Why?* Why is this happening? Can't I just have one moment where I'm not being suffocated or watched? No, because God is always watching. I turn away from James but I can feel his gaze on me as I get out of the car and walk toward the school, following behind Eric who by now is several yards ahead and falling into step with some of his friends.

The halls and voices of students are a blur of color and my head is starting to throb, likely from the lack of sleep. I make my way to class and sit down, taking small comfort in the fact that at least in class no one will be able to talk to or touch me. Students file in as Mrs. Henry makes her way to the front of the classroom.

The smell of cigarette smoke and some kind of spicy cologne fills the air around my head, and I glance up from double checking my homework to see James walking my way. My face grows hot, knowing he just watched me kissing my boyfriend in the parking lot. Knowing that I was kissing my boyfriend after I stripped for him last night. Will he laugh at me? He's wearing a shirt with a red demon on it today and I almost snort at how appropriate it is. Like God is sending me a sign.

Warning—this man is the devil.

The bell rings, and he makes his way down the aisle by my desk with a casual grace. Just like yesterday, his long fingers trail across the edge of my desk, the clink of his two rings knocking together. But then a little folded scrap of paper appears where his hand had been and I suck in a breath. Did he . . . did he just give me a note?

Like a serpent snatching at prey, I grasp the paper, hiding it under my palm and not daring to look behind me where I'm sure he's sitting as cool as a cucumber. Mrs. Henry could very well be speaking Swedish for all I know right now, because the note is burning my skin.

What could he have possibly written? Is it about last night? Is it about today in the parking lot? Is it simply to ask for help with homework? My leg is bouncing so hard, my chair starts to squeak. Finally, after twenty minutes or so, Mrs. Henry sets us our task for the class, reading and answering questions from our history textbook. I make a show of pulling out my binder, but the moment her eyes are off me, I pull out the little paper and unfold it in my lap.

Don't think you can call last night another accident.

A blush spreads across my face, down my neck and all the way to my ears. Before I can help myself, I turn to look over my shoulder where, sure enough, his eyes are on me. He smirks, gives me a little wink, then leans back over his textbook like nothing happened. Some new and unfamiliar feeling starts to spread through my belly, all the way to my fingers and toes. I think the feeling is excitement. The thrill of this flirtation, the fact that he seems to enjoy teasing me and the all-consuming feeling of his eyes and attention.

The mixed messages are piling up like clutter in my mind, blocking out any hope I have of being productive in class. Is he expecting me to respond to this? Because I won't. I can't.

I want to.

I want this game to continue. But I shouldn't because boys like James Walton are dangerous for girls like me. Ignore him and be vigilant . . . I'm stronger than this.

Even as I try to convince myself to toss his note in the trash, my hand reaches for my pen.

CHAPTER 8

California Dreamin'

JAMES

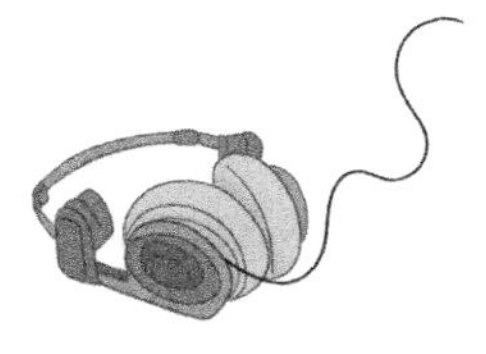

She's wearing another ultra modest dress today and her hair is half pulled back and tied with a white ribbon. The perfect image of modesty, but I know better and there's a twinge of satisfaction that surges through me as I realize I might be the only one who knows the secret part of her.

She snatches the note and looks around, terrified someone might see that we've dared interact beyond her showing me to our second-period class yesterday. As students file in, she seems to clutch the little paper in her lap like a secret, and I can't help but smile at how adorable that is.

It's not until halfway through class that she finally checks what I've written and I'm surprised to see her writing something down. The wait is killing me, the minutes crawling by at a glacial pace. The bell finally rings and she stands to head out of the room, leaving behind the note on her desk. I reach for it, my heart speeding along as I read what she wrote.

Don't think you can say you didn't mean to look.

A laugh bursts from my chest. Maybe little miss goody-two-shoes wants to play after all. I grab my bag and run after her. Spotting her passing the science classrooms, I race through the halls to catch up with her. Within a few feet, I can see her tense like she knows I'm behind her.

"So, are we going to talk about it?" I ask, leaning forward to whisper in her ear. It turns pink, but she focuses on walking ahead.

"Talk about what?"

"Oh, I don't know," I chuckle, looking around to make sure no one can hear before lowering my voice. "How about you taking your shirt off in front of your window last night."

She stops and faces me. "That depends."

"On?"

"If you're willing to admit you couldn't look away."

A wide grin overtakes my face. "That's why you did it? To prove me wrong? Sorry, angel, I didn't realize you'd take it so personally when I said you weren't my type."

"That's not—" She sighs and presses her lips together. "I don't care about that. I have a boyfriend."

She starts to walk again, but I keep pace with her through the halls. "Right, the boyfriend you looked so excited about kissing."

"That's none of your business," she says, her cheeks now turning red.

"Seems like you made it my business when you took your clothes off for me."

She whirls around, bringing us to a stop in the middle of the hallway, nostrils flared. "Even if I didn't have a boyfriend, I wouldn't be interested in you."

"Not sure if I believe that. You took a pretty long look at the goods last night," I say, gesturing to my chest. "I don't think I've ever been so thoroughly eye-fucked before."

Her mouth opens, and whatever retort she had planned to say dies in her throat, her eyes widening. She closes her mouth and pouts, her bottom lip protruding out and, fuck, it makes me want to bite it. Instead, I smile at her. She lifts her arms, but her mouth twitches and she pushes them back down at her sides. Was she about to slap me?

Her throat bobs as she swallows. "I was *not* doing . . . that."

"Listen, there's no shame in looking. What's the problem?"

She pulls herself up as tall as she can, her nose turning up in the air, her lip beginning to tremble. "I—no, I hadn't meant to. I was just . . . Someone like me should be better than that."

I cross my arms over my chest. "Someone like—oh, you mean someone who goes to church."

Her eyes drop to my chest and I look down where we both stare at the demon and pentagram on my shirt. I rub the back of my neck and chuckle. "Right, well . . . it probably won't mean much coming from a sinner like me, but you're not a bad person for looking."

Her head snaps up, eyes darting over my face like I've said something insane. But her face softens, and I watch the way the tension leaves her shoulders. She really is beautiful.

The warning bell rings overhead and I've forgotten we're standing in the middle of a crowded hallway. She seems to have forgotten too, blinking and looking around like she's just remembered we have a class to get to.

"Don't flatter yourself," she says. "I was merely trying to prove a point." She turns on her heel and walks away, her nose proudly turned up in the air.

Shit, that was interesting. And teasing her is fun. In fact, it might be my new favorite thing. I grin wider, then call over the thinning crowd in the hall toward her, "Keep telling yourself that, angel."

DURING SECOND PERIOD, I don't manage to retain any of what Mr. Adams says, and I know I'll kick myself later for that, but every time Rebecca glances over her shoulder at me, every thought about Murdock's collective subconscious theory disappears from my mind. All I can think about is that porcelain skin and that pink bra and the way her lip was just begging to be bitten. Also, the way her face seemed to relax when I told her she shouldn't beat herself up about checking me out.

Fuck. No! This girl is too wrapped up in the "I am holier than thou" bullshit and I don't want to get involved in that. That just screams trouble, and trouble is the last thing I need right now. Especially when there's so much riding on me finishing school and getting the fuck out of here. Besides, I'm hardly a knight in shining armor here to rescue her from outdated ideology.

When the bell finally rings, I look for her without thinking but she's gone, lost amongst the sea of neon pants and plaid. So I head to the cafeteria, aware that most people watch me as I pass them. I wonder what stupid rumors have been spreading through the school since my arrival. Not that it really matters. I'm not here to make friends, and I won't be sticking around for long.

When I enter the cafeteria, I spot Rebecca and her friends sitting at one end of the table they sat at yesterday. Not surprisingly, her boyfriend is nowhere to be seen. For someone who made a big show of letting me know she was with him, he's been oddly absent, except of course when he tried to cop a feel, or when he makes her watch his boring-ass track practices while she freezes to death. The idea of him strolling in here to find me sitting at her table is too good to pass up, and before I can talk myself out of it, I'm walking over, my eyes never wavering from that perfect white bow in her blonde hair.

Coming to a stop right behind her, I look down into the surprised faces of her friends. "Excuse me ladies, do you mind if I join you? No space anywhere else today."

There's a clatter of metal as Rebecca's spoon falls out of her hand onto the table.

"Oh," one of the girls says, her mouth opening and closing a few times before she speaks. She has mousy brown hair and brown eyes, and while not unattractive, she's plain. "Yeah . . . I mean . . . sure."

"Perfect." I smile and take a seat on the bench beside Rebecca.

The two girls opposite me watch for several minutes as I pull the lunch Noreen packed out of my bag.

"It's James, right?" the other girl asks. She's in one of my afternoon classes, but I can't remember her name.

"Yeah, that's right."

"I'm Mary." She reaches her hand across the table toward me. I finish chewing a bit of my sandwich and grasp her hand.

"Nice to meet you."

"This is Amy, and I believe you know Rebecca."

I turn to find Rebecca desperately invested in scraping her spoon around the top of her plastic yogurt container. Biting the inside of my cheek, I say, "Yeah, we've been introduced."

Without missing a beat, Mary leans forward to rest her chin on her hands. "So, why are you here?"

Amy gasps, grabbing onto Mary's arm. "What is wrong with you?" she whispers.

I smile as Mary fixes me with her narrowed eyes.

"Like I said, there weren't many other table options—"

Mary waves at me. "Not that. I mean why are you here, at our school? When there's only a couple of months left in the year."

I set down my sandwich, leaning forward. "Can you keep a secret?"

Amy and Mary nod enthusiastically, but I swear I hear what sounds like a scoff from Rebecca.

"I'm actually here because I'm under witness protection. You see, I helped uncover a secret Soviet military base back home, so they had to relocate me for my own protection from sleeper agents."

There's a long moment as Amy and Mary stare at me, as though trying to figure out if what I've said could possibly be true. It's punctured by a derisive laugh, and I turn to find Rebecca shaking her head.

"What a load of rubbish," she says softly. "Amy, don't believe a word of that. He's just pulling your leg."

I place a hand on my chest with mock outrage. "Are you calling me a liar?"

She turns to face me dead-on. "Yes."

Something flashes in her jade-colored eyes, and I have the funny feeling she's talking about more than just my little Soviet spy story. I hold her stare for a long time before finally raising my hands in surrender.

"Fine, fine," I say, turning back to the other girls. "Afraid the story is not that interesting. Had to move, and just need to graduate, so . . . here I am."

Mary leans back. "You're eighteen?"

"Nineteen."

She tilts her head, examining me. "How—"

"Not my first go at senior year."

Her eyebrow quirks up as though this is an appealing thought. I'm not sure what could be appealing about someone who's had to repeat senior year, but chicks are weird sometimes. A perfect example of which sits next to me, scraping her spoon around her half-eaten yogurt cup.

"I like your tattoo," Mary says, gesturing to the raven on my hand.

I turn my hand back and forth, the leather cuff rotating on my wrist. "Thanks. I do most of them myself. I have a few more, but they're not exactly in places for anyone to see. Just a select few."

Rebecca keeps her head down but flushes a deep pink, her fingers tangling in the gold chain around her neck. I wonder if she's picturing them. After all, she got a pretty damn good view of the tattoos on my chest last night.

I take another bite of my sandwich as Amy shifts in her seat, elbowing Mary. Pretending not to notice, I let the two girls silently work out whatever they plan on asking next.

"So," Mary says, "there's a party happening after the track meet next Friday. It's probably not your scene, but I thought I'd invite you in case no one else does."

I raise my eyebrow at her. I highly doubt this kind of crowd attends the type of school parties I'm used to."Will there be alcohol?"

Mary smirks. "Yes."

"Drugs?"

She blanches. Yeah . . . just as I suspected. Even though I don't do anything hard, it seems as though alcohol is probably as wild as it gets, which I guess if you're as sheltered as they seem to be, is enough.

"Thanks for the invite, ladies, but I actually work Friday nights."

"Oh, where do you work?" Amy asks.

I finish my sandwich and remind myself to hug Noreen as I pull out a couple of Oreo cookies. "The Shipwreck, on Woolbury."

Amy and Mary glance at each other, Rebecca seemingly forgotten.

"What?"

"Isn't that place . . ." Amy starts, her brown eyes wide, "really dangerous?"

I shrug. "I mean, not for me. But, every Thursday they sacrifice a virgin, so I'd steer clear if I were you."

The two girls' mouths drop open, and I feel Rebecca turn to

stare at me so hard I'm surprised my hair hasn't caught fire. I let a grin spread across my face before popping an Oreo in my mouth. I hold one out to Rebecca who blinks at it as if she's never seen a cookie before.

Mary cracks first, a nervous kind of chuckle, followed by Amy and the two of them dissolve into a whispered discussion. Rebecca doesn't laugh, though—she simply stares at the cookie I'm waving in front of her.

"Come on, who doesn't like Oreos?" I whisper, leaning toward her. "Especially after you barely ate that yogurt."

She reaches forward to take it then looks at me like she can't quite believe someone like me knows how to share. I may not believe in God, but I do have manners. I smile at her and nearly fall out of my seat when the strangest thing happens—she smiles back. It's small and she tries to hide it by looking down at the table, but it's there and it's real.

"Oh!" Mary exclaims. "I forgot to tell you both. Guess what came in the mail this morning?" Her voice pitches in a sing-songy way as I open my can of soda and take a long sip.

"What?" Rebecca asks.

Mary pauses for what I assume is dramatic effect before blurting, "My acceptance letter to UIndy!"

Amy shrieks, and I have to pull back, the sound forcing my eyes closed, wishing my ears could do the same. Rebecca looks awestruck.

"Really? It came today?"

Mary and Amy look thrilled, but I don't miss the way that Rebecca looks apprehensive. It vanishes a moment later, replaced by a winning grin that doesn't quite reach her eyes. I can't help but notice how different this one is compared to the one she had over a cookie.

"That's amazing, congratulations!" she says. "I wonder if—"

"What about you, James?" Mary directs her attention back to me, cutting Rebecca off. "What are your plans after graduation?"

I look back to Rebecca, her smile gone, face downcast, and I want to tell Mary she cut off her friend, only . . . that's getting too involved, and I should go anyway. I pack my garbage away, pulling my pack of cigarettes out of my pocket. I shake one out and stand. "San Francisco."

Mary and Amy laugh, probably convinced I'm pulling another fast one on them, but Rebecca is looking up at me with curious, wide eyes.

"Ladies," I mumble, putting the cigarette between my lips, throwing them a two-fingered salute before heading outside. To everyone else, San Francisco might seem ridiculous. An impossible dream. For me, it's a fact. Simply a matter of time.

CHAPTER 9

Livin' On A Prayer

REBECCA

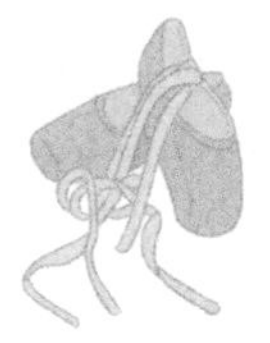

"Dad?"

He barely glances up from his plate as I push my food around, aware my mother is watching and tallying every bite I take. "Yes?"

"Was there any mail for me today?" I say in a rush.

He pauses mid-chew and looks up at me, finally paying attention. "Why would there be mail for you?"

My eyes flick to my mother, who's listening intently. "I just . . . I'm still waiting to hear back from colleges and Mary, um . . . she got her acceptance letter to the University of Indianapolis today, so I thought—"

"No," he says, cutting me off, "there wasn't any mail for you."

It's like a bubble bursts in my chest. I was so sure I would get in, and now knowing that Mary has been accepted—well, sometimes the mail is late, right?

"It's starting to get a bit late in the school year, isn't it?" my father asks, glancing up at me.

I push a potato around on my plate and nod.

"Recently, I'm not sure how much I support you going to

college. It was that Mrs. Henry who suggested allowing you to apply, but she's not one of us. A woman's role is to worship God and to learn in quiet and submission. Colleges these days are leading women astray with all their talk of 'women's rights.'"

My shoulders tense and embarrassment spreads over my skin like bugs crawling all over me.

"I suppose there's probably still a little more time to be accepted," he continues, "but your grades likely weren't good enough."

Why is it never good enough? Why am I never good enough? And why would God give me such a desire for education if it's something I can't have?

"Rebecca?"

I blink and turn to my father. "Sorry?"

His jaw twitches in annoyance at having to repeat himself. "I said, don't you think you could've tried harder in your classes?"

My instinct tells me no. I have a 4.0 grade point average and am taking almost all advanced-level classes. I've worked so hard because I knew that was what my parents expected of me. What God expected of me. What *I* expected of me.

"Maybe," I say quietly.

How could Mary have gotten accepted and not me? She's not even a true believer. She's smart, but she only averages a B+, an A- at most. Plus, she doesn't do any extracurricular activities around the school, whereas I helped set up student-led study groups before finals back in sophomore year. I'm President of the Teens for Christ club at school. I organized the bake sale and clothing drive for the people of Alton when a tornado tore their town apart. But does anyone seem to care about any of that? Apparently not.

Ring ring.

My father huffs irritably as he sets down his cutlery. This is the second time someone has called during dinner. No one ever calls at this time of night. It's simply rude, at least in our community.

"Excuse me," my father says, standing and leaving the dining room to head toward his office.

My stomach clenches hard and my face screws up against the hunger pains. "I think I'm finished," I say, daring a look at my mother, whose mouth curls upward in approval. "May I be excused, please?"

She nods. "Of course, but we should leave for Bible study in about fifteen minutes."

I quickly leave the table, clean up my dishes and head upstairs. Perfect, that's just what I need. I can speak to Pastor Campbell and maybe he'll offer some advice to set me back on the right path.

My hand curls around the heavy wooden door frame of the pastor's office in Holy Grace.

"Excuse me, Pastor Campbell, may I speak with you?"

Pastor Campbell is the type of man who in his youth was probably attractive. He has good bone structure and the tall, broad-shouldered build of an athlete, but now his hair is receding, his belly is protruding, and he smells like something far too sweet. Like lilies past their prime. He's always given me the creeps, but perhaps that's because of how inept and ungrateful I've felt around him. Most of all, I think it's his hands with short, stubby fingers that are too soft. Every time he places his hands on mine, it curdles something in my stomach.

"Ah, Rebecca, finished Bible study?"

I nod and enter the office as he gestures for me to come in. I close the door behind me, terrified of my mother accidentally overhearing what I want to talk about.

"I was wondering if maybe I could ask for some advice?"

He folds his stubby fingers together, the sound of his skin making a shiver crawl up my neck.

I swallow against the bile rising in my throat. "I have . . . Lately, I've been struggling with doubt."

Pastor Campbell's eyebrows knit together and my heart picks up, terrified to be confessing this at all.

"I'm trying to hand everything to God. To trust what he has in store for me, but I feel like I'm staring at a dead end. That there's no way forward that will please him. I just feel so lost."

A creaking of wood as he shifts in his chair to lean forward. "This is what I've been talking about in worship. This is spiritual warfare, Rebecca. The devil is here in our town. Demons are trying to enter our bodies and pull us from God. The end times could come at any moment. When the rapture comes, will you be spit back out because of this doubt you carry? Or are you willing to believe, with everything inside of you, in order to be saved?"

The image of the demons from James's room burst forward in my mind and I shudder. "How is your relationship with Eric Corbley?"

My mouth opens, then closes. I want to tell him no, that it's not just because of Eric that I'm so conflicted. How can I possibly tell him about the pentagram- and demon-wearing tattooed guitarist who lives next door without spilling all the details of our encounters?

"Do you know the most powerful ways Satan tries to lead us away from God?"

I can't speak. I already know the answer.

"Lust. Pride. Greed."

Heat spreads across the back of my neck.

"Have you acted in a way that might lead him to believe you are not a Godly woman?"

I can't possibly tell him I've taken my clothes off for a boy.

What if he were to tell my parents? I just—I can't lie. Not again. "I may not have always acted in a way that would please God."

He tilts his head and narrows his eyes as though convinced I've been strutting around trying to seduce Eric. He sighs. Great, another person I've disappointed. "Your body is a temple for the Holy Spirit. You are not your own. Submit and you will be saved."

My eyes fill with tears, but I blink them back. I knew it. I knew it was my fault. That this body isn't even mine.

He smiles gently. "This will pass. God is wise. Prayer, fasting, and giving are your weapons in the fight against Satan. God will not permit the struggle to be more than you can stand. Corinthians 10:13. I suggest you pray on it tonight, Rebecca. He will always show you the way."

I place my hands on the desk. "But I can't see it. If I can't find the path, how will I know what to do?"

"Put your faith in God and trust that there is a plan for you."

This hasn't helped me at all. I open my mouth but there's a knock on the door.

"Come in," Pastor Campbell says.

My mother opens the door and her eyes widen, glancing between the two of us. "Oh, sorry to interrupt."

"That's all right, we were just finishing up."

I blink furiously, allowing a smile to pull at the corners of my mouth, my cheeks straining from the effort. "Yes. Thank you."

THE DRIVE HOME is relatively quiet aside from the offhand comments from my mother about how tired I look and that she would pack a less heavy lunch tomorrow, because clearly this is God's way of telling me I need to fast more. All I can think about is how stuck I am, how no matter what I do, I disappoint someone. My parents, Eric, even God. How I can never, ever seem to do anything right. If God truly loves me, then why would he set me up to fail?

Every step I take pushes me three steps backward. I should want to submit to Eric, but even when exercising modesty to the extreme, he stumbles and wants me to do more with him physically when I shouldn't. My mother wants me to be her perfect daughter, and I try so hard to please and obey her, but then spends all her waking hours finding ways to point out how flawed I am. And my father—when he's not ignoring me—seems to make his only interest in me how I am serving others. To make me the perfect future housewife and mother. Doesn't he care about my wishes at all? Is it really demons causing me to want *something* for myself? To have a small sliver of ownership over my physical body?

I grab a few crackers and a glass of water from the kitchen once we're inside and my mother isn't watching, then head upstairs. I stuff the crackers in my mouth one after the other, nearly choking on how dry they are before chasing them down with the water. My stomach roils, angry I've neglected it so much all day. Is this torture really want God wants from me? Why does none of it seem to ever make a difference? And the dress—this awful dress. I cross my room to my bed, double checking that the curtains are still closed, I tear off my cardigan then yank down the zipper. I pull it so hard that something pops and I'm sure either the zipper has broken or a seam has ripped. But I can't think about it now. I can't breathe, the plaid straightjacket pressing in on me from everywhere, and I sob as I pull and pull at the dress, terrified for a moment that I'll pass out before getting it off of me. Finally, it gives and I crumple to the floor, taking heaving breaths and clutching at my chest and my ribs where the abrasion is throbbing. I reach around my back, unhook my bra and toss it at my closet. I pull the bow from my hair, letting the strands fall around my face and tickle my neck.

The demand is too much, the control gone, and that frayed rope that's been pulled in too many directions for too long is hanging on by a single thread that could break at any moment.

A discordant noise breaks through my muffled crying. It's not loud, but it's high-pitched and frantic, notes in seemingly no distinct order or pattern but that somehow still make sense. I look over my shoulder to the window, seeing the light from James's room spill across the carpet. I pull myself up, wiping the tears from my face, and grab my robe off the post of my bed, wrapping it around my nearly naked body.

God is supposed to show me the path, yet the only path I can see right now is the one illuminating the way to the sinner next door. I slowly approach the curtains, my fingers curling around the edge of one, pulling it back ever so slightly to glimpse across the way. James is sitting on his bed, one foot resting on an amplifier and the other tapping out the beat. His fingers fly over the strings in a blur, the notes he plays distorting and sliding. His hair is tied back again but he's still wearing the same clothes as he was at school today, and I'm grateful that he's covered up because it allows me to concentrate on his face. His nose scrunches as his body curves in toward the guitar, his tongue poking through his lips as though in deep concentration, and he shakes his head back and forth, the loose strands of his dark hair dancing with the movement.

I gently push the curtains open to watch, impressed by the stamina of his fingers, how they continue to work so furiously for so long. After what feels like forever, his left hand slides down the frets and with a final dramatic strum, he stills. I watch as he grabs a notebook from beside him on the bed and writes a few things down. He tucks the end of his pen between his teeth, his face full of concentration as he considers his notes. I wonder what it feels like to be able to do what you want whenever you choose.

My fingers lose grip on the curtains, the fluttering fabric drawing his attention. His eyes meet mine and for a long moment, we just stare at each other. He runs his tongue along his bottom lip and leans toward the amplifier. The little red power light turns off, and he stands, pulling his guitar off his shoulder and setting it on the stand by the stereo. He grabs the notepad from his bed, flipping a new page over and writing something down. Eyes flicking to me as he writes, I feel a nervous anticipation flood through me and I push my curtains open a little more, as though my view might be obstructed by them. That they're in the way of our connection. Finally, he nears the window and turns the notepad to me.

Are you okay?

Compassion. Care. It's what's been missing this whole time. His words feel like a desperately needed hug. For a moment, I forget about the distance between us, the glass, what Pastor Campbell told me not an hour ago. Forget that he is not what I'm supposed to want, forget that I have a boyfriend who has and always will take away my control, forget that everyone I know would tell me that James is the embodiment of what God wants us to fight against—the worst thing that could ever happen to me.

But he sees me.

James sees that I'm hurt and upset. Sees me as a whole person who's complicated and overwhelmed. Those three little words demonstrate that maybe he actually cares about me—about what I feel and think. All of the confusion and turmoil from the day seems to recede like the tide and I start to untie the belt of my robe.

He looks confused as it comes loose, the notepad dropping

little by little until it hangs at his side. My skin is electrified, vibrating, and my fingers tremble nervously as I grab either side of the opening. I pull the fabric apart slowly and feel the air on my stomach, between my breasts, my collarbone, watching every small change on his face. He doesn't blink as I let the fleece robe fall to the floor. My breasts, shoulders and arms are bare and exposed, standing in nothing but my underwear. My nipples harden from the change in temperature and goosebumps prickle up all over my body.

And even from twelve feet away, I can see his eyes grow darker, hungrier, as they rake over every exposed part of me. See his hands clench at his sides as he drops the notepad to the floor, forgotten. My heart soars as he takes me in. There's so much desire in his eyes that I find myself wanting to do this again, and again. He's not using me for his own selfish pleasure—I'm the one who's in control. He's letting me set the limits, then break them, all without judgment. Not like Eric would. Or my parents. Even God.

He's a sinner. He's turning *me* into a sinner. And I can't help thinking wildly that if James is going to Hell, maybe we can carpool.

CHAPTER 10

Damage, Inc.

JAMES

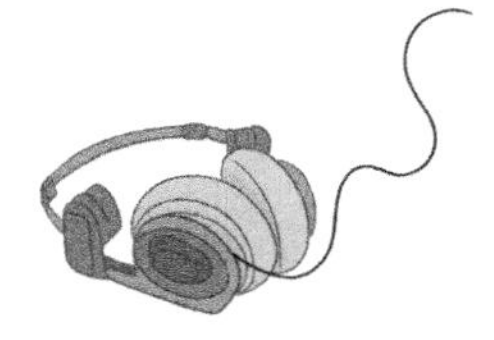

Holy shit. I am in big trouble.

The moment that robe hits the floor, I know I'm fucked. The way she's looking me dead in the eye as she bares herself to me is both exhilarating and terrifying all at once. For a second, I think I must be dreaming. That I've fallen asleep and imagined her pulling back those curtains, but the notepad dropping from my hand and hitting the top of my foot assures me that this is real.

My eyes travel over every inch of her I can see. Her blonde hair is free and tumbling over her narrow shoulders. Even from this distance, her fair skin seems to flush the longer I look. Her small breasts rise and fall with every deep breath she takes and I'm grateful that I'm still wearing my jeans because most of my blood supply is throbbing in my groin. My gaze falls to her stomach and her narrow hips covered in a pair of pink cotton panties. Fuck, she looks like a delectable frosted cupcake.

She's not smiling, though. In fact, her eyes are red. She's been crying. Whatever arousal I feel starts to vanish. Is she crying because of me? The thought makes my stomach turn. As fun as it was to rile Rebecca up, I didn't mean to push her this far. I thought this was just a game she wanted to play. Or is she crying because of something else?

What is she doing? She plays the good girl routine at school and then takes her clothes off for me at night? These last two times have been no accident. She is fully aware that I can see her. And I can't be sure, but she's looking at me like she knows what might run through my mind at the sight of her. Like she wants me to think about those things. And to be perfectly frank, there is both nothing and everything running through my mind right now.

Is she simply trying to make a liar out of me? Throw it in my face that I told her she isn't my type? If that's the case, then call me Pinocchio because my nose, and something else, must be a mile long right now. As much as I've tried to deny it, there is something about Rebecca that fascinates me.

I raise my eyebrows at her, wondering what she's planning to do now that she has my undivided attention. Her head tilts and her hip drops, and I don't think I've ever seen her standing so casually. She is always so straight, like a Barbie doll, inflexible and stiff or sitting as straight as a board. Right now, she looks . . . comfortable. Not relaxed necessarily, but freer. A hand rises to her necklace, her fingers twirling around the cross at her neck, and she winces. Her thin nose scrunching as she inhales then her head falls forward, breaking our connection.

Her face lifts, looking away from me before she turns and walks out of view. The light in her room turns off, then all is quiet except for the blood pounding in my ears. Taking a few steps back from the window, I run my hand down over my face.

Rebecca is like a puzzle, wrapped in knots, wrapped in an enigma. No girl has ever made me question my sanity before. There are usually two kinds of girls—ones who turn their noses up at me and those who make it very clear they are interested. Rebecca does both. I mean, how else am I supposed to interpret the nightly peep show? But it's also the complete opposite of the personality she exhibits in public. The proud, prudish, good girl that always does what she's told even though she doesn't want to. Like some kind of compulsion. If I didn't know any better, I would think maybe she has an evil identical twin.

I rub my eyes. Fuck, I need a smoke. I fit into my jacket and pull my hair from the elastic band before heading down the stairs and out onto the back porch. Pulling a cigarette out of the pack, my teeth hold it in my mouth as I flick the lighter.

"Another one came today."

My head turns toward a voice coming from through the fence to my right—from Rebecca's backyard.

"From where?"

I pull the cigarette out of my mouth and walk closer, my ears straining to better hear what the voices are saying.

"University of Indianapolis."

"Give it here."

There's a pause.

"Then there's the phone calls. They're becoming insistent. I know tithe is demanded but—"

"It's our holy duty. I'm taking care of it, Linda. Remember your place."

What the hell are they talking about? University? Phone calls? Tithe? Isn't that what it's called when they give money their church? Why do I even care? Because maybe it will give me some clue as to what goes on in a beautiful, blonde girl's head.

The sound of metal scrapes against stone and there's a rustling of clothes before the sound of a door shutting echoes out into the night. I take a few tentative steps toward the fence, peering through the small gap of the wood planks. Rebecca's father is sitting on a lawn chair staring up at the house. He must have been talking to his easily offended wife.

Even just sitting by himself, there's such an irritating air of self-importance hanging around him. If only he knew what his daughter was doing a few minutes ago. Not that I'd ever tell. I step back up near the back door and light up the cigarette, inhaling the calming smoke into my lungs. I watch as it drifts up to the sky, blurring the stars that blink down at me. My mom always loved the stars. She'd point out the constellations to me sometimes on a night when our power was out because we hadn't paid the bills.

"Hey, you."

My head whips around to find Rebecca's father glaring at me over the fence. "Yeah?"

"Put that cigarette out. It stinks."

I turn my palms to the sky and gesture around at the empty yard. "Pretty sure it's a free country."

Even though I can only see the top of his face, I can almost hear his teeth grind. He's definitely not used to someone disobeying him. I wonder what would happen if Rebecca ever dared to.

"Do you have any idea who I am?" he says in what I expect he thinks is a commanding tone.

"Umm . . . nope. Don't care either."

"You watch your tone, heathen, and stay away from my family," he says in a low voice, eyes narrowing. Then he turns away, the sound of a door slamming behind him letting me know he's gone.

I take another long drag and rub at my eyes again with my free hand. What a dick.

I glance up at Rebecca's window, which I can see from down here. It's still dark. I wonder if she's already asleep or if she's lying awake staring at the ceiling.

Two hours later, that's exactly what I'm doing. Staring at the ceiling, going back and forth between listening to music through my headphones, listening to the quiet sounds of the neighborhood, and scribbling in my notebook. It's filled with half-written songs and lyrics and random little pictures I've drawn for potential tattoo designs. No matter how hard I try, I can't stop thinking about Rebecca. And while thoughts of her nearly naked body are taking up most of the free space in my brain, I'm plagued with thoughts of what could possibly have been going through her head earlier. So I press my pen to the paper and write.

Dear Mom,

I wish you were here. I wish I had been able to ask you for advice about girls because right now, I really need some. Noreen is great and taking good care of me. Why didn't you tell me about her before? What happened that made you leave everything behind? Maybe if you hadn't—

I pause. If she hadn't, maybe I wouldn't even be here. Maybe it would've been better that way. I rub at my nose and go to write again, but I lose grip on the pen and it tumbles away from me, rolling across the floor into the small closet I haven't bothered to use.

Sighing, I push myself out of bed and walk over, opening the accordion-style door. Picking up my pen I stop, noticing for the first time a large cardboard box packed up in the corner. It's not one of my boxes. Is it Noreen's stuff? Noreen went to sleep hours ago, so it's not like I can ask her right now. I'll ask her in the morning.

I close the door, but I stay gripping the handle, unable to let go. Curiosity consumes me and I open the door again to stare at the box. It's probably just some old books or something. Besides, it's up here. Surely Noreen would've moved it if she didn't want me going through it. I drag it out and sit on my bed before opening the worn, cardboard flaps. Inside are piles of papers and books and pictures—all belonging to my mom.

Something heavy weighs down my chest and I suck on the inside of my cheek to stop the prickling in my eyes. I straighten the box with my toe before taking a long, shuddering breath. There's a few loose papers on the very top. They look like old tests from school and I feel a smile spread across my face as I look at the grades she received. A, A+, A. Wow, I guess she was good at school. My cheeks pull with a grin when I notice the similar way she wrote her *d*'s and *g*'s compared to my own handwriting. I never really bothered to pay too much attention to those details before. And each one feels like a familiar smile staring back at me.

Underneath there's a photo album. The top is covered in paper roses, my mom's favorite flower, and little glued-on plastic jewels. I open up the dusty cover and see a picture of my mom as a baby. Compared to the very few pictures I've seen of myself as a baby, we could be twins. She was all dark hair and dark eyes and round nose, and while I only have a few memories of my dad, I don't see much of him in me. Nope, it appears I'm all Dora Walton.

I flip the page and there she is again. Older this time, her hair is cut short at the chin and she's wearing a frilly little pink nightgown. Her two front teeth are missing adorably. She must be about six years old here. There's a baby next to her who must be Noreen, still in diapers and grinning at the camera with a gummy smile. I've never asked Noreen how old she is but from this picture she must have been at least four, maybe five years younger than my mom. Maybe that's why John didn't know her. If she was several years older they probably wouldn't have gone to high school together.

Digging through the box, there are a bunch of ribbons and

medals at the bottom as well as what look like journals. There's a ribbon for placing first at the science fair in nineteen sixty-four. There's also a medal for placing third at the nineteen sixty-five state cheerleading championships. She was a cheerleader? It's hard to picture my mom with her hair in a ponytail waving pom poms around. That she was in charge of making sure people smiled.

Beneath that are some pictures of her in high school, a few even of her in her uniform, which is good because I don't think I would have fully believed it until it was in front of my face. I stare down at the grainy images of her face. She was so beautiful. With a wide, brilliant smile and dark eyelashes framing her big dark eyes. I shake my head, fighting away the sorrow by forcing a smile to my cheeks. She looked so happy. What happened to her?

What happened after these pictures that was so awful that she ended up shooting-up smack in an abandoned house with my piece of shit dad? I toss the pictures back inside, close the top flaps and kick away the box, watching it slide against the speaker for my stereo system. I can't deal with this right now. Maybe I'll never want to deal with it. But one thing's for sure, I'm not going to be getting any sleep tonight.

CHAPTER 11

Total Eclipse of the Heart

REBECCA

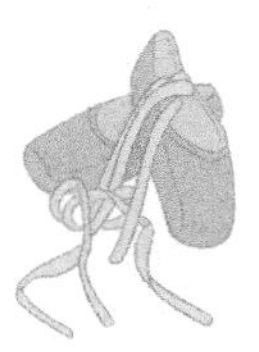

I wish I were at home. I wish I could just curl up in my bed and hide because no matter how hard I try, I can't stop the thoughts of James running through my head. The way his smell reaches me even from where he's seated several rows back. The way every clink of metal and rustle of denim is like a hymn. Filling my waking vision with thoughts of him half naked in his room.

"Hey, Rebecca," Suzanna Martin whispers next to me. Her short dark hair swings under her chin and her brown eyes look at me through round tortoiseshell glasses.

"Hmm?"

"Did you get the answer to number ten?" she asks, pointing to the question in the textbook we're working on for Mrs. Henry.

I nod. "Umm, yeah, I think so. Do you need help?"

She smiles, nods and scooches her chair closer to mine as I explain what I wrote down.

"Hey, by the way," she says, glancing behind me, "do you know the new guy or something?"

I freeze, my mouth going dry. Can she tell he's all I've thought about all day? "Not really, no. Why?"

"Because he's been staring at you all class."

My stomach lurches like I've missed a step going downstairs and my knee jerks in response. "No, no. He moved in next door, that's all."

Suzanna looks back over my shoulder again. "He's kind of . . . pretty, don't you think? For a boy, I mean."

He's the devil.

"I haven't really thought about it." The lie comes so easily that I feel sick.

"Right, you're with Eric. Are you okay? You look kind of pale."

Closing my eyes, I try to calm my racing heart, aware the whole time that James is watching me. "Yes, I'm fine. Just a bit tired, I think." I want to bury my face in the sand. What am I doing? All I wanted was some control but all it's done is made things worse. I don't even recognize myself.

"Before the end of class, I'm wondering if I could get a couple of volunteers?" Mrs. Henry's voice rings out amongst the chaos of my mind. Is it the end of class already? "This box of newspapers needs to be taken to the library after school and cataloged—"

My hand shoots into the air. Perfect. I can do something good as repentance. I can suffer. It'll be dreadfully boring, but atonement isn't supposed to be fun.

"Miss Briar, thank you for volunteering," Mrs. Henry says, smiling sweetly. "One more volunteer should do it. Ah, Mr. Walton, thank you."

No.

Please no.

I turn my head to look behind me where James is sitting, his ankle resting over one knee, his arm in the air. Turning back to the front, I nearly choke on the breath that escapes me, my eyes flicking to the ceiling as I pray for mercy. Pastor Campbell said that God never gives us more than we can handle, but I think the Lord has higher expectations of me than I can manage.

The bell rings and I'm out the door and into the busy hallway before my brain has a chance to catch up. Then that smell—that intoxicating smell—is behind me, beside me, it's everywhere.

"Is volunteering for library tasks your idea of fun, then?"

I jump, his voice in my ear so loud even over the noise of students milling around us. He walks one step behind me, like the other day on the bleachers, just out of sight. If it weren't for the attention he attracts from everyone around us, I might wonder if I imagined him. Like some ghost I've invented to haunt me for all my sins.

I keep my eyes focused ahead. "No."

"That's too bad. I was just thinking last night about how much I wish I could spend hours doing tedious cataloging work for no pay."

I whip around to face him, his smug grin and the mischievous glint in his eyes giving away that he's trying to tease me. "Then why volunteer?"

"Just trying to be a good student, Becks. Isn't that what you're doing?" He leans forward a little. "Or is it what God wants you to do?"

I huff, then turn around to continue toward our second-period class, aware that he's still right behind me.

"Are you all right?"

His voice is quiet, like he wants to make sure only I can hear him.

I swallow, my throat still dry from all the prayers whispered in desperation last night. "I'm fine."

"Because . . . well, last night it looked like you were crying. Or maybe you're sick?"

"You know, it's rude to tell a girl she looks sick."

He chuckles. "I mean, I'd be more than happy to compliment you if I thought you'd accept it."

"I don't need compliments from you."

"Right . . . I'm sure you get enough of those from your boyfriend."

All of this is such a mess. Last night shouldn't have happened. I confused the temptation of the devil for compassion and now I have to pay the price. I wish he would just back off so I can breathe. "Can you just—stop bringing him up, please?"

"Is he the one who made you cry?" he asks seriously.

I speed up, hoping he'll take the hint and let me go. "No."

"It wasn't me was it?"

I scoff. Even though my mind is a mess lately, I won't give him the satisfaction of knowing he ever got to me. He'll never understand what it means to be me. "I would never cry over you."

"Great. I'd hate knowing I made you cry."

Does everything just roll right off his back? If I ever said something like that to Eric, he wouldn't speak to me for a month.

"Becks," he says quietly as he comes around to stand in my way, causing us to stop in the hall. "I understand if you don't want to talk about it with me, just . . . if you ever do, or you feel like you can't talk to your friends—" He pulls on the back of his neck, his eyes shifting away. "I'm here to listen . . . if you ever need it."

I want to retort back something snappy. Something to let him know that he will never be in my confidence, but I can't. "Why would you do that?"

He holds my gaze for a long moment. "Because I wish someone had said the same when I needed someone to talk to."

James catches me off guard. That might just be the most vulnerable thing I've ever heard someone say. He chose to say that to *me*. My soul feels exposed like the beach after the tide goes out. And here he is like an explorer searching through the wreckage for treasure. I find myself staring into his eyes—eyes so dark it doesn't seem like light can escape them, but it does. It flickers somewhere from within and I can't stop my heart from tap dancing in my chest.

"Oh," I say. "Well, thank you. But I have prayer for that."

He grins that smug grin again. "I can kick someone's ass too if praying won't make it better."

Like a bubble bursting, the moment between us is gone, and I roll my eyes before walking around him. After all, I don't need James Walton of all people to rescue me. Only God can do that, and I'm not going to give James the satisfaction of thinking he could.

WHEN THE LUNCH BELL RINGS, I head toward the guidance office, not sure if Eric will be there and on high alert in case James decides to appear out of nowhere. For the third day in a row, Eric isn't here, and while I wasn't overly looking forward to spending our lunch together, especially after he didn't pick me up this morning, the upheaval of our regular routine has me spiraling.

I head into the cafeteria, spotting Mary and Amy at our usual table, and James is nowhere to be found even though I look around for him as though he might swoop down on me like some giant bat, like he did yesterday.

"Becca, you look terrible," Amy says as I sit down. "Did you sleep at all last night?"

I pull the paper lunch bag out of my backpack and set it on the table. "Not really, no."

"Is it because of Eric?" Mary asks.

No, it's because everything is falling apart. "I don't want to talk about Eric right now."

Mary gives Amy a glance I try to ignore while pulling food out of my bag. There's a whole tuna sandwich, cut in half, an orange and some cheese and crackers. I stare at it for a moment. Fasting will cure my lust. That's what Pastor Campbell said. And my mother would be thrilled knowing I waited until dinner to eat. She guides me on the right path. She takes care of me, so she must be right.

Right?

My stomach groans at my indecision. I grab the items and tuck them back into the paper bag and place it in my backpack. I listen to Mary and Amy talk about something that happened during their morning class, trying to relish in the hunger pains.

I don't see Eric for the rest of the day, but when the final bell rings, he's standing by my locker.

"Where've you been?" I ask, genuinely curious.

"Drove into town with the guys for some lunch. Didn't I tell you that this morning?"

"No . . . no, you didn't." He didn't even pick me up.

He offers me a kind of half-hearted shrug. "Sorry, babe. Had a good day?"

No, it's been awful, and it's about to get far worse because I volunteered to help out Mrs. Henry, and I'll be stuck with the devil himself for at least an hour. Eric simply wouldn't understand any of that. "It's been a long day."

"I have practice after school. Stay and watch, and I'll drive you home."

"Actually, I can't. I told Mrs. Henry I'd help her with cataloging some old newspapers in the library. Could you maybe drive me home then?"

His mouth twists, and he rubs his fingers against his chin. "Sure."

He presses a quick kiss to my cheek then heads off toward the gym. I close my locker, my forehead pressing against the cool metal while I collect my thoughts before heading to the classroom. I open the door to find James standing next to Mrs.

Henry, who's eyeing his shirt with trepidation. But as the door snaps shut, they both turn to look at me.

"Miss Briar, thank you again so much for helping out. Ms. Duncan already knows to expect you both in the library."

I force a grin and nod while James picks up the giant cardboard box like it weighs nothing and walks past me out into the hallway. Following along behind him, the halls are quiet with everyone gone. The sound of the chain on his belt provides a rhythmic clinking.

"You'll have to lead the way," he says, tilting his head to look over his shoulder at me. "Afraid I haven't found the library yet."

I roll my eyes and take a couple of quick steps forward so I'm in front of him. Thankfully, he doesn't say much and I'm grateful when the library comes into view.

I follow behind him to where Ms. Duncan is sitting at the front desk. She eyes James up and down, pulling her spectacles down her nose. After a moment, I clear my throat. "We're here for Mrs. Henry with the newspapers."

Ms. Duncan blinks and turns to me, a smile pulling up her face. "Yes, of course. I'll show you the system, then you can work at those tables over there behind the bookshelves."

She leads us through the stacks and quickly shows us her filing system and the cabinet for the newspapers. I hadn't noticed before, but they're all copies of the high school paper dating back years, decades even. I sit down at the table and pull the stack of cards my way. Every muscle in my body tenses as I wait for him to bring up last night again.

"Who says you get to fill out the cards?"

I look up and James is sitting down across from me, his hands folded together on the table.

"Oh . . . I—"

"Relax. My handwriting is terrible. I'll do the grunt work."

I almost smile at that, grateful that I don't have to reach too far or get up and down, because my zipper stings the cut on my ribs with every movement.

"February 18, 1986," he reads, pulling a newspaper from the top of the pile. "Looks like the football team suffered a massive loss last month."

With a shrug, I write on the card.

"I guess football's not your thing either?"

I look up, and he's biting back a smile, fingers spinning one of his rings around. "No, it's not."

He reads off another newspaper from the pile, and while I write out the card, he takes the first one and places it in the cabinet.

"Right, so . . . you're not into track, not into library work, no football . . ." he says, ticking off his fingers, "not into kissing your boyfriend either from the looks of it."

The pen drops from my hand and rolls across the table where James watches it tumble to the floor. "Excuse me?"

He crosses his arms over his chest, and I can see the tattoo of a crow . . . or maybe it's a raven, on his hand. "Yesterday morning. It looked like someone was forcing you to kiss a dead fish." He leans forward. "Is that what it's like to kiss him?"

"I don't—he's not—that's private!" I can't quite grasp the words to tell him off, that it's none of his business and it's killing me. He's doing this on purpose. I can see it on his smug face. He's trying to get a rise out of me. No. Just ignore and be vigilant. Ignore and be vigilant.

"You know, kissing *is* fun . . . if it's done right."

I ignore him, even though I feel a blush spread all the way up to my ears. "Can you pass me my pen, please?"

He leans over sideways dramatically, only to pop back up, pinching my pen between his long fingers. He holds it out for me, but as I go to grab it, he pulls his hand away.

I glare at him, and he just smiles back. He tips the pen toward me again and we do the back-and-forth game twice more.

"Can you stop acting like a child, please?" I ask imploringly.

"But it's so *fun*."

"Well, it's not *fun* for me."

He barks out a laugh. "You know, I'm starting to think you don't actually know what fun is."

"Your idea of fun and my idea of fun are extremely different." I huff, then raise my eyebrow and quickly glance at the red demon on his shirt.

His gaze follows mine and he lowers his voice again. "I can take it off"—he points my pen to his shirt—"if you'd prefer."

The thought of seeing him again with no shirt on—with no twelve-foot distance, or window, or curtains to separate us causes my stomach to clench hard, heat rushing up into my face. Why hasn't he brought up last night yet? Surely he must be thinking about it.

"That's not necessary," I say, and in a moment of desperation I swipe for the pen, but he's too fast and he tucks it behind his ear, his long hair pulling back at one side.

"Okay, what are we? In third grade?" I push myself off the chair, grab the newspaper and walk over to the filing cabinet before grabbing another one from the box and sitting back down. "I just want to get this over with so I can go home."

He leans back in his chair. "Why? Got plans?"

"Yes, actually."

His eyebrows quirk up. "And what does Rebecca Briar do on Wednesday nights? Please tell me it's more than reading your bible."

Ignore him. Ignore him. *Ignore him.*

I grab another pen from my backpack and continue on with the cards on my own while he watches. The front page of a newspaper from 1979 details the winners of the state-wide science fair. Then another, detailing the events of a group at the school protesting against equal rights for homosexuals. I grimace. It's something Pastor Campbell has always drilled into us at church. That homosexuals are sinful, destined for Hell. But they're still people. Is their sin really all that much worse than mine? If God won't forgive them, will he not forgive me either?

James clears his throat and I hastily finish the card. After a few minutes he grabs the papers that I've processed and goes to file them. I take the few moments he's away to try and calm my racing heart.

Fifteen minutes go by . . . perhaps he's finally decided not to bug me anymore because he just keeps quiet. My pen is still being held hostage behind his ear, but he silently continues to help me work. Maybe I dreamt all of that last night. Maybe it never happened.

"So what's the latest rumor?"

My hand jerks, the pen scratching across the card rendering it useless. I look up. "What?"

"You know . . . why I'm here. The weirdo who shows up at a new school with two and a half months left in the year."

I grab another card to rewrite it. "It's sinful to gossip."

"It's not gossiping if the person being gossiped about is asking."

I place the pen back down and sigh. "Fine. I recall there being a conversation about whether you had killed someone, but I told them that was ridiculous."

He narrows his eyes at me. "How do you know it's not true?"

I blink. "Well . . . because you'd be—they would have arrested you."

"Maybe I had a good lawyer."

My lips press together and a nervous shiver travels down my spine, but the next moment he's grinning and I feel like throwing something at him.

"Don't worry, I didn't kill anyone."

I roll my eyes. "There was also talk of you stabbing someone. That—" I glance at the metal rings on his hands, the leather cuff on his wrist, the muscles that flex under the skin of his forearms and I have to swallow the saliva that pools in my mouth. "That you have a knife collection."

He laughs, his head tipping back and his hand moving to rub the back of his neck, stretching his side. His torso lengthens and his shirt lifts a little bit, exposing the flesh of his stomach. Immediately, I feel a pulse throb between my legs and I avert my eyes.

"Well, you've seen my room. I clearly don't have a knife collection," he says. He's seen my room too. He's seen a whole lot more than that. I bite the inside of my cheek as my knee begins to bounce.

"I suppose you could be hiding them under your bed."

He smirks. "Trust me, the only things under my bed are some more records and a few magazines."

I bite back my question of what kind of magazine. If it's music magazines or the type that Melissa from youth group warned us about that depict sinful, loose women with no clothes on. If James was a part of Holy Grace, the black van would come for him for that. How ironic that he drives one when everything he does goes against our beliefs.

With a bored huff, he crosses his arms. "Is that it? I have to say, I'm disappointed. Not very creative. I was really hoping that Soviet spy one would take off."

"I believe there was also mention of you being a Manson cultist," I say, not even looking at his face for a reaction.

"Ah, now that's more like it." He holds out another newspaper for me to check the date and I start writing another card. "Is that what you think I am?"

I glance at the tattoo again, then at the demon on his shirt, my eyes flicking ever so briefly over his face before looking down again. "I think you are laboring under the impression that I think about you at all."

He scoffs. "It's kind of hilarious watching you try to convince yourself that you're not into me. Especially after the last two nights."

My stomach drops. Here it is. He's finally bringing it up. I knew it was only a matter of time. Just ignore him. Ignore. *Ignore.*

I grab another card to fill out and wave my hand at the box, but he doesn't grab another newspaper. He's just staring at me with those dangerous dark eyes, waiting for me to refute him.

"You're not my type," I say punctuating each word.

He blinks for a moment, then laughs roughly, deeply, and it's like a can of worms spills over in my stomach.

"Right, your type is possessive, dipshit church boy. Such a shame."

I narrow my eyes. "He is a man of God."

"Is he? Because it didn't seem that way in the car yesterday."

"What would you know about it?" I ask, my voice pitching higher.

"I know that men of God can also be massive assholes on power trips."

I hold his gaze, my brain spinning and trying to decipher if he's speaking from experience or if this is all some act.

Looking away, I grab another newspaper to distract myself with, I find one from the mid sixties. There's a front page devoted to profiles of the homecoming king and queen nominees. The young faces stare up at me, my fingers running along the names. Dora, Chester, Helen, Jet, Wendy . . . Their hopeful eyes have depth even from the faded, yellowing paper. Their smiles frozen in time. I wonder if they were as carefree as they seem here, or if they too hid all of their darkness behind virtue and a fake smile.

Standing up, I try to rid myself of the uncomfortable feeling—

like they're judging me. I reach forward to grab another paper, the cut on my ribs throbbing angrily, and I wince, my body contracting in on itself and I'm not sure if it's because I stood up too quickly or if it's because I've been so on edge all day, but my vision blurs and my head spins so I clamp my eyes shut.

"Hey . . . are you okay?"

I grip both sides of the cardboard box to steady myself, trying and failing to take deep breaths. A buzzing noise rings in my ears and I feel my hip slam hard into the table. The box slips from my hold but I don't fall because strong hands are grasping my arms. The fingers press into my boiling skin with both enough pressure to keep me upright and enough softness not to bruise.

"Becks!"

My head rolls back, the muscles in my neck just simply too weak to support it. It feels so heavy and the thought of simply falling asleep right here is so appealing. I'm being shaken. The jolting prevents me from descending into darkness and my eyebrows and nose scrunch together from the unpleasantness. I pry my eyes open, finding two chocolate-brown ones wide with fear and surrounded by wild dark hair staring back at me.

He's so close to me that his breath fans across my cheeks, the smell of smoke and mint dragging me back to reality. My pen is still tucked over his ear and I feel my head tilt heavily to one side, curious to know if I were to reach for it, whether he'd pull away. If his hair is as soft as it looks. His eyes dart quickly over my face, pausing for a moment too long on my mouth. His fingers flex against my upper arms and I remember myself, remember that he's touching me.

Realizing that I like it.

CHAPTER 12

Take On Me

JAMES

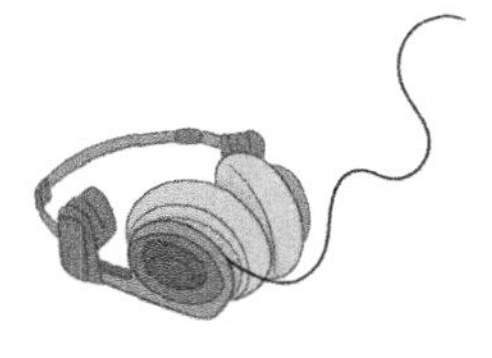

Rule #3 - Never run away from a fight.

"Becks!"

Her head rolls and her eyes flutter, her small body going completely limp in my arms. I shake her, trying to keep her awake all while fighting hard not to panic. Should I yell for the librarian to call an ambulance? Rebecca's face pinches as if she's having some kind of fit or nightmare, but finally her eyes open, pupils so dilated there's barely any green.

She groans and presses the heel of her hand to her temple. "I—"

I gently set her back in her chair before squatting down in front of her so we're at eye level. "Are you okay?" I ask, my voice strangled with worry.

As she blinks me into focus, I register how tightly she's holding my arms. She seems to realize it too and pulls back. She swallows and turns back to the table. "I'm fine. Thank you."

My eyes narrow at her. She almost passed out but she's *fine*? She's so fine in fact that she pulls another card toward her and starts writing again.

"Maybe we should finish this tomorrow," I offer.

She shakes her head. "I told you, I'm fine."

I don't know Rebecca well enough to tell if this is true or not, but my gut tells me there's something else going on here. All of this hot-and-cold behavior? What's going on with this girl? I stand and walk back around the table to sit in my chair. "Maybe your blood sugar is low. Do you want a piece of chocolate?" I reach for my bag. "I think I have a bar in here somewhere—"

"No!" she says, reaching forward to stop me. "I mean . . . no, thank you."

Her eyes flutter a little as she continues writing on the card in front of her. For a few minutes, I simply sit and watch her make her way through the cards for the stack of papers she has pulled from the box. Waiting to see if she starts to look woozy again.

"Can you stop staring at me like that? It's making me uncomfortable."

I look away. "Sorry."

She looks up at me. "Could you—maybe not tell anyone about that?"

My eyebrows nearly disappear under my hair. Why is this some big secret? "Who would I tell? The janitor? I don't have any friends."

"Well, maybe if you stopped telling people that nonsense about why you moved here, you could make some."

I shrug. "Not here to make friends."

She twirls her pen in her fingers for a few seconds, her eyes narrowing as they scrutinize my face. Maybe she thinks I'm lying.

"Do you really work at The Shipwreck?"

My eyebrows lift. I'm surprised that's what she wants to know. "Yeah . . . and don't worry, I was only half kidding about the virgin sacrifice thing."

She rolls her shoulders back, her face twitching.

"Or maybe you wanted to volunteer for the honor?" I tease.

Her eyes flash dangerously. "Absolutely not." She lifts her arms to cross over her chest but pauses midway and pushes her arms back down to her sides. That's the third time she's done that. It's so odd.

I interlace my fingers and rest my chin on them. "Of course not. You're saving yourself for marriage, aren't you?" I say, nodding toward the cross at her throat. "Unless, of course, your boyfriend can't keep it in his pants."

She huffs, dramatically pulling out a new card from the stack, her pen flying over the cardstock.

"Is he good to you?"

"What?"

"Does he take good care of you?" I feel my nose pinch as my mouth twists. From what I've observed so far, he definitely does not.

Rebecca closes her eyes and shakes her head. "Can we stop talking about my boyfriend please?"

"Do you love him?"

She places her pen down again. "I don't want to talk about this. Least of all, with you."

I tilt my head, my nose scrunching. "Kind of seems like you do. Why else disrobe yourself? If that's not a cry for 'I need to get rid of my waste-of-space boyfriend' then I don't know what is."

"He's not a waste of space."

"You want to know what I think?" I say, twirling a piece of hair around my finger. "I think you like me but won't admit it because I'm everything everyone has ever told you to stay away from. And Rebecca is a good girl who does what she's told."

Rebecca's face turns beet red, and her eyes blaze like jade fire. "I have no interest in a Godless degenerate who's only here because he's too big of a loser to pass senior year on the first try."

The moment the words are out of her mouth, she claps her

hand over her face. I won't lie, her words sting and my stomach drops into my boots. I'm not sure why. It's not like I care about her opinion of me. I lean back in my seat as she lowers her hand from her mouth.

"I'm so sorry," she whispers. "I—I didn't mean that."

I look away, my thumb running along the pages of an old yellowing newspaper. "Yeah, you did."

She shakes her head. "No, I—even if I did, I shouldn't have said it."

"Don't worry about it."

There's a shuffling of feet and a moment later, Ms. Duncan appears from around the bookshelves. "Is everything okay over here?"

I wait for Rebecca to say I'm harassing her. In all fairness, I suppose I am.

"Yes, sorry, we're fine," Rebecca says, offering Ms. Duncan a warm smile.

My eyes flick to hers, narrowing. She raises her eyebrows at me and I turn to Ms. Duncan, who's looking at me expectantly. "Sorry about that. We got caught up in some of these old articles."

Satisfied, Ms. Duncan shuffles back out of sight. Rebecca's eyes soften a little as she stares at me, a little wrinkle appearing above her nose. I turn away and open my bag to pull out my notebook and pen, but she just keeps looking at me.

"You should keep going," I say quietly. "I have to work tonight, so can't be here too late. I'll grab more papers when you're done with these."

I pull one knee up and rest the notebook on it like an easel, writing my thoughts down on the page. Feeling her eyes, I avoid looking at her as long as I can. Finally, I gesture back at the cards. After a long moment, Rebecca looks back down and for the next little while we work in companionable silence. She peers up at me every so often, but I pretend not to notice.

"I don't always do what I'm told, you know," she murmurs. "And even if I did, there's nothing wrong with following the path that God has laid out for me."

"So is God the one that told you to take off your clothes?"

Her lip trembles. "Forget it."

I fight the urge to roll my eyes. "Will you just explain it to me, then? I'm here. I'm listening."

Her brows furrow and she shakes her head a bit, her lips tight.

"Maybe that's why you never have any fun. Because you're always doing shit for everyone else. Like this bullshit," I say, grabbing the stack of cards.

"'Whatever you did for one of my brothers and sisters, no matter how unimportant they seemed, you did for me,' Matthew 25:40."

I blink. "Did you just scripture me?"

"I wouldn't expect you to understand—" she says.

"Right, because I'm just some Godless degenerate."

She looks away, her fingers wrapping themselves around the golden cross at her throat.

"And your fucking boyfriend . . ." I mutter. "Is he actually someone you like or did someone tell you to date him and you're so caught up in being the good girl for Jesus that you just went along with it?"

"Enough!" she says, voice shrill. Her breathing is shallow and her hands shake. Her green eyes find mine and I know I've gone too far. I struck a nerve. She starts piling her things into her bag.

"We're not done," I say.

"Yes, we are," she says, standing and pulling her backpack over her shoulders. "I'll come in early tomorrow and finish this by myself."

She turns and heads for the exit, her little white bow bobbing in her hair.

I grab my shit and stuff it into my bag, then toss the papers and cards into the box before running out into the hall after her.

"Rebecca!"

She's halfway down the hall but stops, turning slowly to reveal tears streaming down her face. My chest tightens, the sight of her so upset makes me wish I could kick my own ass. I come to a sharp stop a few feet from her.

"Look, I'm sorry."

Her eyes close and a fresh trickle of tears fall down to her chin.

"I don't mean to make you so upset. I swear. I'm just trying to understand—figure you out. Be your friend."

She sniffs and wipes at her chin. "You said you weren't here to make friends."

"No, but . . . you seem like you need one."

I step closer to her, my hands itching to reach out and brush away those treacherous tears staining her face. She blinks up at me, her quick little breaths loud in the empty, echoing hall. Those jade eyes darting over my face before finally landing on my mouth.

"Becca?"

We bolt apart, turning to see her asshole boyfriend and his friends walking toward us, their gym bags slung over their shoulders. Fuck, they must have just finished practice or something.

"Hey man," he says, eyes narrowing as he approaches, looking back and forth between us. "What are you doing?"

"Eric, it's fine." Her voice is so quiet, so submissive, so very different from how she talks to me.

I back up as Eric wraps his arm around her.

"Babe, what's wrong? Did this guy—Did he make you cry?" He turns to me, his face contorting in anger. "I'll kick your ass, you Satan-worshiping piece of shit."

For fuck's sake. I sigh and roll my eyes. I know exactly where this is going.

The two lackeys at his side step my way and I clench my fists, my knuckles cracking from the gesture as I shrug my bag off my shoulder onto the floor. Never run from a fight . . . even if it's three to one.

"Maybe we want to take this outside?" I suggest, gesturing to the door. "You don't really want to do this in front of your girl, do you?"

"Eric, stop it. He didn't do anything," Rebecca squeaks.

One of the guys steps up into my face. "You dress tough, but I bet that's just to hide what a little bitch you are."

I sniff and rub at my nose. "You sure you want to give me an opportunity to get your blood on me?" I say in a drawling, overdramatic voice. "Who knows what I might do with it? Drink it? Offer it as part of a ritual to Baphomet? You know that's how the demons select who to torment right?"

He seems to blanch at the thought, not quite sure if I'm serious or not, and I'm glad I chose today of all days to wear my Anthrax shirt with the pentagram on it.

As if on cue, a door opens down the hall, and one of the science teachers spots us. "What's going on down there?"

"Sorry, Mr. Tilney. We were just leaving." Eric pulls a wide-eyed and horrified looking Rebecca in the opposite direction. The other two glower at me for a long moment and I stare right back, daring them to hit me first in front of a teacher. But finally, they turn and follow Eric and Rebecca.

My heart is jumping around wildly in my chest, my fingers tight from clenching them into fists. I look away, grabbing the cigarette pack from my jacket pocket and tapping it a little too aggressively against my palm. Looking back up, she glances over her shoulder at me one last time before she's carted off out the door.

"Go on, get going," Mr. Tilney says, gesturing at me with his hat.

I stoop to grab my bag and toss it over my shoulder, silently grateful we were interrupted. Not because I'm a coward, but because it would've really sucked to go to my first shift at The Shipwreck with a black eye. I laugh in spite of myself. Maybe Captain John would find it funny and offer me a spare eyepatch.

Heading toward the parking lot, I look up to the sound of tires squealing as Rebecca's douchebag boyfriend peels away while simultaneously flipping me the bird. I offer one right back, but then they're gone and when I climb into the front seat of my van I quickly pull out my notebook. Finding the page where I've written my rules, I suck on my teeth, an unpleasant guilty feeling spreading over me like cold oil.

I've already bent some of my rules—the ones meant to keep me on track to get to San Francisco to play music. Between being worried about what these assholes will think of my clothing, to relying on Noreen to provide me with food and shelter, to not punching Eric the dickbag in the fucking face when I had the chance—

"Enough," I say. Flexing my hand, the raven's feathers move on my skin. I can't get tied down in the tangled web that is Rebecca Briar. I need to be able to fly freely and getting caught up in her problems is a disaster waiting to happen. And I won't—I can't—let that happen. There's too much at stake.

CHAPTER 13

Mother Stands for Comfort

REBECCA

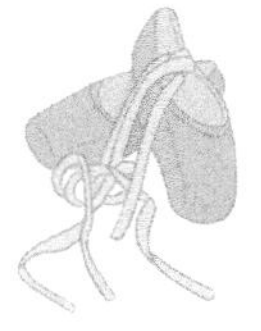

Children, obey your parents in the Lord, for this is right.
Ephesians 6:1

I lean against the inside of my front door, still trying to stem the tears that can't seem to stop falling. Eric drove like a maniac all the way home, ranting about James, but I tuned him out, the words muddling together like a broken record. I vaguely remember him saying goodbye before I walked up the path to the door.

"Rebecca, is that you?" My mother appears in the doorway of the kitchen, her eyes narrowing when she spots my face. "What's wrong?"

I shake my head and turn toward the stairs. "It's nothing, I'm fine." But as I pull myself up, each stair feeling like climbing a mountain, I can hear her hot on my heels. Pushing open my door, my eyes automatically turn to the window, but James's room is dark. That's right, he's working. The sight of that dark, vacant room pinches my heart so hard I gasp.

"I think I know what this is about," my mother sounds out from behind me as she comes into the room.

As I turn to face her, I do my best not to glance at the house next door, knowing that she might put it all together if I give her that one small look. My mouth is dry and my chest aches from panting all day, desperate to tear off this dress and finally breathe. She goes to my closet and fishes out the gray dress from yesterday.

"Do you have something you need to tell me?" she asks, holding it out with a straight arm like it's something covered in filth.

My eyes prickle painfully as I try to keep more tears from escaping down my swollen cheeks. I shake my head, a large lump forming in my throat that's making it hard to swallow.

"Really?" she asks, her eyes flashing dangerously. She turns the dress to show me the damage I did yesterday, the zipper seam broken down the side.

"Mom, I'm sorry," squeaks past my dry lips. "The dress . . . it was too tight, when I tried—"

She takes a few fast steps toward me, waving the ripped dress in my face. "Here I am trying to keep you decently clothed. Keep you modest for God and this is how you show your gratitude? How can you be pure for Jesus when you can't even fit into the clothes I make you?"

My eyes slam shut and there's a dull ringing that starts in the base of my ears. I feel sharp nails and bony fingers clench around my jaw.

"Look at me when I'm talking to you, young lady," she shouts. "Is that what you've been doing when you've stayed late after school this week? Are you sneaking out to stuff your face with those wicked girls you call your friends?"

"No! Mom, I haven't . . . I swear—"

"Probably eating fries and cheeseburgers and ruining your appetite for the dinner I've slaved over all afternoon," she says, throwing the dress across the room.

The tears spill over my lashes like the tide. "Mom, no—I fasted all day. I swear! The dress was too tight, I couldn't—"

"I made that dress with your exact measurements from two weeks ago."

I sob, the abrasion on my ribs throbbing. "Maybe you made a mistake, I haven't—"

There's a moment where her fingers release my chin then a loud sound and sharp crack of her hand slapping across my face. My head whips to the side, my hair flying and sticking to my wet cheeks. I stumble backward toward the bed, my hand coming to rest on the burning skin.

My mother's eyes soften and she sighs deeply. "Oh Rebecca, do you see what you made me do?"

The backs of my knees hit the edge of my bed and I sob as I sink down onto the mattress.

She shakes her head. "Such a disobedient, disappointing, sinful child you are. My mother never would have tolerated such disrespect from me." Walking over, I flinch away as she stops and leans forward. "Don't you understand that everything you do should be out of your love for Jesus?" She steps back and crosses her arms. "Perhaps I should make a call into Mercy Christian Home for Girls—"

The black van.

"No! *Please*," I fall forward, grasping at my mother's skirt.

"It's not that I want to send you away, but—Well, you'll just have to try harder, won't you?"

Even though my cheek stings, my heart races and my whole body aches, I can't feel anything. I'm numb.

She raises her eyebrows at me expecting an answer. My head feels heavy as I nod. She reaches out her hand and strokes my hair gently.

"Children, obey your parents in the Lord: for this is right," she whispers, before pressing her lips to my forehead. I stiffen at the touch and hold my breath, desperate for her to leave. "Your father will be home soon. You'll set the table won't you, dear?"

I blink furiously and nod, terrified if I speak my voice might break. Blessedly, she leaves the room, a simpering smile on her face as she shuts my door. I hear her retreating steps on the stairs and it's like a dam breaks. The air gets stuck as it rushes out of me while the tears burst forth in twin rivers down my face. I yank on the zipper of my dress allowing these great wrenching sobs to rack through me as I fall onto my side and clutch at the comforter. For a long time I just lie on the bed watching the sunlight crawl across the floor as I try to calm down. Finally, I sit up, my head pounding and my face swollen and stuffed up. My stomach growls angrily, but I know at dinner my mother will be watching me like a hawk and I'll hardly be able to eat anything.

There's a damp spot on my comforter from crying, my hand grazing over it as I push myself up on wobbly legs. I step toward the window, staring at the dark room beyond. The shadows of his stereo grow tall across the wooden floor where there's dirty clothes strewn about. Even after everything that happened today between us, I find myself wishing desperately that he were home. That he'd look across and smile finding me here. Maybe he'd notice my teary face and hold up another note asking if I'm okay.

I'm here. I'm listening.

The contrast between James's attempts to understand me versus Eric's roaring indignation when he doesn't even know what happened, or rather wouldn't listen, is startling.

Is he actually someone you like or did someone tell you to date him and you're so caught up in being the good girl for Jesus that you just went along with it?

That's what he'd asked me, that's what crossed the line because I honestly have no idea anymore. I find myself living purely for the sake of others. All that I am is controlled by everyone around me. I'm drowning. And here is this person I should fear, throwing me a life preserver. I wish we were back at school again. I wish I hadn't run away from the library or that Eric hadn't interrupted us. Because I finally know what I would say. What it is that I want. And that's for someone to not demand anything of me. To hug me and tell me everything is going to be okay. What I want is for someone to look at me and see everything that I try to hide.

Ring ring.

All through dinner that blasted phone rings. At first my parents ignored it so I tried to do the same. The fifth time it rang I offered to answer it and all that accomplished was my father barking at me to sit down and a reminder to be silent, that it's none of my business and we don't answer phone calls during dinner. But by the eighth call, he retreated into his office and the phone hasn't rung since.

When I'm finally excused from the table I have to stop myself from bolting up the stairs and into my bathroom. I turn on the shower and strip off the confining clothes. My reflection is hazy from the steam settling on the mirror but as I look at myself, I almost want to cry again. I look like death. My face is pale and gaunt-looking, the little bit of weight I'd put on that Ms. Koysh had noticed on Saturday is now gone and there are bags under my eyes since I haven't managed to get a decent night's sleep all week. My fingers walk down the bones of my ribs, visible under my breasts, which also look like they've shrunk a little. I pull the bow out of my hair, the strands tickling my bare shoulders. My head tilts as I look at myself, trying to find one thing about me that I find attractive, but I can't.

Regret and shame immediately overwhelm me. What had I been thinking, taking off my robe in front of James? So much for proving a point if this is what he saw. This ugly, scrawny, sick-looking girl. Is that why he couldn't look away? Because it was just too awful? Like a car wreck, no matter how terrible, you just can't look away. I replay the day over again in my mind. Every word he'd said to me, and something aches in my chest at the awareness that never once did he admit he was attracted to me. Maybe all of that . . . was just pity. He never said that I was his type after all, and I don't know why that hurts me so badly.

When I get out of the shower a little while later, I pull on a pair of flannel pajamas and head back into my room, brushing my damp hair out as I go. Still no sign of James, but why would there be. If he's working at a place like The Shipwreck, a bar, he'll likely be gone until late. That is if he really does work there after all. He never seems to take much seriously, spouting all of that ridiculous nonsense to Amy and Mary yesterday at lunch. Something about the way he said San Francisco, though, makes me think that it was the one genuine answer he gave during Mary's impromptu interrogation. Why would he want to go to San Francisco? And why is he here with us at all?

Once again I can't sleep, even though my eyes are desperate for it. My brain just won't shut off, and no matter how much I've prayed, the anger and self-loathing coursing through me makes my skin feel itchy. It's well after one in the morning when a light shines through my window, dimly illuminating my room. He's home.

There's a noisy rustling as I pull back the covers and climb out of bed to stand next to the window frame. I peek around the curtains, trying to keep as hidden as possible. He's sitting on his bed, in a T-shirt and boxers, and he must have had a shower because his hair is damp, the curls more defined. Reaching down into his bag he pulls out that black-and-white notebook. I watch as he grabs a pen from his night table and starts writing something down.

I wonder what he writes in there. He's clearly into music, so I would guess that it's music-related. I highly doubt James Walton is the type to write poetry or anything sappy like that. My curiosity seems to make my skin even itchier and I'm suddenly desperate for a peek inside that book, as if it might hold all of his secret thoughts and feelings. I never dared to own a diary for fear my mother would find it, but I've always wanted a place where I could lay myself bare and be honest. James has that, and I'm jealous of him.

He puts the pen away and sets the notebook back in his bag, then his eyes look up at my window. Right at me. He tilts his head to the side and for a moment I think he might smile, but he rubs at his chin instead. Looking away, he clenches both fists and presses them into his thighs before standing. He walks over to the window, and I step out a little more from behind the curtain, before he stops. His eyes lift to mine again and for what feels like an eternity we just look at each other. Then he leans forward, his lips almost touching the glass.

What is he doing? A little patch of fog appears on his window from his breath and I watch in anxious anticipation as his finger reaches out to trace through the vapor. A line, another line and . . . my heart drops through the floor. A pentagram. He drew a pentagram. I don't even know how to react, sure my face is probably adequately showing my confusion. His eyes flick up one last time, before he grabs hold of his curtains and shuts them. The light goes off and I'm left alone.

What just happened? Why would he do that? He said he wanted to be my friend. Tears leak out of the corners of my eyes once again. For a moment, I thought that maybe James saw me, saw how much I'm struggling. Saw a glimpse of the real me and actually cared. But I guess I was wrong. I'm too messy, too proud, too complicated and selfish, and what boy wants to get mixed up in all of that even if he is a sinner?

Honestly? I don't even blame him.

I FEEL like garbage when I wake up extra early the next morning. If I catch the early bus to school, I can duck into the library and probably finish the newspapers before first period starts. After another nearly sleepless night obsessing over James, I've come to the conclusion that somehow I must have built up this fantasy in my head. Maybe that's what God wanted me to realize. That I'm too starved for attention, and am willing to get it wherever I can, even if it's not good for me. The first thing that needs to be removed from my life is our library rendezvous. I won't have to sit or talk to James anymore and I can eliminate the unwanted responsibility from my shoulders of cataloging these darn papers. Kill two birds with one stone kind of deal.

I push open the glass doors to the library and head toward the back area where the newspaper filing cabinet is. But as I round the corner of the bookshelves, the box is gone. Looking around, I think at first that maybe the custodians moved it in the night, but it's nowhere to be found.

"Oh, Miss Briar, what are you doing here so early?"

I turn to see Ms. Duncan pushing a cart covered in books past me.

"I came to finish the newspapers, except they seem to have been moved," I say, gesturing at the cabinet.

Ms. Duncan's brows furrow over her bedazzled spectacles. "Mr. Walton was in first thing this morning to finish those. He left . . . maybe ten minutes ago."

I blink stupidly. "Oh, right. Thanks."

She smiles and continues on her way while I turn back to the empty tables. Had he really come in here this morning to finish on his own? There's a momentary flutter in my chest, thinking he did this for me. But that fluttering is soon stamped out by the memory of that pentagram he drew on his window. No, he didn't do this to help me. He did this so we wouldn't have to spend any more time together.

My fingers twist together in the hem of my sweater as I walk through the halls to my locker. It's still early, the halls quiet except for teachers and a few students involved in band, here for an early morning practice. As I walk, for a moment I think I can hear the clinking of James's chains, but when I turn around there's no one there. I think I'm starting to lose my mind. Less than a week ago, the biggest thing I had to worry about was how to make sure I didn't end up in a compromising situation with Eric.

My tongue runs between my lips and I sigh as I lean against the cold metal locker. I feel heat prickle at the back of my neck, and I wonder what it might feel like for James's hands to wander as he holds me. What it might feel like to kiss him.

It looked like someone was forcing you to kiss a dead fish. Is that what it's like to kiss him?

Is that really what it looked like between me and Eric? There certainly isn't that spark when he kisses me, that moment everyone always talks about in poems and songs.

You know, kissing is fun . . . if it's done right.

Kissing Eric has never been fun. It's been tolerable, but not fun. It started out fine as chaste pecks on the lips. But more recently it's become aggressive, hard and punishing and somehow he's always disappointed. Maybe I'm not a good kisser.

My eyes close and I think about James's full lips, that wild hair and those big hands. The way he had plucked at those guitar strings rushing through my mind like a movie. Heat spreads through my body, my chest flushing and my nipples press against the tight confines of my dress. I can feel my pulse everywhere, the drumming of it loud in my ears. My stomach clenches and for the first time it's not from hunger pains, but from some kind of delicious new sensation that I've never felt before. My imagination plays a symphony of rattling chains and heavy footsteps as my forehead rolls against the cool metal. Then, there's something new, some aching, clenching sensation spreading from between my thighs and I'm nearly breathless.

"Becca?"

My eyes shoot open to see Eric striding toward me, his brows knitted together.

"Why are you here so early? I went by your house to pick you up." He stands with his arms crossed over his chest and a scowl on his face.

I blink rapidly, the throbbing dissipating quickly, and I'm becoming more and more aware by the second that I'm close to panting like a dog in the school hallway.

"Eric, I'm sorry, I forgot to call you—I needed to come in early to finish that job for Mrs. Henry."

He narrows his eyes at me. "Becca, are you okay? You look . . . sick."

I shake my head. "I—I'm fine, I think."

But as the ache starts to dull between my legs, my eyes widen in horror. I'm feeling lust. And not for my boyfriend. My fingers latch onto the cross at my neck, dragging the chain back and forth, feeling it cut against my skin.

"What is with you, lately?" Eric asks.

I grab my textbook out of my locker before closing the door. "I don't know. I think I'm just stressed about college acceptance letters."

Eric's face softens before he wraps his arms around me. Is he hugging me? Some part of me yearns to sink into it, but instead my body tenses, not wanting physical contact from him. He squeezes me with his arms and rests his head on top of mine. "I understand," he says into my hair. "I'm kind of freaking out too.

But it's easier for you. I mean, it's not like you really need college anyway."

His words ring through me like the bell sounding overhead.

"What?" I step back, pushing him away.

"I just mean," he says, his cheeks darkening a bit, "you've already got the church library and daycare job waiting for you. Don't need college for that."

I scoff, my head doing a nervous kind of twitch. "I . . ." My tongue feels like sandpaper. Is that really what Eric thinks? I worked my butt off to maintain a 4.0 GPA, yet I don't need college? Meanwhile, his meager 3.0 would barely get him anywhere decent but he is somehow more deserving than me? That it isn't as big a deal for me because I'm not supposed to see anything of the world outside of what our church has to offer me? That I can't do anything more substantial with my life? "I need to go to class."

He calls after me as I turn away, walking as quickly as I can through the crowded halls. I've never considered myself better than anyone, but out of me, Mary and Eric, I'm definitely the one most deserving of an acceptance letter. I want to see *something* outside of this town. By the time I finally get to class I'm so worked up my hands are clenched so tightly they hurt. I sit down in my seat, trying to slowly ease my hands open before attempting to get a pen or my textbook out of my bag. Then, just as I'm starting to calm down, he's there.

James glances at me, his steps slowing as he enters the room. That clink, clink, clink of his chain evening out. My leg bounces and I think I stop breathing. But for the first time all week, he doesn't smile. He doesn't drag his fingers across my desk and he doesn't pass me a note. He avoids my gaze as he heads for his regular seat, pulling his books out of his bag.

I turn back to the front, feeling like the biggest fool on Earth. He just wanted to play. To lead me down the path of temptation.

That road the devil paved for me with leather cuffs and metal rings and wild, dark eyes. Pulling me in under the guise of understanding and concern. Pastor Campbell was right. Temptation does come knocking on your door. And James? He was kicking the door down.

CHAPTER 14

Owner of a Lonely Heart

REBECCA

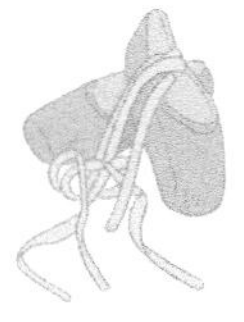

"Are you sure you can't come next Friday?"

Mary and Amy are looking at me as though I've suddenly turned into someone who's actually allowed to go to parties.

"You know they'll never say yes," I say.

"But have you even asked them?" Mary counters. "You're eighteen now. Besides, Eric will be there and they trust him to take care of you right?"

If I'm honest, the fact that Eric will be there is one of the reasons why I haven't even considered asking my parents to let me go. I can only imagine how that would play out. He'd promise me he wouldn't drink, but would anyway. And just like last Saturday, he'd kiss me and try to touch me, and without anywhere to escape to, how far would he try to take it? After what he said to me this morning, I don't want to be around him at all.

"I don't know," I mutter.

Amy rolls her eyes. "Come on Becca, are you seriously going to graduate high school without going to a single party?"

I've never really understood the appeal of parties. The way that Eric behaves when he drinks makes the idea of an entire group of people behaving like that completely unappealing. Not to mention that everyone taking full advantage of no adult supervision to succumb to their base urges is something that God would never approve of. So why would I ever want to subject myself to that?

"Sorry," I say. "But you know they'll say no."

Mary scoffs and leans away. "That's so bogus. Now there's two people that I want to be there who won't be."

My eyes narrow. "Who else do you mean?"

She smirks. "James."

The name ricochets through my body like a bullet. He hasn't acknowledged me since yesterday morning. I even closed the curtains last night because I was starting to lose my grip on reality, the pentagram still visible on the glass pane in the right light. The only indication I have of his comings and goings is the music blaring through the speakers of his van when it wakes me up, followed by the light from his lamp briefly shining into my room at night.

This morning has been the same as yesterday—no smiles, no glances, no notes. And now, even as we sit here for lunch, he's nowhere to be found. Apparently it's like I don't exist to him anymore and it hurts more than I care to admit.

"Mary," Amy says, "you can't be serious."

Mary tosses her dark hair over her shoulder. "I asked him again if he's sure he can't make it. It seemed like if he wasn't working he'd actually come." She rolls back her shoulders intentionally sticking her chest out. "Maybe I'll mention it one more time before the track meet. He can come after he's done."

A burst of jealousy flashes through me as I take in Mary's ample bust, my hand pressing against my almost flat chest. I think about how I'll never look like Mary, or have that voluptuous body that I know appeals to so many men. Does Eric think I'm sexy? I know he must be attracted to me, his wandering hands are as clear an indication as any, but is that because he thinks I'm sexy or just because I'm the warm body next to him?

You're not my type.

James's deep voice bounces around in my skull. I glance down at my bony wrists and knobbly knees and wonder if I'm actually anyone's type. The fact that Mary is probably the exact kind of girl that James is attracted to ignites a kind of compulsion in me.

"Mary," I say, finding it hard to keep the severity out of my voice, "stay away from him. He's bad news."

Mary and Amy roll their eyes at me. "Becca—"

"No, seriously. Wednesday after school I heard him threaten Ryan with some kind of satanic ritual."

Their mouths drop open. "What?"

Why did I tell them that? Jealousy is a sin, knock it off.

When I don't elaborate, Amy starts begging for more details. I leave out most of what happened, particularly the part about James and my little library project. Essentially, all they need to know is that James, Eric, Ryan and Peter nearly got in a fight in the hall before Mr. Tilney appeared.

"Three against one?" Mary says, frowning. "Not very fair."

"Maybe that's why he's not hanging around," Amy says. "Worried he might get jumped. Oh, here comes your lover boy, Becca."

I wish I could simply disappear, that the floor would open up and swallow me, when I feel Eric's arm wrap around my waist as he slides in next to me on the bench. His mouth presses against my ear before he whispers, "Hey, babe. I've missed you."

Turning my face to his, our eyes meet, but that feeling I once had when he would look at me like this is nearly forgotten. I used to feel so excited that he would sit with me, talk to me, and want to hold my hand. That we would one day be married and share our lives together. Was it because I truly liked Eric or was it because he had shown interest and our parents had set us up? Had I simply been doing what I was told to do? Was James right about me all along?

Now, after two years, I want to push him away but I'm frozen, my body tensing under his touch, and I have to stop myself from recoiling. He's still looking at me, waiting for me to say I missed him too, to fall at his feet and submit, so I offer a small smile and, satisfied, he faces our friends.

"Yeah," Ryan says to Amy, "total psychopath. Can't believe they even let him come to school with us."

"Oh please, he was probably joking," Mary says, waving her hand. "We talked to him Tuesday at lunch, and I think that's just his sense of humor."

Oh no, they're talking about James. I feel Eric's hand tighten on my waist.

"What? You talked to him?" Eric asks.

Mary shrugs. "Yeah, he sat with us."

Eric turns to me but I keep my face forward, hoping the heat that has bloomed across the back of my neck and ears don't give away just how guilty I feel at keeping that information a secret.

Ryan presses further. "What did he say?"

"Nothing serious. He spent most of the conversation pulling our legs, right, Becca?"

My eyes flick up. They're all looking at me expectantly to corroborate the story, but all I can think about is how he'd offered me his cookie and it was so sweet I wanted to hug him. "Right."

"Is that why you were crying?" Eric asks. "Did he say something at lunch to upset you?"

Mary shakes her head and holds up her hand. "Wait, he made you cry?"

"No . . . I—"

"He had her cornered after school. We found her crying her eyes out," Eric says, his arm moving protectively around me.

Mary's eyes narrow at me. "You didn't mention that part."

"We're lucky we were there. Who knows what that freak might have done to her," Ryan offers. "And now they're interrogating him about the pentagram spray painted in the boys' bathroom."

"What?" Mary, Amy, and I collectively burst out.

"He's in the principal's office right now," Peter says. "Hope he gets expelled."

My eyes close and I struggle to take a deep breath. Everything is spinning out of control around me and I'm suddenly stiflingly hot. Did James really do that? Somehow I can't believe it. Then I remember the pentagram he drew on the window. I grab my lunch bag that I haven't even opened and stuff it into my backpack before standing. "I think I'm just going to go outside for a few minutes."

"Are you okay?" Amy asks, and I can still feel Mary's eyes burning into me, trying to figure out why I didn't tell them the whole story.

"No," I say honestly. "I think I'm coming down with something."

"Yeah, you look a bit sick," Ryan says.

Mary turns and smacks him on the shoulder. "Ryan, you jerk. You never say a girl looks bad, even if she does."

I feel Eric's hand around my wrist, his body turning in his seat. "You want me to come with you?"

"No, I just . . . I'll be fine." I offer another smile and shake my head, pulling my hand from his grasp as I back away.

"You'll still be there for the track practice after school, right?"

My jaw tightens, but my smile doesn't falter. "Yes, right. Yes . . . don't worry, I'll be there."

I turn toward the door of the cafeteria, making sure to keep my steps even instead of breaking into a run. I'm not even sure where I'm going until I step out into the warm spring air. The sun shines on my face as I lean against the rough brick exterior of the school. I close my eyes and listen to the birds singing. Just two and a half months. Two and a half months until—

No, there wasn't any mail for you.

Maybe I'll never get out of here. Am I really destined to be the subservient housewife to someone like Eric Corbley? Raising a little brood of whiny children and spending all of my time changing dirty diapers and cooking meals that I won't be able to bring myself to eat? I hate to admit it, but James is right about me. I never do anything fun. Never do anything that I want to do, that's just for me, except dance. Which I only get to do once a week. What if, after I graduate, I'm never able to dance again? Surely Eric won't be the type of man to watch the kids so I could take a class on the weekend. No, he'd be like my dad. Too important for that. Too important to spend time with his kids and I'll be all alone . . . and miserable.

Clink, clink, clink.

My eyes shoot open to see James walking toward me across the parking lot, his van in the back corner and a cloud of smoke trailing behind him. Goosebumps prickle up and down my arms as his gaze finds mine. Those dark eyes crinkling a bit around the edges. Time seems to slow down, as though he's walking in slow motion, or maybe it's simply because my heart is beating a million miles per hour.

If he's still here, that must mean he hasn't been expelled. I want to ask him if he really vandalized the school or if he was simply in the wrong place at the wrong time. To ask why he shut me out. All of the questions seem to die on my lips as he approaches, because I simply want him to be near me. I feel myself smile, but he looks down, flicks his cigarette away onto the concrete and passes me to walk back into the school without a second glance.

It's been a week.

A week of pretending he doesn't notice me staring at him, even though I see the way his cheeks turn pink at the back of the room. A week of me watching his closed curtains until I've memorized every fiber of the fabric. The crude pentagram is gone now, washed away by spring morning condensation. A week of more incessant phone calls to my house, my father growing more and more agitated by the day. A week of having to pretend I'm okay when I'm falling apart.

When Principal Jeffries makes an announcement releasing the student body early from fourth period to allow us to go watch the track team meet on the back field, I should feel happy. And for a short moment I am, knowing I'm only a few hours away from my favorite day of the week. But then I remember that I'll have to sit through several hours of watching our school and several others compete for the district track titles before they can move on to the state wide-competition. And it's so dreadfully boring I wish I knew how to sleep with my eyes open.

The day's made worse when, on my way to my locker, I see Mary, leaning up against a wall talking to none other than James. She's pushing her chest forward and batting her eyelashes, the perfect picture of flirtation. And he's smiling at her, and not in that smug way he used to smile at me, his hand pulling on the back of his neck and making his shirt pull up at the waist. Is this a genuine smile? Does he like her? Why shouldn't he? My stomach churns as I mentally kick myself and think how utterly mediocre I am while I watch her flirt so shamelessly. To think I thought that taking my clothes off for him meant something. That he might understand what it's like to hide who you really are from everyone until you're alone. I should have known that wouldn't be the case. James knows exactly who he is and isn't afraid to show it. My jaw trembles and as his head turns to me, I back away and duck into the girls bathroom before his gaze locks on mine for the first time all week.

Only once the halls outside are quiet, and I've stopped trembling, do I venture out of the bathroom. Thankfully, James and Mary are gone along with everyone else. I grab my things from my locker before heading outside, the bright sun making the air warm enough that it's comfortable, but making it hard for me to find my friends. Feeling like an idiot, I spend a solid five minutes searching with my hand up to block the sun before I finally spot them. They're sitting near the top of the farthest bleacher so I make my way over. As I pass, I spot Eric, Ryan and Peter. I wave to Eric, and perhaps he doesn't see me, or the sunlight is shining in his eyes, but he doesn't wave back and my shoulders tense. What if he does poorly and tries to say that he was distracted because of me? I *have* been behaving a bit erratically. My head tilts back as I walk, taking as deep of a breath as I can. I'm just so tired.

I climb awkwardly through the rows of students until I finally reach the top.

"There you are. What took you so long?" Amy asks.

"It took me forever to spot you both, why did you have to pick up here?" I ask, tucking my skirt underneath myself.

"Best view from up here," Amy says. "Anyway, you didn't miss much, except Eric and Jeremiah got into an argument as he was heading out onto the field."

Looking past where Eric is, my eyes scan the crowd to find Jeremiah who sits alone, looking livid. "I wonder what they were arguing about."

Amy shrugs. "Maybe Jer's girlfriend? Stephanie Lawford? They just broke up. I think I heard Eric telling him off that Jer screwed up something perfect."

That makes no sense. Why would that be any of Eric's business? I look past Amy and notice Mary who's been unusually quiet about all this, only to find an annoyed-looking scowl on her face. "What's wrong with you?"

Mary crosses her arms over her chest and looks away.

Amy leans closer to me and whispers. "She asked James out and he turned her down."

"*What*?"

A few dozen students turn to look at me. I'm almost on my feet, my voice high and shrill.

Mary turns to me, her eyes wide and her face red. "It's not like that."

Amy giggles. "It kind of is Mare, you asked him to come to the party after work so you two could hang out"—she lifts both hands to add the air quotes—"and he said he wasn't interested."

My heart is pounding. Did James really turn Mary down?

Mary rolls her shoulders back and lifts her chin. "Whatever, it's not a big deal. He's too weird anyway, and we have *nothing* in common."

There's a lightness in my chest as Mary slumps forward to lean her face in her hands, her elbows resting on her knees.

"Besides, my parents would drop dead if they ever saw us together," Mary continues. "Could you just imagine what my dad would say? You're right Becca, he's bad news."

I have to choke down the nervous giggling that seems to bubble up in my throat. I quickly turn it into a cough to mask it. Somehow the sun seems to shine a little brighter and it feels a little warmer, knowing that James wants nothing to do with Mary. And while he still doesn't want anything to do with me either, it makes that fact a little easier to swallow.

My eyes scan the crowd for his wild curly hair. I wonder if he skipped out with the early dismissal. He made it very plain to me that this kind of thing is boring to him. I wonder where he's been the past week when not in class. Does he just hide out in his van and smoke? I never see him with anyone else. I suppose he meant it when he said that he wasn't here to make friends. There's a loud cheer as people stand up in front of me waving little pennant flags and clapping. I don't even know what happened because I'm barely paying attention. Then I smell it.

The smell of cigarettes and something woodsy hits me and next to my feet I see the smoke blow out in a brilliant white plume. I turn to look to my left, down at the edge of the bleachers. James stands with one arm against the metal scaffolding and the other in his jeans pocket. He has a cigarette between his lips and while I've never before considered smoking as attractive, I stare at the way his lips wrap around the white stick. His shoulders rise and fall, the sound of more cheering fading into the background as I listen for his slow breaths. He lifts the hand from his pocket to his mouth, removing the cigarette, his tongue wetting his full lips.

His arm supporting his weight slides forward, the back of his long fingers brushing against the skin of my ankle and I think I might combust. My eyes softly close as I revel in the subtle pressure of his hand. I breathe a long exhale through my nose, my eyes opening as that clenching, aching feeling returns as quick as lightning and I'm suddenly too warm. He doesn't look up at me, but I'm grateful, because if he did, I might just pass out. My hands wrap around the front of the bench to keep myself upright, my knuckles cracking as they grip the metal. I watch with rapt attention as his lips wrap around his cigarette once more, the ember burning hot as he inhales, and for the briefest of moments I feel his eyes linger on the spot where he touches me and it's as if the world stops.

The noise fades away and that one point of contact has become the center of the universe. I've learned only a little bit about the Big Bang theory. How all of the universe was concentrated in one infinitely small speck before it exploded outward. It had all seemed so blasphemous before, the creation of such a universe without God. Now I think I finally understand. All there is, is the touch of his fingers against my ankle and the heat of his body near mine. The smell of him in the air and his dark eyes brightening to a chocolate brown in the sunlight. I feel my body curl toward him, but then the touch is gone. He's gone. His retreating form walking swiftly across the field toward the parking lot and I feel cold and small, like I'm shrinking. Soon, he's obscured by the bright sun and I turn my attention back to the field. Though he didn't say anything, I feel as if new life has been breathed into my lungs. That maybe he hasn't written me off completely. And when I get home I'm opening my curtains as wide as they'll go so if he opens his, he'll know he doesn't scare me. Not anymore.

CHAPTER 15

Just Can't Get Enough

JAMES

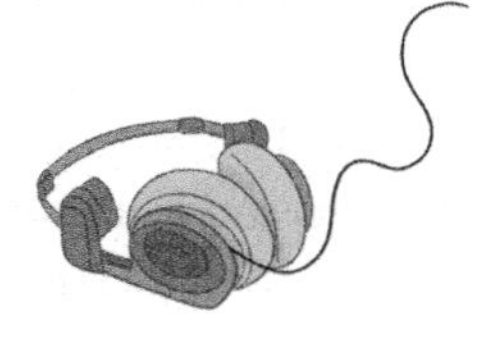

My fingers still tingle hours later. Even when I'm up to my elbows in dirty dishwater, my arms aching from carrying boxes of beer bottles up and down the narrow stairs of The Shipwreck. I tried to stay away. I swear I tried, but Rebecca seems to occupy all of the free space in my brain. Whatever small part of it isn't being taken up by music, she's wedged in there tightly. Even now, as I scrub the grime and grease off of the fridge shelves, all I can think of is her white shoes and green socks, the fair skin of her ankles and calves and the way goosebumps scattered all over her when I touched her.

I hadn't meant to do it. I really planned to stay away. I promised myself I'd keep away from her, but it's been so hard. To feel her presence so strongly through the window every night and every morning. To try and scare her away, sure she'd believe in that satanic bullshit—convince her I'm no good. When I was called down to the principal's office to be interrogated about the pentagram in the bathroom, I thought for a second maybe I *did* do it. They certainly thought so. How it was too convenient that I show up from out of nowhere and the vandalism begins. Thankfully, I had an airtight alibi. Coming in early to finish those fucking newspapers so Rebecca didn't have to was a stroke of luck—I was so sure Ms. Duncan would throw me under the bus.

Part of me hopes Rebecca would know I finished the papers to help her, while the other part of me hopes she believed the rumor that I spray painted that pentagram. She should keep away from me. But all week, I've felt like the negative to her positive. Like the pull of a magnet and I don't know if I can fight it anymore.

I don't pretend to know what's going on in her life—she seems miserable when she's not pasting that fake-ass smile on her face in front of her asshole boyfriend and friends. Perhaps I hit the nail on the head when I appraised how she never seems to do anything for herself. Maybe that's why she got so upset—because it was the truth, and sometimes that's the hardest thing to face. Then there's the whole undressing thing, which . . . I don't even know what to make of all that.

And I find myself wanting to help her. Normally, I don't give a shit about anyone, only looking out for myself because that's what I've had to do my whole life. Through the horrors of foster care and having to take care of my mom . . . But Rebecca has a hold over me like no one has before and it's exactly why I made those rules. To keep me on the path toward my dream. It's terrifying.

"Walton, can you grab another two cases of Bud from downstairs?" John calls from the front where a band playing a cover of Megadeath's *Rattlehead* is blaring through the door.

"Yeah, no problem."

I dry my hands on a nearby rag and push the hair out of my face. I pass through the kitchen, the smell of hot oil hanging in the air mixed with the smell of weed. The joints I bought earlier roll around the metal tin in my pocket. I can't wait to get home.

It'll be a relief to feel that heavy, drowsy feeling again. It used to help quiet my mind when the world got too noisy, when music wasn't enough. It could drown anything out. Sirens, neighbors yelling, and the incessant coughing from the next room when my mom was near the end. Even though it had been annoying as shit and kept me awake most nights, I would give anything to hear it again if it meant having my mom back. Now, at Noreen's, everything is too quiet.

I haul the cases of beer up the stairs and kick open the swing door to the bar with my foot. The loud music is a welcome distraction and the band that's playing is actually pretty decent. I take my time unloading the beer into the fridges behind the bar so I can listen a bit longer. Even though I can't see them play from this angle, I can visualize the movement of fingers across the neck of the guitar. Hear the chord progressions even at breakneck speeds, my fingers curling into the right shapes without even having to think about it.

Switching to filling the boxes with empties, John jerks his chin at me, and I follow him back through to the kitchen.

"You had a break yet?" he asks loudly, pushing his damp hair off his forehead.

I shake my head.

"Take a half hour okay? Feel free to order something. Half price for employees."

I nod. "Thanks."

"You're doing all right, kid."

I smile and head down where the lockers are to grab my smokes. When I come back up, I ask the cook who also supplies the weed to throw a burger and fries on for me. He grunts his understanding, which I'm coming to realize is how he communicates most things, before I push out the back door into the parking lot. One of the waitresses is already out here, inhaling a cigarette and sitting on an overturned milk crate, her short skirt hiked up to reveal a cherry tattoo on her thigh. She looks to be around the same age as Noreen. The beginnings of gray hair and laugh lines on her face.

Lighting up, I inhale deeply before letting out a long billowing cloud into the night. My skin tingles and my fingers twitch from the memory of Rebecca's skin, the little freckle on her ankle bone blazing brightly in my mind.

I wonder what she's doing now. Did she go to the party that Mary seemed so desperate for me to attend? Rebecca doesn't seem like the type of girl who would want to go even if she was allowed, though I could be wrong. Maybe that's what she does for fun. Gets shit-faced on weekends before stumbling hungover into church. No, highly unlikely. She's all about that bullshit "living for Jesus" or . . . how do they phrase it? Anyway, that seems more something Mary would do. I still haven't been able to figure out what Rebecca actually does for fun, but I find myself desperate to find out.

Those five simple rules I wrote for myself as my mom lay dying in that hospital room flash warningly up at me as if the page from my notebook is open right here. I've already strayed from them a bit. They're not broken, but bent. And getting more involved in Rebecca's life puts me in danger of snapping them in half.

I have plans. Big plans. And those plans don't involve getting trapped in this shitty town because I fell for some girl next door. Even if her very presence seems to burn me from the inside out.

"You're James, right?"

I'm pulled out of my Rebecca obsession as the waitress waves her free hand at me.

"Oh, yeah. That's right."

"I'm Eleanor. Help me up, will you?" she asks, stretching out her hand.

I walk over and grab her hand, pulling her to her feet.

"You're Noreen's nephew?" she asks, taking a final drag of her cigarette.

I nod. "Yeah."

"I was sorry to hear about your mom. Dora . . . You look just like her."

I nearly choke on the smoke, coughing and spluttering as I bang my fist against my chest. "Wait . . ." I pause, my voice wheezing. "You knew my mom?"

She gives me a warm smile. "Not well, but yeah. She used to tutor me after school when I was a freshman."

My heart feels like it's bursting. "Really?"

"Yeah, she was so smart. I always wondered what happened to her."

I don't think I've blinked since she started talking. "What do you mean?"

Eleanor narrows her eyes. "Well, she just disappeared. She never told you that?"

I shake my head. Truth be told, my mom hadn't really ever talked about her life before me, and I was a stupid, selfish kid who didn't care enough to ask.

"About two months into her senior year, she just . . . took off," she says, resting a hand on her hip, "never to be seen or heard from again. It was quite the scandal. She was one of the nominees for homecoming queen and everything."

My mom tutored people? And homecoming queen? She was popular too? It feels like Eleanor is describing someone completely different from the woman I knew.

"I think Noreen was pretty cut up about it," she says, eyebrows cinching together. "Were they close?"

I blink rapidly, my eyes stinging. "Umm . . . no. I didn't even know I had an aunt until a couple of months ago."

Eleanor looks surprised by this. "Really?"

I nod again before stubbing my cigarette butt into the ashtray and blowing out the smoke from my lungs. "Can I ask what she was like? My mom, I mean."

Her face softens. "She was beautiful, and smart, and kind—a rare combination."

I smile. When I think of my own troubled history with my mom, it's nice to imagine her this way. I wish I had known my mom how Eleanor remembers—young and without any real difficulties or illness. What must have happened to her to change everything so drastically?

"Anyway, I better get back," she says, pulling down the skirt over her legs a little more, the cherry tattoo disappearing under the fabric.

I nod. "Thanks. For telling me about her, I mean."

"No problem."

Once she's gone, I back up to lean against the brick, glancing at the sky where only a few stars are visible. And while I don't believe in God, or Heaven, or any of that bullshit, it's as though I can feel my mom near me right now.

I reach into my bag and pull out my notebook, flipping to the page where I started writing that letter to my mom.

Why didn't you ever tell me you were so smart? Maybe if I had known, I wouldn't have so easily believed it when people said I wouldn't amount to anything. And cheerleading? There's so much I wish I had asked. So much I wish I knew about your life.

As if she hears me, one of the journals that I found in the box of her things thumps forward in my bag. My stomach tumbles at the prospect of reading her thoughts.

July 4, 1965

Stacey dragged me out to the fair and while I protested at first, I'm so glad I went. We ran into a few of the guys from the football team and I can't believe I'm even writing this but, Jet asked me out on a date. Better still, he spent the whole evening with me at the fair. He even won me a pink teddy bear and took me on the ferris wheel. Maybe Stacey's right. It's senior year. I need to start having some fun or I'll look back one day and regret it.

The backdoor opens.

"Walton!" one of the bartenders calls from inside. "You're needed."

I sigh but I'm smiling. Even just this—this little piece of her, warms me from the inside out. Tucking the journal back in my bag, I promise to read more later, but at least for the time being, I enjoy the small insight into who my mom was.

WHEN I PULL into the driveway a few hours later, sparking the joint between my teeth, I find myself staring up at Noreen's house. I wonder why she hasn't told me any of that. That my mom was so smart—a good student. Maybe that's why she so desperately wanted me to finish high school. So much so that she'd make it her dying wish. Did she want me to because she could've but didn't? Then there's the fact that she had just up and left two months into her senior year. What could've possibly happened to her to make her need to disappear?

The simplest answer would be to just ask Noreen. She seems

cagey talking about her sister though, and since I'm basically freeloading off of her by living in her second bedroom rent-free, I don't want to muddy the waters too much. I feel that familiar relaxing heaviness sink into my bones, the pungent smoke filling the van. My eyes glance over at the dark house next door. I wonder what Rebecca would be like high. I bet she'd be a giggler. She wouldn't be able to stop laughing at something stupid. Girl probably needs a good laugh. Either that or . . . something else to help her relax. She's wound up tighter than a clock, her springs ready to burst loose.

I stub out the joint, leaving the rest in my van for another time, then grab my bag and head upstairs. I rush through my shower and I stumble my way into my room in the dark, looking for my lamp. The light flicks on and I instinctively look to my window where it's just darkness beyond the curtains. I head over and open them wide and freeze. Her curtains are open. Have they been open this whole time? My chest aches thinking about what that simple act might mean. Has she looked out, waiting for me to open mine?

With the towel slung low on my hips and my hair dripping down my back, I notice the faint markings of the pentagram I drew are gone. Good. I don't want to scare her away. Not anymore.

No sign of her tonight, although it is really late. She's probably asleep. I quickly change into a clean pair of boxers and a T-shirt before sitting down on the edge of the bed. Pulling my notebook and pen off the nightstand, I flip through the pages to the very back, where most of them are blank. Except this one, a page of little things I've written about her which she can never know about. If she got a hold of this, I'd probably have to drown myself from embarrassment.

I've never been particularly great at expressing myself verbally. I had a bit of a speech delay as a kid. No surprise there, bouncing around foster homes made me quiet for a long time. But my mom had always encouraged me to write what I thought, so that's what I do. Whenever I can't quite say what I want or need to out loud, I write it down. I glance up at the dark window again. Thinking about that tingle that's still present in my fingers from touching her so recklessly. The way I felt those sea glass-colored eyes on me, so intense that even amongst the crowd, it felt like we were the only two people there. Like it was that Monday all over again when she was cold and I wanted to give her my jacket but didn't.

I inwardly chastise myself. I made those fucking rules for a reason. Am I really so hung up over a pretty face and a bare ankle that I'm ready to disregard them completely? I click my pen and write.

What do you dream about? Would you believe me if I told you I've dreamt of you every night this week?

My eyes scan over the other notes, I've jotted down.

Why did you look so miserable today? Is it because of me?

Your little nose wrinkle is adorable.

And finally,

Why do you fascinate me so much?

I slam the notebook shut and stuff it back into my bag before tossing the pen on my night table. Turning off my lamp, I lie down on my bed and stare at the ceiling. My arms are sore from work and my eyes are heavy, but I turn onto my side to face the window. The curtains are still open. Is she just as affected by me as I am by her? Is she trying to tell me something? I don't fully understand what's going on between us, only that there's definitely *something*. And fuck, I know I'll probably regret all of this later, but I want all her dreams to be about me too.

CHAPTER 16

Danger Zone

JAMES

It's late when I wake up. I'm sure it is. I didn't get in until well after two in the morning and it's Saturday so sleeping in is allowed. Especially when I need to be at the bar again by six. I open one eye to glance at the alarm clock on my night table and sure enough, it's twelve fifteen. I stretch out my long limbs and inhale deeply, swallowing against my tongue which feels thick in my mouth. I turn my head to look out the window, the pastel pinks and yellows from Rebecca's room making the sunlight all the more potent as I squint against it.

She's not there. But what was I expecting? She doesn't live her whole life in her bedroom and I don't think she'd be allowed to sleep in on a Saturday. It's officially been two weeks since I moved here, two weeks since I looked out that window and saw a girl dancing around her room almost naked. Two weeks since Rebecca swept into my life like a tornado, uprooting everything and leaving a trail of emotional turmoil in her wake.

I lie looking through the glass, the clouds in the sky distorting the shadows of her room and making me think on more than one occasion that maybe she is there after all. I sigh and get up. I've got shit to do and can't accomplish any of it lying in bed, but my wandering thoughts of Rebecca have made it a bit hard to stand up so . . . I take care of that first.

Feeling a little more relaxed, I gather up my dirty laundry and toss it in the washing machine at the bottom of the stairs.

"James?" Noreen peeks around the corner of the kitchen at me. "There's some breakfast here if you're hungry," she says, jerking her head toward the counter.

"That sounds amazing." She smiles and I follow her into the kitchen. I'm handed a plate of bacon, eggs and toast. "I uh . . . I really—thanks for this."

"You've been working late. I feel like I haven't seen you in days." Noreen ruffles the top of my head affectionately before sitting down. She pushes a cup of coffee toward me with a smile.

"Thanks," I say, taking it from her and sipping it. "Yeah, I know. But it's a decent gig and the money's not bad. At least I don't stick out there. And the music's killer."

"How's school going?"

I shrug. School was never my strong suit. But so far, I've been keeping up. "Not bad."

"You know, if you need any help with that, I'm here."

Swallowing a piece of bacon, I remember the conversation last night with Eleanor. How my mom had been a tutor. That she was good at school.

"I, uh . . ." I say, not sure if this might be a sensitive subject, "I met someone who knew Mom last night."

Noreen's face tightens. "Really? Who?"

"She works at the bar. Eleanor . . . Not sure of the last name. Does that sound familiar?"

She shakes her head. "Lots of Eleanors around here."

Yeah . . . definitely a sensitive subject.

"What did she say?" Noreen asks, peeking up at me through her eyelashes.

I swallow nervously. "That Mom used to tutor her. That she

was smart, popular even. That she just took off a couple of months into senior year and never came back."

Noreen fiddles with the hem of the crochet placemats on the table for a long time. Just as I'm about to continue eating, thinking she won't reply, she speaks in a low voice.

"Lots of people just disappear around here. You know, they run away. They're sent away. Or they try to escape."

My eyes narrow. "Escape? Escape from what?"

"Holy Grace."

I blink. Mom was trying to escape a church? But Noreen isn't overly religious. In fact, she seems to hate the people who are, like the neighbors. Had she and my mom been raised in it, like Rebecca?

I open my mouth, but Noreen is already up and walking away into the living room, the conversation effectively over. Letting out a long breath, I take another sip of my coffee. If my mom just up and left to get away from the church, my grandparents must not have been good people. I think about how hard things had been for her. Was living here really so bad that she chose that life over this one?

After finishing my breakfast, I switch the laundry and get dressed before grabbing my guitar and hooking up the amp to my headphones. I've been trying to nail down some new song covers and there are a few spots in the solo of *Hell Awaits* by Slayer that are tripping me up. Mainly because I still need to get my fingers wrapped around the down picking, and learning it all by ear isn't easy.

I tie my hair back out of my face then press play on the stereo and my fingers slide over the strings, the hard calluses of my fingertips pressing down on the fretboard. The solo's coming up now, and I feel my heart rate pick up as the speed increases.

When it hits, my left hand flies furiously but controlled over the strings. About halfway through, I've messed up enough to stop. I stand up and rewind the tape, closing my eyes to listen to the notes. Once they're in my head, I pause the song to try and work through it on my guitar. Then, when I think I've gotten a bit more down, I turn the song back on and play with it. It goes on like this for a while. Start and stop, start and stop.

Forty-five minutes later and I think I've finally got it. My forearm is burning and my fingers are a bit cramped. I grab an elastic hairband from my nightstand, and pull my hair back and tie it at the base of my neck before standing up to try it all together. It isn't the longest song I've ever played but it's not short either, and I want to try to get through it once without stopping. I unplug the headphones and turn up the volume on the amp. Not to the deafening level like I'd like to, but loud enough that it'll play overtop of the track.

"Right . . . here goes nothing," I mutter.

I adjust the strap of my guitar over my shoulder and press play before standing back. The first strike of the strings always sends chills down my spine. My head bounces through the chord progression, my teeth sinking down into my bottom lip at the trickier bits, but so far I'm managing to keep up. My fingers are already tired by the middle section, the arpeggios making the movement of my hand a bit easier since it's not skating around for each individual note. I remind myself to breathe, because that solo is coming up.

My eyes close, and the world disappears as the squeal of the notes flies out into the universe. Screwing up my face in concentration, my fingers dance across the strings, hitting every, single, note. Knees feeling like Jell-O, my head falls back as I realize I nailed it. I'm flying high and when the song ends, I'm sweating and smiling so wide my cheeks hurt.

"Well . . ." I say, breathing heavily, "fuck me."

There's a loud knocking on the front door and I quickly turn off the stereo and amp, setting my guitar on its stand before heading for the stairs. I get to the bottom, stopping when I hear Noreen's voice.

"Can I help you, Linda?"

My eyes narrow as I press myself against the wall of the stairwell to listen.

"Yes, you can tell that boy to keep that Godforsaken racket down," Linda says.

"As far as I can tell," Noreen replies calmly, "he's well within the noise level that's appropriate for this time of day on a Saturday. Just because it's noise you don't particularly enjoy, doesn't mean you can stomp over here and tell us what we can and can't do in our own home."

I feel a burst of affection for my aunt and while I know she'd rather listen to the Bee Gees on a loop than thrash metal, I'm glad she's standing up for me. Not many people do that.

"I don't want my daughter exposed to that Satan-worshiping devil music," Linda says darkly, and I realize Linda must be Rebecca's awful mother.

Noreen scoffs. "Your control over your daughter must be fairly weak if you think that hearing a guitar from next door is going to pull her over to the dark side. Or is the *Star Wars* reference lost on you?"

I raise my fist to my mouth and bite down hard on my knuckles. Fuck, Noreen takes no one's shit. She's my goddamn hero.

"You watch yourself, Walton. That boy is going to end up just like his mother."

There's a long tense pause before Linda speaks again. "Oh, you think I didn't know that no-good heathen's mother turned out to be a junkie? You know what this town is like, Noreen, everyone knows something. You just have to ask the right people."

I bite my tongue, but I'm about to burst out of my skin.

"I think you'd better leave," Noreen says in a low, dangerous voice.

There's a pause, followed by the slamming of a door followed by a string of curses. I peek around the door frame to see Noreen, red in the face, leaning against the inside of the front door. Her eyes open and she sees me, her expression softening.

"Oh, hey, sorry about that," she says, pushing off the door.

"It's fine," I say. "I'm used to it."

She stops in front of me and places her hands on her hips, chewing on her bottom lip. "James—"

"I'm going to head into town. I think I'll stop by the music store again."

She shakes her head, stepping forward. "You don't have to leave—"

"Noreen, it's fine. I don't want to cause you any trouble. Besides, it's right near the bar. Plus they have this Gibson SG guitar there, and I think I want to ask it out on a date."

Noreen chuckles a bit. "James?"

I pause as I back toward the stairs. "Yeah?"

"You know I don't think you're any trouble, right?"

I shift awkwardly, my fist pressing into the flat of my other palm as I fidget. "Yeah . . . yeah, sure. I know."

She nods and I spin on my heel, escaping up the stairs to grab my jacket and bag. Maybe I can find a diner or something where I can work on some homework. I look out the window, the darkness of Rebecca's pink room fueling my desire to leave. After all, if she's not there, there's not much of a view.

As I DRIVE ACROSS TOWN, the sun disappears behind dark, heavy clouds. There's a hint of moisture in the air as the breeze blows through my open front window. I stop in at the record store I found and browse for a bit, but most of what they have here I already have at home. I check the message board too, but there's nothing new posted.

It's getting darker, the wind chillier as I drive, looking around for a diner to grab some lunch at where I can get some work done. There's a neon sign in the distance that looks promising, but my eyes latch onto a skinny blonde walking down the street toward me.

"Rebecca?"

Sure enough, it is her. Her hair is in a tight bun on top of her head and her arms are wrapped around herself, a bag slung over her shoulder. What the hell is she doing all the way out here? And where is she going?

I pass her and make a U-turn at the next light. Should I stop? The sky is about to open up, and Rebecca looks like one bad cold or flu would wipe her out. Fuck . . . Okay, here we go.

I pull over on the side of the road ahead of her as she approaches, rolling my window down.

"Hey!" I yell.

Her head jerks up. A panicked look overtakes her gaze as she focuses on the van at first. It softens when it slides to me, before her eyes widen and her mouth drops open.

"What are you doing out here?" I ask.

She looks around as though worried someone will see her talking to me. "I . . ." She trails off, taking a step toward the van. "I'm walking home."

I feel my eyebrows nearly disappear under my hair. "You—Becks, are planning on walking home from here?"

Something tenses in her face, and she blinks a few times before rubbing at her nose. "Yeah."

My eyes narrow. Something doesn't add up. "Do you want a ride?"

Those jade green eyes flick between my face and the seat to my right. “No . . . I’m—I’ll be fine. Thank you anyway.”

I roll my eyes. “Becks, come on. It’s about to rain. You really want to get caught up in that?”

She starts to back up. “I’ll be fine.”

I huff out an exasperated breath before pulling the van into the next driveway, and hop out of the seat.

She pauses on the sidewalk and looks over at me, bewildered. “What are you doing?”

“Well, if you won’t let me give you a ride, at least let me walk with you. There’s some sketchy-as-shit neighborhoods between here and home. Let me make sure you get there okay.”

Her face softens. “You want to walk with me?”

I jog over the last few steps toward her, closing the gap between us and shove my hands inside my jeans pockets. My fingers tingle as the memory of her skin alights my nerves. “Well, I’d rather drive but . . . yeah.”

As if on cue, the first few raindrops fall over top of us and she recoils, like a cat getting wet. “I promise, I’m not going to murder you.”

She looks past me at the van again but her mouth twitches into a small smile. “I guess it’s not Thursday right? So virgin sacrifices wouldn’t be on the schedule.”

Holy shit, did she just make a joke? I grin widely before gesturing to the van. The rain starts to fall a little harder, the sidewalk darkening with every drop. “Damn Becks, I didn’t know you had it in you to be funny.”

She follows me around the van to the passenger side. Her eyebrows lift as I open the door for her, as though surprised by the gesture. “To be fair,” she says, climbing up into the seat, “you don’t really know me.”

“I want to, though.”

Her eyes drop down and I feel my stomach clench as her gaze

rakes over me from my boots to the top of my head. Heat floods my face and I shut the door before jogging around to the driver's side, shaking the rain out of my hair, which is probably frizzing out of control. I take a deep breath, bracing myself against the door. Got to tread carefully here, I tell myself. I'm in the danger zone.

CHAPTER 17

Smooth Operator

REBECCA

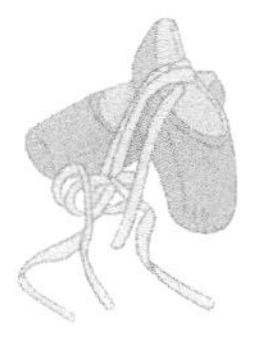

Therefore I tell you, do not be anxious about your life, what you will eat or what you will drink, nor about your body, what you will put on. Is not life more than food, and the body more than clothing?
Matthew 6:25

I'm sitting in his van. The van that terrified me when I saw it first drive down my street two weeks ago, thinking it was coming to take me away. But here I am. Sitting of my own free choice on the soft leather bench. The van smells like James. Like cigarettes and the woods and something a bit more pungent. I watch as he jogs around, the rain tapping on the windshield as it starts to fall. To think I was going to have to walk home in this. Because of Eric.

I was furiously mad. He picked me up this afternoon, and it was so obvious he was hungover. And, even though it bothered me, what really made me mad was that he tried to lie to me about it. As though his pale skin, dark circles under his eyes and the stale smell of beer about him hadn't made it perfectly obvious he had been drinking. Thank goodness I hadn't been forced to watch another one of his awful practices. Judging by the way he'd turned a little green on the drive to ballet class, he wouldn't have been able to do much anyway.

What was worse was he said he would pick me up after dance. Promised he'd be there, but I waited for over an hour, and I seethed for every minute of it. The simplest solution would've been to turn back inside and call my mom to come and get me, but the thought of more time in a car alone with my mother wasn't appealing. Not to mention, she'd demand to know why Eric hadn't turned up and that wasn't a conversation I wanted to have either.

But now here I am, by some inexplicable turn of events, my fingers grazing over the upholstery as James hops up into the driver's seat. And I'm not angry anymore. In fact, I feel more at peace now than I have in over a week. He shakes his hair out, a few droplets of water flying across the dusty dash. He drums a little pattern on the steering wheel before turning to me. His dark eyes take me in, his gaze lingering for a moment on my ankle, and I wonder if he can feel it too. That fiery, tingling sensation that seems to spread across the surface of my skin from where the backs of his fingers had brushed against so gently yesterday.

"So," he starts, a bit cautiously, "are you in a hurry?"

My eyebrows lift. A hurry? Have I not been paying attention? "Sorry?"

"Are you in a hurry to get home, I mean," he asks.

"Oh." Truth be told, home is the last place on Earth I want to be right now. "No, I'm not in any hurry."

He nods, his tongue wetting his lips before he rubs his fingers along his chin, the silver of his rings glinting in the light. "I was just about to stop at that diner ahead when I spotted you. Are you hungry?"

Oh no. "Umm . . ." It's always stressful when the subject of food comes up unexpectedly. I'm usually so careful about what, when and where I eat, but his face is so hopeful and his eyes are kind and I don't want to go home yet. "A little, yeah."

He grins. "Okay."

Turning the keys, the ignition roars to life as loud music blares from the stereo, and I feel my face scrunch up at the noise.

"Shit. Sorry," he says, reaching forward to turn the volume down. He pulls out into traffic toward the neon sign in the distance. I've never been to this diner before. I don't really go to restaurants very often. We always eat at home, my mom insisting it's the best way to keep God in our hearts, by preparing the food by our own hands. Still, I'm only ever on this side of town for dance class, so everything out here is brand new terrain.

He pulls into the parking lot, the rain lashing down now. "Ready to run?"

I grip the door handle and take a deep breath. "Let's go."

We both push our doors open in a hurry, the rain sinking into the cotton fabric of my skirt. I hop out of the seat onto the asphalt, right into a puddle, the water soaking through my shoes. My hands come up to cover my face to search through the rain for the door. I see it ahead and start toward it when I feel James's hand on the small of my back guiding me. My body shivers against the cold, but the spot on my back is burning as though I've just lain against an oven.

A string of curses exit his mouth, but we reach the door and he pulls it open for me as I stumble inside. My wet shoes squeak against the black-and-white checkered floor. Red leather booths line the windows and there's a row of barstools at the counter. The place is empty.

An older man from behind the counter acknowledges us. "Just have a seat anywhere. There's menus on the table already."

"Thanks, man," James replies. He turns me toward a booth by the window in the corner, the heat of his hand making it difficult to remember how to walk straight. I slide onto the seat a bit awkwardly as my dress tightens at my waist. James shrugs off his jacket revealing a black-and-white Raglan shirt. I should look at what his shirt says, but my eyes catch sight of his arms and his hands and all other thoughts fly out of my head.

"All right there, Becks?" he asks, head ducking down to meet my eyes.

Heat blooms across my face, and I quickly pick up the plastic menu to hide behind it. I can practically feel him grinning smugly from here. I've missed it. Shaking my head, my stomach clenching angrily at me with desperation for sustenance, my leg starts to bounce. Fast to combat lust—at this rate I'll die of starvation before this sinful feeling goes away. Everything here is surely loaded with calories and carbs and fat, but maybe there's a side salad I could have. Then a sudden horrible thought crosses my mind and I set down the menu.

"I don't have any money on me," I blurt out.

He shrugs. "No worries, I'll pay."

I shake my head. "I'll pay you back, I promise."

Leaning forward, he lifts his eyebrows at me. "Don't worry about it." He lifts the menu in front of his face, halting the conversation, and I sigh.

My eyes scan the menu again. The salad seems like the best choice, and I wouldn't have to eat all of it either if it's too big.

The man who greeted us from behind the counter wanders over to us. "Can I get you two something to drink?" he asks, eyes focusing on me.

"Just a water, please," I say.

James peeks out from behind his menu. "Same."

The waiter chews on a piece of gum. "You know what you want to order?"

My leg bounces again, my gaze turning back to the menu as I feel James waiting for me. "Umm . . . can I just get a side salad, please?"

"You want dressing with that?"

"Oh." I tap my fingers on the table top. I hadn't thought about that. "Just . . . just some house dressing, on the side?"

"Sure, and you?"

I glance up and James's dark eyes are pinned on me, never wavering from my face as he orders. "I'll get the club sandwich and fries."

The waiter grabs our menus and I suddenly feel exposed. With the menu as a shield, I could hide for a moment if things spiraled out of control. But now, James will be able to read my treacherous face in real time with nothing to protect me.

"I hope you didn't order a salad because it's cheap," he says, clasping his hands together on the table between us. "If you wanted the steak, I would've paid for it."

I'm already blushing. "No, I just . . . I didn't want anything too big."

The waiter returns with our waters and I take a long sip, realizing just how dry my mouth is. The man disappears and with the rain pelting in sheets against the window, we're alone together.

"Thank you, by the way," I say.

He glances out the window, the side of his mouth curling up. "It's no problem. Glad I spotted you. You probably would've gotten washed down a storm drain in this."

I grin, even though my toes are freezing, and I'm fighting the desperate urge to shiver.

"So," he continues, "you going to tell me why you're all the way over on this side of town . . . alone?"

"I was at dance class," I say, my fingers twisting in the hem of my damp cardigan.

He smiles widely, showing off his straight teeth. "So you do have something you do for yourself."

I take a long sip of my water as he leans back against the booth.

"What kind of dance do you do?"

I roll my lips inward before smacking them open. "Ballet."

He chuckles. "I should have guessed. And you're right. Our ideas of what's fun are exactly opposite."

While it sounds like an insult, the look on his face makes me think it amuses him.

"You any good at it?" he asks.

I balk at the question. How can I possibly answer that without sounding completely conceited or so humble I'm annoying. "Ephesians says, 'Be completely humble and gentle; be patient, bearing with—'"

"Yeah, yeah, 'bearing with one another in love,' I know. But what's the real answer?"

I blink, surprised he knows the passage. Then I remember what he told me . . . about men of God on power trips, and I realize James must have more knowledge of my world than I thought. I shrug. "I don't know. No one ever comes to watch me so . . . I wouldn't know."

His eyes narrow. "No one ever—don't you usually have like . . . recitals and shit in dance class?"

My eyes drop to the table. "My parents won't let me take the classes that do that anymore. I take the advanced adult recreational class now."

"Wait," he says, and his hands stretch out across the table toward me. "You don't even get to perform?"

Hearing it said out loud makes it sound more sad than I ever thought before. I press my lips together in a tight smile and shake my head. "No."

His mouth opens in shock. "But . . . but performing is the best part."

"It's fine. I don't really like when a lot of people are watching me anyway. I get awful stage fright."

"You know how you get over stage fright?" he asks.

I blink with surprise. "How?"

He leans forward like it's this big secret. "You practice."

The memory of him playing his guitar the other night, completely lost in the music. How he had bowed when he spotted me watching.

"Is that what you do? Practice?"

He seems to be thinking of the same memory as I am because his head tilts slowly to the side. "That's how you get to the big leagues. Madison Square Garden, El Club, the Hollywood Bowl . . . Everyone who performed there practiced in their bedrooms at some point."

"Are you any good, then?" I ask, turning his own question back on him.

"Yes."

I feel my eyebrows lift, not used to someone being so utterly and completely sure of their talent before.

"And not humble at all, I see," I say.

He shrugs. "I got no use being humble. I want to play music for a living. No point thinking I'm not great at it."

The urge to scoff at his pride—his ambition to be a musician dies out quickly when I see how serious his face is. How dark his eyes are, as though he's challenging me to disagree with him, and the intensity of his look makes my stomach clench.

"Is that . . . why you want to go to San Francisco?"

His tongue runs along the seam between his lips and my heart rate spikes. "Yeah, it is."

There's a long moment, and the spot on my ankle and the small of my back where his hand had been starts to burn, blistering outward over my skin.

"Here we are."

We both look up as the waiter puts our plates down in front of us. James's club sandwich and fries and my . . . gigantic salad.

"Bon appetit," he says a little jokingly, before turning away.

"Umm, excuse me," I say, my hand raising off the table. "This is the side salad?"

"Yeah."

"Oh, okay."

There's absolutely no way I'm going to manage to eat even half of this. Especially with my need to squash the lustful feelings I can't shake. My leg starts to bounce, my shoe squeaking against the tile under the table.

"Something wrong?" James asks.

I look and he's glancing between me and my plate. "No, no . . . I just. It's so *big*."

James snorts with laughter, his ring-covered fingers pressing against his mouth, and I'm left a little flabbergasted. "Have I said something funny?"

He clears his throat and shakes his head. "Sorry . . . no. I just—no, that's on me. I have a bit of a dirty mind."

My eyes narrow, not fully understanding his meaning. "What are you talking about?"

His eyebrows pull together as if he's not sure whether to take me seriously. "You . . . when you said . . . you know, 'it's so big,' my mind immediately went to—nevermind."

His cheeks turn pink, and I realize he's blushing. Why would he blush, wait is this . . . ? Oh my goodness, was this something sexual? I feel that throb between my legs and I clench my thighs together, shifting in my seat.

"Oh . . . sorry." The image of him shirtless in his room in nothing but those sweatpants makes me tremble all over. Now I definitely shouldn't eat. I'm sure he notices because a smirk appears on his face.

"I guess, for someone as small as you, everything must seem big," he says.

I roll my eyes. "I'm not that small—"

He shakes his head. "Nope, you are, look. Put your hand up like this." He rests his elbow on the table and holds his hand out, fingers straight up and palm facing me. "Put your hand against mine."

Oh Lord, those hands. I feel my mouth drop open, my brain desperately trying to think of a way out of this because the danger of his hand against mine is too great of a sin to bear. He wiggles his fingers at me impatiently. Dropping my fork on my untouched plate, I take a deep breath before reaching forward and tentatively placing my palm against his, the heels of our hands meeting first, before my fingers roll up, the tips not even reaching his second knuckles.

"See?" he says. "Tiny."

But he doesn't pull away, and it's like my hand is glued to his, my eyes staring transfixed at our skin touching. My mouth is suddenly dry again, and my heart is hammering. The warmth of his hand spreads through every nerve, singeing down my arm and across my chest. My breathing starts to speed up, the shallow inhales against the tight bust of my dress making me lightheaded.

His fingers shift and I nearly gasp against the rough calluses of his skin as he drags them with exquisite slowness over my palm, my wrist, before turning the back of his knuckles and retracing his way back up. My eyes flick to his face and he's watching me intently, his gaze never wavering as his thumb presses into the middle of my hand, his long fingers curling around the side to grab my wrist. As if I have no control over myself, I feel my eyes flutter closed as his rough thumb traces little circles on the inside of my hand.

I'm burning. I'm on fire. And, oh no, this feels too good, it's too much and maybe this is what Hell feels like. Too hot and too out of control for all of eternity.

Maybe it's not so bad after all.

I force my eyes open and pull my hand back sharply, tucking it under the table as I let go of a long exhale. I avoid his gaze as I try to calm my frantic heart and stare at my untouched salad, worried if I attempt to pick up the fork my hand will shake so bad I'll drop it.

"Don't worry, Becks," he says quietly, and I'm surprised to hear how low it sounds—the sound of it vibrating in my ears. "I've got nothing against small girls."

He picks up his sandwich and starts to eat as if the world didn't just stop spinning while our hands touched. I'm not sure whether to be grateful or offended by his words. Everything he does is a contradiction. I shift in my clothes uncomfortably. The cut on my ribs is nearly gone now but still tender. I finally brave a few bites of the salad, trying to chew down the naked lettuce since I can't chance the extra calories from the dressing. It's harder than normal because the smell of his fries only a few inches away has me salivating.

"How can you eat that with no dressing on it? It's just raw vegetables."

I look up at him, and he's glaring at the salad. I shrug. "I like vegetables."

"You can have some of my fries if you want," he offers, pushing his plate forward.

The gesture is sweet, but I shake my head at him. "No, thanks."

He shrugs. "Suit yourself." He grabs a few and puts them in his mouth, licking the salt off of his lips. "So, do you normally walk all the way home after your ballet class?"

I shake my head. "No, I usually—" I pause for a moment,

feeling my shoulders slump, the memory of my anger turning to a deep kind of despair. "Eric usually picks me up."

James puts his sandwich down on his plate. "But not today?"

"No . . . he—"

The words get caught in my throat, like a web is preventing the syllables from forming and escaping out into the world. Because then they'd be real. And the thought that Eric had just abandoned me there, when he's supposed to be my protector, for who knows what reason feels like something is clawing its way out of my chest.

"Rebecca," James says, leaning forward. "Was he supposed to pick you up?"

I nod, my bottom lip rolling inward behind my teeth.

James's jaw tightens, a muscle twitching in his cheek. "And what? He just left you there?"

His tone is harsh, angry, and I flinch away instinctively because I know somehow it's my fault. Because I was selfishly happy I didn't have to sit through a track practice this morning, this is God's way of showing me I'm failing. Tears sting the backs of my eyes, and I blink furiously to make them go away.

"Hey," James says, his voice softer. "Don't . . . it's okay."

I'm not sure if it's the way his voice feels, like a warm blanket being tucked around me, but my throat unsticks. "He was hungover." I say, rubbing at my nose. "From the party last night. He had been drinking and he looked awful. He said he'd be back to get me and I waited . . ." I take a long, deep breath and look at James. "I waited over an hour and he never came."

James's face pulls back. "Becks, no offense but your boyfriend is a piece of shit."

I scoff at the language but he's unfazed. "He's . . . no, he's not usually—"

"He's a piece of shit who doesn't deserve you." James says forcefully. "I mean, seriously. Why are you even with that tool?"

"We've been together for two years. We're supposed to—"

"That's not what I asked. Why are you with him? Do you love him?"

James asked me that before in the library and I had been too scared to think about my real answer to that question. Not anymore though.

"No, I don't."

"Do you even like him?"

"I thought I did once. But lately, he's just—I don't feel that . . ." My eyes dart around looking for the right word.

"Spark?"

My eyes widen. That's exactly it. Exactly what's been missing between Eric and I. "Yes!"

James smiles a bit tentatively. "Then you should dump his ass. Why waste your time with someone who doesn't set your soul on fire?"

My voice quiets. "Is that what it's supposed to be like?"

His mouth drops open. "Becks, you're eighteen and you've never felt that way before?"

My mouth opens then closes and my face heats furiously. Terrified that I almost just admitted the only time I've ever felt close to my soul being on fire was because of him. Terrified that I may have never felt real love before. I pull on the chain around my neck and look out the window at the onslaught of rain, the wind whipping the trees.

"Wow," he says. I look over and he's shaking his head, his fingers twisting in his hair. "All the more reason to toss that asshole out of your life. No wonder it looked painful to kiss him."

A laugh bursts out of my mouth before I can stop it. My hand clapping over my lips to try and take it back.

"Holy shit, did you just laugh?" James asks, grinning. "I'm seeing a whole different side of you today. Cracking jokes and laughing. Are you sure you weren't abducted by aliens?"

I roll my eyes and push a tomato around on my plate. "Have you . . ." I trail off.

"Have I what?"

"Have you ever felt that way with someone before?"

There's a subtle twitch in his hand before he clenches it into a fist. "Uh . . . not really."

I narrow my eyes at him. "So you've just never dated anyone?"

"Oh no, I've dated. Actually, dated isn't the right word. I've been with girls."

"I don't understand."

He sighs. "Let's just say, I'm not boyfriend material."

"Then how have you been with—oh."

The realization hits me like a freight train. He's been with girls. He's been . . . but not dated.

Heat spreads across my cheeks and down the back of my neck. "So . . . you're not a . . . virgin."

"Nope." His lips enunciate the popping noise.

Something flutters low in my belly and I sit up a little straighter in my seat. The ultimate sin.

He raises an eyebrow at me. "You seem surprised."

I inhale deeply. "I just—"

"Be honest with me, Becks. What about me screams virgin to you?"

I shake my head. All this talk about virgins, and him not being one, and him and his hands, and the heat and—

There's a ringing in my ears and my head feels heavy. In fact I feel heavy all over. My fork drops from my fingers and I feel myself tilting into nothingness.

CHAPTER 18

Let's Make a Deal

JAMES

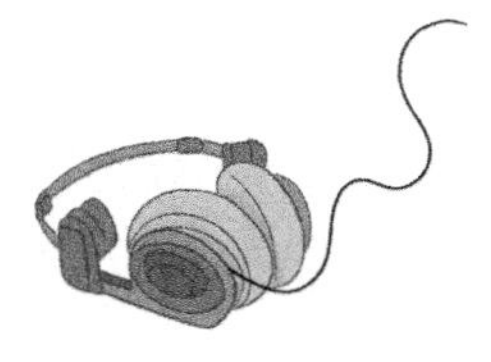

I'm moving before my brain realizes what I'm doing. It's pure instinct as I stand to lean over the table, knocking over the ketchup bottle to grab her head before she tumbles out of the booth.

"Shit!"

Her arms are dead weight at her sides and I carefully maneuver out of my seat to come around to her side.

"Becks!"

Her head rolls back against the bench cushion and I grip her face between my hands, my knee sliding next to her to help keep her upright.

"Rebecca? Can you hear me?"

My heart is pounding and there's an overwhelming feeling of despair that seeps into my chest as the memory of holding my mother like this on the peeling linoleum floor of our old kitchen surges upward through my memory. And just like then, I tap against her cheek, my fingers meeting her skin with a quick slapping noise. This is the second time this has happened. Is she sick too? Fuck, I don't know if that's something I can handle right now.

"Hey, is everything okay?" I look over my shoulder to the waiter and one of the cooks who are approaching from behind the counter.

"I don't—Becks?"

Her eyelids flutter and her mouth parts to take in a breath, her face muscles twitching like she's having a nightmare.

"She's awake," I call to the two men who stop their approach. "Becks, hey . . . look at me."

Those jade eyes flicker to life from behind long, dark eyelashes. For a moment she looks confused, or maybe unfocused, but then her gaze fixes on mine. "James?"

I exhale a relieved kind of laugh. "Yeah, hey, are you all right?"

"I don't—" she says, sitting upright a little more, but I'm scared to let go of her for fear she might tip over again. "What happened?"

I wet my lips, my throat overly dry. "You fainted."

"I . . ." Her eyes narrow on my face. "You're holding me."

My fingers tense and I realize just how close we are. How her face is only inches from mine. How I've thought about hardly anything other than what it might feel like to kiss her since she touched my hand.

"Sorry, I didn't want you to hurt your head," I say, loosening my grip but not fully pulling away in case she faints again.

"Oh."

Her skin is so soft and smooth. There's not a blemish on her, except for the trio of freckles on her neck. Fuck, I wonder what kissing her there would be like. No, not right now . . .

I pull back to squat down next to her so we're at eye level. "Are you okay?"

She's pale but there's a touch of pink coming back into her cheeks now. "Yes. I—thank you."

I take in a long breath then exhale, giving the waiter and cook the thumbs up so they turn back to what they were doing. "Listen, I know it's none of my business, but this is the second time this has happened and—I need to know . . . Are you sick or something?"

"What?"

I shrug. "Like, do you have leukemia or diabetes?"

More color flourishes in her cheeks. "Oh . . . no, nothing like that."

I let go a relieved sigh as I drag my hand down the side of my face. "Shit . . . okay well, what—what's going on then?"

Her shoulders curve in toward each other, for once that rigid, straight posture crumbles. A little smile pulls at the side of her mouth, but it doesn't reach her eyes. In fact, it's sad.

"I think—I forgot to eat this morning before class." She touches her fingers to her temple and waves her hand away, trying to lighten the situation.

My eyes narrow. "You forgot to eat?"

She nods. "Yeah, I was in a rush this morning and now that I think about it, I didn't eat anything."

"But—" I glance at the salad on the table, barely more than a few pieces have been eaten. "You told me you weren't that hungry when we got here. How can you not eat all morning, go to a dance class, and not be hungry?"

I suddenly remember her half-heartedly scraping that half-eaten yogurt cup at lunch. The few apple slices she ate on that first day at school. The way she freaked out when I offered her chocolate, and how I never actually saw her eat the Oreo I gave her. Does she purposefully not eat?

"James, it's not a big deal," she says, trying to brush it off. "It just happens sometimes. Are you telling me you've never gotten so caught up in playing the guitar that you forgot to eat a meal?"

I shift my weight on my heels. "No. The only time I didn't eat was when we had no money for groceries."

Her face drops the fake smile. "What?"

I shake my head. I'm not talking about that now. "Come on, I'm taking you home."

Her fingers clutch onto my arm with hardly any strength and my mind spins out of control, thinking of how she could've been walking home, in this downpour, fainting into the gutter to drown.

"No, please I—I'm feeling better now, see?" As if to illustrate her point, she corrects her posture, sitting up in that typical mannequin-rigid way.

"You haven't eaten and you just fainted, you need to go home. Your parents should know—"

"No!"

I'm startled by the severity of her voice, and something creeps into her eyes. I think it's fear. What's that all about? Is going home scary for her? I can see how it might be with parents like hers. Do they not notice she doesn't eat at home either? And she's so small. How do parents not notice that kind of thing?

Sighing, I push myself to my feet and her eyes travel upward with me, her head tipping back. "Look, I'll make you a deal, okay?"

Her eyes blink up at me, wide and fearful.

"I won't take you straight home right now, if you eat something. And not just rabbit food."

I grab a quarter of my club sandwich and place it gently on the side of her salad plate.

"James," she starts, her eyes downcast. "I'm telling you, I'm perfectly fine."

I shake my head. "No, you're not perfectly fine. Perfectly fine people don't just pass out randomly and not eat all day. It's not healthy."

"Well, you're one to talk!"

I pull my face back, her voice angry, and I narrow my eyes. "What the hell is that supposed to mean?"

"Don't tell me this isn't healthy, when you're the one smoking every chance you get. Those stupid things will kill you."

Her shoulders are heaving and her face is pink, and I know she's just trying to deflect blame but . . . she's not exactly wrong either. I sigh and slide back into the booth across from her, right in the direct line of her glare.

"Fine, you're right. So, how about a new deal?"

Her head tilts a little as my hand fishes inside of my jacket for my cigarette pack. Grasping it, I hold it up in front of my face.

"For every day you eat at least one proper meal, I won't smoke."

She scoffs, a derisive little laugh bursting out of her, but when she sees I'm serious, her eyes dart between me and the cardboard pack in my hand.

"You're serious?"

My eyes widen with surprise at myself. "Yup. Dead serious."

She shakes her head. "It's—it's not that simple."

"It is, though," I say, and push my pack of cigarettes into my water glass. "There. See?"

That little wrinkle appears above her nose again and her eyes start to glisten as she looks between the sodden cigarettes and me.

I offer her a careful, gentle smile. "Come on, Becks. Save my life."

Her hand reaches up to pull on the gold chain around her neck but then she tentatively reaches forward and grabs the sandwich off the plate. I watch, my eyebrows rising as she takes a bite of the toasted bread and something warm fills my chest when her face relaxes ever so slightly. Like she's been desperate for actual food for far too long.

"So," I say, trying to distract her so she doesn't get cold feet, "tell me why you like to dance."

"THERE'S JUST something really beautiful about the lines of the body. The motion of it, you know?" she says.

Twenty minutes later and she's eaten half of my sandwich and a handful of French fries. There's color back in her face, a calmness to her demeanor, and I know the food has done her some good. As much as I've never wanted to talk about ballet before, listening to her talk about it makes the subject tolerable. Enjoyable even.

"So do you really wear those shoes with the wooden blocks in them? Doesn't that hurt?" I ask.

"It's not actually wood. It's actually just layers of fabric or cardboard hardened by glue. My toes are a nightmare but the pain doesn't bother me too much anymore. I guess I got used to it."

"I kind of get that," I say, turning my hand back and forth. At her confused expression I explain, "It took a long time to build up the calluses on my hands to play how I do. Lots of bloody fingers."

"Bloody fingers and bloody toes . . . We'd make a terrifying pair," she says with a smile.

The thought of us as a pair before would have been ridiculous. Laughable even. But as my hand clenches from the tingles that shoot from where her hand touched mine, and the image of her eyes fluttering closed as my fingers trailed down her wrist blossoms in my mind . . . well, now us together is something I can't shake out of my head.

She seems to be thinking about it too, her teasing smile giving way to a thoughtful expression I'm starting to recognize.

"James?"

"Yeah?"

"When you said—what did you mean you only didn't eat when you couldn't afford groceries?"

Fuck . . . she wants to talk about that? Normally, I'd deflect. Change the topic. Straight up tell someone to fuck off. But my eyes flick to the crumbs of the sandwich she ate. She's been vulnerable with me. Surely she deserves the same.

"It's not that complicated. My mom and I didn't have much money. Sometimes we had to choose between paying rent or buying groceries. It's a lot easier to be hungry when you can sleep in your own bed."

She blinks and looks at the table. "Oh . . ."

I shrug. "It is what it is."

"And your mom," she presses softly. "Where is she now?"

I tap my knuckles against the table top, my rings making the noise louder. "She died."

Rebecca's eyebrows droop. "James, I'm so sorry."

Fuck. I didn't want to talk about this. "Yeah, well. Nothing can be done about it."

"And your dad . . ." She pauses. "Is he gone too?" Her face crinkles with worry.

I shake my head. "No. Or yes . . . he didn't stick around. He ditched us pretty early on. I have no idea where he ended up. Foster parents provided plenty of other terrible male role models though."

She tilts her head. "Foster parents? But I thought . . . your mom . . ."

Pressing my lips together, I pause for a moment before speaking. "I—I was in and out of foster care for the first half of my life. My mom, she . . . was unwell."

Rebecca's wrinkle appears. "So, you had to go into foster care because she was sick?"

Looking away, I blow out a breath, the air ruffling the fringe hanging over my forehead. "Yes. My mom . . . was a junkie. At least, she was when I was little."

Her lips part to create an o shape. The world Rebecca comes from—stuff like that only exists in the horror stories parents tell their kids to keep them out of trouble. She opens her mouth to say something, but I lift my wrist to check the time. It's just past five and I need to be at work by six. Plus, I still need to drive her home and come back across town.

"We should get going. I have to work tonight," I say.

"Oh, right. Okay."

I grab my jacket and walk over to the counter to pay the bill. When I turn around, Rebecca is standing by the door. It's still raining but not quite so aggressively anymore.

"Ready?" I ask.

She nods, then we're dashing out into the rain. I wrench open the passenger side door of my van, holding my jacket up over my head while she climbs in. Once again, I'm nearly soaked by the time I hop up into the driver's seat, the raindrops sliding down my face. I look at Rebecca and she's shivering.

"Here," I say. I shrug off my jacket and nudge it toward her.

For a moment, I think she might not accept it, her hand halting for a second. But then she reaches out and grabs the heavy denim fabric, her fingers brushing against mine. Goosebumps scatter up my arm and I let go, reaching for the dash.

"I'll turn the heat on. Don't want you to catch a cold," I say, as she pulls my jacket around her shoulders, the size of it enveloping her.

"Thank you."

I pull out into the traffic, the street lights overhead making each drop of rain on the windshield flare to life. I peek over at Rebecca, sitting straight as an arrow once again. Sitting like that all the time can't be comfortable. Once again, my mind wanders to that night when she let her robe fall to the floor. The way she looked comfortable then, with her shoulders at an angle and her hip popped and her breasts . . . no.

I shift in my seat, my eyes darting back and forth between her and the road. I shouldn't be thinking about how her damp skin glows in the yellow street lights. I shouldn't be enjoying the sight of her in my jacket. I shouldn't want to just pull over and devour her lips like she's my last meal. But fuck, I want to.

"Are you feeling better?" I ask.

She nods. "Yes, thank you. I'm sorry . . . you know, about all that."

"I meant what I said. About our deal."

Her cheeks flush and she looks down at her hands, her leg jiggling nervously. "Oh, that. You don't—" But she stops, her teeth pressing into her lip. She wants to say something, but she's filtering herself. I wish she would just say what's really on her mind.

"So," she continues, "you'll really stop smoking if I eat more?"

A balloon inflates in my chest. Maybe she wants to save me, too. "That's what I said."

"How will we know we're holding up our end?"

"Honor system," I say, shrugging. "I'm guessing you're not much of a liar."

Her lips press into a hard line and her chin juts up indignantly. "It's sinful to lie."

A grin spreads across my face. "Exactly. So, I know you won't try to bullshit me."

She rolls her eyes. "Do you have to use language like that?"

I feel my mouth twist as I try to contain my laugh. "Yes, I do. It's a great stress reliever. You should try it sometime."

She lifts her head and glares at me from the corner of her eye. "I don't need stress relief."

This time I can't contain it. My laughter erupts out of me so loudly she jumps a bit in her seat, a crimson blush spreading across her face. I turn left at the traffic lights and continue down the road, trying to rein in my chuckles. "Oh please, you are like . . . the most unrelaxed person I've ever met. I mean, just look at you."

She glances down at herself then back at me. "What about me?"

I gesture to her with my hand. "I mean, who sits like that. It's like you're auditioning to be a statue."

"I just have good posture—"

"You look like you're sitting on a pinecone."

Her arms lift to try and cross, but she stops again and puts them back at her sides.

"Why do you do that?"

Her eyebrows furrow. "Do what?"

"Go to cross your arms then change your mind. Jesus got something against that?"

She looks down at her hands, balling them into fists and unfurling her fingers, but doesn't answer, her face thoughtful again.

I sigh. "Listen, I don't mean to bug you about it. All I'm saying is, you look like you could benefit from a bit of unfiltered cursing."

She shakes her head. "I don't think I can do that."

I raise an eyebrow. "There are other ways you can relax, too."

Rebecca turns to face me. "Like what?"

"You could try smoking a joint. That would bliss you out pretty quick."

Her face contorts with disgust. "Drugs?"

"It's just pot."

"I'm going to have to say no."

"Why? Are you worried about what God will think? Pretty sure the bible doesn't say anything about marijuana."

Silence.

"Rebecca," I say slowly, "you need to start taking care of yourself. Like eating actual food and doing things that make you happy. You weren't placed on this Earth for everyone else. Doing something just for you—" I pause, trying to reign in the anger that bubbles to the surface at everyone making her believe her only purpose is to serve them. "You're not going to ruin yourself."

She purses her lips. "I think I can walk from here."

Guess I pushed her too far again. "No, it's fine. I can drive you closer, it's still raining."

She shakes her head and reaches for the door handle. "No, it's okay, it's only two blocks—"

She pulls on the handle, but the door doesn't open. She tries again and groans. My eyes lift to the ceiling. "Rebecca—"

"Thank you for today, and I would appreciate it if you wouldn't mention . . . you know, what happened at the diner." She wrenches against the door handle again.

"I won't tell anyone," I say.

Her hand falls from the door handle and her body turns toward me, her shoulders pulled back and her chin pushed forward in that haughty manner she sometimes wears. I think it's the armor she puts on when she's feeling too out of control. "Why are you helping me?"

I scoff. "What?"

"You ignored me for over a week then . . . all of this—today. What do you want?"

I blink, taken off guard by her question. "I—well, I didn't think it was a good idea to get involved in whatever is going on with you."

"Oh." She tugs at her sweater and looks away.

I pull on the back of my neck. "And I thought that you wanted me to leave you alone."

"I thought I did."

My heart is suddenly racing. "And . . . now?"

She freezes, like a deer in the headlights, those green eyes darting over my face. I reach out my fingers to where her left hand is pressed against the leather upholstery of the bench seat. My pinky skims down the length of her hand, and I hear her sharp inhale of breath. Her eyes are fixed on our hands and that familiar burn is back. That blistering, electrifying, thrilling sensation that travels through me at the slightest touch of her.

"Now . . ." she whispers.

My fingers crawl over the top of her hand, pulling it over so her palm faces the ceiling and just like earlier in the diner, I trace up her palm until our fingers are interlaced. My thumb rubs against the back of her hand and I dare to look up into her face. I shouldn't be doing this. I promised myself I wouldn't get involved. But she's like a whirlpool. A vortex. A magnet. And it seems like the harder I fight against it, she just pulls me back stronger than ever.

"I should go," she whispers, but she doesn't let go right away. In fact, she squeezes my hand a little tighter before releasing me one finger at a time. "I—I need to go."

"Right, yeah," I say, annoyed by how my breath catches.

She reaches back for the door handle, pulling on it again, and again, and again.

"What is wrong with this door?" she asks, looking frazzled, a few strands of hair falling out of the tight knot on her head.

"It's a bit screwy, sometimes it sticks, here—"

I shuffle over on the bench next to her to reach over her to jiggle the handle. It catches finally, the door popping open an inch. Pulling back, I realize I'm almost over top of her. Her face is inches from mine, her breath fanning over my cheek. Our eyes meet and it feels like that moment before a thunderstorm, when all of the electricity in the air collects, ready to strike. Then her eyes drop to my mouth and I swallow hard as I realize I'm about to take the biggest risk of my life.

Leaning forward, my lips touch hers. Gently and just once. I pull back from it and I realize my fingers are at her throat, running along the little gold chain that encircles that pretty neck of hers. Her eyes are wide, unblinking, and, fuck, I think I've blown it.

"Sorry, I—"

But she presses forward, her lips crashing back against mine. Her hands fumble in the fabric of my shirt, pulling me closer. My hand slides around the back of her neck, tipping her head back to pull her soft mouth closer to me. My other arm wraps around her, holding her, and I feel that jolt, that spark, the one she asked me earlier if I've ever felt with anyone before. And how I had lied because telling her that simply a touch of her skin sets my soul ablaze would've surely chased her away.

She sighs against my mouth and the tension she carries in her body relaxes just a little. My tongue swipes against her lips, and she gasps, her hands releasing my shirt and I pull back when I feel her tense up all over again. Her fingers come up to touch her dark, swollen lips and I lift my hands off of her, pulling away—knowing I stepped over the line.

"Rebecca," I whisper.

"That was—" she says, looking down.

"I know, I'm sorry." I brush back my hair and move back toward the steering wheel.

"—fun."

I look over, and she's smiling. Genuinely smiling, and it's because of me. And as the sun peeks through the clouds to shine on her face, I realize she's completely stolen my heart. A heart I wasn't even sure I had to lose.

CHAPTER 19

Parental Guidance

REBECCA

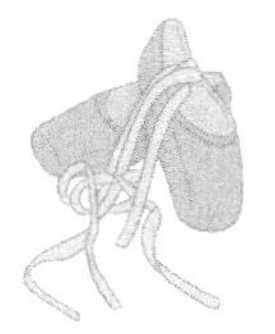

I don't even remember the walk home. There's a pinching feeling in my cheeks that feels unfamiliar. My hand lifts to touch my face and I realize I'm smiling. Smiling so widely it hurts. There's a lightness in my chest that makes me feel like I'm floating, and I'm sure that at some point I might have even skipped. I rein in the desire to grand jeté down the sidewalk or twirl my skirt in the glistening raindrops that periodically fall. My fingers drift from my cheeks over my lips, which are scarred from his kiss. That searing kiss that lit me up like a Christmas tree.

I remember a rushed goodbye, his dark eyes never looking away from my face as I climbed out of his black van onto the side of the road. I lost count of how many times I looked back over my shoulder at him sitting in that van before I finally lost sight of him. And he had watched me go, until the very last moment.

My hair is wet and my dress and socks are soaked, but I don't think I've ever felt happier. The rainbow at the end of the street is like a sign from God that life is beautiful and the storm is over. Then I walk over the threshold of home, leaning back on the front door and my eyes close as my fingers trace over my neck where James's hands were only minutes ago.

"Rebecca?"

The sound of my mom's voice is like a needle to a balloon and my little happy bubble bursts. I catch sight of myself in the mirror above the entryway table and shudder. My hair is a wild nest, my mouth is dark and I look small in the jacket. James's jacket. Oh no.

I tear the jacket off of me and stuff it into the vase by the table just before my mother steps out into the hall.

"Rebecca are you—what happened?" She stops when she catches sight of me. Surely she can tell. Like there's a sign on my head that says I just had the most Earth-shattering kiss of my life with a boy I hardly know. A boy who's not my boyfriend. A boy whom everyone at Holy Grace would condemn me for even speaking to.

"The rain . . . I—" I mumble.

She picks at the damp sleeve of my dress, her mouth pursing disapprovingly. "My goodness, it looks like Eric was driving you around with the windows open."

I open my mouth to tell her that, in fact, Eric didn't drive me home. That he never came to get me. That he probably went to Jeremiah's place again to get drunk and forgot all about me. But she holds up her finger in front of my face.

"I don't want to hear about it. We're having company over for dinner and you need to make yourself presentable and help me clean up."

My eyes roam over the dust-free baseboard, the mirrored surfaces where there isn't a fingerprint or knick knack out of place. As if we live in some kind of a museum rather than a home. My eyes pass over the vase where I've hidden James's jacket and think it's probably too risky to move it right now. Maybe when I come down to help clean, I can move it to my room.

"Go on, then, hurry up. Wear that green eyelet dress, will you?"

I nod and she turns to head back toward the kitchen. "Who's coming for dinner?"

She turns around and smiles excitedly. "The Corbleys."

My stomach drops, possibly straight through the floor. "Eric's parents?"

She nods. "Eric is coming too. Didn't he mention it?"

I shake my head.

"Must have wanted to keep it a surprise. He's so good to you."

With a twirl of her skirt, she disappears and I feel a sharp ache in my hand, realizing my nails are digging into the wooden stair railing. Half-moon shapes are left behind by my grip as I climb the stairs and shut myself in the bathroom. I peel out of my dress, nearly panicking as the tight fabric sticks to my arms, but I finally break free from it. I turn on the shower and wait for the water to heat up, turning to the mirror to pull the bobby pins out of my bun. My blonde hair falls in damp curls around my shoulders and I look at my reflection.

For a moment, I don't recognize myself. I'm still too skinny, still small chested, still bony, except there's a glow to my skin and my face. My fingers pinch at the skin of my stomach, which is full and not aching from hunger. My hand slides over it and I know I should hate it. Should hate how my stomach sticks out a little from eating so much, but I don't. I lightly trace up my skin and I imagine they're his fingers. His lips. And I tremble.

My eyes open and I tear my hand away from myself, blinking at the mirror, terrified by the girl that stares back at me.

I know about that, of course. It's been drilled into us at Teens for Christ. That masturbation is one of those sinful urges that will drag us into a life of degradation and shame. That finding pleasure in our bodies would deprive our husbands of the ability to pleasure us after marriage. That it limits how well we can bond with our one true God-sent partner. That it's a gift for only them and if we indulge in it before marriage then we'll be worthless.

Used up. Like a piece of tape that's been stuck to something and pulled away dirty and covered in grime.

You're not going to ruin yourself.

I shake my head and step under the shower. I wash my hair and face, feeling the heat of the water seep into my bones. What does James know, anyway? He doesn't have faith, so he just indulges in whatever sinful, lustful thing he wants, unaware of the consequences. But me? There's no way. No way I would lower myself to that.

But my lips burn and the memory of his hand heavy on my neck causes my hand to wander of its own volition under the spray of water. I trace over where his hand had been, imagining his long fingers trailing over my collarbone, then down between my breasts. I feel my nipples harden and tingle as my hand trails further down through the fine blonde hair between my legs, my fingers gliding through the hot skin there.

My eyes shoot open as a jolt shoots up and down my spine with such force I have to brace my hand against the shower wall. My legs tremble at the terrifying feeling, and that ache in my core returns in earnest. My heart is pounding and my chest is heaving, hot air rushing in and out of my lungs. I pull my hand away, forcing it under the spray of water as if it's somehow dirty.

But it feels so good. Like how kissing James is so different than how it feels to kiss Eric. When Eric kisses me I feel like a statue, a robot—sinful and guilty. When James did it, though . . . it was like finally being able to breathe. Suddenly once wasn't enough and when he pulled away I chased after it, desperate to satiate that hunger for his lips on mine.

Finally, all the love songs on the radio make sense. Like this is how it's really supposed to be. Maybe I've just lived so long suffocating under their control that I never realized how it should feel.

Kissing James is like being free.

ALL THROUGH THIS AGONIZING DINNER, I want to escape back up into my room. I feel like I'm losing my mind, and what I've been taught about masturbation must be right because all I can think about are excuses to run upstairs and try it again. Thankfully, Eric looks terrible and hasn't tried to speak to me since they got here. I hope his head is pounding. I hope he regrets drinking like he did. I hope he regrets abandoning his duty to me. But somehow I think he regrets that one the least.

My mother's eyes are on me constantly, watching as I pick my way through the rich dinner she's prepared for Eric and his parents. Of course, she expects me not to eat most of it. That she wants the Corbleys to think I have an appetite befitting a Godly woman, but I'm wrestling with the idea of shoving a whole bread roll in my mouth and staring her right in the eyes as I chew it. Daring her to make a scene in front of our guests because I know she never would. No, she'd save that for later. But one of the big problems with eating a full meal like I did today at the diner is that it makes me hungry for more.

There's a moment where both sets of parents are engaged in conversation about the satanic vandalism happening at the school when Eric finally turns to me.

"Becca," he says quietly. "Can we talk?"

I don't even turn toward him. I'm afraid that if I do, I'll either explode at him or revert back into the simpering, submissive girl I've always been. I can't be her anymore. I can't live like that. Something has to change or I might die if it doesn't.

"No," I say simply.

"Please, there's something—maybe I can take you for a drive after dinner? We can talk, go to a movie. Go on a proper date. It's been a long time since we've done that." I feel his hand on my knee and nearly jump out of my seat. His touch is repulsive, his hand cold and clammy. It's not James's touch.

I bite the inside corner of my cheek. "I said no."

"What's wrong with you?" Eric mutters angrily.

"I—" I search for the right words as I turn toward him, pushing away his hand. I look into his face and my stomach lurches nervously. Guilt suddenly overwhelms me. I kissed another man even though I'm dating the one before me, and even though I don't love him, he still thinks I'll one day be his wife. No one deserves to be cheated on. Even if he did forget to pick me up and left me in a rainstorm and hasn't even apologized yet. "I don't feel well. I'll be right back."

Standing abruptly, all eyes turn to me as I walk quickly from the dining room toward the stairs. My hand covers my mouth as my dinner churns in my stomach. I just manage to get the door locked before spilling my guts into the toilet. My stomach muscles clench angrily as I heave, a cold sweat breaking out over my skin. I'm awful. I'm a terrible, awful person who spent most of the last few hours reveling in cheating on my boyfriend. Reveling in sin. I pray silently in my head for forgiveness, knowing I don't deserve any of it.

Once my stomach settles and the gagging stops, I flush the toilet and sit back against the pink tile wall. My muscles burn from the effort of throwing up and my throat feels raw. I wish James were here. Not necessarily because I want him to see me sick, but because he would notice. He saw one of my darkest secrets and instead of judging me for it, he's trying to help me. He made that deal with me, and though I don't expect him to actually give up smoking for me, the gesture was the nicest thing anyone has ever done. Who would've thought that the supposed "devil worshiper" next door would be the one person who actually cared about *me* and not what I can do for *them*.

I push myself to my feet and quickly brush my teeth, before

returning downstairs. I pull a smile on my face as best I can, my cheeks still sore from all my goofy grinning earlier.

"Are you all right, dear?" Vivian Corbley asks.

"Oh, she's fine. She has such a delicate disposition, don't you Rebecca?" my mother says.

I sit back down in the seat next to Eric and politely nod along with my mother's backhanded compliment.

"I don't know about that," Eric says. "She's out there spinning and leaping her heart out every Saturday in dance class, isn't she?"

What? My eyes turn to him and widen. What is he trying to do? He offers me a smile and I realize maybe he's trying to make up for earlier today by complimenting me. I almost want to thank him because his comment has made my mother sneer.

"I certainly hope she's not too delicate," Michael Corbley states. "All of the Corbley babies are big at birth. Wouldn't want her to have any problems that could affect the children."

The glass of water in my hand drops to the table with a loud clatter, the liquid spilling over the tabletop to a rush of gasps.

"Rebecca!" my mother scolds as she reaches across to mop it up with a napkin.

But my heart feels like it's skipping every other beat as I stare into Mr. Corbley's sinister smile. "I'm sorry?"

Eric clears his throat next to me. "She's fine, Dad. Rebecca will make a great mother one day. I know it." He nods at me in what I'm sure he intends to be an encouraging way, but all I feel is dread, unable to remove the shocked expression from my face. Eric's father is talking about me having babies. Why—why are they here tonight?

"I . . . sorry—"

"I don't see why we need to keep things so secretive anymore. Do you?" Mr. Corbley asks my father.

He shakes his head, "No, I don't see why at all. Rebecca,

darling, we've arranged that you and Eric are to be married the week following graduation."

My head spins like I might faint again. I wish I would, because then maybe I wouldn't have to sit here and try to figure out how to react to all of this. There isn't enough air in the room and I feel like I'm falling down a well, the dining room and all its occupants at the very center of a small circle surrounded by black nothingness.

"Oh, come now, Michael," Mrs. Corbley says. "The poor boy probably wanted to tell her himself."

Marrying Eric Corbley? In two months? Babies? My lips are burning. Two weeks ago, I was happy with my parents' choice of husband for me. I would have sat here and smiled politely while the grown-ups at the table decided my future. But this . . . now? I don't want any of this. And Eric . . . he looks as unhappy about this revelation as I do.

My father laughs, and as if from the end of a distant tunnel, it sounds like a demon mocking me. "So sorry, my dear boy. Go ahead."

"*No!*"

I'm not sure how I find the strength to pull myself up, up out of the blackness, out of my seat, the chair toppling over behind me. But five pairs of eyes are watching me and rage burns through every artery in my body. My father has given his permission for me to marry a boy who barely cares about me. Who doesn't notice that I'm hurting. Who abuses his God given power over me. I feel like livestock, like property, and even though I want to get married one day, I don't want it like this.

"Becca?" Eric's voice pierces through the rage, the sound of genuine hurt in his voice. I look down at him from where I stand. For a brief moment, I see the handsome boyish face I thought I had been in love with. For whom I had cared for so deeply that I'd pushed all my own wants and desires away to please him.

How have things gone so utterly wrong? My mother's face is blazing with restrained violence, and my father is glaring like I've never been more of a disappointment.

"I'm sorry, I—this is just such a surprise," I say. Picking up the chair, I sit back down at the table. "I just mean that, I haven't even heard back from colleges yet, and marriage . . . It's a bit soon, isn't it?"

My father's lips tighten. "If you had received an acceptance to a respectable college this could wait, but there's no harm in having a plan in place since it appears no one is interested in you."

An arrow to the heart would hurt less. Even Mrs. Corbley has the decency to look a little shocked by my father's words. She leans forward after a moment, her hand reaching across the table toward me in what I assume she means to be a comforting gesture. "After graduation you'll come work with me at the library and the daycare. Soon, Holy Grace will have its own school and it would be wonderful if you could teach the children."

My cheeks twitch. I don't like children. Snot-nosed, screaming, crying, selfish babies. Years of Sunday school has made me terrified at the thought of being around them as a career. I don't even know if I want my own children someday. Something I know God will likely punish me for. The thought of either being married and pregnant at eighteen or running a daycare at the library makes my already sore stomach muscles churn again.

"But shouldn't you want a teacher who has more than a high school education?" I ask, trying to understand their logic.

Mr. Corbley clears his throat. "We want someone who will instill the correct values in our students. Mrs. Van Houten was telling me the other day about how you spoke up to Mrs. Henry in your history class."

Oh no . . .

"That is exactly the kind of education this country is lacking."

An overwhelming panic settles in my chest. They don't want to educate us, or teach us to think for ourselves. They want to indoctrinate us. What they want is for all of us to follow, blindly, whatever the church elders say is true. And I'm sick to think that is what I've been doing this whole time.

"I think she's just a bit surprised by all of this, aren't you, dear?" my mother says in a tone laced with poison. My eyes catch hers, and I know she's holding herself back from jumping across the table to strangle me.

"Yes," I whisper. "Sorry, it's just a surprise."

"Well, there's still two months until graduation," Mrs. Corbley says. "Plenty of time to get everything in order."

Graduation? I have two months to figure out my entire life before I'm trapped forever?

My mother quickly steers the conversation in a different direction by mentioning President Reagan, but I peer at Eric from the corner of my eye, and he's staring at his plate with a stony expression.

Does he actually want to marry me? I don't think anyone could convince me that he's actually, really in love with me. But the look on his face . . . Maybe he really does care for me, in his own way. The guilt from earlier floods through me and I reach across the table to take his hand. His eyes move from our entwined hands to my face, and he offers me a small smile that doesn't reach his eyes. But as our hands touch, I know that this is not what I want. Someone else has set my soul on fire and it's not the man who is supposed to be my future husband.

CHAPTER 20

Like a Virgin

REBECCA

After dinner, I'm awarded some semblance of freedom as I help clean up while the adults and Eric talk in the living room. Here I don't have to face the disappointed looks of my parents, the eager expressions of the Corbleys sizing me up as their future daughter-in-law and here, I can avoid Eric. But as much as I appreciate the small blessing, I also know that I need to talk to him. I need to tell him that I just don't love him. That us getting married is a terrible idea. But I'm terrified.

I seem to have used up all of my bravery shouting that "no" at the dinner table so I hide away in the kitchen taking way too long cleaning up all the dishes. In order to drag out the process, I don't bother using the dishwasher. Thankfully, once I'm done, the Corbleys are getting ready to head out the door. Eric doesn't say much, just leans forward to kiss me on the cheek, the only acceptable form of physical affection we're allowed. If only they knew what I had been doing hours ago in that black van. That life-changing kiss that was over much too soon.

My parents close the door after waving goodbye to their guests, then they both turn to me—my blood running ice cold at the look in their eyes.

"Rebecca, what has gotten into you?" my mother shrieks.

I flinch. I'm used to her yelling but every time, it feels like a physical assault.

"I'm sorry—"

"Do you have any idea how long this arrangement has been in the works?" my dad asks.

I shake my head, but I'm starting to realize that the path of my life has been decided for longer than I knew.

"You are such a constant disappointment. All we've sacrificed to make sure you have the best, and you repay us with that attitude. You humiliate us in front of one of the most important families in town. One of the most important members of the church," my mother spits, her nose pinching. Then she sniffs. "Do you smell that?"

My heart stops. Oh no. The jacket. It smells like cigarettes and the woods and undeniably someone who doesn't belong in this house. I totally forgot.

She sniffs the air of the foyer—she's always had a nose like a bloodhound. I'm surprised she didn't find it when I first got home, although maybe the smell of rain in the air had masked some of it, or maybe she was just distracted with the thoughts of company coming. She looks under some magazines on the entryway table, then the shoe rack, every second inching closer to the vase where I've stuffed it. She's getting closer and I need to distract them with something . . . anything. Anything would be better than them finding that jacket.

"I don't want to marry Eric," I blurt out. Okay, maybe anything was a bit of a stretch. But it's the truth and even though it's a terrifying thing to admit to my parents, it serves as the perfect distraction.

My mom is looking at me like I've grown another head. My dad, on the other hand, looks oddly calm.

"Why not?" he asks, his voice as smooth as butter.

I try to take a deep breath, my chest and stomach straining against the tight bodice of my dress. Looking down at my fingers, I fiddle with the pleats of the full skirt. "I don't love him."

Saying it out loud feels like a relief, a relief that's shortly extinguished as my dad narrows his eyes at me.

"Love isn't all that's necessary for a successful marriage," he continues, like this is one of his business meetings. "You and Eric are both compatible in the eyes of God. Love can come later."

My face pulls back. "But . . . it won't come later. It's been two years and I don't love him. I won't marry someone I don't love."

"But don't you love God?"

I blink. "Yes . . . yes, of course I do."

"Then why are you rejecting what he wants for you?" my dad says, his voice low as he walks toward me.

Swallowing hard, I step back, my heart hammering so hard I wonder if it's visible through my dress. "I don't—I . . ."

He continues to step toward me, his eyes never leaving my face. "Your calling doesn't lie in secular education. If it did, you would have received an early acceptance to college like the other graduates of our congregation. But that doesn't mean you need to despair."

My back hits the wall and the large presence of my father looms closer to me like a terrifying shadow.

"God wants you to be a dutiful wife and mother and to ensure our values are instilled in the next generation. And really, isn't that the greatest gift you have to offer? What woman wouldn't want to have such an honorable life?"

My neck strains as I look up into his dark face. His hand lifts and hovers over my neck. Tears prick at the back of my eyes as his hand flexes and I think he's going to hit me, or maybe grab my throat, but surprisingly, he pets my hair. His hand is rough on my head, my hair pulling at the root, and my body shudders. He leans down, and my eyes clamp shut as I feel him kiss the top of my head.

"You won't disappoint me, will you, Rebecca? Or perhaps you want to spend the last two months of the school year at Mercy Christian Home for Girls."

Tears fall down my cheeks as I frantically shake my head. God, please don't let them send me away. Not when I've just discovered what it means to feel free. I feel him move away after a long moment, and I keep my eyes closed until I hear the door of his office slam. When I open my eyes, my mother is staring past me. Her face is hard, but there's a strange look in her eyes as she stares after the place my father disappeared. Is she thinking what I am? That my father may not love her like she thought. I can't stifle the sob that tears from my throat, the pain of it tearing at my vocal chords.

"M—Mom?"

She turns to me, her bony finger aimed at my face. "Wake up, Rebecca. You should be thankful Eric wants to marry you at all after how you behaved tonight."

Her lip and nose twitch in an ugly sneer and a retort springs to mind that someone else does want me. Even in spite of my flaws. And even though I'm sure it's not marriage he's after, the thought of his kiss and confidence fills my terrified heart. My eyes flick one last time to the vase by the door, then close so as not to give myself away. But it's already been a horrible enough night and if I'm honest with myself, I'm still fearful that black van will one day turn into the one I've always feared and take me away, so I bite back what I really want to say.

I nod shakily and my mother disappears into the kitchen and out the back door. Once she's gone, I slump against the wall, my fists clenching so hard my knuckles are white and I try to steady myself. On trembling legs, I head for the stairs, but with a quick look at the back door, I reach into the vase in the foyer and dig out the heavy jean jacket covered in patches and safety pins. Then I run upstairs, flinging myself onto my bed to sob, my face buried in the denim as James's smell overwhelms me. If I imagine hard enough, it almost feels like he's hugging me for real.

It's late and I've scrubbed my face pink, my hair is straight and hanging around my face. I've traded the too-tight green eyelet dress to a sleeveless pink nightgown, but I've wrapped myself up in James's jacket. Its size and smell envelop me deliciously. Comforting me when nothing else will.

I could say that I'm still awake because of everything that happened over dinner, but, truthfully, I'm waiting for when James gets home because I simply want to see his face. Will he be happy to see me? Will he be mad that I accidentally stole his jacket? Has he spent all of his shift at work thinking about me?

The house is quiet when the sound of his music rumbles up from the street, and a few minutes later the light of his lamp streaks across my ceiling. He's home.

I shoot out of bed and flick on the light on my desk. Standing in the window, I watch as he enters the room, then turns to me. The smile that creeps across his face makes my stomach flutter and my heart swell. He's happy to see me after all.

He takes a few steps toward the window but stops, almost as if he's forgotten that twelve feet of empty space separate us. His grin widens though, and his eyes trail over me, eyebrows rising. Heat blooms into my cheeks at the way he looks at me and even though he's seen me almost naked twice before, there's something about the way he's looking at me now that has me feeling more exposed than ever.

Backing away from the window, he pulls that checkered notebook out from his bag. He grabs a pen from the nightstand

and flips it open toward the back before scribbling something down.

My breath hitches with anticipation, wondering what he wants to say. He sits down on the edge of his bed and turns the paper around for me to read.

You have something of mine.

What? I look down and cringe. I totally forgot I'm still wearing his jacket. He's going to think I'm some crazy stalker girl. I quickly pull it off and place it on the back of my desk chair.

I grab an old notebook and scribble a reply with a blue marker before returning to the window and holding it up for him to read.

Sorry. I didn't even realize I was still wearing it when I left.

He smiles as he reads the message and turns his notebook back to write again.

You look good in it.

But I would like it back at some point.

I breathe out a laugh and watch as he writes something else on the paper. He hesitates, biting down on his lip for a moment before turning the paper my way.

I've thought about you all night.

Something cracks and I nearly sob, the emotion

overwhelming me. I sit down on the edge of my wooden desk chair and bring my feet up to the windowsill, my cheeks sore from all the goofy smiling I've done today.

I can't get you out of my head.

He runs a hand through his wild hair and rubs at the back of his neck.

I told you kissing is fun if you do it right.

The butterflies in my stomach lurch lower.

Maybe we can try it again sometime.

Even from here, I can see his eyes darken as he gazes at me from foot to face. Even I know he's probably thinking of more than kissing right now, and I'd be a hypocrite if I said that kissing is all I'm considering.

He writes something down again, and I hold my breath as I wait to see what his note says.

You look like you're sitting on a pinecone again. Relax.

My thighs clench together.

You make it sound so easy.

It can be.

He reaches down into his bag and pulls out a tin. Opening it up he pulls out a thin white stick and wiggles it at me, his eyebrows rising suggestively.

What about our deal?

That's for cigarettes. Not pot.

I roll my eyes.

I'm not going to do drugs.

He shakes his head and stretches, his shirt lifting to expose his stomach. A jolt shoots through me from my core without even moving. Looking at him now I can't stop thinking about earlier in the shower. The mere idea of touching myself—of him knowing I'm doing that twelve feet away—sends a thrilling sensation through every square inch of my body, my stomach tightening like I'm on a rollercoaster.

It's okay to do things for you sometimes. You're not going to ruin yourself.

God wants you to be a dutiful wife and mother and to ensure our values are instilled in the next generation. And really, isn't that the greatest gift you have to offer? What woman wouldn't want to have such an honorable life?

My father's words slash through me like a knife. I don't even want kids. And I certainly don't want to marry Eric. Instead, I want James, the freedom he offers me, and I don't want this to end—this day, this exchange between us. Then an idea takes hold of me so strongly I'm not sure I can talk myself out of it.

Maybe I want to be ruined.

He squints at the paper I hold up as if he's not sure he read it right. I place the pad of paper down on my desk and rise to stand in the center of the window. My fingers tremble as I reach for the buttons at the front of my nightgown, pulling them open slowly, one at a time.

James's face stiffens, setting down the notebook on the mattress next to him. His expression is one of utmost concentration, his tongue darting out to wet his lips. The last button pops open and I push the nightgown off my shoulders, letting the soft fabric fall to the floor. I'm bare before him, wearing nothing but my underwear. My hand traces along the skin of my neck where his touch had been, my head tilting to the side as the featherlight touch causes goosebumps to sprout up all over me.

He leans back, his hands behind him on the bed, keeping himself upright as his eyes widen. I don't know what's come over me, but my body is a live wire under his gaze. That beautiful aching feeling spreads between my legs, behind the cotton armor of my panties as my fingers skim over my stomach.

A little voice inside my head screams at me to stop. That I shouldn't be doing this, and my hand jumps away to twist in my hair. What am I thinking? I'm not some sexual creature with a voluptuous body who has men desperate to see me without clothes on. I stoop to pick up my nightgown, quickly pulling it back over me.

When I look back, James is scribbling something in his notebook, his tongue caught between his teeth. He leans forward as though I'm the most interesting thing on television and shows me the note.

Becks, you're like a work of art. I can't look away.

My soul sings at his words and I think of his kiss, his touch, finding something deep inside me to keep going. Maybe I could keep the nightgown on, like the menu at the diner, a crude kind of shield. He mouths, "It's okay," and I can't help but smile. I lift my hand again, pulling up my nightgown just enough to dip my fingers beneath the fabric of my underwear.

I take a deep breath, my eyes fluttering closed for a moment before they reopen to find him, and a smile plays on my lips. He's sitting as still as a statue, like if he moves even a muscle, this will all disappear. I wish he were right here. It's his fingers I want discovering every part of me, for him to touch that place that jolts me like lightning and takes my breath away. I want him to know every part of me.

My fingers skim over that place between my legs and it hits me like jumping into icy water. Mouth dropping open and eyes clamping shut as my body contracts, setting off enough fireworks inside me that it feels like the Fourth of July. My other hand reaches out to grab the window sill for some kind of anchor, my shoulders pulling up and my breath hitching as my fingers move back and forth over the incredibly sensitive skin.

As I look across, James finally moves, and his eyes are as dark as I've ever seen them. Black like a starless night. Too strong to escape from, like black holes. He lifts his arms to grab the back of his shirt, pulling it down and over his head, his wild dark hair covering his face for a moment before he shakes it away. I can see the tattoos on his skin. The massive tree and the rose, and the snake and maybe the demons have hold of me already, or maybe I'm losing my mind, but I want to trace over that art with my tongue. To add an imprint of my teeth to his body—for him to do the same to me.

His hand travels down to the waistband of his jeans which I only now realize is bulging at his crotch. I've seen this happen to Eric and was always terrified by the organ that hides beneath, but right now, I'm practically breathless at the chance to catch a glimpse. My hand stops for a moment as I drink in his image, his fingers deftly unbuttoning and unzipping his jeans with an agonizing slowness. He slides his hand beneath his checkered boxers to grip what I've only ever seen diagrams of in a medical journal at the library. I want to see it but my hands are occupied and I can't write it out.

I don't think he'll be able to read anything I write now anyway and I don't want to stop. He's trying to keep his eyes open to watch me while simultaneously being swept away by whatever he's doing with his hand beneath the fabric. My toes curl into the carpet and tension begins to build inside me, but it's different from the kind that normally plagues me. This kind is like dancing. Like spinning and spinning and spinning and wondering when you're going to lose your balance and topple over. My fingers clench against the window sill, my eyes finding James again. I wish I could see how he likes to be touched so that maybe I might know how to bring that euphoric look to his face with my own hands.

"Rebecca?"

I rip my hand out of my panties and quickly pull my curtains closed before spinning toward the door.

"Just a second!"

I grab James's jacket and the notes from my desk and stuff them into the bottom drawer before grabbing my bathrobe from the closet door and throwing it on over myself. Looking over my shoulder one last time, I can see that James's light is out through the fabric of my curtains, and I try to calm my pounding heart as I open my door.

My mother's sleepy eyes and suspicious face greets me from the other side. "What are you doing up? It's after three in the morning."

I swallow hard, trying to push past the thick film of lust that seems to have settled over me. "Sorry, I couldn't sleep. You know, after upsetting you and Dad . . . I feel awful."

The lie flies from my mouth like nothing, and I'm sure she'll see right through it. But shockingly, her face softens, and she reaches forward to press her palm against my cheek. Can she tell how burning hot I am? Can she feel the thin sheen of sweat that's covering my skin?

"Oh, Rebecca, darling," my mother says in a voice that sounds almost human—sympathetic. The strangeness of it sends a nervous chill down my spine. "We all have a duty to fulfill. Trust me, you and Eric will be so happy together."

I can't say anything. I can't even lie to agree with her so she'll leave me alone. Not when I was just watching James touch himself while I did the same. So I just smile and nod. She tells me to get to bed. That we have church tomorrow and if I don't get some sleep, I'll look tired and that's unacceptable. When my door clicks shut, I collapse against it, finally taking deep calming breaths and pressing my hand to my chest to feel its erratic rhythm.

When I can stand up straight, I head to the window and peek through the curtains, but James is gone. His lamp is off, his bed is empty and I wonder if he ran out of his room to hide or if he thinks I got cold feet and closed the curtains so I wouldn't have to see him. What if he thinks I didn't like it? The anxiety spinning in my head has dissipated that aching feeling and chilled the heat through my body, but I'm more tense than ever. As though touching myself for a few moments made everything ten times worse.

I step away, turning the light off on my desk. My eyes linger on the drawer and quickly glance at my door to make sure it's shut. I pull out the jacket then quickly duck under the covers of my bed. Pressing the rough fabric against my chest, I cling to it. To the smell and the image of him, and a thought settles over me as I smile into his collar. James Walton is like eating real food after starving for so long. The more I taste, the more I crave him.

CHAPTER 21

Escape

JAMES

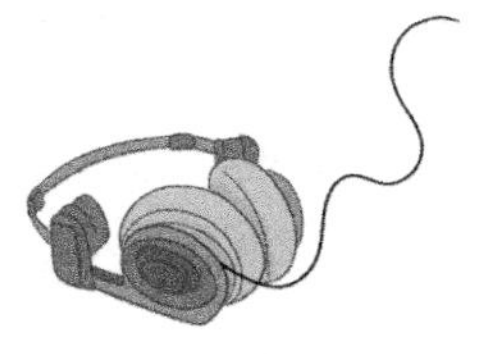

RULE #2 - NO VIRGINS/NO SERIOUS RELATIONSHIPS.

In a flash she's gone, and for a moment I wonder if I imagined it all. But no, my hand is still firmly wrapped around my cock, and I was just watching Rebecca getting herself off. Did she get cold feet? Maybe overwhelmed? Something raw inside of me was desperate to see her face as she came, but I guess that won't be happening now. Whatever the reason, I'm still so hard it hurts, so I quickly duck into the bathroom to finish the job.

I worried all night if she had been okay with our kiss. Even though she was smiling when she left, it's clear the guilt and fear of doing anything against what her church tells her is right plagues her constantly. And . . . she does have a boyfriend. Even if he is a piece of shit loser who doesn't deserve her. That didn't stop me from replaying the day on a loop though, from the moment I spotted her walking down the street to the moment she hopped out of my van in my jacket. It played out like a movie—the flowery smell of her hair mixed with the rain, the touch of her small hand against mine, the look that burned in her eyes right before she kissed me back. My hand strokes up and down as I grip the counter, remembering Rebecca's fingers as they so tentatively trailed down her body to touch between her thighs.

I didn't expect her to do it right there in front of me, but fuck, I'm not complaining. And while I would never tell anyone what happened, no one could convince me that wasn't the hottest fucking thing I've ever seen. Jesus Christ. I'm sweating, fucking my hand like I'm thirteen years old again. Flashes of her flushed face, lips parted and that little wrinkle above her nose swim forward as I imagine it's my fingers touching her, my cock inside of her. My stomach muscles tighten and my jaw clenches as I come hard in a breathless rush.

It takes a few minutes to recover, but finally my heart calms and I clean myself up. When I get back, the light in Rebecca's room is off and there's a nagging ache of guilt in my chest. I feel like I'm always pushing her too far, and I hope when I wake up in the morning those curtains are open because I can't stomach the idea of her shutting me out.

I sink into my bed and take a deep breath, pushing my hands through my hair. What am I doing? Getting involved with Rebecca is reckless and destined for trouble. I mean, what do I really think the end result of this is going to be? That we'll live happily ever after? No. I learned very early on that people like me don't get happily ever afters. All we get is the shit kicked out of our hearts. And I thought I had lost mine after mom died. That it couldn't feel anymore, and it was simply there to keep me alive. But Rebecca has revived me. Like an electric shock to the chest.

No, I know how this will end. And I don't think my heart will survive another brutal beating.

Besides, what am I to her?

Dread and doubt settles into my stomach. Will she break up with her boyfriend? The thought of that prick touching or kissing her after today makes my knuckles pop. Will she expect me to be her boyfriend? I don't do relationships. But I keep thinking about holding her hand. Thinking of seeing her wearing my jacket like she belongs in it. Of her smiling up at me like the adorable creature she is.

Fuck, I wish I could have a smoke, but I can't even do that because of her. It was worth the nicotine withdrawal to see her eat those French fries, anyway. I grab my notebook, glancing over the pages of our window conversation, back to where I've doodled my thoughts of her from today, adding another one from tonight. I trace the back of my pen along the collection of thoughts that have accumulated about her, spreading like inky spider webs across the pages. And even though I'm sure this will all end badly, at least it'll be fun for a while.

When I wake up sometime after noon, she's gone, but her curtains are open and relief floods my chest. A groggy smile creeps onto my face as I think maybe she watched me sleep for a bit. It's Sunday, though and I would put money on the fact she's likely gone to church and all the social expectations that go along with that. I hope she's not being too hard on herself.

I spend the day catching up on homework, making sure I don't fall so far behind that this whole endeavor of another year of high school becomes a gigantic waste of time. Periodically, I set aside my work to jam on my guitar for a bit, either practicing a cover or figuring my way through something original. But she's still not home by the time I have to leave for work. Her family's car is missing from their driveway, and I'm embarrassed to admit that I sit in my van for longer than necessary waiting to catch a glimpse of her when she comes home.

An hour into my shift at work, Captain John flags me down toward the front of the bar. Around seven it's still not very busy, except for a few guys who I've seen almost every shift hanging around with a pint in their hands. The smell of their cigarettes makes me desperate for a smoke.

"Hey, what do you need?" I ask John, pushing through the door to the front.

He glances up at me before his gaze drops, but he points over to where the message board is near the stage. A tall man with a dirty blond mop of hair longer than mine is pinning up something to the corkboard. My stomach flips and my heart skips a beat. I mouth wordlessly while pointing, asking to go over to him, and John simply rolls his one eye and waves me over. A faint look of humor on his face as he does it.

I nearly trip over my own feet with excitement as I head for the man, his back turned toward me and blocking the notices.

Clearing my throat, he turns around.

"Hey, man." I'm forever grateful it didn't come out like a squeak.

He's wearing a denim vest covered in band patches over a Slayer shirt and leather pants. He eyes me up and down and back again and narrows his eyes at me before nodding his head. "Hey."

My head tilts to the side, trying to look around him to get a look at what he posted. "You uh . . . you looking for a guitarist?"

He scratches his chin. "Yeah. You play?"

Fuck, fuck, fuck. Okay, stay cool. Calm.

I give a half-hearted shrug of my shoulder. "Yeah, I do."

"How old are you, kid?"

I take a look at his face, he's hardly much older than me. "Nineteen."

He purses his lips and smirks. "Had to ask. High school kids can look older nowadays. What do you play?"

I swallow. "Lead guitar, but I can do rhythm too."

He sizes me up again. "You any good?"

"Yes."

He grins. "Well, we're going to have auditions here on Tuesday afternoon. John's letting us use the space before he opens. Three o'clock. Can you make it?"

Shit, I'd have to leave school early. One day won't hurt, right?

"Yeah, shouldn't be a problem."

He pulls a cigarette out of the back of his jeans and places it between his teeth. "What's your name, kid?"

"James Walton."

Holding out his hand, he shakes his hair out of his face. "Dave Noblar," he says. I grasp his hand, the metal of his ring clinking against my own.

"Nice to meet you, man."

He jerks his head toward the bar. "You working here?"

I glance down at my Shipwreck work shirt and cock an eyebrow. "Yeah, well, I figured this was better than the Gap."

Dave laughs. "Fucking right. Well, we're looking for a lead. Had to kick our lead guitarist out last week."

"Why?"

His mouth twists like he's trying to decide whether or not to tell me. "Idiot started snorting meth. I mean, whatever, do what you want, but when he was high he was a fucking loose cannon. Stopped showing up for rehearsals and when he did show up he was stoned out of his fucking tree and would just wreck shit."

I nod with understanding, remembering how my mom would get sometimes when she was too high to function. "Right."

"Anyway, we were just sick of it. I mean, dude could fucking shred, but it wasn't worth the hassle anymore. You know what I mean?"

"Sure, man."

"Plus, the plan is to head out west soon if we can, and he wasn't willing to travel."

My heart skips several beats in a row. "Out west?"

He nods. "To California. Nothing for metal musicians in the midwest. Is that something you'd be okay with?"

This is like a goddamn dream come true. "Yes. Absolutely. I was planning on heading out there at the end of the season anyway."

Dave grins widely. "Excellent."

There's a loud cough from behind me, and I look over to see John watching me. He crosses his arms and jerks his head back to the kitchen. "Listen, I have to get back to work. But I'll be here on Tuesday."

"Good to meet you, James."

I turn but spin back on my heel, remembering I forgot to ask. "Anything in particular you want to hear on Tuesday?"

Dave shrugs his shoulders. "Up to you, come to impress though, yeah?"

I grin, holding up my palms. "I always do."

I FEEL as light as a feather when I get home, even though it's late and I'm exhausted. When I enter my room, my eyes instinctively flick to the window as I turn on my lamp. Rebecca doesn't make an appearance but her curtains are open, so I take that as a good sign. I thought maybe she'd wait up for me, only it's a school night. I hope she had a good day. I hope she thought about me and knows that I thought about her too.

I lie on my bed and pull out my mom's journal.

> *July 12, 1965*
> *Jet kissed me! He kissed me and it was wonderful and romantic and I'm so nervous Mom and Dad will find out, but I wouldn't trade tonight*

for the world. He even told me he wants to go steady! He's such a wonderful guy. Sweet and charming and I know Mom and Dad will approve because he's always at church. I feel like the luckiest girl in the world.

Warmth spreads through my chest. Knowing that at least for a while my mom was happy. That she was just a regular teenager who was excited about a kiss. I read on.

August 15, 1965

Today at school, Jet introduced me as his girlfriend. I think I might just die of happiness. He really is the best boyfriend ever. Will he ask me to go to homecoming with him? What color dress should I wear if he does? Noreen always tells me I look best in blue but she's just a kid, what does she know?

My smile starts to fade. It's clear from this journal that at one point Noreen and my mom had some kind of relationship. What happened that led to their estrangement? Will she ever tell me what happened? Why did my mom run away? What was she trying to escape?

I flip through my notebook to where I've been writing to my mom.

Mom, I wish you could meet Rebecca. You'd really like her. Maybe you would have some advice on how

I can help her. I think she's trying to escape something too.

Tucking the notebook away, I lie in bed, my eyes locked on the window where Rebecca is surely sleeping. Is Rebecca trying to escape her strict parents? Or her boyfriend? Or maybe just the expectations that come with being Rebecca Briar. Whatever she's trying to get away from, I make a silent promise that I'll do my best to help her.

CHAPTER 22

You Give Love a Bad Name

REBECCA

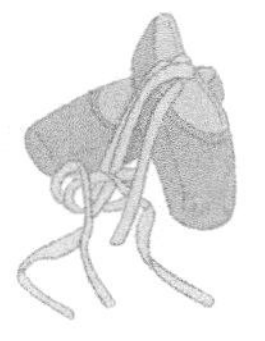

Sunday is still my least favorite day of the week. And today just keeps proving why I hate it so much. Not only have I been forced into a dress so tight I can't even manage to get the zipper closed all the way and have to hide the gap under my cardigan, but I'm also helping to run the Sunday school program.

I've tied dozens of shoes, wiped several runny noses and even though I've only been here for an hour, I think I have permanent damage to my eardrums from the shrill screaming.

I try my best to smile and be patient, but every moment I'm here feels like physical torture. The one good thing about it is it distracts me from thinking about last night. I'm amazed no one knows what I've been doing in secret. What James and I have is like a sanctuary that I can go to in my head when things start to close in too tightly.

Another shrill scream, and my eyes pinch shut.

"Claudia!" Mrs. Corbley scolds. "Little girls are to be seen and not heard."

She bends the girl over her knee and spanks her, again and again. Claudia stops her screaming but begins to cry and something visceral punches me in the chest. I see myself in this little girl who can't be any older than five. Remember the way I was disciplined to ensure I submitted and stayed quiet. Is it really because that's what God wants from us? Or is it to keep us from realizing the hypocrisy of their entire system?

Mrs. Corbley continues until the girl finally goes quiet. It feels like part of me dies. She lets Claudia go, and the girl runs toward me. Instinctively, I open my arms to her. Pulling her in tight like I can somehow protect her from all the things she'll learn. The things I'll be expected to teach her. The fight that will be beaten out of her.

I might be sick again.

If I marry Eric, they'll expect me to have babies right away. They'll expect me to raise them this way—how I was raised—and the idea of one day becoming my mother or Mrs. Corbley is perhaps the most terrifying thing of all.

"See?" Mrs. Corbley says with a smile as she watches me with Claudia. "The children love you. You'll do great here."

I PRACTICALLY RUN out of the backroom into the nave when Sunday school finishes, but out here isn't much better. The constant disappointed looks from my parents are about to send me over the edge. Between my father's stoic glare and my mother's disapproving sneer, I feel feverish. It doesn't help that Pastor Campbell and Eric's father, Michael Corbley, took today to remind the congregation that, now more than ever, tithing and planting the seed money is the holiest investment we can make.

On top of all of that, Eric seems more determined than ever to keep me close. His hand snakes its way around mine in a possessive manner the moment he finds me, and when I try to pull away, his grip tightens until my knuckles turn numb. Worst of all is when we're called to a meeting with the Pastor after service, in which he informs us that Eric and I should start attending his pre-marriage counseling sessions. The idea of it all makes me nauseous—marriage counseling with someone I have no desire to be married to. I can only imagine how painful this will be to endure.

Trapped. That's how I feel. Like the walls are closing in around me. Walls painted with good intentions and family duty and God's plan that I want to tear to shreds with my fingernails. But amongst the walls there's a window. A singular point of salvation. James. And while I don't think he'll ever know how much that window means to me, it's the only thing keeping me sane right now.

He isn't home when we finally walk through the door just before dinner time. His van is gone and I'm reminded that he's probably at work. I hope he doesn't think I ran away from him. This morning, I left my curtains open so that when he woke up he'd know that my disappearing last night wasn't because of something he did. I even watched him sleep for a while, one arm flung over his face against the sunlight that streamed into the room. I closed my eyes to imagine what that arm would feel like wrapped around me, what it might feel like to wake up next to him.

Now, as I sit on the edge of my bed staring out the window at his empty room I realize something. I'm never getting out of here. No college acceptances. An arranged marriage immediately following my high school graduation. Destined to work in a job I hate until God blesses me with a baby.

The thought of just running away is suddenly so enticing I almost reach for a bag to stuff clothing into. But where would I go? I have no money to get anywhere. Even if I did manage to get far enough away that my parents couldn't find me, I don't even have a driver's license or any useful real-world skills to get a job. I wonder if James would drive me somewhere far away if I asked him to. Plus he already thinks my parents are the worst, and he doesn't even know the half of it.

"Just accept it. You're stuck," I mutter.

The tears don't even fall. I shed my clothes and stand in front of the window. Even though he's not there, the memory of his eyes on my body is a comfort I've not had all day. My eyes close and my breathing deepens, my heartbeat reeling back from the edge of panic. Clarity starts to dissipate the fog in my mind.

If I really am doomed to this unhappy domestic life then I should spend every last minute before graduation doing what I want. And what I want the most right now is James.

Would he be okay with spending time together, knowing it'll be over in two months? He said himself, he's not boyfriend material, and he's . . . been with girls. I swallow hard, my stomach flipping over at what that statement means. How he is so much more experienced than me. How if I'm to be sold off like cattle to Eric, maybe I don't want to go without having some of that experience myself first. Maybe it would feel good to go to Eric as ruined property. On top of that, James is leaving too. Going to San Francisco after graduation. This time, the tears *do* come. The thought of him leaving causes hot tears to spill from the corners of my closed eyes and drip onto my bare chest.

So two months is all we can have. Can someone survive the rest of their life on two months of happiness? One thing's for sure. I'm going to try.

I'M up early and out the door to get to the bus stop. The last thing I want is to have to get a lift from Eric. Normally, I'd be terrified of him being angry with me, or disobeying him, but last night I came to a decision. I'm going to do what I want for the next two months. At least as best as I can.

When I step off the bus in front of the school, I quickly head for my locker, ignoring Eric's incessant call of my name from the far end of the parking lot. Maybe if I'm quick enough, I can hide out in the bathroom before class starts so I won't have to deal with him until at least lunch. But it seems God has other plans as Eric jogs up next to me in the hallway in front of my locker. He is a track star, after all.

"What the hell, Becca?" he asks, flushed and annoyed.

"Leave me alone, Eric." I say, swapping out the books I need for the morning.

His hand slams against the locker next to me, the bang shattering the bravery I managed to conjure for myself and my books topple out of my hands onto the floor. Stepping over them, he closes the gap between us until I'm pressed against the lockers. My heart leaps out of my chest, my pulse fluttering in my neck, and I think wildly of how Claudia was spanked for her disobedience. How he might hit me for mine.

Eric's never behaved like this before. Looking around, no one seems to be bothered by this at all. How can no one think this is wrong? James would think this is wrong, and I find myself glancing over Eric's shoulder, hoping to catch sight of him.

"What's gotten into you?" he asks, voice low.

"I just—" All of my resolve seems to vanish in an instant and I nearly burst into tears. "I'm feeling . . . really overwhelmed."

His eyes narrow. "Overwhelmed?"

My lip trembles as his arms cage me in, but I push on as best I can. "This whole getting married thing—and so soon—it's a surprise. I just—"

"You're overwhelmed with the thought of marrying me? I thought you loved me, Becca."

I thought I did too. The words are on the tip of my tongue but my mouth is frozen.

He sighs. "You know . . . I'm a little disappointed."

My breathing stutters, I almost can't believe it. "Re—really?" Is he feeling pressured by all of this too? I mean, surely he doesn't want to get married immediately out of high school either.

Petting the top of my hair, a sympathetic smile pulls at his lips and he nods. "Yeah, of course. I mean . . . wouldn't you be disappointed if the person you love shouted out 'no' when the subject of marriage came up? And in front of their parents, too? Do you have any idea what I had to go through when I got home?"

An icy chill slithers down my spine. "Eric, I—"

"Where did you go on Saturday?"

I blink. We haven't had a single moment to talk about that gigantic fiasco and I'm surprised he isn't trying to make me forget it ever happened.

"What?" I ask breathlessly.

"I came to get you, but you weren't there. Where did you go?"

I shake my head. Why would he lie about that? "Eric, no you didn't. I waited for you for over an hour and you never came, so I walked home."

He laughs sardonically. "That's bullshit, Becca. Where did you actually go?"

"I went home!" I say, my voice rising, regaining some of that lost courage. "And even if I didn't, it's none of your business where I go. Especially when you ditch me!"

His hand slams into the locker next to my face and it feels like time stops. "It *is* my business."

"Where exactly were you on Saturday?" I throw back at him. "Out drinking again? At Jeremiah's place? What do you even do there for hours on end?"

Eric's face reddens with rage and he swallows hard. "What I do in my free time is none of your business."

My mouth drops open. "Don't you understand how hypocritical that sounds?"

“You’re going to be my wife and that comes with certain obligations.”

I want to shrink down and hide in my locker. He’s been mad at me before, but never violent, never made me afraid he might hurt me, but now I’m not so sure. “And wh—what about your obligations to me?”

His eyes narrow. “What?”

“Husbands, love your wives, as Christ loved the church and gave himself up for her,” I say with surprising steadiness. “You also have a Holy obligation to me. A marriage isn’t just a woman doing everything for a man like a slave. It’s a partnership. But you don’t care about me at all!”

He opens his mouth to retort when he’s interrupted by the warning bell ringing overhead.

“This conversation is over,” I say, my eyes darting over his face, wondering if he’ll try and keep me here. Something ticks in his jaw and for a moment I’m reminded of my father on Saturday, when I thought he might hit me. But Eric doesn’t—he backs away and disappears through the crowded halls as I scoop up my books and try to get air into my lungs. Every part of me feels tense, vibrating with anger, but I slam my locker closed and head down the hall for class.

Sitting down in my seat, my ribs ache against the ever tight, squeezing fabric. I’m still seething when I feel warmth come over the room, like a summer breeze. I look up and there he is. James. And I can’t stop the grin from spreading across my face, my eyes blinking furiously, trying to keep myself together as he walks toward me with a grin of his own. Calm exudes out of him with every step. The clink of the chain on his hip keeps time with my heart and his hand reaches out to touch my desk. That fluttering feeling in my chest quickens as I spot the paper in his hand and I reach forward to grasp it. Our fingers touch and that single point of contact is calm and fierce all at once. Something that steadies me yet burns at the same time.

I watch him walk toward the back of the room, that smug smile something I now look forward to, every moment we're apart. Not wasting any time, I quickly pull the note into my lap and check what it says.

I missed you.

Three words. How can three words mean so much to me?

NEARLY BOLTING out of my seat when the bell rings at the end of class, James is next to me a moment later, his breath in my ear.

"You all right, Becks?"

I want to fall against him and have him wrap his arms around me. I want to tell him everything. I want to tell him just how much I've missed him, but my tongue feels too big for my mouth so I simply smile and nod, following him out of the door. In the crowded hall we're able to be close to one another without anyone asking any questions and every few steps I feel his hand brush against mine.

"Did you have a good—"

"I missed you too," I blurt.

The smirk on his face flickers out for a moment, changing to a warm smile that soothes my soul. I feel him tug on my hand and the next second he pulls me into the alcove of a door to one of the science labs. He stands in front of me, the size of him likely blocking anyone from being able to see me.

"I can't stop thinking about you," he whispers, and my knees buckle at the confession.

Looking up into those beautiful, dark eyes, it feels like we're alone. Like the only two people to ever exist are the two of us. And it's dangerous and thrilling at the same time.

"I can't stop thinking about you either," I breathe.

His fingertip runs along the gold chain on my neck, his finger hooking into the necklace which pulls me forward, tipping my head back.

"Please tell me you dumped that asshole."

I'm so desperate for him to kiss me right now, I can barely think. But luckily there's at least one part of my brain still working, and that part reminds me that Eric could see us if he walked by. Anyone could. And I need James to understand what I decided I want before anything else can happen.

I grab his fingers and gently pull them away. "It's complicated."

His eyes narrow. "It's complicated?"

I sigh. "Can we talk? After school maybe? Away from . . . everyone?"

He nods. "Sure. I could drive you home?"

My eyes close with relief and I nod, my hand lifting to rest on his chest. I can feel the beating of his racing heart behind the hard muscle and the memory of him from Saturday night opens like a floodgate. Him with no shirt on, his hand beneath the waistband of his pants, stroking that most secretive part of a man I'm absolutely desperate to see—to feel.

The warning bell rings and I jump away, saddened by the cold air that comes between us. He clears his throat then backs up, holding his arm out for me to lead the way. "After you, m'lady," he says in a dramatic accent.

My smile pulls my cheeks and I walk ahead of him toward class, his warm presence always just a few steps behind me like a friendly shadow.

I SUPPOSE one good thing about not being accepted into any colleges is that I don't have to worry about my GPA plummeting. Ever since James walked into my life, I've hardly been able to concentrate on anything the teachers have said. Today is the hardest yet. It's made even more difficult when James's pen rolls off his desk and he quickly comes up the aisle to grab it from rolling under my chair. The backs of his fingertips grazing up my calf to my knee have me nearly shivering out of my seat.

When the bell rings for lunch, James lingers behind me in the classroom ensuring we're the last to leave.

"So I'll see you after school?"

I turn and nod. "Yes . . . I'll—I'm looking forward to it."

His fingers grasp at a strand of my hair, twisting it around his finger slowly, before dropping it and backing away. My body instinctively leans forward as if chasing after the magnetic pull of him. Grinning, he disappears out into the hallway and after taking a few moments to compose myself, I pull my bag over my shoulders and head toward the cafeteria.

Amy and Mary are sitting at our usual table speaking in hushed voices when I enter, their heads close together. When I drop my bag on the bench across from them they jump apart and look up at me. I freeze, my eyes darting between them and the half-concealed looks of guilt on their faces.

"What's wrong?" I ask, sinking into my seat. My heart rate spikes. Do they know about James?

They glance at each other quickly and Amy looks away, tucking her bottom lip behind her slightly large teeth, but Mary leans forward. "Becca, we—something happened at the party on Friday."

The tension in my shoulders eases slightly. Thank goodness, this isn't about James. "Oh?"

Amy is practically jumping out of her skin, her arms slamming down on the table in front of her and leaning so far over the table, her nose is only inches from the surface. "Jeremiah caught Eric hooking up with Stephanie Lawford."

A loud, short laugh bursts out of my mouth. Like this is just one of the many tidbits of gossip I don't normally engage in. Then it starts to sink in. Like being boiled alive slowly and before you realize it's too hot, it's too late.

"I'm sorry, what?"

To her credit, Mary actually looks sad about it. Like it hurts her to tell me this juicy piece of gossip. "I'm so sorry, Becca, but he—Amy and I walked in on the three of them and . . . well . . ."

"They were arguing. Next thing we know, Jeremiah is telling us how he and Eric are done. That . . . that he screwed his ex-girlfriend behind his back," Amy adds, flushing scarlet.

Time seems to slow down. If this had been a few weeks ago, it would have devastated me. But now, I'm floundering for a normal reaction to finding out my future husband cheated on me.

"Okay," I say, drawing out the word.

A long silence stretches between the three of us, Mary and Amy looking at each other nervously.

"Are you okay?" Mary asks.

I blink rapidly, looking up at them. The muscles of my cheeks are straining to keep me from grinning like a loon. Wanting to hug both of them for the best piece of news that's come my way in months. "Me? Oh, yes . . . umm . . . that's awful. I can't believe he would do that to me. Excuse me."

I stand and grab my backpack and turn toward the exit. On my way, I spot Stephanie Lawford who takes one look at me and hangs her head. And although she did a terrible thing, I wish I could run over and tell her thank you. But for the first time in weeks, I'm actively looking for my jerk boyfriend. Maybe God is granting me a miracle because as if by my thoughts alone, Eric and Ryan stride into the cafeteria. And while I hadn't wanted to do this publicly, I don't think I can pass this up.

"Eric?"

He stops in his tracks just inside the doors, Ryan halting behind Eric's shoulder. He glances sideways at his friend then back at me. "What's up, babe?"

"I know about what happened on Friday."

Ryan lets loose a low whistle and backs away, heading around us toward where Amy and Mary are likely watching with rapt attention.

Eric shoves his hands in his pockets and shrugs. "What are you talking about?"

I try to cross my arms over my chest indignantly, but the zipper of my dress pops loudly. Cool air brushes against a small exposed area of my back that thankfully my cardigan is still covering and my joy at finally having some leverage over my current situation disappears.

My mother is going to kill me!

My mouth opens and closes like a fish gasping for air. Eric tilts his head at me, waiting for what I'm trying to say. But I can't seem to put what I want into cohesive sentences. Then, over his shoulder at the end of the far hallway, I see James speaking to the principal and Ms. Flora, the guidance counselor, by the doors to the parking lot. He looks over at us, his expression unreadable as he takes in what Eric and I must look like. But his presence inspires me to be brave.

"Eric, we're done."

His face turns splotchy in an instant, his teeth clenching hard. "What?"

I lower my voice and step closer, my heart rate spiking intensely. "You had sex with Stephanie Lawford?"

Eric looks past me, probably to where Stephanie sits. He seems . . . confused, his nostrils flaring widely—a tell of his I've become well acquainted with over the years when he's caught off guard. His lips roll over his teeth and he readjusts his face as he looks back down at me. "So what?"

I blink. "What do you mean, so what? You cheated on me."

He shakes his head. "It doesn't matter."

"It matters to me. It matters in the eyes of God!"

"It won't matter to our parents, though."

A lead balloon drops in my stomach. And the look on Eric's face tells me he knows that it's true. That even if I run home and tell my parents, they'll turn it around on me. Say that Eric stumbled because I wasn't modest enough and the lustful temptation led him astray. That I should forgive him. That God would forgive him. My mother will probably tell me it's because I've gained weight, the popped zipper on my back giving her exactly the kind of ammunition she'll need to starve me until I can barely walk to school.

I see James in the background, taking tentative steps toward us like he knows something serious is going down. Does he know my face—my emotions, that well already?

"You know it, don't you, Becca? Even though I might have screwed up, this marriage is still going to happen. Our fathers made sure of that."

His statement adds fuel to my anger. My nails dig into my palms, my fists clenching painfully hard. "Maybe so. But if I tell our parents, your parents, Pastor Campbell about what you did . . . you can say goodbye to all the precious freedom you seem to be enjoying so much."

His eyes widen, and for the first time, he seems genuinely concerned.

"That's right. The partying? The drinking? Sleeping around?

All of that will be gone, and they'll send you to the Samson Academy for Boys until the end of the school year."

His eyes flicker with fear. He's just as afraid of the black van coming for him as I am. Chest rising and falling, his seething breaths are loud, and I realize almost everyone is watching us. Leaning close, straining to hear our whispered conversation.

"So what now?" Eric asks, eyes narrowing and beads of sweat appearing on his forehead. "You going to tattle on me? It's just something *you* would do. Are you sure it's a good idea? It'll only make things more difficult for you too."

I shake my head, my blood pounding in my ears and pushing away a nauseating feeling in the pit of my stomach. "No, we're going to make a deal."

He takes a step closer. "What kind of deal?"

"For all intents and purposes, we're still together. But you won't touch me. You won't kiss me. You won't even talk to me. You can do whatever you want until graduation . . . and I'll do whatever *I* want."

His eyes seem to wander over my face, what I've proposed taking a few moments to permeate that thick skull of his. "And you'll—what the hell do *you* want to do?"

"Like I said this morning," I say, smirking at him, "you don't care about me at all. If you did, you'd know what I want."

He crosses his arms. "Seriously, Becca, what the hell do you want to do?"

"Nothing that involves you."

Sniffing loudly, he rubs his jaw with his hand, the wheels spinning in his head. He's wondering if his freedom is worth our secret. Worth letting me have two months to do as I please.

I'm barely breathing, wondering if this is all going to blow up in my face. But his chin dips sharply in a nod. "Fine."

Restraining myself from jumping with joy over my small

victory, I settle for a tiny shimmy, aware that my back is still exposed under my sweater.

"See you around, Eric."

I step away, but his hand closes around my wrist tightly. I look back over my shoulder and his face has turned menacing, a sliver of fear wedging its way through my split second of joy. "Two months, Becca, then you're mine."

I try not to think too hard about the threat behind that statement. Pulling my wrist out of his grasp, I turn my gaze to the gorgeous boy at the end of the hall whose face is full of concern. I feel like crying. Crying with joy or anguish, I'm not quite sure. My emotions simmer so close to the surface, they're just trying to escape any way they can. I smile at James anyway, tilting my head toward the parking lot hoping he'll follow me. He does, the clinking sound of the chain on his hip keeping time with my steps as I burst out of the doors.

The sky is gloomy, but it might as well be sunshine and rainbows.

"Becks, what's going on? Are you all right?"

As I spin around, James watches my face, his eyebrows pinching together. I grin and reach forward to grab his hand, the metal of his rings pressing into my palm. Pulling him away from the door, I step toward him. And maybe he sees it in my face because the side of his gorgeous mouth curves up and his pupils dilate before I back him up against the brick wall and step onto my tiptoes to kiss him.

CHAPTER 23

Girls Just Want To Have Fun

JAMES

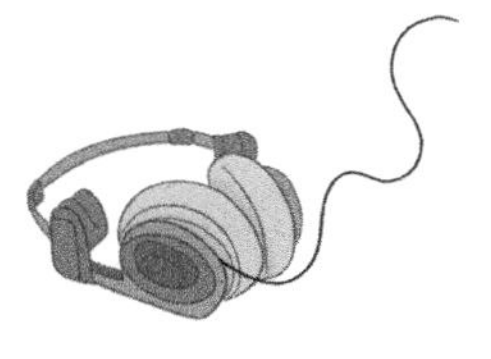

Rebecca's lips press against mine and a wave of bliss sweeps through my muddled mind. Kissing her is soft. Her lips are smooth and delicate like flower petals, and she smells just as sweet. And . . . holy shit, she's kissing me. In public, where anyone can see. Granted, there's no one around outside at the moment but . . . did she dump her boyfriend?

"James?" she breathes out, and the sound of her voice like that makes my brain short circuit.

"Yeah?"

"Can we go somewhere?"

I pull back to look into her face. Her green eyes are darker than normal, her cheeks are flushed and her warm little hands are pressing against my chest pleasantly. "Go somewhere?"

She swallows and nods. "I just mean . . . I want to get away. Not be here right now. But—it's fine. I don't want to make you skip school."

The fact that this girl thinks I'd rather sit in that stuffy classroom, listening to teachers who already think I'm a waste of space drone on and on, than go wherever she wants me to take her reminds me just how innocent she is. The fact that she's probably never in her dizziest daydreams thought of all the filthy things I want to do to her. The thought of ditching class to take her somewhere to be alone is the most appealing thing I've heard in the last year. However, girls like Rebecca don't just skip school. What's the real reason she wants to disappear for a few hours?

"Angel, I don't care about skipping class. It's just . . . are you okay? Did something happen? I saw you talking to *him*."

Saw him grab her too, and my vision flashed red, but thankfully my brain managed to convince my body to wait, and she pulled away from him without issue.

She nods again and smiles. Genuinely smiles, all of her perfect white teeth gleaming. "Yes, I'm fine. Great, actually. I just really don't want to be at school today. I want to be with you."

My pending graduation status creeps up on my conscience. I'm here to finish school for my mom. That should be my focus. Then there's the additional headache of the repeated vandalism that I keep getting blamed for—three pentagrams in just over two weeks. I was sure Principal Jeffries would find some way to blame it on me. Thankfully, one of the guidance counselors convinced him that without evidence there was no way to prove I did it. Right now, though? Rebecca needs me, so I quickly squash it back down. It's just one afternoon, and so far all my grades are above average.

I push off the brick wall, kiss her quickly on the lips and pull my van keys from my pocket to dangle them in front of her. "Then let's go."

Grabbing her hand we jog across the parking lot as the warning bell rings for the end of lunch. I pull open the passenger door for her and give her a hand up into the seat, the sound of a giggle escaping behind her hand. On my way around the van, I try to take a deep breath. Okay, cool it, Romeo. She probably just wants to talk and kiss a bit. Don't push her.

I hop up into the driver's seat and start the engine. The stereo blares to life, drowning out her startled squeak as I race to turn the volume down.

"Sorry about that," I say.

She shrugs her shoulders. "It's fine, just surprised me, that's all."

"So . . . where to?"

That little wrinkle above her nose appears. "I don't know. Other than dance class there really isn't anywhere that I can just go to hangout. Can we just go somewhere we can be alone?"

My fingers tap rhythmically on the steering wheel, trying to think of where we can go. Can't be anywhere we might risk running into her parents, then the perfect idea pops into my head. "Yeah, I think I know a place," I say, throwing the van into reverse, my palm spinning the wheel. I hear the bell ringing in the distance as I pull out onto the busy road.

We're silent for a few minutes. The quiet always made me uncomfortable, but with her here, it's growing on me. As we drive further away from town, the trees become denser and the air is different. I roll down my window, letting the wind whip my hair around my face. The smell of it is invigorating. Just as I'm about to head toward the interstate, I pull right onto a narrow, unpaved road lined with trees, bouncing around on the seat as I drive slowly over the uneven ground. I drive to the very end of the deserted road and park.

"Come on," I say, opening my door. She blushes to the roots of her hair and grins. I grab her hand and pull her along the bench. I turn, my fingers sneaking under her sweater to grip her waist before helping her hop down. Hands on my shoulders, her body slides down my front until her feet meet the ground. I take a step back and grasp her hand.

Walking toward the back of the van, through the trees, she finally sees why I brought her here.

"Wow," she whispers.

I smile wide and pull her through the wild grass and tall trees until we're standing on the shore of a small, secluded lake. It's calm and beautiful, the wind rustling through the new leaves on the branches.

"It's nice, huh?"

I turn and look at Rebecca who's gazing across the water. "It's beautiful. How did you find this place?"

"My mom." At her questioning look, I continue. "I found a box of her old stuff. It's full of journals and pictures and trophies. I haven't gone through it all, but in one of the journals, she mentioned finding this place. How she loved coming here." I swallow hard and look out at the water. "I get why she liked it."

"Me too," she says, squeezing my hand and I pull her a little closer. "So," she teases, "is this how you 'didn't date' those girls back home? You bring them to a beautiful place and get all sentimental?"

I laugh. "Hardly. I never told any of them much about myself."

"Why not?"

A muscle ticks in my jaw. "Guess they never really bothered to ask." Is that what makes Rebecca so special to me?

"This is probably going to sound really lame," she says, her cheeks turning pink. "But, I really like getting to know you. You're unlike anyone I've ever known."

"And you," I say, pulling her to face me, "are not at all what I expected."

She reaches for my other hand and tugs me closer. I pull her gently against my chest, my hands dropping hers to wind around her waist as she tucks her head under my chin. She nuzzles her face against my chest. "Are you really going to San Francisco after graduation?"

The way she's curled into me right now, wrapped up in my arms, makes me hesitate. Inwardly, I curse myself. I knew this would happen. Knew getting attached to her would fuck up everything. The answer spills from my lips anyway. "Yes."

It's quiet for a moment, then she pulls back, looking up at my face. "That's perfect then."

That—that was not the response I was expecting at all. "Wait . . . what?" My arms loosen from around her body.

"I just mean, you're leaving and I have commitments after graduation too. So we can just be casual. You know? Have fun together until then."

Something odd twists itself in my stomach. She just wants this to be casual? Why is that so contradictory to everything I know about her? Even her face betrays her. There's something hollow in her eyes as she looks at me now, but maybe I don't know her as well as I think I do. "Oh."

"Is that okay?"

My right hand pulls away from her to rub the back of my neck. Truthfully, I should be thrilled. Here's a gorgeous girl willing to commit to a fun, casual, two-month-long relationship with no expectations of it becoming anything more. I should be whooping it up and cheering like a maniac at my good luck. It means that, miraculously, my number-one rule can stay unbroken. But no matter how much I want to, I can't feel happy about it.

"I mean . . . are you sure that's what you want?"

She nods enthusiastically. "Yes, it is."

There's a lead stone in my stomach. A lump of coal. Like that one Christmas morning when I came rushing out of my room to find the electricity had been turned off again and there were no presents under the dark tree.

"And what about Eric? Are things still complicated?" I generally don't like to make a habit of hooking up with girls in relationships, but I've got no moral quandary over sneaking around behind her douchebag boyfriend's back.

“It’s over between him and I,” she says, a touch of darkness flashing through her eyes.

“Oh,” I say. “Is that what was happening in the cafeteria?”

She nods. “Can—” Hesitating, she bites her lip. “Can we keep this—us—quiet though?”

I raise my eyebrows.

“Not because I’m ashamed to be seen with you!” she says quickly. “It’s just, my parents would never let me leave the house again if they found out we were even speaking to each other. And if we’re going to have fun, I can’t exactly do that while locked in my room.”

Something ticks unpleasantly inside of me at the thought of Rebecca wanting to keep me a secret. It’s uncomfortable, which is strange because it’s what I’m used to. Most of my hookups have been secret rendezvous, yet I can’t really disagree with her. Her parents definitely wouldn’t be cool with us being together. Hell, they might even try to get me arrested if the two previous warnings from her father to stay away from her were any indication.

“Yeah, that’s cool. Don’t want you getting into trouble.”

But the sight of her smile pushes all of those feelings and doubts deep down. My hands inching their way up to cup her face. “Does that mean I can kiss you without you feeling guilty now?”

Her fingertips brush against my collarbone and my stomach muscles contract as her hand pulls on the neck of my shirt to bring me closer.

“I sure hope so.”

CHAPTER 24

Part-Time Lover

REBECCA

In one swift movement he scoops me up at the thighs and tosses me over his shoulder. My surprised shriek echoes off the water and a flock of birds take flight on the opposite bank. "James!" I giggle. "Put me down, I'm too heavy to carry around."

He's heading back toward the van and my heart starts to pound. "Oh please, if you were any lighter you would blow away on a light breeze."

Plunking me down next to the sliding door of the van, he opens it, then turns to me.

"Speaking of which, how's our deal going?" he asks.

"Huh?" I've been so preoccupied with the way his fingers had gripped my thighs that it takes me a minute to remember what he's talking about.

He faces me with a serious expression. "You've been eating more, right?"

My face drops. "I've been trying, I swear, but . . ."

"But what?"

My eyebrows pull together with the shame of it. "My mom packs my lunches and stuff. I can only eat what she gives me."

His face pulls back, his brows furrowing. “So . . . then you eat everything she gives you.”

My hand shakes. He doesn’t get it. That my mom insists that restricting my food is the way to be closer to God.

“Becks?”

“She usually only makes . . . a small amount.”

His head twists to the side. “What do you mean, a small amount?”

“Please . . . I—I can’t—”

He lets out a huge sigh and opens the driver’s side door, reaching up to fold down the sun visor where a new pack of cigarettes falls into his hand.

“No!” I say, my hand darting out to push them away.

He pulls out of my grasp and opens the pack. “That was the deal.”

I watch anxiously as he tears into the pack, pulls a cigarette out and places it between his teeth, his eyes scanning my face before he pulls a lighter from his pocket.

“Wait!”

He stops, eyebrows lifting and waiting for me to continue.

My knee bounces and I huff out a short burst of air. “Hand me my backpack,” I say.

Eyeing me a little suspiciously, he leans over the seat into the car, the next moment he pulls my bag out to hand to me. Opening it, I grab the paper bag my mom gave me for lunch today and hold it out for him.

“What’s this?” he asks.

“My lunch.” My voice treacherously cracks on the delivery.

He slowly reaches out and takes it, opening the bag and peering inside. For a moment he’s confused, tilting the bag back and forth, but I know what he’ll find in there.

“Where’s the rest?” he asks.

I swallow hard. “That’s it.”

His hand clenches around the bag and he tears the unlit cigarette from his mouth. "Your mom sends you to school with half a granola bar for lunch?"

I'm not going to cry. I'm not, even though my eyes are burning as I nod my head.

James face contorts, his nose scrunching and his fist comes up to his mouth. "Rebecca . . ." he says, voice quieting, "why—why would your mom only give you—"

"Look, it's fine," I say, snatching the bag away from him. "I just . . . I don't get any spending money so I'm stuck eating whatever I get and that usually means it's not much. So I'm just saying, it might be hard for me to eat as much as you expect."

It's quiet, and I avoid his eyes, tucking the paper bag away into my backpack. For a long moment we stand in silence. Even the birds have stopped chirping. I should just climb into the front seat so he can take me home. I may not be what he expected but I don't think he expected me to be this damaged and maybe it's too much for him. Then I feel his hands wrap around my shoulders and I'm being pulled into his chest. His hair tickles my face and my shoulders shudder as I sink into him. The few tears I've been holding back escape down my cheeks. My hands weave around his waist, and I squeeze. Terrified that if he lets me go I'll never recover.

"Becks . . . I'm sorry. I didn't know. That's . . . that's messed up."

My fingers clench a little harder. The smell of him is so soothing and for the first time in a long while, I feel safe.

"You can have some of my lunch, okay? Noreen always packs me too much. I'll split it with you," he says, whispering into my hair.

I shake my head and tilt my face up to look at him. "No, it's fine, I don't—"

"Let me watch you eat so I don't kill myself by smoking, all right?"

I sniff and nod. "Okay."

He turns and sits me down on the carpeted edge of the open sliding door. For the first time, I look at the inside of the back of his van. It's actually really nice. There's a mattress with lots of thick blankets and fluffy pillows. A small fridge and fold-down counter. The walls of the van are tufted leather. It's all a little imperfect, like he did it himself. Maybe he did.

"Did you upholster the inside of your van?" I ask as he grabs his bag from the front seat.

"Oh, yeah . . . last year most of the courses I wanted to take at school were full so they stuffed me into the home-ec class." He appears from around the door, his paper lunch bag in hand. "The ladies weren't exactly thrilled that I was there at first, but I actually learned a lot. Like how to do some cooking and sewing and shit. When my mom was in the hospital, I spent most of the time making the buttons for in here." He points to the walls where the hundreds of leather covered buttons crease the fabric.

"Did you buy the van yourself?"

"I saved for the down payment myself. Then after my mom died, I basically sold anything and everything worth any money from our apartment to pay off the balance. So she's all mine now." He affectionately pats the door frame.

"I have to say, you are full of surprises, James Walton," I say, smiling.

He sighs as he plunks down next to me on the edge of the door. Pulling out his own paper bag, which appears full to the brim, he retrieves a wrapped-up sandwich. He tears off the plastic wrap and hands me half. "Here. Turkey sandwich."

I take the sandwich in my hands, looking at all of the layers while he bites into his half next to me. There's piles of turkey, cheese, mayo, tomato, lettuce, and my hands start to shake as I think about all of the calories, not to mention the bread. James is watching me now, so I take as deep a breath as I can and bite into it.

The taste explodes on my tongue. I've had turkey plenty before, but never this good. My eyelids slowly close, and a moan of delight escapes my throat as I chew. The tang of the mayonnaise and tomato mixed with the savory turkey is like heaven in my mouth.

"Yeah, I could watch you eat all day." James chuckles in my ear.

I swallow and open my eyes. "You say that, until I end up as big as a house."

He purses his lips and shakes his head. "You've gotta knock that off, Becks. I get why you probably think that with your mom and the shit she's doing to you, but you're gorgeous. You'd be gorgeous even with an extra twenty, thirty, hell, even fifty pounds on you."

My heart swells as my stomach twists. "Well, hopefully everyone else thinks so too, because I'll end up having to come to school naked. I already don't fit into my clothes since we made our deal on Saturday."

His brows furrow. "What are you talking about?" he asks through a mouthful of food.

"I . . ." I press my lips together and feel the blush spread across my cheeks all the way to my ears.

"What is it?"

I wave at my back, where my sweater is covering the broken zipper of my dress, moisture building up in my eyes. My knee begins to bounce, and James slides a little closer to me, the backs of his knuckles brushing against my burning cheek. "It's okay, you can tell me."

I sniff, look up and take a shaky breath. "The zipper . . . on the back of my dress—the zipper popped open."

"Oh. I hardly think you gained so much weight in two days that your zipper broke because of it. It's probably just faulty."

I don't say anything, but I take another mouthwatering bite of sandwich. I can already feel the tightness of my dress around my waist as my stomach fills with food.

"Is that why you wanted to ditch school?"

My eyes shoot up. "No! I mean . . . partly, but . . . no." I would never want him to think I didn't want to be here with him.

He takes a bite too, then sighs after a minute."Do you want me to try and fix it? I mean, I'm no zipper expert, but I can try."

Biting down on my lower lip I think for a moment. I am going to have to go home later and the conversation I'll have to endure over a popped zipper won't be remotely pleasant if last time is anything to go by.

"Okay."

I pop the last bit of sandwich into my mouth and chew while unbuttoning my cardigan. Pulling my arms out, I can feel his eyes watching my every movement. I feel the cool air on the exposed skin of my back as I fold up the sweater and set it down next to me. James finishes his half of his sandwich and brushes his hands off before shifting on the edge of the van to turn to me. I reach over and pull my hair over my shoulder so it's not in the way, revealing the gigantic hole in my dress. Turning my back to him, his knee bumps into my backside as he shuffles closer.

Then his fingers brush against the exposed skin of my back, and I shiver. Goosebumps spread all over my body all the way to the crown of my head.

"Hmm, okay . . ."

He tugs on the zipper, but it doesn't budge. Yanking it up and down doesn't do anything and all I can think about right now is getting out of this dress. Realizing I'll never be able to get out of this thing on my own. A phantom slap on my cheek makes my heart race, the feeling I had of utter hopelessness as my mom stood over me resurfacing.

"James, forget it—"

"It . . . won't . . . budge . . ." he mutters, the pull of the fabric tightening around my chest. "Also, why is this so tight? Jesus, can you even breathe in this thing?"

The combination of his touch and the pulling around my ribs is making it hard to breathe. Like I'm buried alive in my own clothes. Still trapped even outside of my bedroom's four walls. Trapped by everything and everyone except him. My larynx tightens and my head feels light.

"I think you should buy some new clothes, Becks."

I shake my head. "I can't . . . my mom"—*gasp*—"she makes them all." The effort to form the words is dwindling and my heart feels like a frantic animal desperately trying to escape my chest as the tufted leather buttons on the wall start to spiral.

"What is this? Little House on the Prairie? Has she never heard of a department store before?"

I'm going to be stuck in this dress forever. I'll be married in it—buried in it. My mom is going to slap me again. Oh no, what if she tells my dad? Will they call for the black van to take me away while I suffocate in this dress?

"Becks, are you okay?"

It feels like a noose is slowly tightening around my neck. A ringing fills my ears and I grope behind me to grab onto him. Things start to go fuzzy but clear as day is the face of my mother with her hand raised. Then there's my dad's disappointed look of disdain as he glares at me down his nose from above. The eyes of the congregation at Holy Grace watching me as I sink into the shadows of the cross on the altar.

"Becks, can you hear me?"

What if this is all a mistake? Maybe I shouldn't have confronted Eric. . . Now I've missed school and I've eaten something bad. Maybe that makes me bad. God is punishing me. He's watching all of this—there's no hiding from him.

My chest is spasming, the zipper digs into my back and James is in front of me, saying . . . something. He looks so worried, but I don't want him to worry. I want him to look happy and relaxed again, I just can't get the words to reassure him to come out.

The edges of my vision darken. I think I'm going to faint again. James looks down at my chest, his mouth moves but I can't hear anything. Everything spins and I'm falling back.

Rip!

Gravity catches me and my hand shoots out to catch me as the leafy green and tufted leather world comes back into focus. There's a rush of blood to my head as air enters my lungs.

"Breathe . . . breathe . . ."

There's a warm hand on my face, and another around my waist, the ringing in my ears subsides as his thumb strokes my cheek.

"I'm so sorry, Becks, but you were panicking and you couldn't breathe. You were so pale and your lips were almost blue. I had to rip it."

I can hear James's shallow panicked breaths and I can't stop the tears now as I hold myself up on shaking arms. I should feel embarrassed, but I'm just so relieved. Relieved to be able to breathe for a moment. Relieved that he's here. That someone finally knows.

I flinch as something touches me, only it's soft and warm. James lays my sweater over top of my shoulders, his hand gently rubbing my back through the fabric. Then I feel him pull me against him. His arms wrap around my disheveled and tormented body, pulling us further into the van. He leans against the opposite wall and I fit between his legs, curled up like a child as his hand smoothes down my hair soothingly. The rhythm of his heartbeat pulses against my spine, allowing my sobs to slowly extinguish and my breathing to level out. My head tips back against his chest as my heart falls into step with his.

"It's why you don't cross your arms," he whispers. "Because the clothes are too tight. Because they're *made* too tight."

I nod, the reality of what my mom does to me too horrible to say out loud.

"And . . . it's why you sit the way you do. Like a statue. Because that bitch puts you in a straight jacket every time you leave the house."

The shame of it all settles into my skin, and I close my eyes as I wait for the moment that he finally says he's had enough. That he has his own problems and can't possibly take on mine too. But he doesn't. He's just quiet and continues to hold me.

"James, I'm such a mess . . ." I whisper.

His chin nuzzles into the crook of my shoulder and his nose glides over my neck, his breath sending a shiver through me. "I like your mess."

CHAPTER 25

Beat It

REBECCA

I press up onto my knees and spin around to face him. And I'm suddenly so overwhelmed with the urge to kiss him. For a moment, we look at each other, then I'm surging forward, my lips touching his and it's like a tidal wave crashing in my chest. The horrible thoughts of all of the Teens for Christ purity meetings, the countless hours of bible study, the daily prayers to prove I'm worthy of Jesus's love surge upward from the depths of my memory. Shame and terror for what I'm doing right now clawing at me like some dark creature threatening to pull me under the surface. But I kick against it. Kick toward that shimmering surface as his lips move hungrily over mine. Then his tongue runs along my bottom lip and I break through to the other side.

Some wanton, animalistic need is driving me as our tongues meet, and that throbbing sinful sensation returns between my legs. I lean into his chest, my fingers pulling at the fabric of his sleeves as his hands settle on my waist. My hands trace their way up his arms, over his strong shoulders, to wrap around his neck. Our noses brush against each other, the desire to get closer and closer an overwhelming addiction. My fingers tangle in the hair at the base of his neck, twisting and pulling a little on the strands as he groans against my mouth. His hair is so soft.

The sounds he makes cause my entire body to pulse. He tastes like that delicious turkey sandwich, and I gasp against his mouth as his fingers tighten on my skin. One hand slides down my waist to run down the back of my thigh, under my skirt, and my breath hitches. My face pulls back for just long enough to catch his gaze. His eyes are black, pupils blown wide and hooded in shadow but burning like coal.

Never looking away from me, he pulls my leg over his thigh and with his hand still on my waist, pushes me down to sit on him. My eyes grow wide as I realize the only thing between my throbbing core and his leg is my underwear. But the pressure there feels so delicious that my eyes close, and my head tips back and away from him. His lips press against my jaw, my neck, and soon I'm panting. The sound of it loud in the back of the van. Kissing was never like this with Eric. I never even dreamed it could be like this. It feels like insanity—like the most glorious sin.

"James," I breathe.

His lips break away from where they're latched onto the hollow of my throat. "Do you want to stop?"

"No. It's so . . ." His fingers tighten on my leg, and my hips buck against his thigh. I gasp. The chain from his wallet directly beneath where my pulse is throbbing relentlessly between my legs. "Oh—"

He kisses me again, sucking my bottom lip into his mouth and I think maybe this is what it's like to be possessed. The noises coming out of me are unlike anything I've ever heard before. But that chain, oh, that chain on his thigh is hitting exactly the right spot. Heat spreads across my whole body, and a moment later I'm pulling my sweater off of me. I'm burning up, my own private preview of what awaits me in the afterlife for allowing myself to get swept up by him. It feels too good to care right now. The air against my bare back where my dress is still torn open offers me momentary relief before his fingers move from my thigh to trace up my spine.

"Becks . . ."

His fingers on my hip are lightly pushing and pulling, and with a sudden burst of clarity, I realize I'm grinding against his thigh. The tightness and pressure in my belly building like it was Saturday night when I'd touched myself in front of him. Only this time it builds so much quicker. Like I've been on the edge of it for days. My heart is pounding like the drum beat of the music he loves so much. I gasp, stopping my movement and pulling away from his mouth, embarrassment washing over me. But James's gaze is boring into mine, his grip tightening on my hip and back.

"Don't you dare stop," he says. His voice is lower than I've ever heard it. It's commanding and sends a jolt of electricity all the way through my veins to settle in that throbbing center. The fact that he's here, touching and kissing me, rather than twelve feet away has every nerve crackling and ready to explode. He lifts his thigh, pressing it harder against me and my breath stutters, my toes curling in my shoes as my sweaty forehead presses against his.

"James," I gasp, my fingers digging into his shoulders as I race toward that peak.

His hands grip my face as I continue to chase this unbelievable feeling on his muscled thigh. "Come on, Becks. Fall apart for me."

I tip over the edge. Like falling off a cliff, my muscles spasm and my legs tremble. Clinging to him with sharp panting gasps, stars burst behind my eyelids, pleasure ricocheting through my body like thousands of tiny bullets. I'm floating outside of my own body and time seems to stand still. Then I open my eyes to find James staring at me.

"I . . . I—"

His mouth crashes against mine, arms wrapping around my body to squeeze me tight. I slump against him, all of my limbs feeling heavy. My cheek resting on his shoulder as I come down, my breathing returning to normal.

"Are you okay?" James asks quietly, his voice rough.

"I didn't know it would be like that," I whisper.

He pushes my face back to look at him, his brow furrowed. "Have you *never* . . . ?"

I shake my head. His eyes soften and he kisses me gently before pulling me back in. I smile for a second before I cringe with shame. I feel like the biggest idiot in the world. What must he think of me? Will God forgive me? "I'm so embarrassed."

James pushes me back, gripping my chin in his hand to look me in the eyes. "Don't be. That was the hottest fucking thing I've ever seen."

I scoff with disbelief, but he rolls his hips beneath me and I feel . . . it. My mouth drops open and my eyebrows lift as I feel his hardness against the top of my thigh.

"Oh," I stammer. I look down and see the bulge in his jeans, the way James's eyes flutter with every movement I make against it. Does he want me to touch it? Should I touch it? What do I do? He's probably waiting for me to do something for him, right? But I have no idea what I'm doing.

Nervously, I reach down, but just before I touch him, his hand captures my wrist.

"You don't have to do that," he says.

"But, I—"

He shakes his head. "No, this was about you. I was the first person to see you come. To see you fall apart and—fuck. If I died right now, I'd be okay with that."

My face burns with a mixture of embarrassment and feeling unbelievably desired. "But you didn't . . ."

"Don't worry." He swallows, his Adam's apple bobbing deliciously. "I can take care of that later."

I'm not sure where it comes from. Maybe it's because I've never felt more safe with anyone else before. Or maybe it's because I'm still riding the high of my first orgasm after humping his thigh like a wild animal. Except I feel beautiful, dirty, and brazen all at once. "Or you could take care of it now."

"What do you mean?"

"I mean . . . I could watch. Like the other night? I've thought about nothing else all weekend. What you looked like when—" My eyes flick down for a second then back up. "Show me what you do. Show me how you do it . . . so I know for next time."

Something flares across his eyes. "Next time?"

He promised me casual fun until graduation. And surely this —today—is the most fun I've ever had. I nod.

"You sure?"

Nodding again, I gently kiss his lips. "Yes."

His face flushes like he's nervous but he takes a deep breath. Reaching between us, he unbuttons the top of his jeans and a fresh wave of excitement skitters across my skin, my finger freezing from where his hair curls around it.

"You should play with my hair some more," he whispers. His lips brush along my jaw as he unzips his black jeans.

I push my fingers into his beautiful mess of dark curls exposing his ears and the side of his neck. Leaning down, I press my lips to his jaw. The sound of his sigh and his breath on my collarbone causes heat to spread all over me again. The shuffling of his pants against my thigh alerts me that this is really happening. That I can watch.

"Becks?"

His right hand grasps my chin. "Yeah?"

"Can you do something for me?"

Is he going to ask me to touch him? Part of me wants him to.

Part of me wants to finally look down, to take him in, to participate in what he's about to do. "Sure."

"Suck on my fingers, angel," he says.

I think I've stopped breathing. The request is so foreign to me, but it's like my body has been dying to do exactly that. I open my mouth wide, my tongue pushing out before his fingers slide into my mouth, and for the first time, I'm holding back a string of curse words. Because this is the most erotic thing that's ever happened to me, and as James groans and my lips close around his long fingers, I feel that aching need come back to life between my legs.

"*Fuck*," he mutters. "Open up."

I open my mouth, and he removes his fingers, a string of saliva still connecting them to my mouth.

"Such a good girl."

I whimper at his praise, not fully understanding why it makes me tremble all over. But then I feel his hand reach down between us and James's eyes roll back in his head and his mouth drops open. And for a few minutes, I just watch his face, twirling my fingers around in his hair like he wanted me to, because his face is so euphoric I can't look away.

His teeth bite together and he hisses. I'm pulled from my daze, finally glancing down at that part of him that's been so elusive to me ever since I learned what sex was. I'm shaking, worried it'll scare me, all the warning tales we've been told at church about the male body skipping through my mind on a loop, but when I see James's fist wrapped around his length, something primal switches in my brain. And it's not scary in the slightest, simply fascinating, and maybe a little intimidating and not at all like how that medical textbook depicted.

His hand sliding up and down over himself has me hypnotized and clenching my thighs around his leg. I barely register that my tongue is swirling around my own two fingers before they're halfway down toward their final destination. When my fingers touch his hand, James's eyes shoot wide open. I touch him and he gasps. The skin is soft and hot as I wrap my hand around him, the saliva making it easier for my small hand to slide down his length.

"Becks—"

I lean forward and kiss him. Pouring all of the desire I have for him into this kiss and after a moment, I feel his hand on top of mine. He moves our hands up and down and up and down in the rhythm he craves. As I suck on his lip, another moan leaves him, and I swallow it down. I feel his hands tighten around my ribcage and that's when I realize he's not guiding me anymore, both of his hands on me instead. And the sounds he's making are because of me, and me alone.

A few more strokes and his hips buck forward and I watch his beautiful face contort. He groans and pants, his teeth sinking into his bottom lip and his fingers pinch a touch too hard around my ribs causing me to gasp sharply. I feel something wet and slippery and I look down where his semen is spilled all over my hand.

I dare not move. I'm worried if I say something then this will all come crashing down around me, so I simply watch his face. Watch as his quick breaths start to slow and the tension in his forehead disappears. Finally, he opens his eyes.

"Shit," he mutters, reaching to the side to grab what looks like an old towel. "Sorry, Becks, didn't mean to get my cum all over you."

I blink and tear my eyes away to look into his face. "Cum?"

"Yeah, just—" His eyes narrow, finally catching on to my confusion. "The uh, the semen, it's called cum in every other context than the medical kind."

"Oh." I lift my leg off of him so he can clean up but when I look down there's a dark wet stain on his jeans. With horror I realize that my underwear is damp and, oh no, did I pee myself? "I . . . I—"

"Don't worry about that. It's perfectly normal. Don't be embarrassed," he pleads.

My face burns and I likely look like a tomato. "I'm so—"

"Don't you dare say you're sorry," James says. "You're not ruined, okay? You're perfect."

Something about the way he's looking at me now feels so intimate. And while I'm still embarrassed, I find myself wanting to believe him. But as one emotion fades, another takes its place. The guilt starts to flood in. Like a dam that I've been holding for too long. Guilt and shame bubbling up under the surface. I lost control of myself here in this van with James, and while I don't regret anything that happened, I'm anxious about it.

"Come here," he says, pulling me into his chest again and pulling my cardigan overtop of me like a blanket. He kisses the top of my head and entwines my fingers with his.

"James, are you sure that's, well, normal?" I ask, my eyes locked on the wet patch of denim.

He smirks. "Yes. Don't worry about it, angel. Maybe next time you can do it on my fingers."

CHAPTER 26

Material Girl

JAMES

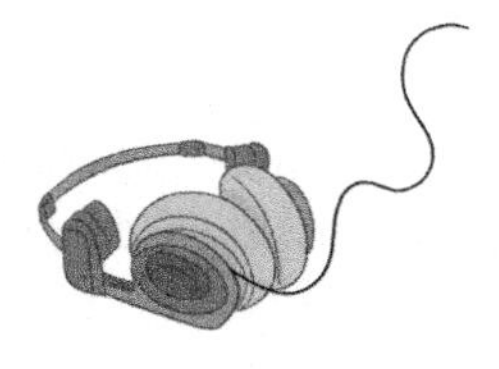

Rebecca never ceases to surprise me. She humps my thigh only to help jerk me off a few minutes later. I was just expecting to make out, maybe feel her up, but it's like she's speeding toward a finish line somewhere I can't see.

The reminder of our agreement floats to the surface. Casual, until graduation. Is that why this all happened? But then there's also the way she hides what's going on in her own house. That fucked up shit with her mom. The bitch who starves her own daughter and forces her into clothing that's so fucking tight she can barely breathe. It makes me want to kick down their front door and smack some sense into them.

I wonder what the father thinks of it all. I already know he's an asshole and seems hell-bent on controlling everything around him. Maybe he knows.

"James?"

I look down where Rebecca is cuddled up next to me on the bench seat as I drive back toward home. She's got her sweater back on, her hand tangled up in my right one and her face nuzzled into my chest.

"Yeah?"

"I'm terrified to go home," she whispers.

My heart aches. "Because of your dress?"

She's quiet but eventually nods.

"Listen, I have an idea about that," I say. I've been thinking about it since my mind cleared from my post-orgasm bliss. "I was thinking I could ask Noreen if she has any extra clothes you could borrow. They might be a bit big on you, but at least you'd be able to be comfortable."

She turns her green eyes up at me. "My mom won't let me leave the house in anything she doesn't approve of, James."

I shrug. "So wear what she wants and the moment you're out of sight of the house, I'll be here in the van and you can change."

"You'd do that for me?"

"Of course."

She blinks, her long eyelashes fluttering, then pushes up to kiss my cheek. "Thank you. So does this mean you're also planning on driving me to school?"

I smile. "Of course. If I only get a few weeks, I want to spend every minute I can with you." She opens her mouth, her eyes widening, so I quickly add. "Don't worry, I can be discreet." I don't very much like the idea of being a secret, but . . . if that's the only option, I'll deal with it.

A gorgeous pink blush spreads across her nose and cheeks. "Okay."

"Oh, by the way, I have an audition tomorrow. I have to leave a bit early from school to make it there. Do you want to come?"

Her eyebrows lift. "An audition?"

I nod. "Yeah, for a band. They need a guitarist."

"Does that mean I'll finally get to hear you play?" she asks, eyes brightening.

I tilt my head down. "Desperate to hear me shred on a guitar, angel?"

She nods. "Yes."

My cock twitches in my jeans at the eager look on her face. “Then, yeah, you’ll get to see me play.”

She settles back into my chest, letting go of my hand to wrap around my waist. And maybe it’s because I’ve been so starved for affection for most of my life, but the thought of having to say goodbye to her in a few weeks makes my stomach turn. The other girls hadn’t been like this. For them, it was purely lust, attraction —they didn’t care because they were too cool and I thought I was too. But Rebecca is different. Her touch is soft and maybe it’s because I’ve gotten to know her, but she’s dug in like a tick under my skin. I kiss the top of her head, the flowery scent of her hair staining my memory.

As we approach our street, I pull over on the side of the road. “This is where I’ll be tomorrow morning to pick you up, okay?”

She sits up and nods.

“Here,” I say, lifting her backpack up. “You can run right upstairs when you get in the door so she won’t see the hole in the back.” I pinned the top with a safety pin, but the dress still pulls open.

Rebecca nods, pulling the bag over her shoulders. It does a good job at hiding the problem as long as someone isn’t staring for too long. I smooth her hair down and say, “There. She won’t notice.”

She’s quiet for a while. Her fingers fiddle nervously with the fabric of my shirt. Maybe it’s because she’s terrified to go home to those monsters. Or maybe she just doesn’t want to leave me. I hope it’s the latter.

“Thanks for everything today,” she says finally. “I had a great time.”

“Me too.”

I pull her to me and kiss her deeply. A goodbye kiss with the promise of more tomorrow. And with each passing second that her lips are touching mine, I feel like she's healing all the rotten parts of my life and replacing them one by one with joy.

I watch her until she's too far around the bend to see anymore then wait some more. Taking a deep breath, my hand glides down my face. This day has been a whirlwind, and I'm still not entirely sure it's not a dream. And while I know I should be overjoyed by the fact that I've managed to land myself in the perfect situation with Rebecca, I can't help but feel a touch of disappointment that she doesn't see a future with me. Then again, no one ever has, so why am I so surprised?

I finally pull into the driveway as the sun starts to dip low above the horizon. My stomach flutters nervously, hoping she made it inside okay.

"James?"

As I close the front door behind me, Noreen peers around the entrance to the living room where she's listening to *Dreams* by Fleetwood Mac.

"Hey," I say, sitting down in the living room trying to figure out how best to approach my request.

"I ordered pizza for dinner. You good with that? I wasn't in the mood to cook today."

I nod my head. "Yeah, pizza sounds great."

"Principal Jeffries called me into the school today."

My muscles tense.

"Some more vandalism at the school."

"I swear it's not me." I sigh, sure she won't believe a word of it.

She smiles. "Don't worry, James, I believe you."

"You do?"

"Of course. You haven't given me any reason not to trust you. If you say you didn't do it, that's good enough for me."

Something tightens in my chest. No adult has ever said they trust me before. "Thank you."

"Besides." She smirks. "I saw the polaroids of the damage and . . . those pentagrams look like they were drawn by amateurs."

I snort out a laugh, and Noreen laughs too. She's in a good mood. Maybe now is the best time to ask her for help. "Umm . . . Noreen? I wanted to ask for your help with something."

"What with?"

I know she's not a fan of the Briars. What if she refuses to help? "I need help with a girl."

She freezes. "Oh no. I didn't think we needed to have that talk—"

Realization hits me like a brick to the face. "Oh! No! Oh my God, no. It's Becks." Noreen's eyes widen and her eyebrows shoot up and . . . shit . . . I just called her Becks, didn't I? "I mean, Rebecca."

She arches an eyebrow. "Becks?"

I can't hide the heat spreading across my face. Noreen's eyes close in one long fluid motion. "James, you say you have no interest in making friends, then you pick her? Of all people?"

"No, it's not like that," I start, but then clamp my mouth shut, realizing I'm just going to open a can of worms for Noreen to sift through.

It clicks, and her face becomes deadly serious. "Oh, James, no . . ."

I hold my hand up. "I know what you're thinking, but—"

"You best hope you don't know what I'm thinking, because I'm thinking that"—she looks over at the window then lowers her voice—"I'm thinking that you're getting it on with the absolute worst possible person for you."

"She's not! And we're not . . . I mean, not *that*, I just—" I'm stumbling over my words, digging myself deeper and deeper into the hole of shit I've landed myself in.

Noreen heaves a heavy sigh. "This is only going to end very badly."

"She needs help."

She pinches the bridge of her nose. "What do you mean?"

"I mean, her mom is starving her. Making her wear clothes that are so tight she can't even breathe properly."

Noreen's face pales a little and there's a long pause as her eyes scan my face for the truth. "Are you being serious right now?"

"I wanted to ask you if you have any old clothes you wouldn't mind lending her. I'm trying to help her eat more because she's fainted—twice. But she's got very limited options, since her mom is a sadistic bitch."

She crosses her arms over her chest and bites on her fingernails. Finally, she nods and drops her arms. "All right, I'll help."

Hope floods through me. "Can you call someone?" I ask, thinking out loud. "Like, isn't that child abuse?"

Noreen shakes her head. "If she's over eighteen, child services won't help anymore, and . . . I'm not sure if calling the police is a good idea either since her father and his friends are all buddy-buddy with the cops." She sighs. "I'll try and find out if there's something we can do, okay? In the meantime, I have some things you can give her."

I smile and rush over to throw my arms around her and squeeze. She chuckles into my shoulder and when I release her, she's pink in the face.

"You really are just like her, you know?" At my confused look, she explains. "Like your mom. She was always trying to help people too. Except—"

She cuts herself off and her face darkens a moment later. "Except what?"

The doorbell rings, and Noreen stands abruptly. "That'll be the pizza," she says, striding over to the kitchen and grabbing her purse. I want to press Noreen about what she means, but she takes her time paying the delivery guy then disappears into the kitchen again.

"Hey, Noreen?" I ask, walking into the kitchen. "What did you—"

"I'll pull a couple of things for Rebecca tonight before I go to sleep," she says through a mouthful of pizza, effectively bringing our earlier conversation to a close. "Just promise me one thing?"

"What's that?"

"Be careful with . . . whatever it is you're doing with her." Noreen hands me a plate and spins the pizza box toward me.

"Don't worry, I will."

REBECCA'S all smiles as she sits with her friends in the cafeteria at lunch today. Thankfully her mom hadn't noticed the broken zipper and Noreen came through spectacularly with a whole bag full of stuff for Rebecca to try on. She nearly broke down in tears as she sifted through the bag, ultimately settling on a multicolored pastel button-down shirt and a pair of jeans, which of course were too big on her, but she tightened them at the waist with a wide black belt.

Respecting her wishes to stay discreet, I sit at a table nearby. It's close enough that I can hear her conversation but far enough that any onlookers won't think that there's anything going on between us.

"You look amazing today, Becca," Amy says.

Rebecca grins at the compliment. "Thanks!"

"Where did you disappear to yesterday?" her friend asks her. "I didn't see you in Calc after lunch."

Rebecca shrugs. "I wasn't feeling well so I went for a walk around town."

"Were you sick? Or just upset about Eric?"

My spine stiffens.

"I'd rather not talk about that."

"Well, we're going to," Mary interjects, and for once I'm glad that Mary doesn't take no for an answer. "You find out Eric is cheating on you, skip an entire afternoon of school which you've never done before, then today you waltz in here looking like you haven't got a care in the world."

Wait, Eric was cheating on Rebecca? Is that what they were talking about yesterday? Is that why she needed to get away from school and came to me? Something sours in my stomach at the thought that she only spent yesterday with me because she needed to get away from her cheating asshole ex-boyfriend. Was everything that happened in my van by the lake simply because she was upset about what Eric did?

"Mary, all you need to know is I've simply decided that I don't want to spend the last few weeks of high school not doing exactly what I want, when I want, since that's what Eric's doing. I'm not going to sit around sulking about his bad choices when he obviously doesn't think about me when he makes them. And yesterday? I did *exactly* what I wanted."

While I can't see Mary's face, I can imagine her dropped jaw and shocked expression, and I smile—glad that Rebecca is finally standing up for herself. And partly because *I'm* what Rebecca wanted.

"We were just worried about you," Amy says, "but you seem . . . great actually. Happy."

My chest swells, a burst of pride bubbling upward at the thought that maybe I've contributed to that happiness. Not only that, but Rebecca looks relaxed for once. Comfortable in her skin.

"Thanks, Amy, I feel great."

"I don't think I've ever seen you in pants before. Isn't that . . . like . . . against the rules of your church?"

Rebecca takes a bite out of her turkey sandwich. Noreen had

made an entire extra lunch for her when she handed me the bag of clothes this morning, and I nearly crushed her with a hug.

"Yeah, sort of. Don't tell my mom, okay?" Rebecca tells her friends. "You know what she's like, and I'm sick of being her little doll to dress up."

"I have to say," Mary says, crossing her arms and leaning back from the table. "I'm kind of enjoying this new version of you, Becca. Does this mean you might actually come to a party?"

Rebecca shrugs her shoulders a bit, her eyes flicking over to me for a split second. "If I can convince my parents to let me stay out that late. I still have no interest in drinking or anything like that, but . . . yeah, I think I might."

Mary claps her hands together. "Yay! It'll do you so much good to get out there and just let your hair down! We can dance and play games and . . . well, okay no alcohol, but you can pretend. I make a mean Shirley Temple."

A snort bursts out of me, and Mary and Amy look around at the noise. Mary places a hand on her hip, her eyes narrowing at me.

"Something funny, Walton?"

I grin. "Quite a few things are funny, actually. I have to say though, I'd pay good money to see little miss goody-two-shoes over here let loose over a Shirley Temple."

Rebecca's eyes flash mischievously. The corner of her mouth twitches as she suppresses a grin, but she doesn't say anything.

"That would mean you'd have to come to one of our lame parties," Mary says. "And you're too busy for that, right?"

I pop a cheese puff into my mouth and chew. "I could maybe change my schedule with enough notice."

Rebecca holds my gaze for a long moment before looking down and taking the last bite of her sandwich. Mary, on the other hand, looks murderous.

"Freak," I hear her mutter under her breath. Ironic that Mary uses that word when less than a week ago she was tripping over herself practically begging me to meet up with her at that party. I salute them all before walking away, spotting the tiniest hint of a smile gracing Rebecca's mouth.

"YOU WEAR pants for one day and all of a sudden you're agreeing to go to parties?"

My arms snake around Rebecca's belted waist, my nose grazing the shell of her ear as she comes up to the far side of the van. I feel the sudden tension in her body relax when she realizes it's me behind her. She leans into my chest, her hands closing overtop of mine.

"You said you'd pay good money to see me let loose. How much are we talking here, Walton?"

I place a kiss behind her ear and feel her shiver against me. "If it's anything like how you looked yesterday in the back of my van, then that shit is priceless."

She spins in my arms and presses up onto her tiptoes to kiss me, her smell overwhelming my senses. Her fingers push into my hair and her touch sizzles my skin. My heart begins to race and I feel the overwhelming urge to throw her in the back and kiss every inch of her skin that I can right here in the parking lot. But . . . I have somewhere to be.

"We've got to go, angel."

Her face is flushed, she's breathless, and her hooded eyes look up at me through long lashes. "Okay."

"Don't worry, I'll kiss you senseless later," I say, opening the door for her.

"Promise?"

I chuckle as I help her climb in. "Promise."

We're quiet on the drive toward The Shipwreck. My knee bounces and my hands grip the steering wheel a bit too hard.

"Are you all right?" she asks, placing her hand on my knee to settle it.

I nod stiffly. "Yeah, just a bit nervous."

She grins. "You? Nervous? I was under the impression James Walton never got nervous."

I laugh in spite of myself. "For all my confident demeanor, I do still get nervous sometimes. Everyone else will likely be much older than me, more experienced . . ."

Rebecca brushes my hair aside to kiss my neck. "You'll be great."

"Now who's confident?"

She shrugs and laughs. "Maybe it's the pants."

I laugh loudly. "Must be." Her earlier conversation in the cafeteria springs to mind. "Hey, Becks?"

"Yeah?"

"Why didn't you tell me Eric cheated on you?"

She looks out the window at the passing cars. "Because it didn't matter. I don't want to be with him."

"Yeah but . . . it still hurts."

She shakes her head. "Can we not talk about him?"

I blink at the edge in her voice. "Yeah, sure."

Something tells me there's more going on there, but she just wants casual. Casual relationships don't get into the messy stuff. Even though we've already tackled her eating disorder, parental abuse, and my fucked-up childhood. Somehow, her boyfriend cheating seems to be too much for her.

I pull into the parking lot of The Shipwreck and turn off the ignition amongst a few other vans and cars of likely other musicians here to audition. Rebecca winds her fingers in the lapel of her shirt, her bottom lip tucked behind her teeth.

"Look, are you sure you want to come in? You can stay in the van if you want."

She shakes her head. "Why wouldn't I want to come in and watch you?"

Her smile makes my heart swell.

"It's just . . . this place is a little rough around the edges. And while you seem like a new woman in those pants"—I gesture at her thighs—"I don't want you to be nervous."

She kisses me softly. "I wouldn't miss it for anything."

I grasp her face in my hands and fall deeper into her kiss. The nervous butterflies settle as I focus on her pulse, racing beneath my fingers. Finally, she breaks away and I take a deep breath. "Okay. Come on then."

"Wait!" she says.

Maybe she doesn't want to come after all. "What's wrong?"

She turns on the seat and opens her backpack, pulling out my jacket. Smiling sheepishly, she hands it over. "You should have this back. For luck."

I grin widely, taking the denim jacket from her and pulling it on. It smells like her now, and for that alone I feel lucky. "Thanks."

I help her down out of the van and open the sliding door to pull out my guitar, slinging the strap of the case over my shoulder. I grip her fingers in my hand and pull her toward the bar. Walking in, it's dark compared to the bright sun outside, and I blink as my eyes adjust. I can see John sitting with a stack of papers at the bar. He looks up and sees me, but does a double take when he spots Rebecca. His mouth twitches a bit, but he just nods at us and jerks his head toward the side where the stage is.

There are a few guys sitting at a small table and I recognize Dave, the man I spoke to the other day who hung up the poster. Behind him there are half a dozen guys with guitars and my stomach rolls, like missing a step going downstairs. Rebecca must sense my stress so she squeezes my fingers, and I tug on her arm a bit to pull her closer to me as we walk over.

Dave spots me and rises from his chair, holding out his arm, and I have to drop Rebecca's to shake his hand.

"Hey, it's James, right?" Dave asks.

Out of the corner of my eye, I see Rebecca going to sit at one of the tables near the stage. "Yeah. James Walton."

He grins and turns to the two other guys sitting at the table. "Guys, this is James."

The other two nod in greeting at me but then return to their conversation.

"Don't mind them," Dave says. "Right, well, since you're last here, you'll be at the end."

I nod. "No problem."

Dave's eyes wander over to where Rebecca's sitting. "She your girl?"

I glance over, and while she isn't sitting quite like a statue anymore, there's no denying that her posture is a little more refined than the bar's usual patrons. Smiling at the way she folds a napkin again and again, I nod. "Yeah."

Dave chuckles. "How the fuck did you manage to score Strawberry Shortcake over there?"

I grin widely. "It's a long, complicated story."

Dave shakes his head. "Well, we're about to get started. So get yourself situated."

"Or you could just send all these other posers home."

The two moody band mates stop their hushed conversation to look up at me, and Dave laughs. "If your talent is half as big as your ego, then this is going to be fun."

CHAPTER 27

Dream On

REBECCA

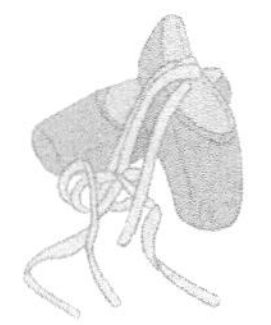

I might not know anything about metal music other than what James has played for me, but even I can tell that the first two guys to audition aren't what the band is looking for. If it weren't for the looks on their faces, all of them trying to hide their true thoughts and failing, then all I'd have to do is glance over at James whose ringed hand is covering his mouth as he tries to hide his laughter.

It isn't necessarily that they're terrible . . . Okay, yes, they're terrible. Plus, they're a bit older, like my dad's age, and don't seem to be playing anything that sounds like what James listens to. After each guy performs, the three band members discuss for a few seconds, then thank the guy for coming out and say that they'll call them. They seem put out by that, as though they know deep down there's no chance they're going to be called.

The next few guys seem a lot more talented. They're playing the type of music I would expect, and the band members sit up straighter in their seats. The next two are sent on their way, but after the fifth one, the band members have a very long conversation and they seem to argue about it. I look past them at

James, who is trying not to stare too much as he fiddles with his guitar.

Gazing over at him, I feel my mouth go dry. I've never seen him standing and wearing the guitar before. He's always been sitting on the edge of his bed, kind of hunched over it. But right now, it's slung low on his hips, the strap pulling on the fabric covering his chest and his forearms are—

"Can you stick around for a bit?" The band member who James spoke to when we got here addresses the guy on the stage.

He nods, and the second-to-last guitarist gets on the stage. Only thirty seconds in and it's clear that he's very good. The band's faces light up and they lean forward in their seats as they watch him. James's face is ultra serious as he observes as well. After a moment, his eyes flick to me and that smug smile pulls up the side of his mouth as he winks.

An entire conservatory of butterflies releases in my belly, and my whole body grows hot. Something about that smile and the way he's holding that guitar makes it difficult to focus on whatever that guy is doing on the small stage. I only have eyes for James, and I'm nearly salivating with the desire to see him get up there and show off.

I've been so caught up in admiring James that I didn't even realize that the sixth guitarist is finished. The band don't even discuss it amongst themselves and ask the sixth guitarist to hang around as well. I wonder what they want them to stay for? Will they make them try again? Maybe play a different song? I bite my nail and say a silent prayer that they like James even more.

It's finally James's turn and my knee is bouncing so hard the table shakes. I wonder if he's still nervous. If he is, he definitely doesn't show it. That cocky smile radiates confidence. There's a touch of feedback as he plugs his guitar into the amplifier then his fingers are moving a mile a minute.

I don't know what song he's playing, or even if he's doing it well, but I cannot take my eyes off of him. I might be biased, but James Walton is unbelievably sexy when he's playing guitar. He also has something that I didn't see in anyone else who got up there today, and that's stage presence. It's like the guitar is an extension of himself. His hair whips about in time with the music, and I don't even think he has his eyes open for most of it.

Realizing I'm gripping the little wooden table so hard my fingers hurt, I finally tear my gaze away from James. The band members are staring at him either slack-jawed or grinning widely, their heads nodding along to the beat. I feel my cheeks pull into a wide smile and look back up at the stage. My teeth sink into my bottom lip as I watch his hands. Thinking about how big they are, how nimble.

Don't worry about it, angel, maybe next time you can do it on my fingers.

His words from yesterday zing through me. My thighs press together at the thought of him touching me. The memory of his face as I helped him get off surface so intensely I close my eyes and drop my head back. All the purity stuff they shove down our throats at church hadn't mentioned just how empowering it would feel to watch James's face as he came. How vulnerable but safe I would feel in his arms. How I felt closer to God in that moment than ever before sitting on the hard wooden pews.

James finishes his song with a loud, dramatic strum of the strings, the neck of the guitar bouncing up and down. He shakes his hair out of his face and looks up at me. My pulse hammers in my chest as I think, maybe, he wanted to impress me too. The difference between him and Eric is startling. While Eric would force me to watch his practices, he barely acknowledged me. James, on the other hand, asked if I wanted to come, made sure I was comfortable coming into this new world and the whole time I've been here he's been looking over at me, checking on me, playing for me. He bites his tongue then smiles and looks over at the band members, who are nodding appreciatively.

"Your boyfriend's pretty talented."

I look up and nearly jump out of my seat. An older man with an eyepatch is standing next to me. I didn't even notice him approach. He was sitting at the bar when we entered, and I have a feeling he probably works here.

I swallow against the lump stuck in my throat at hearing James referred to as my boyfriend. Even though it's not entirely accurate, a warm feeling spreads through me at the sound of it. "Yes, he is."

"I'm John, by the way," he says, holding out a hand. "I own the place."

Smiling a bit nervously, I shake his hand. "So you're James's boss?"

He nods. "Yeah. He's a good kid. Hard worker. I'm a bit surprised he's got a girl like you, if I'm honest."

I'm not quite sure if he means it as a compliment or an insult. Is it that obvious that I'm completely out of my element here? Are James and I so different that it seems impossible to imagine us caring about each other? I shrug. "It's complicated."

"I don't mean no offense, darlin'," he continues. "Kid just seems like he's only got one thing on his mind and that's making it big in music."

"Oh."

"Hard life." At my questioning look, he continues on. "Being a musician, I mean. Always on the go, on tour. Late nights, money's tight or nonexistent unless you make it big. No time for . . . distractions. Not if you want to make it."

"Right," I say. My eyebrows furrow, trying to make sense of what John's telling me.

"Anyway," he says, "I think he could actually make it, don't you?"

I turn my gaze back to James, who is speaking to the band members and the other two guys who were asked to stay behind. His eyes flick over to me and as he smiles, I nearly melt into the floor.

"Yeah, I do."

I BURST out of my chair as James runs over to me, grabbing me around the waist and swinging me around, his lips planting wet, sweaty kisses to my temple.

"You were amazing!" I say into his shoulder as he sets my feet back on the ground.

His grin is so wide as he pulls away from me I find myself matching it. "I can't—I can't believe they picked me."

I place my hand on his cheek. "How could they not? You were clearly the best one up there!"

He laughs nervously. "I don't know about that. I fumbled the bridge a bit—"

"I bet they hardly noticed. I couldn't take my eyes off you," I say, my fist pulling on the front of his shirt.

His smile turns hungry. "Oh, yeah?"

I swallow as his dark eyes take me in, and I'm instantaneously breathless. When I nod, he gives me a quick kiss on the lips and backs away. "You're looking at the newest member of Carnal Sins."

There's a sharp drop in my stomach. I can only imagine my parents' reaction to learning James doesn't just play guitar but now plays in a band called "Carnal Sins".

"I just have to chat with the guys for a few minutes, then I'll make good on that promise from earlier."

The thought of him kissing me senseless causes goosebumps to prickle up all over my body. I'm jittery, bouncing around between sitting and leaning and pacing while he talks to his new bandmates. The anticipation of his lips on mine builds and builds until I'm ready to burst when he says his farewells and waves at John the owner with that crazy huge grin still on his face.

"Ready to go, angel?"

He grasps my hand, interlacing our fingers, and lifts it up to kiss my knuckles. I feel giddy and nod as he pulls me out of the bar, heading for his van.

"I'm so happy for you," I say. "What will happen now?"

James opens the side door and puts his guitar inside before helping me into my seat. The excitement in his voice is tangible. Electric. "Now, I'll be able to play with an actual band. Play for a crowd. Maybe collaborate on some original songs. Maybe it'll be the start of something bigger."

John's words run through my mind, deflating my excitement. *No time for distractions. Not if you want to make it.* But I won't be a distraction. We're just casual. Just having enough fun so it'll sustain me for the rest of my life.

"You all right?"

I inhale as my eyes meet James's and I realize my smile has fallen away. "Sorry, yes . . . I'm just thinking about all the amazing things you're going to do!"

He hops into the seat next to me and starts the engine, his fingers tapping on the steering wheel. A habit, I've noticed, when he's excited or anxious. "I think I promised to kiss you senseless, didn't I?"

My pulse quickens and a smile tugs at my lips. "You did."

"By the way, I have band practice on Saturday afternoon. But I'll still be able to drive you to and from your dance class if you like."

My heart swells. "You thought about that?"

"Of course," he says, lowering his brows. "Why wouldn't I?"

I blink at him, then finally shrug. "I guess I'm just not used to being a priority for anyone."

The smile on his face falters as he pulls my forehead toward him. He places a gentle kiss on my temple and my heart skips.

James pulls into the lot of an old drive-in theater. I remember coming here once as a child, but it's been closed down for a while. After turning off the engine, he grabs my hand and pulls me into him.

My heart starts to race—aware that we're alone and no one knows where we are. The thought of what happened yesterday when we were alone makes the hairs on the back of my neck stand on end and my core start to ache. The thought of him no longer around to bring about this feeling is suddenly terrifying, and I tremble as his hand grips the side of my face.

"Becks?"

My stuttering breath escapes me. "Yeah."

His eyes soften. "We don't have to do anything. Yesterday was a lot. I don't want you to think it always has to be like that."

Simultaneously, I both want him desperately and I'm also frightened that if I give him too much of myself, when he leaves, there'll be nothing left.

"No, it's not like that. I was just thinking . . . What about San Francisco?" I ask, my voice trembling as his fingers trace over my throat. "Will you still leave? Now that you're in the band?"

Something changes in his eyes, but the next moment his lips are against my throat and I gasp, my body arching toward him, into his hands which pull me forward.

"If all goes well," he murmurs, his kisses trailing up my jaw, "then we'll go together."

My heart almost stops at the word "we" but then it plummets when I realize he's talking about the band and not us. This is such a bad idea. I'm falling too hard and too fast for a man who's just going to leave me behind to pursue his amazing dreams. And I'll forever be stuck here with just the memory of him and desperately wishing he had taken me too. But I can't tell him that. Like John said, the life that James wants doesn't include some silly girl with no real knowledge of how the world works trailing after him like a lost puppy. Distracting him from his ambitions. And I want him to have the life he dreams of. At least one of us should get that.

"Will you write to me?" I whisper. "When you're a famous rockstar?"

He pulls back to look at my face. "Would you want me to?"

I grip his wrists and nearly sob, thankfully able to keep the tears from running down my cheeks. "Yes."

There's a beeping noise, and James looks down at his watch. "Shit."

The loss of his touch makes me feel cold, lonely. "What?"

He rubs a hand through his hair. "The audition ran longer than I anticipated. It's five o'clock. I've got to get you home."

Thinking about leaving James right now to go home so I can be dragged to Bible study is such a repulsive thought that my eyes automatically begin to fill with tears.

He places a finger under my chin and tilts my face up. "I promise I'll make it up to you next time," he says.

"I'm holding you to that." Leaning forward, I capture his lips with mine, the salt of my tears mingling with his taste. His arms wrap around me, pulling me into his lap. "Why do I always seem to kiss you when you're crying?" he asks, laughing.

I smile and brush some of the hair away from his face. "For what it's worth, I've never smiled as much as I have since I met you."

"So, I have some new material for us to go over today."

Vivian Corbley gestures to a stack of books behind her on the table. She holds one up in front of her and smiles. "*Embracing Godly Sexuality*," she says proudly before passing out copies around the circle.

I freeze on the metal folding chair. My mother passes me a copy and when our eyes meet, I wish I could shrink down so small that I disappear all together. Am I going to have to discuss sex with my mother in church? I might actually die.

Mrs. Corbley resumes her seat, her gaze finding me across the room as I gingerly hold the text in my hands. She winks at me, and I want to throw up. I'm about to discuss sex with my future mother-in-law *and* my mother.

"Now, remember, girls," Mrs. Corbley says, pointing her finger at the other unmarried teens sitting pink faced and anxious. "For you this is just for educational purposes. You need to keep yourselves pure for your future husbands." She smiles, the married women of the group nodding in agreement, and I don't think it's possible for my face to get any redder. "How about we all take time to read the first chapter on our own? Then we can discuss it."

Most of the ladies in the circle eagerly open their books, the stiff spines creaking in the quiet room. There are a few other teenage girls here too, maybe a couple of years younger and older than myself, and we all give each other sideways glances before opening the book ourselves.

Okay, maybe this won't be so bad. Sex, after all, isn't itself evil. Sex is supposed to be an expression of love, a way to increase spirituality and be closer to God . . . as long as we follow their rules. I think of the way James made me feel. How I made him feel. It causes me to wonder just what more with him could feel like.

"Hm-hm." My mother clears her throat when she notices I haven't started reading yet.

I quickly look down, and as my eyes scan over the words it feels as if I'm suddenly able to understand another language. What's written here is . . . awful. Three pages in, and I'm horrified—even more so when I look around the room at the married women who seem to be eating this up as if it's the bible itself.

A good Christian wife will never turn down the advances of her husband. A good wife is responsible for fulfilling all of her husband's physical and emotional needs. For keeping herself clean and beautiful even if she's too tired. And if she is "not in the mood," she should simply pray to God for strength because her body belongs to her husband and not herself.

I can't read anymore. I've seen enough and more nausea rolls through me at the thought that only a few weeks ago, I would have accepted this. The old Rebecca would've laid down in her marriage bed after cleaning and cooking and taking care of babies all day by herself to then allow her body to be used by a man who doesn't care. I can't imagine someone like Eric would ever make my pleasure his priority.

But James does.

I need to get out of here. I stand so quickly my book nearly falls out of my lap. My mother and Mrs. Corbley look at me questioningly.

"Problem, dear?" Mrs. Corbley asks.

Don't freeze. Don't freeze. *Don't freeze.*

"Sorry, I just need to use the bathroom. I'll be right back."

Doing my best not to run from the room, I shut the door behind me and walk along the dark hallway to head for the restrooms. I press a hand to my chest, my heart beating wildly as I approach the back of the church. I'm nearly breathless as I shut the heavy wooden door and almost miss the murmur of voices that trickles down the dark hallway.

"I think it's beneficial for everyone involved," a male voice says. "He needs the money and I need to solve a problem."

"Yes, and you're very generous to make such an offer. God demands so much of us."

Not wanting to get caught eavesdropping, I walk louder than normal to announce my arrival. The discussion stops abruptly and I turn the corner to find Pastor Campbell with Eric's father, Michael Corbley, and another man the same age.

"Ah, Rebecca, is Bible study over already?"

I swallow the lump in my throat as all three men's eyes focus on me. "No, sorry, I didn't mean to interrupt. I just came out here to use the restroom."

He claps his dry hands together, and I fight against the urge to cringe.

"Rebecca, have you met Police Chief Miller before?" Pastor Campbell gestures to the brawny man next to him.

"No, I don't believe so." I've seen him on Sundays of course but I've never spoken to him myself. "Nice to meet you."

"And you know Mr. Corbley."

What a ridiculous statement. If you come to Holy Grace, you know who Michael Corbley is. My eyes meet Mr. Corbley's, and they're the same icy blue as his son's. "Yes, of course. How are you, sir?"

He smiles, the expression unsettling as he takes a few steps toward me. "Such a well brought up young lady. Your parents raised you well."

I swallow against the sour taste in my mouth. At least one thing seems clear, he doesn't seem aware of the arrangement Eric and I have made. "Thank you."

"Appearances are everything, Rebecca," he continues. "If Eric is going to be in a position of power, an elder of the church one day, he needs a well-brought-up woman of God at his side. Someone who has wholly given themselves up to Christ." He takes another few steps and stuffs his hands in the pockets of his fancy dress pants, then leans closer and lowers his voice. "You'll both do your duty for Jesus, won't you? Make sure he doesn't stray from his purpose."

His tone is calm but his eyes are hard. Threatening. What is he talking about? In what world have I ever been able to influence Eric into doing something he doesn't want to? I mean—other than through my recent foray into blackmail. Not quite knowing how to respond, I tentatively nod. "Yes, sir."

He looks me up and down then turns back to Pastor Campbell and Chief Miller. "So, we're still on for the committee meeting this weekend?"

The three of them leave me in the hallway, the sound of their voices laughing like old friends echoes off the walls as I try to catch my breath. What was that all about? Is that what's expected of me? To be some sort of trophy wife just so Eric can be successful?

A daunting realization spreads through my mind like wildfire. That this marriage is just one more thing that I'm doing for someone else. My body is for someone else. I'll never be able to make a decision or pursue what I want. It'll always be for everyone else. It will never be about me—nothing ever will be.

It makes the limited time I have with James all the more precious.

CHAPTER 28

Break the Rules

JAMES

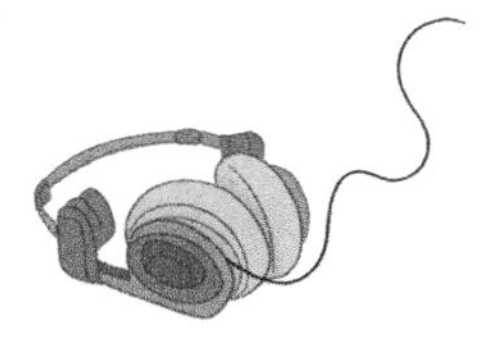

The next morning when Rebecca climbs into my van, she's glowing. Her eyes shine and her cheeks appear a touch fuller. She quickly kisses me, before disappearing into the back to change into some of Noreen's clothing.

"So, was Bible study a revelation last night?" I ask, pulling out onto the road toward the school.

She snorts derisively. "It was enlightening."

I glance in the rearview mirror and hear a muffled response as she pulls a checkered corduroy dress over her head. Her hair stands on end from the static, her cheeks flushed from the exertion of pulling the tight clothing off, the tops of her breasts peeking out from the—

Focusing back on the road, I take a deep breath. "So what do you do at Bible study, anyway?" I ask, clearing my throat.

"I'd rather not think about it, if that's okay." Her voice is flat. "It's just the usual, do as you're told, be virtuous, stay away from men with dark curly hair who play the guitar."

Her lips press against my cheek and I smile. She uses my shoulder for support as she climbs over the seat next to me. She's wearing a pair of red crepe pants and a black-and-white-striped sweater today.

"You look really pretty," I say.

Her face lights up like a Christmas tree, and I grin from ear to ear. When Rebecca smiles I smile too, like I could be happy like this—with her. Forever.

She twirls her finger around a strand of my hair. "You look really pretty too."

I cock an eyebrow. "Me? Pretty?"

She wraps her arms around me as we drive toward the school. "Boys can be pretty and still be manly. You happen to be both."

I laugh. "Well, thanks. I guess."

"You know, when I first saw you, I thought you were the devil."

"Who says I'm not?" I smirk.

She shrugs. "I suppose even the devil was an angel once."

I kiss the top of her head. "I have to go to work after school, so unfortunately we won't have much time to hang out until Saturday. But," I say quickly when her face falls, "I think I can schedule a quick makeout session during lunch."

She smirks. "What if I can't wait that long?" Her lips press feather light against my neck and I shiver.

"Maybe I *am* the devil. Look how corrupt you've become."

She giggles. "Maybe this was just who I was always meant to be."

The thought of simply ditching school to take her back to that secluded spot by the lake grows more and more desirable in my mind. But I inhale sharply and shake my head. "Stop distracting me, Becks. How am I going to graduate if all I can think about is bringing you over to the dark side in the back of my van?"

Her head tilts a bit. "Can I ask you a question?"

My brows furrow at the request. "Sure?"

Putting some space between us, she clasps her hands in her lap. "Why bother graduating at all?"

I blink at her then turn my attention back to the road. "What do you mean?"

She shrugs. "I just mean. Have you even applied to colleges? You haven't mentioned wanting to do anything like that. Surely you don't need a high school diploma to go to San Francisco and play music."

Shifting in my seat, I grip the steering wheel a little tighter. "You're right, I don't. But I—" My vocal chords seize. Do I tell her it's because it was a dying woman's last wish? That I never would've come here if it wasn't for that promise.

Her eyebrows lift as she waits for my response.

I sigh. "I promised my mom—you know, before she died—that I would graduate high school."

"Oh. James," she continues quietly, her face softening, "that's really sweet."

I shake my hair away from my face. "Well, there isn't much else I can do that would make her proud."

She snuggles back into me as I turn into the school parking lot. "Don't be ridiculous," she whispers. "I'm sure she was very proud of you." She kisses me. A long, lingering kiss, and I'm back to thinking about turning this van around and stealing her away to the lake. She pulls back, placing another soft kiss on my cupid's bow.

"I should go first. That way, no one sees me getting out of the van."

My stomach drops. "Oh, yeah . . . right." Secret. She wants to keep this secret. And I'm cool with that, right?

"I'll see you in class."

She tests the passenger door to see if it'll open today and it does. She slides along the bench to get out, but I reach out and grab her hand.

"Hey," I call and she stops to look at me. "If you can't get away, I'll see you after school. I'll still drive you home before I have to go to work."

She nods with a smile before grabbing her backpack and jumping down out of the seat. I watch in the side mirror as she enters the school, grabbing my own bag and heading for the doors. But as I walk, there's a growing anxious feeling in my stomach. While I promised discretion, thinking it wouldn't bother me being Rebecca's secret lover, I'm starting to realize it does bother me. It bothers me more than I ever thought something like this could.

When I take my place behind Rebecca in class, and those gorgeous green eyes find me through her curtain of blonde hair, I pull my notebook out of my bag. I flip to a page near the front of the book. A page where I'd written myself five simple rules when I was sitting in that hospital room waiting for my mom to die. Rules I wrote when I decided that I would graduate to fulfill my duty to her before pursuing my dream. Rules that would ensure I couldn't be distracted from having the life I've always dreamed of.

Rule #5: Always be yourself and never apologize for it.

Rule #4: Never rely on anyone else.

Rule #3: Never run away from a fight.

Rule #2: No virgins/no serious relationships.

Rule #1: Music before anything else.

Rebecca may not know these rules exist and be under the impression that what we have going on between us is casual—but it dawns on me that I want more. That I've wavered on each of these rules over the past few weeks for her. That I've crossed a line or two, thinking it wasn't a big deal. That I blurred my very set limits, forgot my promises to myself, destroyed the five principles I should live by.

Worse than that, I don't regret any of it.

Because I've not only broken rule #2—I've obliterated it.

I'm crazy about Rebecca Briar, and I want much more from her than two months of casual, secret hand holding and stolen kisses. I want all of her.

CHAPTER 29

Your Song

REBECCA

"You look good, Rebecca," Ms. Koysh says, grinning at me.

I nod. "Thank you."

My dance teacher tugs at the skin of my cheek. "Yes, you are looking much better. Healthy. Happy."

It's true. The past two weeks have been some of the happiest of my life. James being the main reason, of course. Every minute I spend with him, I feel lighter than air, and every minute we're apart I find myself counting down the seconds until I can see him again. We haven't been able to see too much of each other. James works five evenings a week and a lot of his weekend is taken up with band practice now as well as homework. But he still takes the time to drive me to and from school every day. Ensures I have an adequate lunch and clothes that fit.

The clothing I have to squeeze into every morning and sit in at dinner I can't even get the zippers up on anymore, and have resorted to wearing every cardigan in my closet to hide where the gaps are. But, when I'm out of the house, I feel free and beautiful. I feel like myself.

"Yes," I say. "I've been feeling good the last couple weeks."

"Is it the new boyfriend?" she asks.

My eyebrows lift. "What?"

She jerks her head toward the windowed wall past which are the changerooms and front office. And there, looking like the sexiest devil in disguise, is James.

Happiness bursts through my chest at the sight of him. Not simply because I missed him from only a few hours ago when he dropped me off, but because he's here. In the building. Did he see me dance?

I turn back to Ms. Koysh who is wearing a knowing smirk.

"I—yes. That's James."

"Do your parents know—"

"No!" I say a little too vigorously. Oh no, she's not going to call my mom is she?

"Don't worry, my lips are sealed." She chuckles, miming locking her mouth and throwing away the key. "He is good for you. Tell him he is welcome anytime."

I sigh with relief then head toward the door.

"What are you doing here?" I ask, a wide grin pinching my cheeks.

He scoops me up into a hug and twirls me around before setting me back on my feet. I try to push him away, suddenly self-conscious of the sweat on my skin. "James, stop—I'm all sweaty."

His smile only grows. "I'll bet. All that dancing looks like hard work."

"You . . . watched me dance?"

He tilts his head. "No, I thought I'd come in and stare at the wall for thirty minutes. Of course I watched you dance."

My heart is swelling and my stomach flutters. "Really?"

He nods. "Yeah! You're amazing. How do you turn so fast? Don't you get dizzy? And don't your toes hurt?"

A thousand answers bubble up my throat waiting to spill out.

No one has ever been interested in my dancing before, and the fact that James wants to know about it is like a drug. But the answers get caught in my mouth like a traffic jam and for a moment, I just stand staring at him.

"Becks?"

I rush forward, wrapping my arms around his neck, and pressing up in my pointe shoes to help me reach his lips. We stumble back into the wall by the water fountain but then his hands grip my waist and he pulls me against him. I don't even care that the other ladies from class are probably watching us as they exit the changeroom. All I care about is him and having more of this.

"James?" I whisper.

"Hmm?"

"Can we go back to the lake?"

He pulls back, those dark eyes flickering with flame and he swallows hard. "Sure, angel. Anything you want."

"Let me just get changed and we'll go."

I take a little longer than normal, anxious for the first time about what I look like after my ballet class. I've always been too self-conscious to use the attached showers in front of the other ladies, but with James, I find myself ducking into the last stall to clean myself up. When I come out of the change room, James is there waiting for me.

"Ready?"

I skip over to him and grasp his hand before waving at Ms. Koysh and heading out the door.

"You're in a good mood," he says as I buckle my seatbelt and he starts the engine.

"I guess I'm just excited that you came to watch me dance."

"I told you I would," he says, and I recall the promise he made that day at the diner when everything changed between us.

My mouth burns with the memory of that first kiss. "I still have to hold up my end of the bargain though," I say.

His brow furrows as he turns the corner heading out of town. "What do you mean?"

"I mean, I want to see you play."

"You have seen me play."

I shake my head. "No, I saw you audition. It's not the same. I want to see you perform for a crowd."

He laughs. "I doubt your mom and dad will let you out late enough to see it."

"Well," I say, "maybe I'll just have to sneak out to see you."

James tenses. His toned arms under my fingers turn rigid and something ticks in his jaw. My stomach drops. Does he not want me to come watch?

"I don't think that's a good idea."

I sit up a little straighter and pull my hands away. "Why not?"

His face softens. "I just don't want to be the reason you get in trouble, that's all."

Perhaps I'm imagining it, but there's something in the tone of his voice or the way he glances at me out of the corner of his eye for a moment before turning back to the road that makes me think there's more going on. I'm not sure why it upsets me so much. After all, I'm the one who told him this relationship can't be serious.

Maybe he's telling the truth. That he just doesn't want me to get caught and suffer the punishment that goes along with that. Looking out the window, the trees get denser the closer we get to our little secluded spot.

"Hey," he says, grasping my hand. "I think I can make it up to you, okay?"

My eyebrow lifts, intrigued. "Okay."

The smell of the forest and the water is calming as I jump down out of the driver's side door. James's hands grip my waist and the smoky, earthy scent of him makes me nearly forget our earlier conversation.

He opens the side door of the van and to my surprise, there's a cooler and his guitar.

"What's all this?" I ask.

A blush spreads across James's cheeks and he reaches up to pull on the back of his neck. Is he nervous?

"I thought . . . well—a date?"

My heart nearly bursts. "What?"

James grabs my hands and steers me to sit down on the soft quilt that is laid out on the carpeted van floor. "I know this is just casual, but I realized we hadn't really been on a proper date and I wanted to rectify that."

A tingling sensation floods my face and I try to contain my smile but it's so wide my cheeks hurt. "Really?"

He sits down next to me and opens the cooler to reveal bottled soda, sandwiches and a box of chocolates.

"James . . ." I whisper. "No one's ever—thank you."

He grins and grabs one of the sandwiches from the cooler and hands it to me. It's turkey again, the taste divine on my tongue. I mentally remind myself to try and find a way to thank Noreen for all of her kindness. James pops the top off of one of the sodas and hands it to me.

"This is—" I start. "This is wonderful."

"Hold on," he says, reaching behind him. "I almost forgot the best part."

Grabbing the guitar, he places it in his lap and strums the strings a few times before turning the tuning knobs at the top. "I wrote something and it kind of reminds me of you. Do you want to hear it?"

He wrote a song that reminds him of me? My heart might actually leap out of my chest. "Of course I do."

Plucking the strings a few more times to make sure the sound is right, he starts to gently strum the strings with a pick. I sit at his side, listening to the hauntingly beautiful notes that he creates. I can barely breathe. The loveliest music I've ever heard and I remember that he said it reminds him of me. I've never been compared to a song before, but I'm suddenly overcome with emotion if this is the song he chose to represent me. That burning feeling creeps into my face. No, I won't cry. I cry too much. A trickle of tears escapes anyway, and even though I inwardly curse at their treachery, they're somehow fitting. The music is beautiful but sad. Like the ballerina in my music box, forever trapped and spinning to that sad song. Just like me.

James strums a final time and looks up at me expectantly but his smile drops as he notices the tears. "Hey, you okay?"

"Yes, sorry." I smile and wipe my cheeks. "It was just so beautiful."

He puts the guitar down behind him and moves closer to me. Reaching out, he grabs my face with his talented and calloused hands and wipes the tears away. "Always crying," he chastises with a small smile.

I breathe out a laugh. "But also smiling, see?"

Smiling because I'm falling for him.

His lips touch mine and my skin tingles all over. His hands hold my face and the feel of his skin and the way he kisses me are all at once everything I've ever needed and not enough. I pull him against me and he follows. His tongue swipes against mine, and my skin feels like it's burning hot as my pulse races in my veins.

I shimmy back into the van, my fingers tugging on the hem of his shirt to keep him with me until I feel the soft mattress beneath us. His body crawls over mine as I sink into the foam, the delicious weight of him pressing against the parts of me that are so very hot. He groans as my knees widen enough for him to sink his hips against mine.

That little voice that says I shouldn't be doing this starts to claw its way toward the surface again, but the image of James watching me dance, the picnic lunch date he planned as a surprise, the song he wrote that reminded him of me, wind their way around the guilt and doubt and spur me onward. The fact that he's shown more care for me than anyone else has in years solidifies the decision to keep going. That this isn't something bad.

My fingers trail down his back until they find the hem of his shirt. He breaks away to pull it over his head, his hair falling back over his shoulders in soft waves. My chest is heaving, my breathing erratic, and my heart pounds so loud it could be the percussion for his band. The tattoos on his chest are finally fully visible and I trace along the branches of the tree.

He leans back down to kiss me, but instead of my mouth, his lips trail down my jaw. Eyes closing, I gasp at the touch of his fingers on my stomach.

"Is this okay?" he mumbles into my neck.

I swallow hard against the nerves and reach down to cover his hand with my own. He stills then I move his hand further up and up until his hand is on my breast, and my mouth drops open at his touch.

He breathes deeply, his body shuddering. James grinds his hips into me, and I feel his hardness press against my core. My stomach clenches and my back arcs upward into his touch as his thumb brushes over my nipple.

The cool air that blows through the open van door is soothing to my overheated skin as James pushes up my shirt. I lift my head off the mattress and it's off. Even though he's seen me naked before, it's different now. Now he can touch me. It's gone from simply showing to something much more.

His kisses trail down my neck and I feel both sublime and aching all over. I jolt as he pulls down the cotton cup of my bra, exposing my breast and before I even realize what's happening, he takes my nipple in his mouth.

I cry out, and if there was anyone around, I would be terribly embarrassed, but we're alone in the woods and I'm suddenly overwhelmed by the fact that he isn't touching me where I want him to most.

"James," I mumble, half delirious and pulling on his hair.

"Is it too much?" he asks. His face is flushed and his eyes are black.

I shake my head and exhale. "No, it's not enough."

He seems confused for a moment, before I grab his hand and slowly push it down my body toward where his erection is pressing into me.

"Are you sure?" he asks.

"Yes. Touch me." The words steadier than I thought they'd be. "Please."

He shifts, kissing me while coming to lie by my side, our bodies still pressed close together. I feel his fingers on the button of my jeans and while I'm desperate to be touched, I'm unbelievably nervous.

"You're shaking," he says.

"I'm all right."

He kisses my nose. "Remember, you can tell me to stop at any time."

I nod and smile. "I know."

The jeans Noreen gave me are fairly loose and James easily slides his hand beneath the denim fabric, inching underneath my underwear. I tilt my head back against the mattress, my hands tight against his biceps. Then his fingers touch me, and I nearly scream.

Eyes wide and panting, he exhales a long breath as his hand moves through the slick skin between my legs. This is so much better than doing it myself. I don't know if it's the unpredictability of his movements, his rhythm or if it's simply because it's James, but pleasure rockets through my body.

"Shit, you feel so good, Becks," he gasps.

But I'm like a runaway train and just like on his thigh, my hips start moving on their own. Grinding against his hand with desperation as my grip tightens on his arms.

"Pl—please," I stammer.

"What do you need?" he whispers against my ear, his teeth grazing the lobe.

"More . . . I need more."

His hand moves, and I feel a digit circling my entrance as the heel of his palm continues to press against that bundle of nerves. "Tell me you want this."

My eyes open to find him watching me intently. His face is so serious I almost don't recognize him. "I want it." Still though, his finger touches the edge of my entrance only and I feel like I might go insane.

"Tell me I'm the only one who's touched you here."

It's not a lie, but at this moment, I feel like I would tell him anything he wants to hear. "It's only been you. Please."

"Tell me he never made you feel like this."

Something shakes loose in my head. Why is he bringing up Eric right now? But then his finger slides inside me and it's just James. Only James and only ever will be him. My back lifts off the mattress to press against his bare chest, his finger pumping in and out of me. The sound of the slick action intoxicating as he plays me like his guitar—seeking out the pleasure chords of my body.

"Oh God!"

"No God here. Just me."

My legs shake until I'm shattering into a thousand tiny pieces of myself, held together only by him. His lips encase mine possessively as his hand slows until it's gone from inside me.

His hand brushes against my stomach, the wetness from my orgasm trailing up until he grasps my throat. I can smell myself on his hand, in the air of the van, it's everywhere. The kiss ends and I look into his eyes. His dark, flaming, beautiful eyes and as his breath evens out he gently traces my skin with his hands. "Are you okay?"

"I'm okay," I whisper. "I'm not going to break."

"Yeah, I know," he whispers back, lips pulling up at the side. "But I might."

CHAPTER 30

I Want to Break Free

JAMES

Fuck! The things that shoot out of my mouth when I'm around this girl are dangerous. How can one woman hold such power over me that I'm losing all control. This is going to end badly, I know it. She might be able to walk away at the end of all of this but I can't. It might kill me.

Her face and body are flushed, her chest rising and falling rapidly as she comes down from the high. Eyes scanning my face, I can tell she's trying to decipher what the fuck I said.

"I just mean . . ." I say, sitting upright and clearing my throat. "You make me want to lose control. That's all."

"Oh." She sits up grabbing my shoulder and fixing her bra. She pushes me back against the upholstery. "You make me want to lose control too."

Her green eyes are dark and peek up at me from under her long lashes. Her mouth is swollen and . . . good lord, I want to do unspeakable things to that mouth of hers.

"James?"

I'm so hard I'm nearly delirious. "Yeah?"

Fingers grasp at my belt, my stomach clenches and my cock throbs, but her gaze never wavers. "Will you tell me what to do?"

"Wha—what?"

Her fingers fumble with the buckle, that adorable wrinkle appearing above her nose. I grab her hand.

"You don't have to do that."

"Shh—" she says, leaning over to kiss my chest, sending goosebumps scattering all over me. "You made me feel good. Now, I want to make you feel good too."

Something wicked flashes across her face, and as she starts to trail kisses down my stomach, my brain finally catches on to what she's planning to do.

"Becks, wait . . ." *Shut up!* I yell at myself. This gorgeous girl is willing to suck my cock, and I'm trying to convince her not to? I shake my hair away from my face as she looks up with those innocent eyes.

"But I want to. I've just—never done it before, so you'll have to tell me if I'm doing something wrong."

The button at the top of my jeans comes loose, and I let out a shaky breath trying to regain some kind of composure. "Promise me you're sure?"

She smiles slyly and nods. "I'm sure."

Thank fuck!

Her fingers pull on the waistband of my boxers and I gasp. "Just—just do what you think you want to and . . . be careful of teeth."

She nods again, her face beautifully determined, and I take a deep breath as she pulls down the fabric for my cock to spring free. Then, before I can even think about it, her tongue flicks out to lick me.

Breathe, I remind myself. *Breathe.* But I think I've stopped breathing altogether as her lips wrap around me and her tongue swirls around my tip.

"Jesus H. Christ!"

I feel like I'm fourteen, getting head for the first time behind the portable of my old high school.

"Becks . . ." I gasp. "That feels—shit that feels so good."

She hums with approval and the vibration shoots through me like a taser. She bobs her head a little, up and down, up and down, and my eyes roll back as my head tips against the wall. I collect her silky hair in my hands and hold it out of the way for her, the loose grip giving me just a little bit of control.

"I'm not going to last long," I whisper desperately. My chest heaving and my leg shaking. Normally I can drag this out, hold out a little longer, but not with her. Maybe it's the possessiveness I feel overtaking my senses at the fact that she's never done this before. That mine is the first cock she's sucked. Touched. That I'm the first to touch her. First to watch her come. That it's all for me. And that selfish part of me wishes I had been her first kiss too. That it'll only ever be me forever.

"Becks, I'm . . . I'm—"

I pull her hair a little harder than I mean to, but she backs off as I come hard onto my stomach. A shiver runs down my spine as the cool breeze hits the wetness on my skin, then I feel something soft being pressed into my hand. I open my eyes and look down where Rebecca has passed me some tissues.

She smiles a bit nervously, sitting back on her heels.

"Thanks," I whisper.

"Was that," she starts, "okay?"

I clean myself up and tuck myself back into my pants before grasping her face and pulling her toward me. Our lips crash into each other and for a few moments it's like I've forgotten myself, forgotten to be gentle because I simply want to devour her.

When I pull away, her mouth is red, and her eyes are glazed.

"That was incredible, Becks."

"Really?"

"Where the hell did that come from?"

Her cheeks darken. "I may have borrowed Amy's cosmopolitan magazine at lunch yesterday."

I laugh. "Well, remind me to thank Amy."

She blinks and I realize what I've said.

"Sorry, I wouldn't—" I say. "It's just a turn of phrase."

Rebecca nods but her smile falters a bit. "Right. I know that."

Even though she's still smiling, I can tell that something's shifted. She's not blissed-out anymore, and if I'm honest, neither am I, my high crashing like I've jumped out of a plane without a parachute.

Rebecca sits back and pulls her shirt back on over her head. I suppose that's the signal for me to put mine back on too, so I do. We both pull ourselves together in an awkward silence that's never really occurred between us before. I start to think maybe she wants me to take her home, but I remember that she hates home. Maybe she's not saying anything because she doesn't know where to go, but the only option is to be with me. Something sharp twists in my chest at the thought that she's only here to escape.

I think about the way Eric might look if he knew she was here with me. Of all people, I want him to know the most.

"Hey, I meant to ask you . . ." I start. Rebecca looks up at me with wide eyes, as though she's stunned I've spoken at all. "Has Eric said anything to you?"

Her eyes scan my face. "Eric? No . . . Why?"

I shrug and pull at the hem of my shirt nervously. "Well, he's your ex and he cheated on you and—"

Rebecca places her hands overtop of mine and the gesture is all at once soothing and anxiety inducing. "I told you. I don't care about him."

She leans forward to kiss me. Gently. Her body folding into mine so effortlessly it's like the past few minutes never happened. It's disarming.

"Thank you," she whispers as she pulls my arms around her. "For today. For everything. It's been the best day of my life."

Kissing her forehead, I squeeze her until she squeaks. The doubt drains away a little but somehow I'm still drowning in it. I want to tell her that I wish I could make everyday just as perfect. That I want to be with her through all of her days, even the bad ones. That fuck casual because I'm falling in love with her. But I don't.

"Yeah, me too."

"Walton. John wants you up front."

I set down the two boxes of beer bottles I brought up from downstairs with a sigh and nod to Benny, the cook, who disappears behind the counter. Stretching out, my back cracks down my spine before I head out front into the busy bar. It's much darker out in the front than it is in the kitchen so I have to squint to find where John is at. I finally spot him in the far corner of the room passing out a tray of shot glasses.

His eye finds mine and I gesture to him to ask what he wants. But rather than signaling that he needs a refill of Jack Daniels for the bar rail, he points to the wall opposite the stage where I see Dave, my bandmate, watching the current act.

I push my way through the drunken rowdy crowd, momentarily remembering how Rebecca sat so prim and proper at one of these very tables a few weeks ago. I wonder if she'd still like the place after seeing it on a night like tonight, full of punks and bikers. But next thing I know, Dave spots me and grins so wide I can almost see all his teeth.

"Hey, man!" he says, pulling me into a brotherly hug.

I reciprocate happily with a smile. Even though I haven't

known him for very long, I really like him. He seems genuine and, like myself, willing to do whatever it takes to make it.

"What are you doing here?" I ask over the noise.

He leans closer to yell in my ear. "Booked us a gig."

My eyebrows shoot straight up and my stomach flips over, nearly causing my sub from earlier to launch out of my stomach. "No shit?"

Dave is still grinning. "That's right. Third weekend in May, we're going to be right up there on that stage."

He points to where the mediocre hair metal band is playing and my nerves are jittery with excitement.

"Hey, can I talk to you about something quick?" Dave asks, shouting again over his beer. "Come on outside, it's too noisy in here."

I look back over to John who's watching me intently. I point to the door and he nods, understanding I'll be right back. I follow Dave out onto the lit patio, the smell of cigarette smoke burning deliciously in my lungs and my hand reaches for my pocket instinctively but then I remember . . . Becks.

"Want a smoke?" Dave asks, turning back to me and noticing the way I pat my pocket.

"No thanks. Quit."

He nods. "Good for you."

My knuckles clench and I want to scream at him to tell me what's up, because he's started pacing nervously.

"Listen, I want to run something by you."

"Yeah? What's that?" My throat is instantly dry. Fuck, I wish I had a cigarette simply so I had something to hold onto.

"I booked this gig for a reason. I mean, a reason other than simply playing and getting paid for it," he says, before taking a long drag.

"I don't understand."

He shakes his head. "Before we kicked out our last guitarist, I sent a few demo tapes to some studios in California. It was almost a year ago. I was sure they'd probably chucked us in the bin. Until I got this yesterday."

He holds up a typewritten letter on official letterhead from what appears to be—

"Holy shit, Megaloud Records?"

Dave seems to revel in my enthusiasm. The truth is, I'm about to burst out of my skin.

"A producer happens to be coming to town next month for a memorial . . . a funeral? Doesn't matter. He's coming here. He said he got our demo and liked it. Wants to see us perform live while he's in town."

"Fuck!" I yell, and several bar patrons turn to stare. "Fuck, fuck, fuck, this is insane!"

Dave takes another long drag of his cigarette and blows the smoke out slowly as I read over the letter. A letter that very well may change my life.

"But, I'm not the guitarist in the demo," I say, my excitement suddenly deflating.

Dave scoffs. "Please, and I say this with no desire to stroke your ego, but you're way better than the demo. Ricky was always too heavy-handed and had lazy fingering skills. Ha . . . maybe that's why his wife left him. Anyway, with you, we'll have an even better shot at making it. This guy is going to show up here thinking we're some small town hick band and we'll blow him out of the water!"

I can't speak and my cheeks are hurting from grinning so widely.

"Oh, and I spoke to John because I know you work Saturday nights, but he's cool with you taking the night off to play."

Fuck, right. Work. "Oh, thanks man. Appreciate that."

Dave claps me on the shoulders excitedly. "This is it man.

We're going to impress him and he's going to tell us to pack up our gear and head out west."

But while this should be the happiest moment of my life, all I can think about is the fact that, if this works out like I want it to, I'll officially be leaving. Officially headed to San Francisco like I always dreamed. Officially leaving Rebecca behind.

Two hours later I'm sitting on an overturned crate out back finishing off the last of an order of chili cheese fries on my break. My notebook is spread open over my right knee, my pen tapping the paper aggressively. There's so much I want to tell my mom—to document in this moment. Dave coming to the bar to tell me we have our first gig, to him showing me the letter from Megaloud, to thinking this might all actually . . . happen.

But funnily enough, even after writing down all the amazing things that have happened tonight, my pen traces and retraces over the lines of Rebecca's name.

Rebecca, if I asked you to come with me,
would you?

It's an idea that's been circulating in my head for over a week now. She hasn't ever talked about what she plans on doing after high school, and while I assume she has college or something lined up, part of me wishes she didn't. That if I ask her to come to San Francisco with me she'll leap into my arms and without hesitation tell me she's been waiting for me to ask. That it was a stupid idea to tell me this was just fun for her. That she loves me.

I click my pen and slam the notebook closed, opening my bag and stuffing it back inside. It hits another book and I pull out the aged journal. It's worn at the edges and swollen on the one side from water damage. The name Dora Walton smeared a little across the front in blue ink. My mom's journal.

I've been making my way through them, just enjoying a bit of insight into who she was before everything fell apart. I find comfort in the fact that she used to write down her innermost thoughts, just like me, but I've been so busy I haven't looked at the journals in a while.

I open it up, passing over the pages I've already read.

September 7, 1965

Jet asked me to go to homecoming with him! It's official, I am the coolest, happiest girl in the world. Even Mom and Dad approve. We're having him and his parents over for dinner on the weekend and I'm so nervous Noreen is going to embarrass me. Maybe if I threaten to take away her record player she'll behave. Or better yet, maybe I can arrange for her to go to a sleepover at a friend's place and remove her from the situation altogether.

I laugh out loud at the idea that if Noreen wanted to embarrass her sister, I don't think anything would've stopped her.

September 20, 1965

Tonight was confusing. I thought Jet understood that kissing is the most that can happen between us. Did I give him the impression that I wanted more? He was so mad when I pushed him away. I don't want him to break up with me. Mom and

Dad will be so disappointed. It's not like I don't want to touch him, but God forbids it before marriage. As someone who goes to church every week, you'd think he of all people would understand.

My stomach churns with nausea, the chili cheese fries suddenly unsettling themselves from the comfort of my stomach and as I turn the page, my hand is shaking.

October 1, 1965

I'm so excited for tonight. I can't believe I was nominated for homecoming queen. I bet Jet will look so handsome in a suit. He looks handsome in everything. My dress is sky blue and so pretty, I wonder if he'll bring me a corsage to wear. I'm just a little worried about whether the dress shows too much cleavage. I don't want Jet getting the wrong idea. I know it's my job to keep our relationship pure in the eyes of God.

The way this reminds me so much of Rebecca is painful. Is this how she felt too? On the next entry, the date is hard to read, a splotch of ink where it seems like water has dripped and dried on the words.

October –, 1965

I just want to die. Everything hurts and I'm still bleeding. I told him to stop, that I didn't want to sleep with him. That I was saving myself for my husband, and reminded him that he promised he understood. But then he took everything from me. Holding me down in the dirt to muffle my screams while he took what he wanted. Then dropped me off at home, my dress torn and my underwear lost in the woods, acting like we'd just gone down to the diner for a milkshake. I want him to pay for what he did, but right now I just want to sleep. Better yet, maybe I just won't ever wake up.

I'm not sure when it happened but I'm standing, the milk crate and the order of fries knocked over on the ground of the alley. My heart is thumping so wildly and out of rhythm that I think I'm having a heart attack. I blink rapidly, trying to force the world back into focus as the journal falls from my hands to splay across the cement, and I realize that the ink splotches and wet marks aren't water damage, they're tears.

Tears my mother cried while she wrote about her boyfriend raping her.

CHAPTER 31

Love is a Battlefield

REBECCA

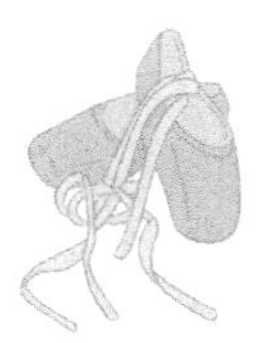

I can't sleep. My mind is racing and even though every part of me is exhausted, I can't seem to shut everything off and finally fall asleep.

Tell me he never made you feel like this.

James's words run through my head on a loop. Why would he say that? He knows I never loved Eric and besides, there's no need to be jealous. I'm with James now. Unless . . .

No, there's no way that James knows about what's happening between Eric and I after graduation. If he knew, I'm sure he would've mentioned it. But what if he does, and he just hasn't said anything? I feel a sharp, angry pain in my stomach and it doubles me over in bed until I'm curled up into a ball and breathing through my nose. Is it cramps? My period has been erratic the last few years so I never really know when it'll happen but this doesn't feel like the usual discomfort that signals Aunt Flo is coming.

This pain is guilt.

For the first time in my life, I'm lying. Well, not overtly, but I'm withholding the truth and from the person who means the most to me. He will never understand though. And I can't burden him with the truth because somehow I know deep down that he would abandon everything he wants for his life to make sure I am okay. I can't let that happen. James deserves to live his dream. He's talented enough to accomplish it and I know that I can be happy in the knowledge that he's achieving it, even if I'm not there with him.

There's a crash from next door and the light from James's window floods into my room. I didn't realize it was so late or that he was even home. I spring out of bed and race to the window to see him. But two of the milk crates holding his records have been knocked over, the sleeves scattered on the ground and he's sitting on the floor at the end of his bed holding his head in his hands.

My hand rests against the glass, desperate to reach out to him, to call him and find out what's wrong. Then I see the blood dripping from his knuckles. My insides are in knots, horrified. Did he hurt himself? Did he punch someone? Is he mad? What if he's mad at me?

I grab a pad of paper and a marker from my desk and scribble out a note.

Are you okay? What happened?

Holding the paper up against the window, I wait and wait and wait for him to look up. I don't dare try to make any noise to get his attention. I'm honestly astounded my parents didn't wake up at the noise. My insides feel like a bucket of eels until he finally looks up.

His face is splotchy and swollen and his eyes are red where he must have been crying. When he spots me, he tries to smile. He sees my note and gestures at his bloody hand before shaking his head like he's ashamed of himself. What could have happened?

Leaning over, he grabs that notebook from his bag and flips it open before writing back.

Found something out about my mom. I may have punched a dumpster.

There are two sides warring within me which makes my stomach hurt even more with guilt. Part of me is sympathetic, saddened by what he must have learned about his mom. And the other is unbelievably selfish, relieved that he's not mad at me. That what's grieving him isn't about us. That at least we're okay.

I'm sorry. Tell me at school on Monday?

He nods and pushes his hair away from his face. He writes something down on his page but then stops abruptly. His eyes glance up at me for just a moment before he chews on his lip then flips the page and writes something else before holding up the new note.

Okay. Sorry I scared you. Sweet dreams.

I smile before he leaves the room flexing his hand. I place the notepad down on my desk and get back into bed, but if I thought I couldn't sleep before, it's nothing compared to now.

What had he been writing before he changed his mind? I wish I could see what he keeps in that notebook, but I don't dare ask. It's obviously the most private part of him and since I have access to almost every other part, surely he deserves some semblance of privacy.

What am I even talking about? This is becoming so

complicated. All I wanted was to feel alive—free. And here I've gone and fallen in love with James.

Love.

That's it. This is why I can't sleep. Why the guilt of being less than perfectly honest with him is eating me alive. Why when he's upset, I am too. How the closer I get to him leaving is like a knife that slowly twists its evil way deeper into my heart. I wish I could just tell him to please take me with him wherever he goes. But my love for him is also exactly the reason why I won't.

"REBECCA."

I look around to find my mom staring at me expectantly. "Sorry?"

Her mouth tightens impatiently. "Rebecca, don't forget that you have your first counseling session with Pastor Campbell."

Again, I'm drawing a blank. Counseling session?

"With Eric?" she adds through gritted teeth.

I feel all the blood drain from my face. The pre-marriage counseling. I totally forgot. My mouth opens and closes as I gape at her church friends who are grouped around me. My mom's face is getting redder and redder by the second and I can tell I'll pay for embarrassing her later.

"Right. I'm sorry. I was just so caught up in today's sermon, I can hardly think of anything else," I say, pulling a wide smile onto my face.

Everyone but my mother looks appeased, as though they really do believe that I was overcome with emotion for today's sermon focusing on charity, rather than daydreaming about being in the back of James's van again.

"You must be so excited," Martha, one of the older church

ladies, says. “You know, I got married to my high school sweetheart too.”

I nod, my cheeks hurting desperately with the smile plastered on my stricken face.

“Had our first baby nine months later. Are you excited to start a family? Your children will be so beautiful.”

“I—” I start. No, not kids. I don’t want kids. Someone save me from having to breed with Eric Corbley. “I haven’t really given it much thought.”

The ladies laugh. “That’s what everyone says, then the honeymoon’s over and next thing you know you’re tossing your cookies in the alley behind the supermarket.”

I’m about to toss my cookies right now.

“Rebecca?”

Maybe someone has come to save me after all. I turn to look where the voice has come from, but I see Eric standing next to Pastor Campbell, who is waving at me to come to the front of the altar with a look of stern impatience at being kept waiting. My stomach heaves. No one is coming to save me.

“Eric will drive you home after,” my mother says, grabbing my arm. Her grip is tight, bruising through the fabric of my too-small dress concealed under the yellow cardigan.

“What?”

Her nails dig into my skin and I flinch. “I said,” she snarls, “that Eric will drive you home. Your father and I have things to do and we can’t wait around for you all afternoon.”

I would rather walk home than get in a car with Eric.

“Sure.”

Finally she releases me. I stagger backward before turning and heading up the aisle to where Eric and Pastor Campbell are waiting for me. Eric’s eyes are like ice but he smiles politely and gestures for me to go first. Something prickles down my spine at having him behind me, and as we walk through the dark, windowless corridors to the back office, I can feel his breath on the nape of my neck.

Don't cry. Don't cry. *Don't cry.*

We enter the office and situate ourselves on the uncomfortable leather chairs—squeaking and groaning beneath us with every movement. Luckily, I have years of experience sitting still, so thankfully it's just Eric that looks uncomfortable. Meanwhile, I'm ready to jump out of my skin.

Pastor Campbell groans as he sits down at his desk.

"So, Eric," he starts, "are you excited about getting married?"

Eric's eyes shoot to mine and hold my gaze. "Absolutely."

What kind of game is he playing? He's the one who cheated on me. And sure, I may have kissed James before I knew that, but he's treated me like garbage for years. Suddenly, because I don't want him, he's obsessed with the idea of marrying me?

An awful smile appears on his face and I don't see how Pastor Campbell doesn't see right through it.

"I see here—" He continues talking but I zone out. I guess he's just going to skip over asking me if *I'm* excited about getting married. This is going great so far. I wonder what James is doing right now. I hope his hand is okay. I wonder what he found out about his mom. It must be bad if he was so upset about—

"Rebecca?"

I look up. "Hmm?"

Pastor Campbell folds his hands together, the sound making me cringe. "I can see we're going to need to discuss how to communicate in a marriage. It will only lead to fighting and unhappiness if you're not focused and willing to listen."

My nails dig into the leather of the seat and I feel heat sear across my face. "I—yes, sorry. I'm just not feeling very well."

He tuts at me. "You may not be feeling well for several months when you start having children, but listening and respecting your husband are key to a happy, healthy marriage."

I think I might be sick.

"I think she's just nervous."

Turning my head, I blink at Eric. Is he . . . no. He's not standing up for me. This is just like when he was trying to save face when he forgot me after dance class. Making me think he's standing up for me only to blindside me with some backhanded compliment later.

"Plus, she's been very *busy*."

It feels like time has stopped. Am I even breathing? The way he says it and the look on his face—he knows. He knows about James and I. He has to. That smug smile on his face is practically glowing like a neon sign that says "busted."

"Is that so Rebecca?" Pastor Campbell continues. "Have you been busy?"

A long breath leaves my lungs and I swallow before turning back to him. "Oh, yes. Just with school stuff. I'm always trying to be charitable if the teachers need volunteers for anything."

I smile at him and he smiles back, apparently appeased, as indicated by his awful, watery smile.

"Well, life will get busy, I'm afraid. But today I'd like to look at Genesis 2:18. 'It is not good that the man should be alone.'"

AN HOUR later and I'm sitting in Eric's car staring out the window. I never noticed how uncomfortable the seats are. Or maybe it's just because I've been so tense the past hour that I'm sure my muscles have seized. It's like he's torturing me. He keeps looking over. He has something to say but won't say it and part of me wishes he would just spin out into the ditch and end all of my suffering right now, forever.

It isn't until we turn down my street that he finally clears his throat.

"We need to talk, Becca."

My arms tighten across my chest, pulling at the open side zipper even more than normal. "I have nothing to say to you."

He pulls up in front of my house and parks the car. My eyes flick on instinct to the next driveway. James's van is gone. I try to hide it but Eric catches me.

"Really, Becca?" he says in an angry whisper. "The freak?"

My fists clench at the name. "I don't know what you're talking about."

Eric slams his hand on the steering wheel and I jolt in my seat, spinning around to stare at him. "Knock that shit off, Becca!"

He's breathing hard as if he's been holding this in all day and only just now lost his composure. "I saw you together in the school parking lot, and after your dance class, and—"

"You're following me?" I cry, outraged.

"You're going to be my wife! What you do and *who* you do is my business!"

"Wha— We're not—We haven't . . . it's none of your business what I choose to do with my life *or* my body!"

Eric leans toward me and I spring back. "It absolutely is my business! And what's worse is you aren't even being discreet about it!"

"Oh, like you were?" I throw back.

He runs a hand down his face. "That isn't—" He pauses and takes a deep breath. "It was a mistake. I was drunk—"

"That's no excuse—"

"I was drunk, Becca!"

"You're pathetic," I whisper.

His eyes widen. "Me? I'm pathetic? Says the girl chasing after some wannabe-punk going nowhere so she can slum it in the gutter before marriage?"

"Don't talk about him that way!"

"Does he know?"

I blink. "Know what?"

"Does he know about your—*our* little arrangement?"

"Of course not! James knows that he and I are just . . . hanging out. Just casual. He's leaving anyway." My voice cracks, betraying me, and I'm sure Eric can tell that it hurts me more than I'm letting on.

Blinking furiously I look back to James's house thinking how once he's gone I'll see this house every time I visit my parents. How I'll remember our late night notes through the window. How he made me feel free.

A hand grips my shoulder painfully. I turn and Eric presses his face toward me.

"You listen to me, Becca," he says, low and menacing. "You know as well as I do what is expected of us and what will happen if we don't make this work. If you want to fuck your little freak, be my guest. All the better for me not to have to break you in on the wedding night, but keep what you're doing a secret. I'm amazed no one knows about it already with the way you both drool over each other all day."

I can barely formulate a response. What he said—I'm appalled. "Eric—"

"You keep that shit under wraps or I'll make his life a living hell, do you understand me?"

My brow furrows. "What do you mean?"

Eric leans back from me and loosens his grip on my shoulder. "I'm saying, keep your little arrangement a secret, or I'll have my dad make a call to the sheriff's department. You know he has half of the police in his pocket already."

My mouth falls open. "For what? James hasn't done anything wrong!"

Eric laughs. "Like that matters? Just look at the guy. Like anyone would believe his word against mine."

"You—how could you even think to do that?"

He presses his lips together and rubs at his nose, before looking away out the window.

My blood is boiling. I'm so angry I'm vibrating in my chair. Every muscle is like a trap readying to spring apart. "I hate you."

Eric turns back to me. "Perfect. You can include it in your wedding vows. Now get out."

CHAPTER 32

The Evil That Men Do

JAMES

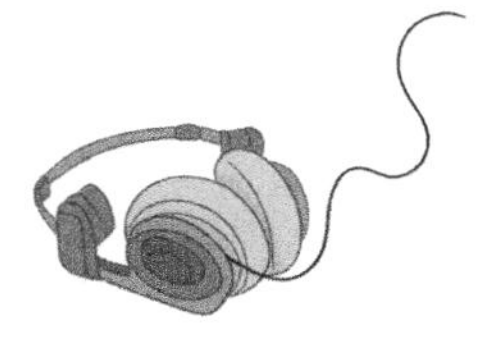

I've barely slept all night and as the sun starts to lighten the tops of the trees I get up to make my way downstairs. Journal clutched tightly in my sore and bruised right hand, I put on a pot of coffee and sit at the kitchen table waiting for Noreen. She doesn't take long and a few minutes after the scent of freshly brewed coffee hits the air, she wanders in wrapped in her fluffy bathrobe.

"Oh! James! I didn't expect you to be up at this hour. What's—"

"Did you know about this?"

I hold the journal up in my hand. It shakes and I'm not entirely sure if it's because of my fucked up hand or how angry I am. Noreen stops midway through the kitchen.

"Know about what?"

"This!" I say slamming the journal down on the formica table. She jumps and for a fleeting moment I'm ashamed to think that maybe I'm scaring her. But I also want answers and Noreen has been withholding information about my mom since I got here.

She takes a few tentative steps toward the table, her eyes fixed on the journal. "What is that?"

"It's Mom's journal."

"Where did you get that?"

"There was a box of her stuff in the closet of my room."

Noreen blinks and takes a deep breath. "What does it say?"

"It says she was raped."

There's a silence that hangs over us for a long moment, permeated only by the chugging of the coffee pot and the drizzle of liquid into the carafe.

Several emotions flicker across her face; denial, anger, sadness. At least it answers my question—she didn't know. Finally, her eyes become misty, and I slump back in my chair. A long exhale escapes me before I bury my face in my hands, the hot prickle of tears clawing their way up into my eyes.

The kitchen chair scrapes across the floor and I feel Noreen's presence as she sits down next to me.

"I didn't . . . James, I didn't know." Even though she's right next to me, her voice is barely audible. "Does it say who—"

"Who did it?" I ask, looking up. "Yeah, it does."

"Who?"

"Someone named Jet." The name is like acid burning my tongue.

Noreen sits back, her brows furrowing. "Jet? Jet who? Is there a last name?"

My stomach drops. I have been clinging to the hope that maybe Noreen knew who this Jet fucker is so I can track him down and bury him alive. "No . . . there isn't. I've looked through it a hundred times and never once is he referred to by anything other than Jet."

"Is there a date?" Noreen asks, gesturing to the journal.

I shake my head. "No, it's all smudged out, but it was around homecoming during her senior year."

About two months into her senior year, she just . . . took off, never to be seen or heard from again. It was quite the scandal.

She was one of the nominees for homecoming queen and everything.

"I think," I say, remembering the conversation with Eleanor at The Shipwreck, "I think it was after the homecoming dance."

Noreen stills, her face draining of color.

"What's wrong?" I ask.

She shakes her head, tears leaking from her eyes as her hand comes up to cover her mouth. Like a dam breaking, she's suddenly sobbing. Crying so hard the table beneath my hands is shaking. Then, as quickly as it started, she stands, the chair tipping backward onto the linoleum floor.

"Goddamnit, Dora!" she yells.

I'm on my feet a second later. "What? What is it?"

"They told me—and I believed—oh God! What I said to her—"

She wraps her arms around herself and cries, slowly sinking to the floor. I sit down next to her and wrap my arms around her heaving shoulders as she cries, knowing it's pointless to try and ask questions before she's ready.

When it's quiet again, I reach up onto the counter and grab a tissue before handing it to her. She takes it, wipes her face and blows her nose. "I'm so sorry, James. I'm so . . . God, I'm such an idiot."

"Noreen," I say cautiously, like approaching a deer I don't want to scare away. "What happened between you and my mom?"

She sniffles loudly and turns to me, her face blotchy and her eyes red. "She started seeing some boy that summer. I vaguely remember meeting him, but he looked just like every other midwestern jock asshole around, so I never really thought about him much. Mom and Dad approved, though. In fact, I think they were over the moon about her choice of boyfriend. Which means only one thing. He was either rich, or heavily involved in our church, or both. With the way they talked about him, though, my money is on both.

"I remember being so resentful of him. Dora and I had been close and even though she was much older than me, she always looked out for me and made time to hang out. But once she met this guy, she only had time for him. I was stupid and hurt that my big sister was choosing some loser over me. Then the morning after homecoming, something was wrong. Our parents were furious that she had been out so late. Thinking back on it now, she was basically catatonic. And she was never one to get into trouble—always the perfect daughter. Feminine and quiet . . . not like me. So naturally, I thought she must have done something terrible for them to be so mad at her.

"Next thing I knew, they were all screaming at each other. I remember sitting on the stairs trying to hear what they were yelling about, but Mom had shut the door to the living room. After that, Dora locked herself in her room for three days. I tried to talk to her. Find out what had happened. I tried asking my parents, but they kept telling me it was none of my business. That Dora was a sinful, wicked daughter, and I wasn't allowed to talk to her.

"Then . . . they canceled all my piano lessons and locked up my roller skates. I hadn't even done anything wrong! They said all of this stuff is what led Dora away from God. That they didn't want me to follow down the same path of wickedness as she had."

She takes a shaky breath. "James . . . my parents—they were awful people. Religious zealots who cared more about how they looked at church than loving their own children. But I was young and angry that I'd lost all of my very limited freedom because of something *she* had done. I heard a rumor at school that Dora had seduced and slept with her boyfriend. And in my anger . . . I *believed* them. I wanted something and someone to blame.

"One day, a black van turned up our driveway. All the windows were dark, and two men in white uniforms came to the door. They broke down Dora's door and carried her, kicking and screaming, away from the house. My parents were the picture of devastation. I thought they genuinely wanted what was best for her. To help her. But Dora was screaming that she hadn't done anything wrong. And before they shut her in that van, she looked at me and said she would run away. That she would come to get me and we'd run away together."

Noreen presses her shaking hand to her mouth. "And do you know what I said?"

I'm barely breathing, my stomach so twisted it hurts, and lightning is shooting through my clenched jaw.

Noreen shakes her head with a dark laugh. "I said, 'I wouldn't go anywhere with a whore like you.'"

My eyes close, and my hand clenches, the knuckles cracking. I feel like punching something again.

Noreen drops her head into her hands. "Of course, my parents were thrilled. They'd turned me against her, knowing they'd be able to control me. I watched that van drive away to God knows where, with the only person who ever actually cared about me, and I never saw her again. After a week, I wasn't angry anymore, and I regretted every day what I said to her. Another week went by, and my parents were insufferable now that I was on my own. I started to wish she really would escape and come rescue me, just like she said she would. Surely she knew I didn't mean it—that I was just mad.

"My parents got word a few weeks later that she ran away from wherever they had sent her, and every day for two months I would sit and stare out of my window at night with a bag packed and ready, hoping to see her face behind the tree in our yard, waiting to take me away. But she never did—she never came.

"My parents died three months after my eighteenth birthday, a head-on collision with a transport truck. I got the house and my freedom, but I had no idea where Dora ended up, and worse, no idea how to find her. Until a few months ago when I got a letter telling me she was dying and needed someone to help take care of her amazing son so he could graduate."

My mind is racing. It's all too much to take in at once, and we sit there quietly for what feels like an eternity.

"Noreen," I say, "it's not your fault. You're not the one who attacked her. If she had told you what really happened . . . You're not the one who tried to lock her up for something that she wasn't to blame for."

"But what I said—"

I grab her shoulders and look into her pained eyes. "You were so young when it happened. What you're doing now . . . helping me—I'm sure she would forgive you if she were here. I'm sure she already has."

Noreen starts to cry again, and just when I think I can't shed another tear about it all, that anger is replaced by sadness. I feel the warm trail of tears down my own cheeks.

After a while, I help her off the floor and pour her a cup of coffee. I show her the journal entry and the handful of others afterward that outlined how her parents hadn't believed her. That they blamed my mother for seducing a good Christian boy. Noreen excuses herself after that one to go to the bathroom and I don't say anything, but I think I hear her throw up. It's while she's gone from the room that something occurs to me and it spreads like a virus, making me ill with the thought. Is my dad really who I met all those years ago, or am I the result of this horrendous, violet act?

Noreen wipes her mouth as she reenters.

"Is Jet my dad?" I ask in a breathless rush.

Noreen blinks but rushes over to me. "No! No . . . James, this happened in October. Your birthday—" She ticks off her fingers.

"You would've had to have been conceived in the spring, not the fall."

I breathe deeply. "Okay. I—I just wanted to know." Even though my dad is a worthless piece of shit, somehow this would've been worse. "And do you . . . " I start, not quite sure how to ask what I desperately want to know. "Do you think this is why—why she started doing drugs and stuff? Why she ended up such a mess?"

She reaches across the table and grasps my hand, her fingers warm from the mug of coffee. "I'm no expert, but . . . I'd say it's pretty possible. When someone suffers such a traumatic experience but has no healthy way to cope with it, I would imagine that yes, drugs probably offered a reprieve from it all."

I nod and my face twitches.

"James."

I look up. "Yeah?"

"I know what you're thinking."

"What?"

"There's no point in trying to find him. It won't do anyone any good."

My eyes narrow. "And just let him get away with what he did?"

"It was twenty years ago. And the only proof you have is a few journal entries. That's hardly enough to prosecute someone."

"I've got no interest in prosecuting—"

"Exactly," she says, pointing a finger at me. "I'll be damned if I let you get hauled off to jail for murdering the piece of shit who did this. You know that's not what she would have wanted."

I sit back in my chair and blow out a long breath.

"You should try and get some sleep, James," she says kindly. "You look like shit."

A laugh bursts out of my chest, and I nod my head. "Yeah, likely."

"Are you working tonight?"

Suddenly, the memory of what Dave had told me springs back like a slingshot. "Oh, holy shit!"

"What?" Noreen asks, startled.

"I—my band. We've got our first gig happening. It's the third week of May."

She smiles brightly even though her face is swollen from crying. "Oh James, that's amazing."

I pull on the back of my neck. "There's more too. Dave got a letter from someone at Megaloud Records. He listened to the band's demo, and he's going to be passing through here and is going to come watch us."

Noreen reaches forward and grabs my hands, pressing her forehead to them. "James, that's—that's amazing. I'm so excited for you."

She breaks away, and I shrug. "I mean . . . I'm trying not to get my hopes up or anything but this could be it."

Noreen smiles slyly. "Then, maybe I should give you your graduation present early."

"What do you mean?"

She grins and leaves the kitchen for a minute. I rap my knuckles against the table top impatiently, then Noreen reenters carrying a guitar case.

I stand up so fast, this time it's my chair that goes flying as she sets the long case on the table.

"What—" I stammer.

She tucks her folded hands under her chin and bounces like a little girl on Christmas morning. It might as well be, because I'm about to lose my mind. "Well, go on. Open it."

My hands shake as I reach forward and click the latches open. I take a long deep breath and open the case, my eyes landing on a brand new Gibson SG. The same one I've been admiring for weeks.

"Holy shit!" I yell. "But how did you—"

"I asked the guy who works at the music store by the bar which one was your favorite."

My fingers trail reverently down the strings, testing them, feeling them sink against the frets. The body is so shiny I can see my reflection. "But . . . this must have cost a fortune. Surely you don't—"

She shakes her head and waves me off. "Consider it nineteen years' worth of birthday and Christmas gifts together with your graduation present."

I'm nearly in tears again. This day has wreaked havoc on my emotional stability. I turn to Noreen and pull her into a crushing hug. "Thank you," I whisper into her hair.

"Just promise me you'll put it to good use, okay? When you're a famous rockstar. For me. For your mom. Don't waste your energy and future on a horrible man who already took so much from all of us," she says as she pats my back. Maybe finally talking about what happened with my mom has eased some of the guilt she's been carrying with her for two decades.

"I'll make sure I can come and see your show. I'm sure Rebecca will be excited to see you perform too."

And like a balloon popping, my excitement bursts.

"What's with the face?" Noreen's eyes are locked on me, her gaze probing.

"Nothing."

"Is everything okay with you and her?"

I nod my head a little too enthusiastically. "Yeah . . . yeah, everything's fine."

Taking another wistful look at my beautiful new guitar, I shut the case and lock it before trying to make a break for the stairs.

"Oh no, no way are you racing out of here like that."

Busted.

I spin around to find Noreen standing with her arms folded across her chest. "Come on, spit it out."

My gaze drops to the floor. "It's nothing. We're great. Going along exactly as planned." I can't keep the irritation out of my voice though, and Noreen catches it.

"What does that mean?"

I take a deep breath and push the hair away from my face. "Rebecca just wants a fling. Just some fun until the end of the school year. She knows I'm leaving so she said that works out perfectly for her."

Noreen's fingers tap on her arm. "But . . . you don't want a fling?"

I try to say yes, that it's all I want from her, but standing here now, after someone has asked me point blank how I feel about her, the truth bubbles up like word vomit.

"I'm in love with her."

The lines of Noreen's face soften. "James . . ."

"Anyway, it doesn't matter."

She steps toward me. "Doesn't matter?"

"We'll go our separate ways and—"

"Tell her how you feel!" Noreen yells at me.

"No . . . no way. If I tell her and she doesn't feel the same way it'll make everything awkward between us, and if all I have is four more weeks then I'm going to make the most of them."

I turn to go but Noreen's hand grasps my arm. "James, has what happened between my sister and I taught you nothing?"

I don't turn, but I stop, an ache throbbing in my heart.

"For twenty years I wondered what happened to Dora. Wishing I could tell her I was sorry. What she really meant to me. That I loved her so fiercely it nearly killed me when she left. That every day, I regretted what I said out of anger, wishing to replace it with all the beautiful ways she made me feel special. If you love Rebecca, then for the love of God, tell her. If you don't, you'll always regret it, and you'll never know if she felt the same way but was too scared to tell you."

Her words hang in the air and when she finally lets go, I don't look back, simply carrying the heavy guitar case up the stairs. When I enter my room, I set the case on top of the milk crates and take the guitar out. It's so beautiful and I can't wait to see how differently it plays compared to my old Epiphone. I set it on the stand by the stereo then look out the window. Rebecca doesn't appear to be there, or perhaps she's still sleeping. It's still early morning, but I'm exhausted, emotionally and physically.

With the truth that's been revealed, I feel like I've been torn apart and glued back together. Other than Noreen, there's only one other person I think will understand—one person who I'm desperate to share this with. I think about Rebecca and the note I wrote last night when we exchanged words through our windows. The note where I almost confessed that I love her. How I shut it up in my notebook instead. I can't tell her. Noreen doesn't understand, either. It's not the same.

Rebecca deserves so much more than me. And she should have it. She'll have her fun with me then go off to college, marry some smart, preppy guy that can provide her with everything her heart desires. Besides, after Rebecca comes out of this exciting new relationship phase she'll remember that I'm just the freak. The lonely, broken boy who gets left by everyone.

So I won't tell her. Then when this is over, I'll cry my broken heart out into a case of beer and I'll make sure that one day I record that song. The one I said reminded me of her. But that's not entirely true because I wrote it *for* her. I'll record it and one day when she's done college or even ten years from now, she'll hear it on the radio. Maybe then she'll think of me and what we were for a while.

CHAPTER 33

Paranoid

REBECCA

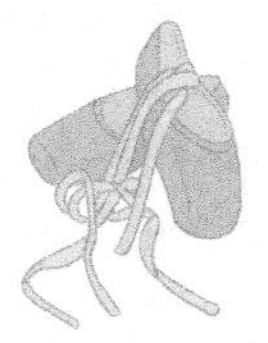

April changes into May and with it brings unseasonably warm weather but even that doesn't brighten my mood as I walk down the street toward James's van. Eric's threat from last night is hovering over me like a gigantic bat—pervading every thought and action. When I spot the black van idling on the side of the road, that desperately needed joy doesn't bloom in my chest like it normally does. No, now it's accompanied by fear and I find myself looking all around me to make sure I'm not being watched or followed.

"You're late. I thought maybe . . . Hey, are you okay?"

James's dark eyes capture mine, the sunlight filtering in through the windshield highlighting the chocolate brown in his irises.

"Sorry," I say, shaking my head. "I didn't sleep very well last night, I'm a bit spaced out."

He tilts his head at me. "Are you sure? You look—"

I lean forward quickly to kiss him, effectively stopping his line of questioning, then pull back. "I'm going to get changed."

One of my favorite parts of the day now is picking out something to wear from the bags of clothes Noreen provided. It's like being a little kid again and getting to play dress up. I sway from side to side as James pulls the van out into traffic. I spot an adorable pair of brown corduroy pants with suspenders and pull them on.

I pair it with a cream peasant blouse, the suspenders hooking over my shoulders, and climb back into the front seat.

James eyes me up and down and smirks. "Very high-fashion today, huh?"

I pull my shoulder forward a bit bashfully. "You think so?"

"Very hot."

Heat floods my cheeks. It feels absurd that he should say something like that. After all, I've been taught to believe over the past few years that no man in his right mind would want me like this. That I had to be the peak of femininity and modesty. But, even though I'm wearing pants and I've put on a few more pounds, James's attention has never wavered. In fact, even now I catch him stealing looks at me, his fist tightening on the steering wheel.

"Hey," I say, reminded when I see the cuts and bruises along his knuckles, "what happened Saturday night? What did you find out about your mom?"

James sighs. "I found—she wrote in her journal that she was . . . raped."

An icy chill spreads across my entire body. "James, I—" But I don't even know what to say.

He reaches over and grabs my hand, his calloused fingers lacing through mine. "He was her boyfriend, and we're guessing it happened after homecoming."

My tongue unsticks. "Did it say who it was?"

His fingers squeeze mine a little and I gently rub my thumb over the red blisters from where he punched the dumpster .

"Some asshole named Jet. But there's no last name and Noreen didn't recognize it."

Something flickers in the back of my memory. Like a firefly in the reeds across a wide lake. Bright enough to know it's there but too little to distinguish. Unfortunately, it's as if James can see the recognition on my face.

"Do you know him?" he asks desperately.

I shake my head. "I think I've heard the name before—maybe once, as a kid. But . . . I'm not sure. I'm so sorry."

He nods and turns back to the road. "It's okay. Probably for the best anyway. I'd kill him then get hauled off to jail."

Eric's threat boils up to the surface of my mind, and I feel sick.

"Are you sure you're okay?" James asks.

I nod and smile, hoping he doesn't see the sweat over my brow. "It was just a long day yesterday." So much has happened recently it's hard to choose which thing to stress over. Not getting accepted into college, my impending marriage, Eric threatening me, God's judgment, and now James's mom and the horrible thing she endured.

"Right, yeah."

"I'll be fine. Are *you* okay? After learning all of that? It's so awful. Is there anything I can do?"

He blinks rapidly, his eyes turning glassy for a moment, but he shakes his head. "There's nothing really that can be done," he says. He tells me about Noreen's confession, about the black van that came to take away his mom when she'd done nothing wrong. My knee bounces and my hands tremble.

I swallow against the hard lump in my throat. "You know," I say, a dark smile lifting my cheeks, "I thought that's who you were."

"What?"

"That first day, when you pulled down the street in this van. I was sure it was the dreaded black van coming to take me away for something I'd done to upset my parents. That's always what scared me the most when I got in trouble, being sent away."

He nearly slams on the brakes. "Wait . . . your parents have threatened to send you away if you disobey them?"

I shrug my shoulders. "I mean . . . yeah."

"Becks, that's messed up. Your parents are evil."

Snorting out a laugh, I turn away. "They're not evil!"

Approaching the school, he pulls over on the side of the road and stops. "Yes, they are. Look at what they've done to you!"

I'm thrown off guard by the anger in his tone. "James, it's fine. It's normal—"

"Jesus, Becks, starving you, squeezing you into clothes they know don't fit so you can hardly breathe, threatening to have some maniacs come and take you away if you step out of line? That's not normal."

"You don't understand. At Holy Grace . . . It's like that around here—"

He huffs. "Just because it happens a lot around here, doesn't make it right! Look at what happened to my mom!"

I open my mouth to retort, to defend, but nothing comes out. Finally, my lips press together. James looks away then lets go of my hand to squeeze the steering wheel.

Sitting like a child who spilled milk on the floor, I wait, shame radiating out of every fiber of my body. Finally, he tilts his head back and sighs. "I'm sorry. I just—fuck, Rebecca. Thinking about what they do to you . . . it kills me."

Like a match strike, my heart bursts like fireworks and I want to tell him. Tell him I love him. That I never want to be away from him.

"Thank God you'll be able to get away to college next year."

Icy water soaks my soul and douses out the light. I consider lying, but I'm already keeping so much from him. I can't lie about this too.

"I—I'm not going to college."

He laughs. Genuinely laughs. His hair tossing back and forth as he clutches at his chest.

"Ha! Good one, Becks."

But I shake my head. "No, I'm serious. I'm not going to college."

His face goes rigid and serious. "What? Why the fuck not?"

I look down at my shoes, my voice dropping to a whisper. "I didn't get in."

There's a long pause.

"Bullshit."

I look up and his eyes are black.

"It's not!"

"There's no way you didn't get into college."

My mouth works furiously, trying to form the words. "Well . . . believe it! I didn't. I didn't get a single acceptance letter."

"That's impossible." His jaw is twitching and his eyes narrow on me as if trying to discern if I'm lying. "You work harder in school than anyone I've ever seen. I've seen your test marks, Becks, there's no way *you* didn't get in and Mary did!"

Tears rush up treacherously in my eyes. Truthfully, it's been eating away at me for weeks. The fact that Mary got into Indianapolis and I didn't. Not that I don't think she deserves to go, but I know for a fact that my GPA is better than hers . . . by a lot.

"Are you sure they even got your applications? There must be some mistake. What was the reason they gave for not accepting you?"

"I—I don't know." Every muscle feels like it's spasming and my chest feels tight. Why do I feel like he's mad at me? Like this is somehow all my fault.

"They would've put a reason in the rejection letters. Like . . . too low of a GPA, or your references were bad or whatever—"

But my heart nearly stops. “Rejection letters?”

He blinks. “Yeah.”

“But . . .” Am I really that stupid? How did I not think of that myself? My head shakes, my hair whipping about my face. “I never got any rejection letters.”

Something dark passes over his face and a sudden chill enters the van. Looking out the window, a dark sky has rolled over us, the trees whipping back and forth in a sudden strong wind like my inner turmoil has turned even the weather on its head. When I turn back, James is looking past me, his eyes unfocused.

“Indianapolis . . .” he mutters as a tremor shoots down my spine. “Becks,” he says, “I think—I think your parents have been taking your mail.”

“Why would you say such a thing?” The sound of my voice is hollow. I can’t even convince myself that it’s nonsense.

James closes his eyes for a long moment and retakes my hand. “A few weeks ago, I was in the backyard smoking when I heard your mom say to your dad that ‘another one came’—from the University of Indianapolis. I didn’t think anything of it at the time. When Mary mentioned she’d gotten accepted at UIndy, I never drew the connection.”

My head starts to shake, and even though I know it’s probably true, a primal part of me can’t believe it. The part that desperately hopes my parents are loving, and supportive, and living for God like they claim to be. Not this sad excuse for a family . . .

James is right. They *really* are evil.

“But . . . how—”

“Think about it,” James says seriously, “mail probably comes in the morning, right? After you’re already at school. You could’ve been getting letters for weeks but wouldn’t know unless they told you.”

No, there wasn’t any mail for you.

“Take me home.”

James blinks. “What?”

“I need to know. It’s Monday. The mailman will have come by now. My mom will be out all morning and my dad will be at work. I can’t sit in class wondering if my parents are deliberately lying to me about getting accepted into college.”

He rubs his free hand along his jaw. “Okay.”

The warning bell rings in the distance. “Wait, James . . . this won’t—you’re still on track to graduate, right? I wouldn’t want to be the reason you fail.”

He grins at me. “Don’t worry. Surprisingly, I’m holding a pretty decent average considering how distracted I’ve been at school.” He wiggles his eyebrows and just like that, the tension releases from my shoulders.

Turning the van around we head back home, and my leg bounces faster the closer we get. I reach forward and turn up whatever music James has in the stereo system. I never fully understood the appeal of such loud and aggressive music before, but after only a few minutes, my leg has stopped bouncing and my head feels clearer and for the first time in my life, I am unabashedly furious.

I barely need the confirmation at this point. I’m certain that this is exactly the kind of thing they would do to manipulate me into doing what they want. That they would do such a heinous thing as hide my college acceptance letters from me. As we pull into James’s driveway, I nearly explode out of my seat.

“Becks!”

But his words barely register as I race for the mailbox at the end of the driveway. Wrenching down the metal door, my heart hammers. Inside is a singular letter and there’s a ringing in my ears as I rip open the letter and stare at the words.

Dear Rebecca Amelie Briar,

Since we have not received an answer on our offer of

admission, your acceptance has been rescinded. As you know, we are a highly competitive program . . .

It's right here. Right in front of my face, and now I have to accept the reality of it all.

"Hey, are you okay?" James gently squeezes my shoulder, but I head for my house.

I throw open the front door, the clinking of James's chain not far behind. I pass the living room and the dining room, not a thing out of place as usual, and head straight for my father's office. It's the one place in the house I've always been told to stay out of and therefore, if my parents are hiding something from me, it's the first place they would put it.

My father's mahogany desk sits in the center of the room. The papers and folders are obsessively organized on the top as I use my fingertips to scan through the various bills and documents.

"Your house feels like a museum," James mutters, out of breath. I glance up for a moment to see him taking in the surroundings.

I open the first drawer of the desk. "Actually, it feels like a prison."

"Do you want me to help?"

I shake my head. Nothing in the first drawer or the second.

"I don't think you're going to find anything," James says, rifling through some papers on the desk. "Why would they keep them?"

"Maybe because they think I'm too stupid to ever come looking." My face grows hot, the tears brimming in my eyes as I try to accept the reality of it all. My parents lied right to my face. Kept this from me and made me believe that I wasn't good enough. That I didn't work hard enough. That I was a failure and not destined for anything more than being Eric Corbley's wife.

"Becks?"

I look up into James's dark eyes and a painful ache spreads through my chest. Realizing that none of this matters. That I'm reliant on my parents to pay for college. And even if I confront them about all the lies, they'll simply say it's what God wants for me. No, they want me to get married immediately. So I can—what? Have babies? Be the uneducated teacher at their new school? Not be their problem anymore? It doesn't make any sense.

"Hey," James says from across the desk. "Is your dad in some kind of financial trouble?"

I'm pulled out of my thoughts as I look up and find James reading a letter from the top of the desk.

Shaking my head I ask. "Not that I know of. Why?"

James's eyes flick between me and the letter. "This letter is from a debt collector. I recognize the company. My mom had a bunch of these come in. They used to call the apartment all the time."

My hands shake. "The phone calls . . ."

"Huh?"

Those incessant phone calls that suddenly stopped. What did my dad tell them? They stopped . . . right before the Corbleys came over for dinner. "What does it say?" I ask.

His eyebrows shoot up and disappear under his fringe. "It says your dad owes . . . two hundred and fifty thousand dollars to the bank."

"Two hundred and fif—"

But the sound of the front door opening and closing has my heart leaping from my chest. The sound of my mother's heels clicking down the hallway as she passes the office toward the kitchen. I'm frozen—panicking, worried I might pass out again. But James lifts his finger to his lips signaling me to be quiet. The door is shut and I could kiss him for the instinct he had to close it after us.

He nods toward the desk, and I take the hint to put everything where it was while he slowly and silently replaces the debt collection letter onto the pile. Thankfully, my mother's commotion in the kitchen hides the creaking of the desk drawer as I slide it closed before coming around the desk to grasp James's hand like a lifeline.

"What are the chances she goes out again?" James breathes into my ear.

"Slim to none," I whisper. "But if we're lucky she'll head into the sewing room and turn on *The Gospel Bill Show*, then we can escape out the front door."

He nods and entwines his fingers with mine as we hold our breath and desperately hope my mother doesn't feel the urge to check on anything in here. Closing my eyes, I lean into James's strong body. Everything is such a mess. My life is splitting apart at the seams and I feel more trapped than ever. His thumb brushes against the top of my hand, and I glance up at him. His eyes are closed, his chest rising and falling rapidly, and I think about how lost I would be without him. How simply the act of his hand in mine is what's keeping me from falling apart right now. How loving him is the only thing making my life worth living. The words are there. Sitting on the edge of my tongue trying to burst past my lips—I love you. But my jaw is frozen. I love you. Just say it. My jaw unhinges and my lips part.

"James?" I whisper.

He opens his eyes and looks down at me and the words are right there. Just tell him.

The sound of the TV blaring from the living room followed by the noisy thrumming of the sewing machine needle makes me swallow down those three words.

"Now's our chance," he whispers and pulls me along behind him. For the briefest moment I can see the words I didn't say hanging in the empty air behind us. As quietly as possible he turns the door handle and I'm surprised at how stealthy he is. The noise of the TV increases as the door opens inch by inch and before I can blink I'm being torn down the hall, out the front door and across the lawn to the other side of James's van.

We try to catch our breath, but even out here we're exposed, the little old ladies on my street having nothing better to do with their time than watch out their windows for anything out of the ordinary.

"Someone might see us," I wheeze.

James's brow furrows then he looks around before his gaze meets mine. He opens his mouth but stops himself from saying something. His lips press together then he nods and jerks his head over his shoulder. He pulls me toward his front door, and I'm not sure if it's the adrenaline rushing through my veins or if my emotions are on the fritz, but I'm suddenly giddy with the idea of being in his house.

Once we're inside, he leads me through to the kitchen, grabs a few sodas from the fridge then pulls me upstairs. I've seen his room before. Hundreds of times. For hours I've looked over his things through the window, but somehow being here—surrounded by him, the smell of him, all of his possessions—feels so intimate. He moves across the room to shut the curtains. The room falls into darkness, the sunlight through the dark fabric casting a golden glow over his skin.

"Sit down, you're shaking."

I blink rapidly as I'm led to the edge of his bed. Once I'm sitting, I realize he's right. I'm practically vibrating—a level of anxiety I've never felt before taking control of my limbs. If only I could relax.

"Becks, take some deep breaths with me, okay?"

James's dark eyes find mine as he crouches in front of me. He mimics a deep breath in and out and I try. Really, I do, but my body doesn't seem to want to cooperate with what my brain is trying to have it do.

"I think . . . I might be in shock?" I whisper.

His fingers massage the insides of my palms, the gesture distracting and relaxing at the same time. Continuing the breathing exercises, our rhythms finally sync up.

"Better?" he asks.

I nod and he smiles warmly before sitting down next to me and pulling a box out of his nightstand. When he opens a bag and pulls out a cigarette I open my mouth in outrage.

"Hey! We had a deal—"

He places it between his teeth and smirks. "Not a cigarette, angel. And after all that? I need to take the edge off or I'm going to break something and between you and me, there's nothing in here I want broken."

My stomach flips over. "Oh . . . you mean that's—"

He pulls a lighter from his pocket but stops. This is what he does to relax, and he's not an addict. Maybe I had it wrong about pot. "I can go outside if it bothers you. I know it doesn't smell the best—"

"Can I try some?"

The words just run, like freed hostages from my mouth. Maybe it's because nothing apart from him seems to matter anymore or the fact that the idea of getting high with him, in his room, after so many lies seems like the most honest and normal thing I could do right now. I just want to float away with him.

He stares at me for a long moment. "Are you serious?"

I roll my shoulders back and nod.

"What happened to, 'I'm not going to do drugs?'" he says.

"I trust you," I say simply.

His eyes dart over my face, hesitating. The joint bobs up and down between his lips. Finally he nods and flicks the lighter, the tip of the joint sparking to life.

"Right. You want to take a tiny inhale and hold it in your lungs before you blow it out."

He passes it to me, and my fingers aren't shaking when I take it. I put the joint between my lips and suck, the glowing ember brightening.

Then I can't breathe. I cough and cough, spluttering endlessly as my eyes and nose water. Something cold is pressed into my hand and my eyes refocus to find the soda can open. I take a drink after the coughing passes, and James is smirking devilishly.

"Not bad, for virgin lungs."

"You—could've—warned me . . ." I splutter.

He shakes his head with a smile. "Nope, got to figure that out for yourself the first time, I'm afraid. It does get easier though."

"Did I do okay?" I whisper.

James's hands cover mine to release the joint from my grip. "Yeah, angel, you did great."

My eyes feel heavy and I lay back on the bed, my head finding his pillow. The smell of him is everywhere. "You smell so good."

He chuckles, and I feel his hands removing the shoes on my feet before the heavy drop of his own boots hit the floor. Lying down next to me, he wraps his hands around my body and pulls me close. It's possible I fall asleep, or maybe I just lose track of time. Or maybe it's only been a few minutes before he speaks next.

"Becks?"

"Hmm?"

"Are you okay?"

I am okay. For just a few moments, lying here, I am okay. Or at least I was until James reminded me of the horrific truth of my own life. "I—I know I'm supposed to say yes, but . . . I don't think I can."

He pulls his face back to look down at me. "You're not supposed to say yes unless it's the truth."

I shake my head. "It doesn't matter. It doesn't make any

difference."

"Doesn't make—what do you mean?"

"It's true, it doesn't."

He blinks at my harsh tone, but he needs to understand.

"They may have lied and hidden the truth from me, but it doesn't matter. I can't go even if I went behind their backs. Who would pay for it?"

"We could figure it out—"

"No."

Acceptance seeps into my bones. I resigned myself to my fate weeks ago, but this has helped me accept it for the truth it really is. That this is a deliberate attempt by my parents to control me. It's never been about God. And even if I wanted to escape, Eric would see to it that everything I care about is ruined.

"Then why not leave?"

His face is so beautiful, so expectantly hopeful, that I blink at him stupidly for a long moment before shaking my head. "I can't leave."

"Why not? What could possibly be keeping you here?"

An arranged marriage. No money. The threat from Eric that if I don't follow through on what I promised, he'll dash all of James's dreams with a single word and it'll be all my fault.

A giggle bubbles up from out of nowhere. I feel so mixed up. My body is laughing when all I want to do is cry. "I've already got a job lined up at Holy Grace. In the library and the daycare. That's—that's what I want to do. Work in the community and help people."

James watches me but I look away. Finally he rolls over onto his back and scoffs angrily.

"What?"

He shakes his head. "Nothing."

I push myself up onto my elbow to try and catch his eyes. "No, tell me."

His tongue rolls around the inside of his cheek before finally turning his face to me.

"You know, I really hoped you'd gotten over your martyr bullshit."

My stomach clenches. Wait, he *is* mad at me. "What?"

His eyes are burning coals and heat prickles the back of my neck. "You told me before you hate that shit! Now that's what you're planning to do as a career? That you don't want anything more for yourself than to run around doing bullshit jobs for someone else and taking care of everyone but you?"

I shake my head. "I—"

"You need to get away from here, Becks," he says pleadingly.

I want to, desperately, but I can't. If only he knew how much I want to run away with him. "I—I want to stay."

James's mouth twists unpleasantly before finally dropping his gaze and turning to stare up at the ceiling. "I thought . . . but—nevermind." He shakes his head and looks away. "I find it hard to believe anyone would want to spend any longer in this piece of shit town than necessary."

"You didn't grow up here. It's not all bad—"

"If it weren't for that fucking promise I made my mom, I'd be gone already."

I feel as if an ice pick has been jammed into my heart. I turn away from him onto my side and curl inward on myself like a wounded animal. The reminder of why he's even here like a nuclear bomb, exploding the fantasy of him somehow rescuing me from this hell.

"Shit—I don't mean . . ." His voice trails off like he's not sure what to say.

The tears fall, and I don't even try to stop them. With my face turned away, maybe he won't know. "No, it's fine. You're going to be a famous rockstar, and I'll go to the record store and listen to your albums—"

"Becks—"

"And I'll remember how you used to practice right here, in your room, and the way you smiled when you caught me watching."

"Don't—"

"I'll be fine, James." I say it sharply, as though I need to convince myself as much as him. "You don't have to worry about me."

He rolls toward me and sighs, his forehead resting on my shoulder blade. Warm breath scatters over my back igniting the physical desire for him somewhere low in my belly.

"You told me this is what you want," he whispers.

"It is." It was. But I was so wrong. I want so much more. But I want him to have everything he ever dreamed of even more than that.

His lips are on my neck and his fingers curl into the flesh of my waist. I need the distraction he can provide, and the inhibitions I normally carry around with me like a chain have flown out the window with the help of my high. Shuffling back into him, I press our bodies together and grab his hand, tracing it down between my legs.

"Touch me," I whisper.

But he stills, even though I can feel his erection growing against the back of my thigh. "Becks, wait—"

I roll over, lifting my leg to straddle his stomach. Surprise flashes in his eyes before I lean down and kiss him. "Please, James. You're the only one who makes me feel good. Don't take that away from me too."

"Okay."

As James's fingers and lips bring me over the precipice of pleasure, I can't help but think that it no longer scares me that God is watching my sins unfold like a story. Rather, I'm scared God was never there to begin with.

CHAPTER 34

Flight of Icarus

JAMES

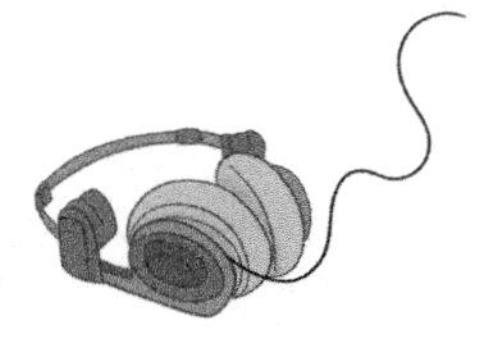

RULE #1 - MUSIC BEFORE EVERYTHING ELSE.

"You okay, man?"

I look up to find Dave, Keith and Joel's eyes on me.

"I, sorry . . . yeah, I'm fine."

"You're okay with that set list then?" Joel asks as he plucks idly on the E string of the bass guitar slung over his chest.

Nodding, I try to grin. "Yeah, man, I think it's solid."

It's been a week and a half since I found out my mom was raped. A week and a half since Rebecca discovered her parents were hiding her college acceptance letters, and a week and a half since I realized Rebecca is lying to me about something.

Or maybe it's many somethings—I don't know.

For the past ten days, I've felt like I'm being pulled in too many different directions. I want to be with Rebecca all the time, but I have work and practice, and she has appearances to keep, so we can only steal small moments together. But when we do have time together, she seems on edge—always worried someone will see us. And I get it . . . I really do. Her parents would lose it and probably have her sent away in that horrible van if they found out we spent time together, but that deeply broken part of myself still thinks it's because she doesn't want to be seen with me. That she doesn't actually want me.

And while being physical with Rebecca is something that is always on my mind, after that time in my room—it feels somehow wrong. My heart and brain constantly warring with my body to tell me this isn't right. That I should walk away because all I'm doing is getting closer and closer to having my heart torn to shreds.

I haven't even told her about the gig Dave landed us, or the fact that an exec from Megaloud Records is coming to see us perform. I mean, how could I? When everything around her is falling apart, how can I ask her to be happy about something that's happening in my life? That will take me away from her? It should be exciting and I desperately want to share it with her, but each time the urge strikes to tell her, all I hear is her response when I told her she needs to get away from here. *I want to stay.*

"James, listen," Dave says, circling around the drum kit and turning off my amp. "I know we're all trying not to put too much stock in the Megaloud boss coming to the show, even though . . . that's pretty much impossible."

I laugh and nod. "Yeah, that's pretty much impossible."

"So, I made some calls into a few ads I saw in the paper. There's no point in us sticking around here much longer. Everything for us is out west. If this goes well or even if it doesn't, we could head to San Fran by the end of May. There's a few house rentals we could all chip in on together. What do you think?"

Here it is. Everything I've ever dreamed of doing is being served to me on a goddamn silver platter. I'm in an awesome band, playing live, moving to San Francisco to pursue music—what more could I possibly ask for?

"That sounds perfect. I'll have my diploma before then too."

Dave smiles then tilts his head. "And your little Strawberry Shortcake girlfriend? What does she think about all this?"

Shaking the hair back from my face, I look down and fiddle with the tuning knobs. "She knows I'm leaving. She's cool with it."

Dave narrows his eyes at me. "Really?"

My lips press together tightly before taking off my new Gibson guitar and putting it in its case. "Yeah, really."

"Sweet thing like her? It's hard to believe that."

"Yeah, well . . . you know how it is. Good girls want to be corrupted then they go back to their cookie-cutter lives." The moment the words leave my mouth I regret them, and while Dave laughs and shakes his head as he walks away, I feel like ramming my skull through the bass drum. Because that's not how I see her at all.

OVER THE NEXT week as I force my ass to sit in Mrs. Henry's history class, I can't stop from obsessing over it. I know she must feel something for me. And what I said to her—*If it weren't for that fucking promise I made my mom, I'd be gone already*, it makes me feel nauseous every time I think about it. She tried to hide it, but I know I made her cry. I've made her cry so many fucking times now, but I don't want her to have to hide from me.

I want to stay.

Rebecca doesn't want to leave. It won't make a difference if I ask her to leave with me or not. She said she'll be fine, so why am I obsessed with trying to save her?

And what could I possibly give her? I have nothing. Rebecca's never known poverty like I have. Not knowing whether there'll be heat when you get home, or where your next meal is coming from, and while I've saved almost every dollar I've made since moving here, it won't go far. It won't buy her the college education she deserves. It won't pay for the dance classes she loves. It won't provide the comfortable home she should have where she can be happy with a family she chooses for herself. A family who appreciates her.

I can't give that to her. Because I'll be chasing after my stupid fucking dream, living out of the back of my van and playing all night in dirty, run-down night clubs, living with a bunch of other guys doing the same thing. Becks deserves better than that life. So even if she wanted to run away with me, how could I put her through that?

My hand slams down on the desk in my frustration, and I feel every eye in the class spin around to look.

"Problem, Mr. Walton?" Mrs. Henry asks over her glasses.

I shake my head. "Sorry, no, my hand slipped."

Feeling Rebecca's jade-green gaze on me, I keep my eyes fixed on my desk. Pulling out my notebook, I flip through to the last few pages. If anyone were to find this, they might think it belongs to Dr. Jekyll and Mr. Hyde. There's anger scattered across the last few pages. My frustration and pain fill the margins after learning about what happened to my mom. Trying to catalog clues that might tell me who Jet is. But there are words from my aching heart that scream out in black ink across the page.

I'm still holding onto the shred of hope that maybe you'll change your mind. That you love me as much as I love you and are willing to risk it all to be with me.

When the bell rings for lunch, I head to the table next to Rebecca, where she sits with Amy and Mary. Some days we simply pass each other like we're strangers, choosing instead to wait for the ride home from school to get our daily dose of each other. Then there are other days when I can't stop staring at her, and for anyone who might be paying attention, it's probably creepy. Then I spend the rest of the day trying to steal her away for a few private moments because I simply can't help myself.

"So, what do you say, Becca?" Amy says.

My ears perk up at the mention of her name.

Mary scoffs. "Oh come on, Ames, Becca's not going to come—"

"Actually, I was thinking I will. Come to the party, I mean."

It takes everything in me not to spin around in my seat.

"But . . . how will—what?" Mary asks, flabbergasted.

I can see Rebecca shrug out of the corner of my eye. "I mean, I'll need your help, of course. Convincing my parents to let me stay out late, but I really want to come. The last high school party before prom? Before graduation? I want to be there."

There's a pause, then a deafening squeal causing several onlookers to turn our way.

"Oh my goodness! Yes, Becca! I'm so excited. Okay, well . . . I can have my mom call your mom and say you're going to sleep over at my place. You know my mom is in bed by seven, out cold from the pills, so she won't even know we've gone out—"

"You know Eric will be there," Amy interjects.

"Yeah, I know."

"So what if he's there?" Mary says. "It's good he'll be there. He can see how much he blew it by being a lying, cheating asshole."

"Well, where is the party again anyway?" Rebecca asks.

"Jeremiah's place."

"So there'll be alcohol?"

"It's Jeremiah, so obviously."

"Wait, Becca, are you saying you want to drink?"

A long pause. "I mean, one drink won't hurt, right? Just to try it?"

My stomach turns. This party is a bad idea. Becks getting high in the safety of my bedroom during the day is one thing. Drinking at a house party where everyone can see? That sounds like trouble. Not to mention she's been acting . . . different, and this seems reckless.

"What are you going to do about prom now anyway, Becca?"

"What do you mean?"

A pause. "Well, you and Eric aren't together anymore. Aren't you worried about going without a date? It's only two weeks away and almost everyone's paired up already."

Rebecca laughs, a musical, delicate sound that I haven't heard in a while. "I'm hardly concerned about bringing a date to prom. To be honest, the idea of prom seems somewhat ridiculous now."

I can practically hear Amy and Mary's mouths dropping open indignantly. "How can you say that?"

A sigh. "It's just . . . dressing up in a fancy dress and dancing around isn't exactly what I would picture as the culmination of my high school experience."

Mary splutters. "Well, what would?"

But Rebecca stays quiet until Amy and Mary carry on their conversation, reassuring each other that prom will be everything they've ever hoped it would be. And I keep thinking that dancing with Rebecca in a beautiful dress doesn't seem like a bad way to spend an evening.

"So you want to drink and party now?" I ask Rebecca as she climbs over me to sit in the passenger seat, the door handle on the fritz again.

She stops and narrows her eyes at me. "Is that something I'm not allowed to do?"

I hold my hands up in surrender. "No, I—it's just that . . . I'm worried you—nevermind."

Her expression softens. "I'm sorry. I don't mean to snap at you. I guess I'm just realizing high school is almost over. There's less than three weeks left and I don't want to miss out on anything."

"Yeah . . . right," I say, running a hand through my hair.

"Besides, you'll come, won't you?"

I turn to her pretty face smiling at me so expectantly. "I—well, I usually work Fridays, you know."

Her face drops. "Right, I forgot."

"But I can ask for it off. I can maybe work Tuesday to make up for it."

She smiles again and leans forward to kiss me. Wrapping her arms around my neck, I quickly glance around, but we're out of sight of the school. Another thing she's added to her requests is that she doesn't want to be picked up and dropped off on school grounds anymore, and while it tears my chest open day by day, I don't want to lose her, so I agreed.

My hands cup her face as she straddles my lap, her hips rocking against mine.

"You know," she whispers against the shell of my ear, "I was thinking that maybe after the party we could . . ." Her voice trails off but she leans back—dark eyes and flushed cheeks, her teeth biting into her pouty lip.

"We could . . . what?" My heart is racing—sprinting.

She smiles nervously, tucking her hair behind her ears. "You know . . . we could do something that we haven't done yet." Her eyebrows lift, willing me to understand. Then her hips roll torturously slowly over mine and it clicks.

"Oh! Fuck . . . I, uh—" My throat is suddenly like sandpaper and my cock swells beneath her. "Are you sure you want to? I mean, I haven't been pressuring you, have I?"

She leans forward to kiss along my jaw. "No, you haven't. I want to."

My eyes close as she sucks gently over my pulse point. "We don't have to rush it." A voice inside my mind is screaming at me to shut the fuck up, but my heart is finally in control for once. "Your first time . . . it should be special."

"Was yours?"

No it wasn't. To be honest, my first time was at a house party and it was rushed and awkward, and I don't even know the last name of the girl it was with. "No. But yours should be."

She sits back on my thighs. "Why wouldn't it be special with you? I want it to be you."

I cup her face and hold her in my palms. Her eyes are sparkling again. They haven't in so long. Not since before she found the letters, and I would do anything to keep that sparkle alive. She wants it to be me. "Okay. If that's what you want."

She smiles nervously. "Okay."

Tell her. Tell her. *Tell her.*

I clear my throat and shift in my seat, pushing the vision of her naked body trembling under mine aside. "I, uh . . . there's something I want to tell you."

Her eyes dart over my face, her posture tense, anxious.

"I . . ."

I love you. I want to be with you. I'll give up everything I've ever wanted to take care of you.

"I just . . . my band has a gig in two weeks—at the bar," I say, the words spewing from my mouth, hatefully knowing they're not what I truly want to tell her.

Her face lights up and she clasps her hands together. "Oh James! Really? That's amazing!"

"It's the same night as prom."

She blinks. "Oh." Then shakes her head and smiles. "That's okay, I'd much rather come and see you play."

Sighing, I shake my head. "You know that's probably not a good idea. It's one thing for me to take you after school . . . during the day. It's another to go at night on your own. What would you even tell your parents?"

The wrinkle above her nose appears, and she pouts. "They'll think I'm at prom! It's perfect, I can—"

"The chaperones will notice you're missing."

She shakes her head. "Well, I can ask Mary to cover for me—"

"But what would you tell Mary? She doesn't know about . . . us. Besides, you can't miss prom."

"I don't care about prom, not if you're not there."

She's getting upset again, the moisture brimming in her eyes. It's moments like this where I feel so confused I want to scream. How she can sit here and cling so desperately to wanting to spend our time together, then turn around and convince me so completely that she only wants that until we graduate. That she'll be happy here once I'm gone.

"Don't cry, angel, please. You're breaking my heart."

My thumbs wipe at her lash line as she sniffles then a short laugh bursts out of her. Her hand grips mine and places it over her chest, the beating of her heart thundering beneath her skin. "Mine was broken, but I think you fixed it."

I wish I could just quit. That I didn't need the money, because I just want to keep Rebecca wrapped up in my arms, her face buried in my neck. My number-one rule taunting me in the back of my mind. *Music above all else.* Because even though I know she never would, if she asked me to give it up for her, I wouldn't hesitate. And while she's made it clear that sex is on the table, all I can think about is staying like this forever. That if I can forget about our time running out, how she keeps me a secret, how I know she's keeping something from me, and how I can't fucking tell her how much I love her—I'm actually happy.

I guess the only question that remains is, am I strong enough to leave her when the time comes? When she doesn't want me anymore?

Too soon it's the time that I need to get her home so I can head to work. I turn on the engine and pull out onto the road, Rebecca heading into the back to change back into the torture devices her mom calls clothes. The sunlight is heavy and orange, reflecting off of the cars as we make our way through the busy streets. After the third right turn, I notice an eighty-five Monte Carlo following along behind me. Something prickles up the back of my neck, and I take an unnecessary right turn, wondering if they'll continue to follow.

I hold my breath as I wait, but the car just passes by, the setting sunlight making it too difficult to discern if it belongs to anyone I know. But Rebecca's hand is on my shoulder a moment later as she climbs back into the front seat, her body restricted and trapped beneath the fabric. My hand runs along her spine, my fingertips brushing over the open zipper hiding beneath her cardigan.

"Are you okay?" I ask as she fidgets.

She sighs. "I just wish I didn't have to pretend so much. It's exhausting."

I want to ask if she just means the clothes, but I'm too much of a coward. "I understand now, you know."

Her eyes focus on me. "What do you mean?"

"Why you were naked. Why you took everything off for me—before we were . . ." My voice trails off.

Her chest rises and falls quicker by the second as though her heart is sprinting to hear what I have to say.

"You wanted someone to look at you and see everything you were hiding. You wanted to be free."

Rebecca's lips begin to tremble and her nose scrunches, so I know she's trying to keep her emotions from overwhelming her. And maybe I can't say those three words I want her to know, but maybe I can say something else.

"I just want you to know that when I look at you, I see someone worthwhile. Someone who deserves everything they could ever want."

Her kiss is fierce and bruising, and I give it right back to her as a way of spilling what I can't say from my mouth to hers. Like maybe our lips will interpret what my heart needs her to hear. But then she's out of the van and disappearing around the corner and I'm turning the van around in the opposite direction as Noreen's words echo around the inside of my skull.

If you love Rebecca, then for the love of God, tell her. If you don't, you'll always regret it, and you'll never know if she felt the same way but was too scared to tell you.

It's true. If I don't tell her, I'll spend the rest of my miserable life wondering what could've been. How I was too much of a fucking coward, terrified of being left and abandoned by the people I love to take a shot at being happy. But as I try to convince myself to take the plunge, consequences be damned, I can't help but hear her words.

I want to stay.

So I pour more of my soul into ink and paper instead of handing over my heart.

CHAPTER 35

The Writing on the Wall

REBECCA

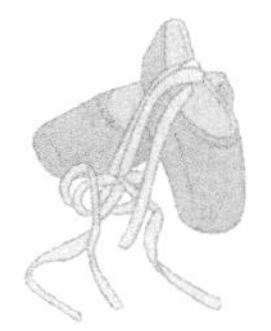

It's surprisingly easy to convince my mom to let me stay over at Mary's house. In fact, she's been in a good mood for the past two weeks, and if I cared enough, I might even ask why, but I have a feeling I'll know eventually. Even my dad has been . . . well, not friendly, but he's been around more, and while our conversations consist of prayer and belittlement, I'm not overwhelmed by the crushing anxiety I normally feel when he's in the room.

"It'll just be you and that worldly girl? Mary?" she asks at the dinner table Thursday night. Her smile is full as she watches me push around the potatoes on my plate, having no idea that James brought me a container of leftover spaghetti for lunch.

I nod. "Yeah, and Amy, of course."

"I imagine they're getting excited for prom and all that."

"Yes, it's all anyone can talk about."

"Will Eric be picking you up that night?"

My fork clatters noisily onto my plate as I fumble at the mention of his name. "Sorry?"

My mother narrows her eyes. "Prom. Eric's driving you?"

I hesitate, then blurt out, "Oh, yes. And he'll drop me off after. He's such a gentleman that way."

It nearly kills me not to roll my eyes as my mother nods, satisfied, and after our nightly family prayers, I'm able to escape from the dinner table to my bedroom. James's room is dark and empty but even so, I stand at the window and stare into it because I know our time is running out.

Now that he has a performance with his band coming up, it's even more imperative that I'm mindful of Eric's threats. I could never forgive myself if I were the one to stop James from achieving his dreams. It's simply too awful to think about, and it keeps me awake in bed. So I try to distract myself with something else. Something which, in some ways, is even more nerve-wracking.

I meant what I said when I told James I want to have sex with him. I'm in love with him and even though he can't know that, it's likely that it will be the only time in my life that I experience that kind of love. So I want all of it, in every capacity, in every facet, in every part of my body. Even though everything I've ever been brought up to believe is telling me otherwise. I want to be bonded to him forever and express how much I love him even though I can't say it. And I know that he'll be kind and gentle and take things as slow as I need. Eric would never extend me the same courtesy. No, Eric wouldn't care about making sure I feel good.

Thinking about James and me together floods my body with heat and my hand traces down my body between my legs. I imagine it's his touch, and it's not long before my orgasm has me trembling underneath the sheets. And simply because I can, I release a breath into the darkness. "I love you, James."

A secret whispered between me and God.

AN HOUR and a half into the party at Jeremiah's house and I'm . . . bored. It smells like stale beer in here and while I've tried a couple of sips from the keg in the corner, I still do not understand the appeal of alcohol. It tastes awful, and even though I'm not even remotely drunk, I still don't particularly like the way that the people around me are behaving.

Their destructive, lewd behavior makes me uncomfortable, but nothing makes me feel as anxious as Eric standing in the doorway, watching my every movement. That is, until Jeremiah says something to distract him. He hasn't said anything, but I know he's just waiting for me to do something. Anything. And I start to feel like this was a bad idea. Maybe I should just tell Mary and Amy that I'm not feeling well and we should head back to the house.

"What do you think?" Amy asks, her drink sloshing around in her cup. "Fun, huh?"

I take another miniscule sip of my room temperature beer and nod politely. "Sure, fun."

"You know," Mary says, "I'm happy you're here. I feel like we hardly see or talk to each other anymore."

A small smile pulls at the corners of my mouth. "I know. I've been a terrible friend lately. I'm just—I've been going through a lot at home and—"

"Oh my gosh, what is *he* doing here?"

The hairs on the back of my neck stand on end, and I feel his gaze on me before I find him through the crowd.

Amy scoffs. "Mary, you're such a hypocrite. You were the one begging him for a week to come to a party."

Mary's cheeks darken. "Yeah, well, that's before I realized what a freak he is. Still hot though. Don't you think, Becca? Becca?"

But I'm barely listening as James's tall frame makes its way through the cluster of bodies between us. My body is alight as his dark eyes travel up and down over me, never wavering until he's standing two feet away from me.

"Hi."

"Hi." A smile blooms across his face. He finally looks away and glances at Mary and Amy. "Hi, ladies, enjoying your evening?"

Mary looks like James has personally insulted her by simply saying hello, but thankfully Amy smiles back, albeit a little nervously. "Good, thanks."

"I thought you were too busy working at that dive bar to come to one of our lame parties," Mary says with a sneer, earning a sharp jab to the ribs from Amy.

James turns back to me and shrugs. "Plans change."

My eyes flick past him to where Eric was watching me, but he's gone. I take a deep breath, thinking maybe he finally got bored with watching me standing here doing nothing. I turn my gaze back to James. He's staring at me and my breathing stutters as I think maybe he's trying to tell me something more, but Mary clears her throat and straightens her back. "You want a beer?" she asks.

His eyes flick away from mine. "No, thanks. I've got some weed though if anyone's down?"

Pulling the joint out of his pocket, a thrill speeds through my veins. The beer might be awful, but maybe this would help me loosen up and have fun. I can see Amy and Mary looking at each other nervously, the two of them trying to converse through raised eyebrows and knowing stares.

"Actually, we don't—"

"I'm down." I say, interrupting Mary. I want to loosen up, but also, it gives me the perfect excuse to keep James nearby without my friends getting suspicious.

James grins at me again, and it makes it easy to ignore the incredulous looks from my friends. Something about the way he looks tonight, the way he's looking at *me,* makes me forget that this is a bad idea. All I want is him everywhere. To shout how much I love him in the middle of the party.

"Becca, you're not seriously thinking about this, are you?" Amy asks.

I shrug. "Why not? What could happen?"

"Isn't your church like . . . really against that?"

But I'm not even listening as James places the joint between his lips and lights it. He inhales deeply, the ember glowing on his skin. He steps toward me, right up against me and leans down. For a moment, I think he's going to kiss me, but he says, "Breathe in, angel."

Without even thinking, I start to inhale and as I do, he blows the smoke from his lungs toward my mouth. There's a collective gasp from around me as the smoke billows out of him, into me. I fight the tingling sensation to cough and hold my breath for as long as I can before I release, and the white plume of smoke surrounds us like a cloud. James grins at me, his dark eyes burning as wisps of smoke escape his nose.

He looks like a dragon in human form and I have to stop myself from leaning forward to check if he tastes like flame.

I can feel the looks of everyone around me, but my head is light and airy and the world is moving in slow motion. James backs away from me but his gaze still burns, and the ache I get between my legs pulses desperately as I think about what I want him to do to me later.

"See you around, ladies," he says, then backs away into the crowd before I can protest. Why is he leaving me? Oh, right. Because I told him we can't be seen together.

I stumble back and glance around. Amy and Mary are staring at me, shocked, and a few other people are watching too, as though they not only can't believe I'm here, but that I just let a boy blow smoke in my mouth and I liked it.

"Becca, what the hell was that?" Mary says, gripping my arm in a painful vice.

"What?"

"You sucking the smoke out of Walton's mouth? Are you crazy?"

A giggle bursts out of me, and I shrug.

"Oh my goodness, are you high already?" Amy asks.

"Wasn't that the whole point?" I ask.

Looking down at my cup, I have no interest in finishing this disgusting beer, but maybe I can find some bottled water somewhere.

"I'll be back," I say, heading through the throng of sweaty bodies drinking and undulating to the overly loud music. When I squeeze my way into the kitchen, there isn't any bottled water so I grab a plastic cup and fill it from the tap before taking a long sip. Fingertips find my hip and squeeze gently. His smell fills my head and I close my eyes to hover in my blissful slow motion moment.

"Come with me." His voice speaks against my ear and before I can even tell my body what to do, I follow behind him as he pulls on my wrist. Every time I blink it's like I've jumped forward and time doesn't make much sense right now. Then I'm in a dark room, the door closing and blocking out the noise from the rest of the party.

Calloused fingers are in my hair, tugging on my head before his lips find mine in the dark. Grasping onto his denim jacket, I pull him in as he kisses me until I'm sure my lips are swollen and bruised. I'm lifted up onto a counter, or maybe a dryer, and instinctively wrap my legs around him. Everything is just a throbbing, gasping, groping mess as James pulls away and brushes his thumb along my lip.

"I want you so badly," I whisper.

He holds my face, and I can just see him through the light from around the edges of the door. "Becks—"

I grab his hand and let it slide down my body over my breast. I breathe into his touch and gasp sharply. My mind is trying to play catch up as my body goes barrelling ahead of me.

"Do you have a condom?" I ask.

James stills. "What?"

"Do you have—"

He backs away. "No, I heard you. And yes, I do, in the van but not here."

"Let's go then."

"Wait," he says, pushing me away. "I—I want to tell you something first."

His fingers feel like they're trembling, or maybe it's because my leg is bouncing so much on top of the dryer. The room spins in the dark without him up against me. I feel like I might fall over, so I try to pull him closer, but he stops me.

"Please, Becks, it's about me playing at the bar next weekend."

I blink rapidly, trying to bring the room into focus. "What about it?"

"It's a—well, someone from Megaloud Records is coming to watch us and it could—"

But what James says next turns to a buzzing drone in my ears. As if I've been doused in icy water, my dizziness is gone and the dark is somehow darker than before. I thought we had more time. I thought we had a few more weeks before we had to say goodbye.

"You're leaving."

"Yes, but I told the guys I would stay until—"

Nausea turns my stomach. "You're leaving me."

"No, Becks, listen to me for a second . . ."

I was sure I could do this. Let him go when the time came. But now that it's here the air is pressing on me so tightly I can't breathe. My throat closes and my muscles lock up.

"Breathe," I hear, "just breathe!"

How can I breathe when James is about to leave? I've known this whole time but maybe part of me deep down always thought he might stay. That there could be a happy ending to all of this where I finally escaped the hell I'm living in.

"I need air," I gasp, my hand fumbling for the door. I'm nearly blinded by the light, the noise level assaulting my ears. I look around, squinting for the direction to the patio, when I feel James right behind me. I finally spot the door, but my blood turns to ice as I spot the furious eyes of Eric from across the room. James's hands are wrapped around me and several onlookers are watching, whispering.

Heat floods my cheeks and mercifully my throat opens up in order to get some air in. But everyone saw. Everyone just watched me stumble out of a dark room with James's arms around me and his kisses bruising my skin.

This time, it's not slow motion. No, this time Eric stalks toward us through the crowd like a panther after rabbits. In my panic, I push James away, stumbling out of his grip and nearly knocking over someone's drink. Eric's fingers dig into my forearm as he yanks me forward.

"Rebecca, you're going home," he says, his voice like venom.

But James is there a second later. "Get your hand off her, now."

"I fucking warned you, Becca," Eric whispers dangerously. "Yet here you are, making a spectacle of yourself."

James's hands are on Eric in a flash, his grip on my arm disappearing as he's pushed back against the wall. "What the fuck is your problem, man?" James growls. "She's not yours."

Whatever high I've been feeling is instantly gone, as the most gripping sense of dread crawls its way inside of me to strap a vice around my heart.

"Are you all right?" James asks, his beautiful face creased with worry as his gaze darts over every visible inch of me.

"She's not yours either."

James lets me go before whirling around. "Let it go, man. You fucked up. Move on."

But Eric is smiling. "But that's just it. She will be mine, even after everything."

This isn't happening. I'm frozen in place. It's like watching a terrible car accident. I can't do anything. I can't look away.

James's hands are in Eric's shirt, nearly lifting him off the ground. "Shut the fuck up!"

"Haven't you wondered why she keeps you such a secret?"

I see it. The moment James realizes Eric isn't just trying to get him going. That there's truth to this. He glances at me out of the corner of his eye.

"You know it, don't you? That she's keeping something from you? That she's just using you to be a dirty little slut—"

James's fist collides with Eric's mouth and blood sprays over the wallpaper. I think my hands cover my mouth, but I can't feel it. I'm frozen from terror. James stands over Eric, fist raised ready to punch him again. "Say that again and I'll knock your teeth out."

"Do whatever you want. She's still promised to marry me."

Even though it's noisy, all of the sound suddenly disappears. And while I'm sure the music and chatter of the party is still going on, right now it's so quiet I could hear a pin drop.

James's fist lowers. "What did you say?"

Eric spits the blood from his mouth to the floor and glares up at James. "I said, she's going to be my wife. After graduation."

"You're fucking lying!"

"But I'm not. She and I made a deal. That we'd both do whatever we wanted until graduation. And while I wasn't a fan of her whoring around with you, I knew she'd be a good girl and come back to me. Just like she promised."

Tears of anger and despair and betrayal are burning down my cheeks like lava. James lets go of Eric, who topples back into the wall and rubs at his jaw. It takes forever for him to face me, and even when he does, he's not looking at me. No, he can't bring himself to look into my traitorous face.

"Tell me he's lying, Becks."

It's barely above a whisper and my jaw is trembling so hard I don't think I'll be able to form the words. "James, I—"

"Tell me it's not true!" he yells.

But the words won't come because I can't lie anymore. Not when the truth is laid out like this and all I can do is shake my head, wishing and praying that this is all just a bad dream. His dark eyes flick up to me for a moment and for the first time, they are black as death. No life to them, no burning brightness in their depth. Just empty.

Then he's leaving. He turns and I watch as he pushes his way through the crowd toward the door and the front of the house. My feet unstick themselves from the floor and I tear after him, shouting his name over the noise that has suddenly resumed. The front door bangs open and I'm running after him down the long, dark driveway.

"James, wait!"

He stops and whirls around, his face contorted with rage and his eyes shining with tears.

"All this time? All this time, you were planning to go back to him? To *marry* him?"

My mind races, trying to come up with a way to explain myself. That even though Eric has ruined everything, it could always get worse, so I simply whisper the truth. "Yes."

"So I was just what? A way to get some sort of itch out of your system before you settle down into nuptial bliss?"

My hair whips across my face as I shake my head desperately. "No! No, it isn't like that—"

"You just wanted fun, right? Fun with the freak you knew was leaving anyway."

"James, please—"

"No, I get it. I'll never be able to give you what you want. A nice house and a family that you can dress up for church on Sundays—"

"That's not what I want!"

"This whole time you felt nothing. And to think I was going to ask you to come to San Francisco with me."

I stumble forward. Perhaps the earth has stopped spinning because my entire universe halts when I hear those words. A sob rips past my throat.

"You . . . you were—?"

"But you've had this planned out all along." Tears are trailing down his cheeks. "I hope you'll be very happy together."

He turns and pulls his keys from his pocket. I run after him, my fingers grabbing the denim of his jacket. He spins around and I cling to the front of him. Desperate not to let him leave, fighting against my anguish to try and explain that this is not what he thinks. That it has to be this way. That I love him so much, I'm willing to condemn myself to a life of misery so he can be free.

"Please . . ." I whisper.

But his hands grip my wrists and it forces me to release him as he takes a step back.

"I just—" he stammers, and I dare to look into his face. But he's broken, the remnants of his shattered heart all over his expression like some grotesque mosaic. "I broke all my rules for you."

There's nothing to say. I don't even understand what he means, but I collapse into a heap on the dewy grass as he leaves.

The sound of his van roars to life, then the crunch of the tires on the gravel, then silence. He's gone.

Time passes as the party continues on behind me. Continues as if the world didn't just fall apart. I suppose that's what it feels like when a heart breaks. Like so does the world—a crack in the earth so deep it creates a chasm to the underworld.

I hope Hell will swallow me whole, because it's where I belong.

CHAPTER 36

My Last Words

JAMES

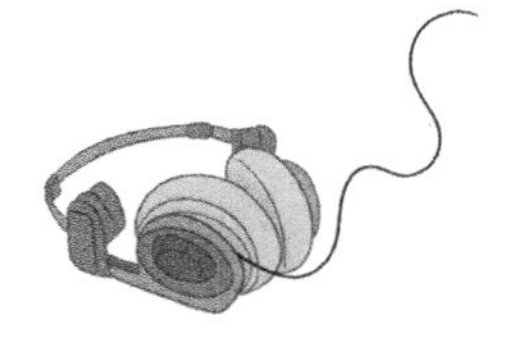

Fuck.

Fuck it.

Fuck everything.

Fuck every single one of them.

And fuck me for thinking it would ever be different than how it's always been. To be dismissed. To be used. Abandoned. Made to feel like I'm not worth anyone's time or love. Maybe I'm not. Maybe it'll never happen for me. That's what I've always thought anyway . . . until she came along.

When I first spotted her through the window, I should've ended it there. I never should have given her that note, or volunteered in the library so I could spend time with her. I never should've gotten involved in any of her bullshit. I should've shut my curtains tight and kept them like that.

A car horn blasts and I swerve as I see the lights coming toward me on the dark road. I hit the patch of dirt on the side and the van fishtails. Gripping the steering wheel I slam on the brakes, the van screeching to a halt as everything in the back shudders and topples over.

"God fucking dammit!" I shout, my fist slamming into the

dash as the stereo blasts to life. I quickly shut it off. There's no drowning out this noise.

All this time, you were planning to go back to him? To marry *him?*

Yes.

I shove my fists into my eyes to stop the hateful tears from spilling down my cheeks, but I can't stop the trembling in my shoulders as my body fights the desperate urge to sob. So I finally let it take control of me. Years and years of rejection—a lifetime of it consuming me all at once until I can't breathe and the world goes dark and I think maybe finally it'll be over. That someone will find my van in the morning and I'll be dead. That's where everyone thinks I'll end up anyway. Dead or in jail. Would anyone be surprised? Would anyone care?

THE DRIVE between the party and Noreen's house is a blur—somehow I end up where I planned on going. I quietly make my way through the house and up the stairs to my room. *Her* room is still dark. There's no sign of life, but I can't stand the sight of it, so I close my curtains with a snap and grab a duffle bag out of the closet. I catch sight of the box of my mom's things and grab the photo album from the top. I look into her young, pretty face, my finger sliding over the glossy paper.

"I get it, Mom. Maybe not in the same way . . . but I get wanting to die without really being dead." I'm sure it was worse for her, but if this is even a fraction of how heartbroken and betrayed she felt that night, then I think I can finally understand what drove her to poison herself with heroin to the point it almost killed her.

Grabbing the duffle bag, I start shoving whatever clothes I can find inside until it's full to the brim, then I grab my guitars and put them in their cases before getting my backpack and heading for the door. I can't—I won't stay here another night. Not when her room is twelve feet away. Even with the curtains closed and the fact she's likely still at the party or at her friend's house, I can't rid myself of her presence. It's like beetles crawling under my skin and eating my soul.

When I get down to the kitchen, I take a piece of paper and scribble out a quick note to Noreen to let her know where I've gone. That I'll stop by before I leave for San Francisco for more of my stuff but that I can't sleep in this house any longer. Then I'm out the door, in the van, backing out of the driveway and heading toward Dave's house.

I pull the visor down, the pack of cigarettes I stashed there falling into my lap. Opening the pack, I pull one out and place it between my lips as I reach for a lighter from the console. It takes a few tries and the lighter finally bursts to life, but as I bring it toward my face, I can't light the cigarette.

Rebecca's thin, pale face looks back at me and I'm transported back to the diner when I found her and it poured rain. The day I made the deal with her that I'd quit smoking if she ate more. The first day I kissed her.

I flick the lighter closed and toss it and the unlit cigarette into the console. Fuck this. I can't even smoke anymore because of her. She has permeated every single cell of my existence.

Dave doesn't ask any prying questions when I show up at his house at three in the morning. Just offers me the couch and says I can stay as long as I want. I desperately want to sleep, to wake up and discover that this has all been just a terrible nightmare, yet when the sun begins to shine in through the windows, I realize I have to come to terms with the fact that last night really happened.

That Rebecca lied to me. That she's going to marry that piece of shit. That she was always just using me before the rest of her life began. Even though I didn't drink a drop of alcohol, I feel like I have the worst hangover of my life.

SATURDAY, I get up. I eat. I practice with the band. I go to work then go back to sleep on the couch.

Sunday, I get up. I eat. I practice with the band. I go to work then go back to sleep on the couch.

But at least in that time, I manage to come up with some sort of plan. When the sun comes up on Monday morning, I head out the door to get to school as soon as they open the doors. Luckily the guidance counselor, Ms. Flora, is there and welcomes me into her office.

"What can I do for you so early on a Monday morning, Mr. Walton?" she asks, taking a sip of her coffee.

I take a deep breath. "I want to check if I'll still be able to graduate if I stop coming to school."

She blinks at me for a long moment. "Well . . . what do you mean?"

"I mean, there's only two weeks left in the school year and most classes I've already turned in my final assignments and papers. It's just the exams that I would miss."

"But—" she stammers, "you'd miss prom and graduation."

I give her a look. "Let's be honest here, Ms. Flora. Does it really look like I care about prom? Or wearing a gown and walking across a stage for a phony blank piece of paper wrapped up in ribbon?"

She chews the inside of her cheek. "No . . . no, I suppose not."

"My average is decent and since the exams are only worth fifteen percent of my final grade, by my calculations I should still have at least fifty percent in all my classes, and be able to get enough credits to get my diploma."

Pulling on her glasses, she turns to her computer screen and starts to type. My fingers tap idly on the armrest as I wait. The halls are starting to get noisy now and all I can think about is wanting to wrap this up before Rebecca shows her face. I don't know what I'll do if I see her. Or that fucker she plans to marry.

"Well," Ms. Flora continues, "I suppose you're correct. You have a high enough grade that missing the exams wouldn't put you below a D."

I grin. "Excellent."

"But is that really what you want? You wouldn't be able to apply to any colleges with a D average."

I stand and pull my bag over my shoulder. "No offense, Ms. Flora, but going to college was never something I intended anyway. You'll mail the diploma to my aunt?"

Startled at my abrupt attempt to leave, Ms. Flora stands as well, then nods. "Of course."

"Great. Thanks for your time."

Without looking back, I leave the guidance office and head toward the parking lot. The chorus of whispered voices that follows me down the hall makes my teeth grind, and I start to sweat as every corner I turn around, I'm worried I'll see her. Then the doors are ahead of me and I'm finally free—I haven't seen her. My hand is on the door handle, but I stop.

Just go. I made it. I'm done. I never have to see her again. I never have to step inside this high school again. I fulfilled the promise to my mother and I have everything laid out ahead of me. The gig. The Megaloud exec. San Francisco. It's all there, just waiting for me to grasp it.

Then why can't I leave?

Because I want to see her—one last time. Maybe to try and understand why she did what she did. What it was about me that was never enough. Why she couldn't risk it all to be with me. Why she didn't love me.

Because I love her more than life itself. More than music. More than making my dreams come true. I would've thrown it all away for her. I almost did.

"Hey, kid, you okay?"

I look over and it's the custodian I met on my first day when I was lost and had no idea where I was going. Somehow, this moment feels full circle because I'm lost and have no idea where I'm going.

I turn and find the halls empty. The bell must have rung but I've been standing here with one hand on the door handle unable to leave.

"Uh . . . no. Not really."

"Want some coffee? I just made a pot in my office. You look like you could use a cup."

My fingers release from the metal bar, and I step back.

"Come on, son. I think I've got some cookies around here too."

I almost laugh, if laughter were something I was still capable of, but I find myself following behind him anyway, toward the end of the hall where there's an open door, the smell of coffee wafting out.

He gestures for me to sit and pours me a cup and places a stack of thumbprint cookies in front of me.

"Wife made those. They're a bit bland, but she tries."

"Right . . . thanks."

"Do you want to talk about it?" he asks.

I take a sip of my coffee and finally look up at his face. "Talk about what?"

"Why you look like someone killed your dog?"

My hand rubs against my jaw. "Oh. Not really, no."

"It's not about those pentagrams someone keeps spray painting around the school is it? You haven't gotten expelled, have you?"

My brows furrow. "No. It's . . . something else."

"I never thought it was you, by the way," he says before taking a sip of his coffee. "Have a pretty good hunch as to who's been doing it, but with the school year almost over, I probably won't be able to catch the little bastard before graduation."

I should be thanking him for not assuming it was me because of how I dress and what I look like, but I can't bring myself to speak.

"You know," he says, sitting back in his chair, "I'm not the wisest of people, but whenever something shitty happens in my life that I don't want to talk about with anyone, I find that writing it down helps. Maybe you should try it."

This time I do grin . . . at least a little. It's exactly what my mom would say. Maybe she's here, channeling her wisdom through the janitor. But this time do I really want to? Why would I ever want to put on paper what I've felt in the past fifty-eight hours? I glance down at my bag, my notebook just visible. I don't want to write down how this feels. But I have been writing down how *she* makes me feel. Since the moment we met, I've scribbled my thoughts of her on those pages. Let my heart and hand express the words that my mouth couldn't say. And she should know. She should know the truth.

"Hey, do you have one of those big brown envelopes?" I ask, glancing at the shelves behind him.

He nods. "Think so. Hold on."

He fetches an envelope for me and watches silently as I open my notebook and tear the words out of the binding. It takes me longer than I thought it would, but before I seal it up, I write one last note and stuff it inside. "Thanks," I say, not sure how else to appreciate the help.

"Anything else I can do for you?"

"Yeah. Can you tell me which locker belongs to Rebecca Briar?"

CHAPTER 37
True Colors
REBECCA

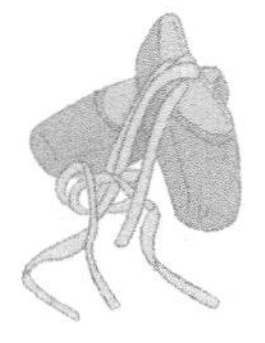

Can someone die from a broken heart? My whole body hurts and is numb at the same time. There's sound but I don't hear anything. I speak but I don't say anything. His windows are closed and his van is gone and the small sliver of hope that I had at the possibility of seeing him in class this morning is now gone too.

I keep trying to convince myself that he's just late. Or he'll be here tomorrow. But deep down I know he won't be. He's left. Gone. And the look on his face when he realized I lied to him will haunt me until the day I finally die. God, I hope it's soon.

And to think I was going to ask you to come to San Francisco with me.

I've considered running away, but I don't know where to go. Has he already left the state? If I somehow manage to get there, I wouldn't even know how to find him. Besides, this is the punishment I was promised for my sins. I deserve to live a miserable life. I resigned myself to it, and after what I did to James, I *should* suffer.

One day, I hope I see his name in lights, or see his picture on the cover of *Rolling Stone* magazine. Because maybe then I'll know that it was all worth it. And though I secretly hope he doesn't, he'll likely find someone who will love him. Maybe she'll love him more than I did, and that thought provides me with the smallest shred of comfort.

At lunch, I don't even bother to open the bag from my mom. I know I promised James I'd eat and I want to uphold that, but I can't keep anything down. The constant anxiety has my stomach churning like the sea. I've hardly eaten anything in three days. It hurts, but it's what I deserve, and I relish in the hunger pains to remind myself that I'm still alive. That I'm still horrible.

"So, he just left?" Amy asks. My heart feels like someone is trying to jump-start it with a car battery. But there's not enough power to restart this heart of mine.

"Of course he left. After what he almost did to Rebecca? The track team alone would run him out of here." Mary interjects.

Wait . . . what? "What do you mean?"

"Everyone's talking about it, Becca. That if Eric hadn't been there to stop him, who knows what that Satanist would have done to you. We should've kept a closer eye on you. I'm so sorry."

"He didn't hurt you, did he?" Amy asks.

I have no words. Is that really what everyone thinks? That James tried to take advantage of me? The thought is despicable. But what can I really say? If I tell them the truth and Eric finds out . . . "No, he didn't hurt me."

They both offer me sympathetic smiles. Amy reaches across the table and grabs my hand. "Eric was so brave to come to your rescue like that."

Angry tears begin to build in my eyes at the mention of his name. But then I remember, this is my fault. "Yes, he was."

"See?" Mary says. "I knew this would all work out. He still loves you, Becca, I know it. Do you think you can forgive him for what happened with Stephanie?"

But I can't say any more because if I open my mouth surely

I'll shout the truth to the rafters. That Eric is a piece of garbage. That I'm garbage. And that James was too good for all of us. Perhaps my mouth will just close over on itself. After all, if I can't use them to kiss James, what's the point in having lips anyway?

"COME ON, BECCA," Eric says as he pulls out of the school parking lot. "At least pretend to be excited about prom. You know my mom will want to take a hundred pictures."

I need to take a deep breath. I don't even know why I agreed to let Eric drive me home, but I might be trying to sabotage myself.

"Look, the freak is gone. No one thinks you're a slut. Everyone thinks I'm a hero. It's a win-win. Plus, Walton gets to stay out from behind bars. That was the deal, right?"

Maybe I should just throw up in Eric's lap. At least that would make me feel better on several levels.

"Becca?"

I turn to look at him. "What?"

He rolls his eyes. "You better snap out of it. I don't want to spend the whole night of prom dragging you around a dance floor sulking." Facing the window again, I hear him sigh with annoyance. "You know he was just trying to sleep with you, right?"

Maybe. But, God, do I wish I had let him. At least then he would have a part of me that no one else could ever take. A part of my innocence to keep safe and protected forever.

I'm not sure how I do it, but my parents seem none the wiser that anything Earth-shattering has transpired. I suppose that says volumes to how much they actually pay attention to how I feel or what's going on in my life. My mother seems happier than I've ever seen her. She watches me gleefully as I hardly touch anything on my plate, and my dad seems content that the game of deception he's playing on me is continuing without a hiccup. Sometimes I think about screaming about the college acceptance letters at the top of my lungs as we pray around the dining table. But I'm not sure what that would achieve. Sometimes I want to bring up the money he supposedly owes the bank, but I'm too afraid to know the answer. So I just sit there, like an open wound silently bleeding out onto the floor.

Standing in front of my bedroom window, I watch James's curtains, waiting for the moment they might be torn open. That he'll look across at me and smile. That he'll hold up a note for me to read. But day after day, it never comes, and every time I look in the mirror I feel like I'm wasting away to nothing. It's not just the fact that I've lost the few pounds I gained while eating properly, but my soul feels like it's in tatters—my skin the only thing keeping all of me from dissolving.

I broke all my rules for you.

The amount of hours I've agonized over this one sentence. I don't know what he meant, only that it meant a lot to him and that somehow not only did I hurt him, but I also managed to convince him to destroy the value system he had for himself—and that maybe is the worst of all.

BY THURSDAY, I've managed to get into a routine. I think I even managed a small smile yesterday when Mr. Adams accidentally said orgasm instead of organism. But it's when my mom knocks on my door Thursday night with a bubblegum-pink taffeta prom dress that I realize just how broken I really am. Because it's so easy for me to agree to try it on. When the stiff fabric zips up my back without a hitch I know I should feel disgusted by how thin and sickly I've become again. My mom's radiant smile makes it even worse.

"Wow," she says, standing back to appraise me, "for once something fits you on the first try."

I try to swallow, but the lump gets stuck in my throat.

"You've been fasting."

"Yes."

"Just wait to see what else I have in store for you," she says with a wink, patting my cheek. If I could feel something, I'd be terrified by that statement, but I expect it'll just continue my misery, so I push that terror down for a later time. She sighs. "Just think, by this time next year, I might even be making baby clothes."

Bile rises in my throat, and I press my hand to my lips to keep it down. My mother gives me a simpering smile, clearly misinterpreting my upchuck reflex for anticipation. I don't even know how a baby will be possible. I haven't had a period in months, and if she thinks I'm not going to be doing everything in my power to prevent Eric from impregnating me, then she's as delusional as I think. But after she's left my room, I find myself standing in front of my bathroom mirror holding a bottle of Tylenol and wondering if I were to swallow the whole bottle, would I be dead by morning?

No. No, no, no, no. The bottle of pills drops from my shaking hand into the sink and I scoop it up quickly then slam it back into the medicine cabinet. My heart is racing and I can barely breathe, but I don't want to die. Not when what might come after presses in on me like a wool blanket—smothering, itchy uncertainty. Is there a Hell? Will I really go there? I've been brought up my entire life believing that is what awaits sinners, and in the past few months I have sinned more than the rest of my life combined.

And what does it say for the existence of God that the only

time in my life where I've felt truly cared for and happy was when I was with James? I sit on the edge of my bed, open my nightstand and pull out my bible. It's been weeks since I've looked at it, the longest stretch since I've been old enough to read. But, maybe it'll offer me some kind of comfort, even if I don't deserve it. I flip through the pages until I find what I'm looking for. First Corinthians 10:13 says, "God won't give you more than you can handle," but I don't know if I can handle this.

"I'M SO happy you and Eric have worked things out," Mary says.

Lunch is over and we're walking toward my locker. There's a final exam in my calculus class this afternoon, but I'm seriously considering just hiding out in the bathroom. The last thing I want to think about right now is an exam. Besides, even if I got a zero on it. I'd still get my credit, and it's not like I'm worried about getting into college.

"Right," I answer.

"Eric's a regular knight in shining armor. Thank God that freak is gone. Good riddance."

If only she knew that my knight wears leather and chains.

"You're such a forgiving person, Becca. But now it'll be like it was always meant to be. All of us together at prom. It'll be so much fun!"

I'm hardly listening anymore as I open my locker and dig around in the bottom for my calc notes. In another life, I'd be ashamed of the state of my life, my locker, my GPA, but it's not like any of that matters anymore. The freedom and control I thought I finally had was just a pipedream—a fantasy. Finally, I spot the periwinkle blue folder on the top shelf and pull it toward me, when something else falls with it that I don't recognize—a brown envelope.

My eyebrows furrow as I turn the envelope around to turn the writing right side up.

This is everything I never said.

Heart pounding, eyes wide, I brush my thumb over the familiar handwriting—his handwriting. Glancing at Mary, she's checking her makeup in her pocket mirror, so I tuck the envelope under the folder as the bell rings overhead.

"Becca, hurry up or we're going to be late," she says.

I nod, closing my locker, and the two of us head toward class. My stomach is in knots and my heart is beating so fast and hard that I'm surprised Mary can't hear it. She walks a step ahead of me as we push past the throng of students in the halls. We pass a bathroom and I stop, my brain whirring so fast I don't even know what I'm doing until I've ducked inside the tiled room and locked the door.

My loud panting echoes off the tile walls as I race over to the corner of the room and slump down to the floor. The bell rings again overhead. Class has started, but I can't wait. Not for this. Even if it's a letter about how much he hates me, it's still from him. One last shred of his existence to cling to. After all, I don't even have a picture of him.

I pull the envelope back out and look at the words. My hands are shaking and it takes a few tries to get it open. When it finally rips, I peer inside to find dozens of scraps of paper—all in varying sizes. My forehead wrinkles as I wonder what this could possibly be. I upturn the envelope, allowing the scraps of paper to fall into my lap. The first one I pick up is short, his messy handwriting a little smudged.

Becks, the way you dance is mesmerizing.

My face grows hot and I gasp for air. The knife twists in my chest. I put the note aside and grab another one from the pile.

Your little nose wrinkle is adorable.

This time a laugh that's half a sob escapes. I reach up and touch the spot where my nose touches my forehead and feel the wrinkle of skin there. The memory of a kiss he placed there once burns brightly in my mind. I grab another.

Why did you look so miserable?

My head tilts to the side. When did he write this? Was it back before that first kiss? Is this what he was always writing in his notebook?

I don't want much, but I want you.

A smile tugs on my lips.

I think about you way more than I probably should.

I can't explain to you how good it feels to look out my window to find you standing there.

Tears silently trail down my cheeks, but I'm smiling. For the first time in a week, I'm smiling.

You are too good for half-assed love. He doesn't deserve you.

I think there's been a place for you in my heart since we first met.

The notes continue.

You've made me feel things I never thought I could.

I never expected to get this attached to you.

When this is all over, don't forget me and all the things we did. Please.

I cover my mouth and squeeze my eyes shut. My lungs feel ready to burst and my body aches from trying not to shake so much. Something in my broken, shattered heart stirs.

I tried not to, Becks. But it just happened so fast and I fell for you so hard.

I wish I could just tell you how much I don't want this to be just casual between us.

My hand cramps from holding the paper so tightly.

The truth is I'm fucking in love with you.

I stop breathing. The world stops as I read the note over and over and over again. The words replaying in his voice again and again in my mind like the most beautiful song.

"James . . ." I whisper, the sound echoing around the empty room. "You should have told me."

I cling to this note but reach for the last few in my lap.

If I asked you to run away with me, would you?

I'm still holding onto the shred of hope that maybe you'll change your mind. That you love me as much as I love you and are willing to risk it all to be with me.

Why can't you just tell me how you feel? Why can't I tell you?

"Oh God, how I wish I had," I whisper. I can taste the salt of my tears on my tongue and it reminds me of all the kisses he gave me. How he always turned my chaos and sorrow into beauty and passion. I can barely bring myself for this to end, but I pick up the final note.

My biggest mistake wasn't falling in love with you. It was thinking that you loved me too.

CHAPTER 38

Runaway

REBECCA

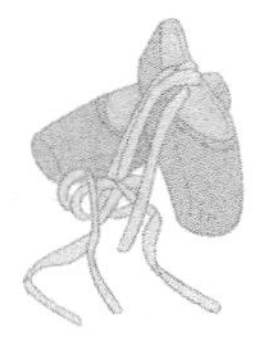

As if caught in a gigantic wave, I feel everything at once. I feel all my grief and all the pain at what I did to James. How I made a mess of everything out of fear. But I also feel joy—that crack in the earth that swallowed me somehow spits me back out. Maybe everything isn't lost after all. James loved me. He loved me all along.

I need to tell him I love him. That even though what happened between us is probably beyond repair, he needs to know that it was never casual for me. That all I want is for us to be together. Even if it's impossible. Maybe, even with Eric's threats, we can somehow run away together and actually win—be free.

Grabbing the envelope, I tuck all of the beautiful notes inside, each one as precious as gems in a treasure chest. I kiss the brown paper before putting it in my bag and unlock the bathroom door, nearly colliding with someone.

"Oh! Rebecca, I'm sorry. You scared me." It's Stephanie Lawford, the girl Eric cheated on me with.

I take a step back to let her pass. "It's fine."

"How are you?"

I look around, surprised she's even speaking to me. "I—okay, I guess?"

The bathroom door swings shut and she lowers her voice. "I heard about what happened at the party."

My chest tightens. "Yeah?"

"About how Eric rescued you."

I want to scream. To tell her what really happened. That James isn't some deviant, and I needed no rescuing. Quite the opposite. "You shouldn't believe everything you hear."

Her round face lowers. "Yeah. I know that. It's sinful to gossip." Her eyes start to shimmer and for the first time I wonder if *she's* okay. I didn't care enough to think about what happened between her and Eric beyond giving me a chance at freedom. Maybe she feels guilty about it.

"It doesn't matter to me," I say, reaching out to touch her arm. "What happened between you and Eric. I forgive you, and so will God if you ask."

She tilts her head. "What are you talking about?"

"That . . . you slept with Eric. At the party after the track meet."

Her mouth drops open and she turns red all the way to her ears. "I did *not*! What are you—I never slept with him! I would never even dare."

There's a long silence that stretches between us. "What do you mean? Amy and Mary said that Jeremiah caught you *together*."

"You . . . don't know?" she whispers.

"Know what?"

"Jeremiah and Eric . . . they're"—she looks around as if to check we're actually alone—"they're gay."

Laughter bubbles up at the absurdity of it. "Eric is—that's ridiculous!"

She shakes her head. "Why do you think Jeremiah and I broke up?"

"What are you talking about?"

Her watery eyes dart over my face. "Listen, I didn't believe it at first either. The three of us used to hang out when Eric dropped you off at your dance class. We'd have a few drinks and just play cards or whatever. But then Jeremiah stopped asking me to come, and it was just the two of them."

My heart is about to burst out of my chest. What is she saying right now?

"I didn't suspect anything. I was just hurt that they didn't want to hang out with me anymore. So, one day I showed up unannounced. I found them with their shirts off. On his bed. Kissing."

Thank goodness there's a wall behind me, because I might just have toppled over without its support.

"They tried to convince me it was just because they had been drinking. That it was nothing and"—she laughs darkly—"like an idiot, I believed them. But I couldn't shake the feeling that something was wrong. Jeremiah never wanted to touch me or kiss me anymore, he had just lost all interest. So I broke up with him."

"The day of the track meet . . ." I whisper. "Eric and Jeremiah were arguing. Amy mentioned you had just broken up with—Eric was mad at him." I'd been so preoccupied with Mary attempting to ask out James that I completely forgot.

Stephanie nods. "Then at that party—I walked in on the two of them and they were . . ." She trails off as tears run down her cheeks. "I didn't know what to do! I wasn't going to tell anyone! You know as well as I do what would happen if someone found out they're gay. Jeremiah and his family, they're pretty worldly. They might just kick him out, but Eric . . . I know enough about Holy Grace to know what would happen to Eric if they found out."

The black van would come for him.

"And I knew my parents would find some way to blame it all on me if they found out that Jer was gay. Somehow it would be my fault."

My stomach clenches. Stephanie and I have a lot more in common than I thought.

She wipes at her cheeks, sniffling and her expression changes to one of anger. "I told Eric he had to break it off with you. I didn't want to put you in the same position I was in. When I saw you confronting Eric in the cafeteria, I was sure that's what had happened."

"He—he didn't deny sleeping with you." I'm breathing so hard I can feel the seams of my dress splitting. I want to tell her she's wrong. How can Eric be gay when he was always trying to kiss me, to touch me, pressure me? "He was always drinking . . ."

"What?"

I swallow, my head spinning. Is this why he was always drunk when trying to kiss me? Why he's been so hell-bent on keeping me for himself? To push a marriage that neither of us wants? To hide being gay? Did his parents find out and they're forcing him just as much as mine are forcing me? "I have to go," I say, pulling on the door.

"Wait! Rebecca!"

But I can't stay here any longer. Whatever has been going on with Eric is going to have to wait because he's not leaving—James is, and I'm running out of time. It might already be too late. The bell rings overhead, but before anyone can enter the halls I burst out through the front doors and run toward home with the echo of James's words spurring me on.

I DON'T KNOW how I don't faint on the way to Noreen's house after hardly eating anything for a week. Perhaps I get here on adrenaline alone. When I turn the corner of my street, I spot exactly the person I mean to find.

"Noreen!"

She's walking to her door, rifling through a stack of mail. At the sound of her name, she looks up and around. Spotting me, her eyes narrow and she frowns.

"Rebecca?"

"Hi," I say breathlessly.

After a moment she blinks, then crosses her arms, her expression overtaken by one of irritation. "What do you want?"

"Do you know where James is?"

She eyes me up and down. "Why should I tell you?"

"I need to speak to him, please!"

Turning back to her house, she starts walking away. I follow after her until we're both standing on the front porch. "I don't know where he is or why he left, but something tells me it has something to do with you."

I hang my head in shame. "I—you're right. I'm so sorry I hurt him. What I did—it was truly unforgivable."

We stand in silence, the spring wind lifting my damp hair off my forehead. I can barely lift my head, the weight of what I've done hanging heavy around my neck.

Finally, she sighs. "Well, you might as well come on in."

Holding the door open for me, she steps aside. I enter the house and my heart swells. It smells like him. Even though he's not here—hasn't been here all week—I can still feel him around me.

Noreen passes me and sits at her small kitchen table before gesturing to me to join her. I sit down and my knee begins to bounce. Where do I even begin?

"You know," Noreen says, "if you've come here just to make yourself feel better, I'm about to kick you out of my house."

"No! No, please, I never meant to hurt him."

"But you did anyway."

My eyebrows pinch together. "I thought—I didn't know how he felt. He never told me and I . . . I thought this was what he wanted. He told me from the beginning that he was leaving and I knew I would never be allowed to follow him. I just thought that we could —" I stop and take a deep breath, my mouth has been moving a mile a minute. "I can't let him leave without telling him the truth."

"And what truth is that?"

My eyes meet hers. "That I'm in love with him."

Noreen's mouth twists as she studies me for a long time. Then she sighs, reaching forward to grab my hand and squeezes.

"He went to stay at his band mate's house. I'm not sure of his name or the address. I don't think he wanted me to be able to find him, so he didn't leave any specific details. But he hasn't left the state yet."

My heart begins to swell and hope rises in my chest like a hot-air balloon. Maybe there's still a chance.

"But after the gig they're all leaving for San Francisco."

"Gig?" I could slap myself. I'm such an idiot! Of course, he wouldn't leave before performing. I totally forgot about it. "But what about his promise?"

"The school called me. Apparently, he stopped by first thing Monday morning and asked if he were to miss his exams whether he'd still get his credits to graduate. They said yes, so that's it. He's fulfilled that promise."

He was there. That must have been when he left me the envelope and stupid me, I let it sit in my locker for five days.

"Do you know where they're playing tomorrow?" I ask.

"At The Shipwreck."

"Noreen," I say with trepidation, "You've already done so much for me. But, I have a favor to ask."

I'VE DECIDED I hate pink. Well, maybe not all pink. But definitely this exact shade of pink that looks like Pepto Bismol. The taffeta prom dress rustles with every movement and while it doesn't squeeze me as badly as the clothes my mom usually makes for me, there is still a suffocating discomfort in the way the fabric feels against my skin.

My mother has painstakingly curled my hair and pinned back the front before adding a custom headband in the same pink as the frilly layered dress with a gigantic bow on the hip. When she finally stands back to take a look at me, she tilts her head, her brows knitting together.

"Well, I suppose it's the best we can do with what we have to work with, right, Rebecca?"

It's hard to imagine how someone can be so critical, so cruel. After all, she's the one who made the dress—made me. She's the one who picked the shoes, did my makeup, did my hair. James was right. This was never what God wanted, it's about her trying to control me. Control me to the point that I would never be able to have the confidence or knowhow to fight back. Unfortunately, knowing that doesn't make the harsh critiques hurt any less. Because to her, I'll never be enough, and it kills me that I've spent eighteen years of my life desperately trying to please her. But I have plans for tonight, and none of those will be possible if I piss off my mom so much that she doesn't let me go to prom.

"Thanks, Mom," I say as cheerfully as I can manage. "I couldn't have done this without you."

She steps forward, touches the golden cross that hangs around my throat, and takes a deep breath.

"You know, Rebecca, prom night is a time where many young women are encouraged to participate in lewd, sinful behavior. But you'll behave, won't you?"

"Yes, Mom."

She pats my cheek sharply. "Remember, Eric may try to convince you, but God is testing you. Can you be virtuous enough to resist? You've always had a hard time with temptation, I mean, just remember how you used to gobble down your food."

An overwhelming urge to laugh tries to burst its way forth as I think about everything I learned from Stephanie. Eric is gay. The more I think about it, the more it makes sense. How he would only try to push things with me physically if he was drinking. How he never seemed to care about me. How he's always hanging out with Jeremiah. How he would forget about me while being there like he lost track of time—the same way I did with James. But laughing about it won't help me so I swallow it down, choosing instead to smile and nod.

The doorbell rings and my heart hammers.

"Looks like Eric is here. Grab your bag and come right down, you don't want to keep your future husband waiting."

She turns and leaves the room and without even realizing, I turn to look out the window. His curtains are still closed, but I feel lighter than I have all week. Like maybe this will work. But as I watch the curtains hang there like they have, a creepy crawling feeling starts to find its way all over my skin. What if this doesn't work? What then? What if he refuses to listen to what I have to say? I suppose it would be exactly what I deserve.

"Rebecca!"

I spin around. I've been standing here for too long. Grabbing my little handbag from my desk, I steel myself before stepping out and down the stairs. Eric is standing at the bottom in a dark brown suit and tie, speaking to my dad, when I appear on the upper landing. Surprisingly, Eric holds out his hand to me, and because I know my parents are watching, I smile and take it. He leans forward and kisses my cheek, and maybe it's because I know to look for it now, but I can see the way his body recoils at touching me.

"You look beautiful, Becca."

"And you . . . look very handsome."

There's no point in lying. He is handsome. He's always been. And I know he might be fighting his own inner battle with who he is, but I can't look past what he's done. What he's threatened to do.

"Here," he says. He holds up a small box with a corsage inside. I'm taken aback. Did he really think to do this on his own? No, likely his mother bought it for him to give to me. Eric isn't thoughtful like that. At least not with me.

Taking out the small purple and white floral arrangement, he pulls me closer to slip the band around my wrist. He smiles at me, and for a moment he looks like the boy who gave me my first kiss at sixteen. A chaste peck on the lips that made my face turn bright pink and made me so nervous that God had seen and would punish me for it.

"Thank you," I say.

"Your mom told me to take lots of pictures," my mother says while grabbing the polaroid camera from the hall table behind her. After a dozen or so flashes, spots begin to pepper my vision.

"Okay, I think that's enough," I say.

"Of course, of course. Don't want to be late. You two have a good time."

Eric turns to my dad, who hasn't said a word this entire time. "I'll make sure we aren't out too late."

My dad grasps Eric's hand and shakes it, then glances at me, my bag, my shoes and back to my face again. "Have a good night, Rebecca."

Ice freezes my veins. Something about the way he said it

makes me feel like something dreadful is about to happen. But there's no way he can know. Right? No, I'm probably just so paranoid that I'm reading too far into things again.

We walk to Eric's car and I stop in my tracks when he opens the door for me.

"What are you doing?" I ask.

He tilts his head. "Opening the door for you?"

I narrow my eyes. "Why?"

"Because isn't it the gentlemanly thing to do?"

Taking a deep breath, I continue down the walkway and fit my ridiculous pink dress into the front seat of the Monte Carlo. Eric gets in a moment later then pulls out of the driveway and heads toward the school. It's a beautiful night. The sky is clear, not a single cloud, and the stars are bright and blinking down at me. It's even unseasonably warm for the end of May.

"You look nice."

My head turns to look at Eric. "Excuse me?"

He pulls on his collar. "I said, you look nice—pretty."

I cross my arms. "What are you doing?"

"What? Can't I pay you a compliment?"

"As if I want a compliment from you."

He scoffs. "Is this really how it's going to be for the rest of our lives? You don't have to hate me."

"I don't need to like you either."

"Then this is going to be a very agonizing marriage."

"Then call it off. You can't possibly want to be married to someone who can't stand you."

His mouth twists and he grips the steering wheel but says nothing.

"Don't you want to be with someone you actually love? Someone who loves you back for exactly who you really are?"

Eric glances at me out of the corner of his eye for a fleeting moment then turns away.

"You know you don't have to do everything your parents say, right?" I press gently. His dad must know. Is that what he had been talking about when I overheard him speaking after Bible study? That my dad needed the money and Eric was . . . a problem. It must be why he and my dad moved up the wedding. After all, what a scandal that would be—the only son of Michael Corbley, an elder of Holy Grace—gay. Maybe Eric is just trying to do everything he can to keep himself protected. To keep the black van from coming for him. "Eric, you can—"

"Just shut up, Becca!" he yells, slamming his hand against the steering wheel.

I lean back against the seat and sigh before turning to look back out the window at the passing houses. I spot a few limos picking up other seniors dressed in their best and heading to prom as well. Wide smiles and bright eyes and my heart aches with the longing to want that same feeling. An image of James in a suit jacket over his Metallica tour T-shirt makes me smile.

He would grip my waist in his big hands and press his forehead to mine to a Cyndi Lauper song as we sway under the lights of the disco ball in the school gym. Maybe there would be remnants of paper streamers in his wild hair and he'd probably wipe away the tears of joy I'd cry at being there with him. And I'd kiss him there in front of everyone to make sure no one could think I didn't choose to kiss him. That he isn't preying on my vulnerability, that he's the most decent human being I've ever met.

"We're here," Eric says.

The daydream is gone, replaced by laughter and shouts as we pull into the parking lot and maneuver around the colorful bodies heading toward the gym. Eric and I smile at everyone as we pass them arm in arm, but all I can think about is what James would write in his notebook if he saw me right now.

THE PARTY IS in full swing two hours later. People are dancing, chatting, and I'm pretty sure I saw someone trying to spike the punch. If I weren't so nervous, it might actually be fun. Glancing at the clock above the score board, my fingers tap against the table cloth. Jeremiah came over at one point to talk to Eric and after only a few moments it was clear that everything Stephanie told me was true. The way they looked at each other—the way their bodies moved like magnets. They love each other. So when the two of them disappeared to get a drink, I take it as a blessing that Jeremiah is distracting him for me.

When the clock finally hits nine fifteen, I stand up from my seat. Glancing around, no one is paying attention to me. The teacher chaperones are enjoying their glasses of spiked punch as much as the students and anyone who's not dancing is chatting amongst themselves.

"Just act casual. No one's going to see you unless you act shifty," I whisper.

Slowly, I start to make my way toward the gym doors that lead outside. I realize probably most people won't care if I stay or leave, but the last thing I want is a chaperone to notice and call my parents because I'm missing. Or Eric knowing where I might have gone. Hopefully, he'll think I went to the bathroom and by the time he realizes I'm actually gone, I'll be far enough away that he won't be able to stop me.

The doors to the gym are in sight, the streamers swaying subtly to the vibrations of the music and the breeze from outside. Just a few more feet until freedom. Just a few more feet until James.

"Becca!"

My heart plummets like a stone sinking beneath the waves

and my eyes close. When I open them, Mary is headed my way, followed closely by Amy. At their smiles, I mirror their expressions—after all, I'm supposed to be having the time of my life.

"Hey," I reply, leaning on the nearest table so it doesn't seem suspicious that I'm over here for no reason.

"We just heard the news!" Mary squeals excitedly.

My lips purse and I tilt my head. "What news?"

"That you and Eric are getting married!" Amy shouts. Thankfully, her voice doesn't carry far over the music. But even if it had, I would feel the same intense dread.

"What?"

"Yeah, Mrs. Van Houten just told us!"

I look over to where Mrs. Van Houten is sipping on her punch and dancing a little too enthusiastically to be sober.

"How did she—"

"Well, she's friends with Eric's mom, right?"

The curse of living in a community where everyone knows your business.

"But, I—"

"Why didn't you tell us?"

"Are you excited?"

"Did he give you an engagement ring?"

"You're such a forgiving person to still love him after everything that happened."

My teeth clench. "Yes, I am."

"Oh, and speaking of school gossip," Amy continues, "we just found out who's been spray painting those pentagrams around the school."

This grabs my attention. "What do you mean?"

Amy leans forward to whisper. "It's been Jeremiah this whole time. Isn't that crazy?"

My breath stutters.

"We were so sure it was Walton," Mary continues. "But, I mean . . . Can't blame anyone for thinking it was him."

"I wonder why Jeremiah would do such a thing?"

"Anyway, you won't tell anyone, right Becca? He could get expelled."

I shake my head. "No . . . no, of course not."

Mary grabs my hand. "Doesn't matter anyway. A bride! It's so exciting. Will we be able to come?"

"It'll be such a beautiful wedding."

Something starts to splinter. Like a dam that's been cracking and the pressure just keeps mounting and mounting until one day everything finally bursts.

"A beautiful wedding?" I ask. The words feel jagged in my mouth.

Mary and Amy stare. "Of course, I mean, you're so—"

"I'm so what, Mary?" I spit. "Skinny? Or have you not noticed that I've been starving myself so much I almost passed out on Thursday?"

Her and Amy's mouths drop open.

"All those lunches, you've sat there while I've picked at my food. While I've eaten nothing at all. While I've looked so gaunt, I'm practically a skeleton and you never once thought that maybe something was wrong?"

The two of them look at each other, their eyes traveling over me as though they finally see my real appearance. How I've hardly eaten anything in a week—that it's the only reason this dress zipped up tonight.

"Becca, we—"

"And you really think I'm happy?" I whisper dangerously. "Do you really think I've been happy since the party? Since Eric and I supposedly got back together? Because I am miserable!"

Mary steps toward me. "Why didn't you say something?"

"Because neither of you have ever seemed to understand me.

Even when I do say something is bothering me, you brush it aside! How could I possibly think you wouldn't do the same this time."

The music continues in the background, and I glance toward the door.

"You're . . . really unhappy?" Amy asks.

I press my lips together to keep them from trembling—to keep the tears at bay. "I've been so unhappy I considered killing myself this week."

Amy's eyes become glassy, and Mary is paler than I've ever seen her.

"Becca, I'm so sorry. We should've been there—"

"And of course you would assume the worst about James. Everyone always does," my voice breaking, and I have to grasp at my stomach to keep from hyperventilating. "But he is the best person I have ever known and I . . . we didn't deserve him."

The girls stand horrified and teary eyed as my breathing settles.

"It doesn't matter." I shake my head and glance at the door, then up at the clock. It's nine thirty now. I'm running out of time. Mary seems to notice.

"Where are you going?"

I sigh. "To try and find happiness."

"With him?"

I nod. "Yes."

She looks at Amy then around the room. "Then, we'll cover for you as long as we can. But, Becca, once he knows you're gone, he's going to be looking for you."

I grab their hands, their help filling my heart up with hope. Maybe I should have pushed harder to tell them before. Maybe I should have had more faith in my friends. "Thank you."

They stand shoulder to shoulder to do their best at hiding me as I slip through the streamers and into the lobby. Mercifully, there's no one around and I make a run for the door. Panic starts to grip me once I'm outside and don't see Noreen's car. Did she leave, thinking I changed my mind? I'm not that late—only fifteen minutes. Surely, after yesterday, she wouldn't leave me stranded here. As I edge around the building, I can see her car parked behind a few trees on the side of the road outside of the parking lot.

A grin splits my face and I run for it, the curls in my hair bouncing and blowing in the spring nighttime air. She unlocks the door once she spots me and I throw myself inside. Not a moment later, she's driving out into traffic, a smile on her face.

"I thought for a minute or two that you'd had a change of heart."

Catching my breath, I shake my head. "No . . . I had to get away quietly."

Glancing over her shoulder at the school she smiles. "You know, I hated my prom."

"Did you? Why?"

She rolls her eyes. "My boyfriend ditched me to make out with Tammy Jordan."

My mouth drops open. "What did you do?"

Her mouth twitches. "I broke into the office and tried to hijack the PA system."

A laugh bursts out of me. "What?"

She laughs too. "Yeah, I wanted to tell everyone he was a cheater then blast Nancy Sinatra's *These Boots Are Made For Walkin'* for everyone to hear, but alas, I was apprehended before I was able to do it."

I smile. "That would've been totally awesome."

Noreen pats my hand as she speeds through the streets heading for The Shipwreck. My adrenaline is pumping so hard I'm sure it's the only thing keeping me from passing out. What if I get there and he doesn't want to see me? What if he can't forgive me? What if he doesn't love me anymore? Oh God, what if he gets in front of the microphone and tells an entire audience how I broke him?

"Just say what's in your heart," Noreen says, as though she can read my thoughts.

"But what if—"

"Then you'll know you tried."

My hands clench into fists as The Shipwreck comes into view. The parking lot is packed and my stomach flips as I spot James's black van. Noreen circles the parking lot, but it's quarter to ten and they'll be starting any minute.

"Here." Noreen stops in front of the door. "You go in while I find parking."

"Okay."

I jump out of the car, bubblegum taffeta dress and all, and head for the door as Noreen pulls away. The largest man I've ever seen in my life stands in front of it, arms crossed. He takes one look at my approach and holds up his hand.

"ID?"

I freeze. I didn't consider this. Of course, they won't let me in. I don't look twenty-one. Especially not in this ridiculous dress.

"What's the matter?" some girl jeers from the patio area. "Got lost on your way to prom, sweetheart?"

I turn back to the giant of a man blocking my way inside. "Please, sir. I need to see Carnal Sins."

"Under twenty-one? You'll have to wait until they have an album come out, princess."

I shake my head so fast my headband almost falls off. "No, you don't understand. Please. I know James. Walton. He's my . . . or, he was my . . . my—"

"It's okay, Bruce, you can let her in."

I peek around to find John, eye-patch and all, and I push past Bruce to him. "Thank you! Thank you so much!"

"Come on," he says, chuckling. "I'll take you back. They're about to go on."

The bar is dark and incredibly noisy inside. The air is hazy from the smoke and it smells like beer but my eyes are focused on the back of John's head as he winds a path through the crowd of people until we're walking past the bar and into the kitchen.

"Just down those stairs to the green room," John says as he points to a narrow doorway in the corner.

"Thank you," I say as I run for it. My heart is hammering so fast my pulse throbs in my temple, in my jaw, in my fingers and toes. As I come down the stairs, I can hear voices, laughter. There's a painted green door ahead of me with the word "Talent" written across it in black paint. I almost laugh, thinking of how fitting a word that is for James. My entire body is jittery, jumpy, and I worry for a moment that I might combust before I get the chance to see his face.

Lifting my hand, it shakes terribly as I rap my knuckles against the peeling green wood.

"Yeah, yeah, we're coming," a voice calls. His voice. James's voice.

Then the door opens.

CHAPTER 39

Sweet Dreams are Made of This

JAMES

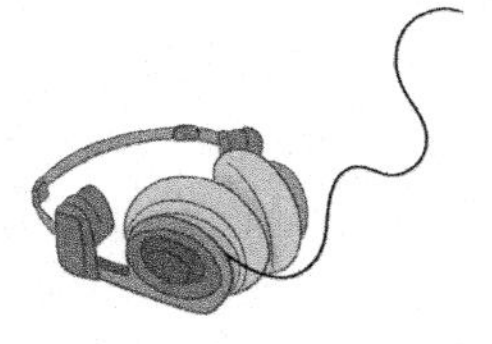

"Becks?"

Rebecca stands before me dressed like a Barbie doll and for a moment I think I might have smoked something stronger than pot.

"Hi," she says.

The noise from upstairs and behind me goes quiet. Is she really here? "What—what are you—"

"I love you!"

Her words hit me like an avalanche. Emotions ripping through me, tearing me apart only to put me back together in a way that somehow feels better, happier—complete. They're words I've been waiting weeks for her to say.

Her eyes are bright and shining as she tries to hold mine.

"I love you, James. And I'm so sorry I didn't tell you. I didn't know how you felt, I didn't think—but then you left me those notes and—" She shakes her head and looks at her feet. "I knew they'd make it so we could never be together. I thought two months would be enough, but it'll never be enough. I'm sorry I hurt you—"

I grip her face in my hands and crash my lips against hers as we fall against the wall. Euphoria floods my brain and something good finally pierces through the agony I've felt for the past week. Lips, tongues and hands ravage one another as though we've been starving. When it feels like I might pass out, I pull my lips away, but our noses still touch. I don't want to be away from her ever again.

"James, I—"

"I love you, Becks."

A happy sob escapes her mouth. "I love you, too. So, so much."

"Carnal Sins!" a voice yells from the top of the stairs. "You're on in five."

Remembering where I am and what I'm supposed to be doing in five minutes rushes back at me. My adrenaline is pumping and I'm nervous and calm all at once. Turning back to Rebecca, she's smiling so brightly she outshines the pink of her dress.

"I uh—I've got to go play . . ." I whisper.

She nods. "I know. I came to watch you."

A wide grin spreads across my face. "How—how did you even get here?"

She takes a deep breath. "It's a long story, but Noreen drove me."

"Noreen's here too?" I ask.

She nods. "Yes, she's just parking. But, I had to see you before—to tell you . . ."

I kiss her again. "I can't believe you're here. That this is real. It *is* real, right?"

She smiles. "I sure hope so."

The green door behind me opens and Dave appears, along Keith and Joel, holding his drumsticks. Their eyes take in the sight of me and Rebecca in her bubblegum dress.

"Hey, Strawberry Shortcake, you better not be here to break

his heart again," Dave mutters. He says it jokingly, but I hear the tone of caution behind it.

Rebecca shakes her head. "No, definitely not."

Dave smiles. "Good, because Jamsey's been downright depressing to be around since you two broke up."

I turn to him and cock an eyebrow. "You knew that was the reason?"

Dave rolls his eyes. "Oh please, you were the picture of a poor sap who had his heart broken."

Laughing, the three of them pass us and head up the stairs. Dave turns halfway and looks back. "Come on, we've got a show to do."

"Coming." Turning back to Rebecca I still can't believe my eyes. She's here and she loves me.

Her cheeks darken. "You should go."

"You'll watch?"

"Of course."

"Then, after . . . ?"

She swallows. "After, I'll tell you everything. No more secrets."

I gently kiss her again. "I love you."

"I love you."

I JOIN the others standing off the side of the stage. Dave nods at me as I crack my knuckles.

"You good?" he asks.

I grin, and with complete honesty, I say, "I've never been better."

He smirks. "I knew she had you wrapped around her little finger."

I shrug. "It's not so bad."

Joel calls out, "Make this count, okay, guys?"

We all nod our heads. We know what's at stake. What this could mean if we're good enough.

John walks out onto the stage and steps up to the microphone. "Please welcome to the stage, Carnal Sins!"

There's some decent applause as Dave and the others walk out. I follow behind, squinting against the bright lights that shine down on the small stage. I grab the guitar that Noreen bought me and move the strap over my shoulder as Keith speaks into the microphone.

"Shout out to The Shipwreck for having us. We've got a few covers, but mostly all original music for you tonight. Let's make some noise."

My eyes adjust to the lights as I scan the crowd. I wonder who the Megaloud exec is. Maybe it's better if I don't know. There's one face that I simply can't miss, though. Rebecca is standing at the back in that bubblegum-pink dress. A pink cream puff in a sea of black. My heart swells and I smile at her, noticing Noreen at her side. She gives me two thumbs up and I grin at them both.

The sound of drumsticks bang together—one, two, three, four.

A strum of strings and music blares through the speakers and through the crowd. Fingers fly over strings, cymbals crash and that double bass beats in my chest. I was sure I would fuck this all up. That there was no way it could work out. That somehow this was all going to go spectacularly wrong. But maybe the universe has decided to give me a break.

Despite having learned their songs in only a few weeks, the four of us play like we've been together for years. Riffing off each other, goading each other on to show off, everyone is on their A game. And through it all, Rebecca watches with wide eyes and the brightest smile on her face. My adrenaline is pumping through my veins and I'm riding the biggest high of my life.

When we're nearing the end of the hour, the crowd is on their feet, shouting and cheering and I'm sweating, my hair stuck to my forehead and the back of my neck. There's one song left and I wonder if she'll recognize it. It's the only song of our set tonight that I wrote. The one I played for her by the lake. The one I wrote for her. It won't be an acoustic version tonight, so I would understand if she doesn't remember, but when I downpick the melody, she perks up in her seat, the recognition instantaneous on her face.

And I play it just for her. Every other face in the crowd disappears. I know the future ahead of us is unknown and will likely be difficult, but I'll do anything to make her smile. In a world where I was drowning, never opening my heart up to anyone, she threw me a life preserver. She made me care about something other than music. Something I never thought could be possible. She's my salvation

The song ends, the crowd roars and both Rebecca and Noreen are on their feet, jumping up and down in support. The lights dim as the stereo system blares an Iron Maiden song and after my guitar is back on its stand, I'm being rushed off the stage. Dave and the others grasping my shoulders and bouncing around like kids who just hit their first home run. Before I can stop them, they usher me back down the stairs to the green room where we open the door to find a man with gravity-defying curly hair and a burly beard.

"You guys sure know how to put on a show," he says.

Dave steps forward, obviously the least nervous of the four of us, or maybe he simply hides it the best. "Hey, I'm Dave. Thanks for coming out."

"If I'd known you were this good, I would've come sooner."

My hands are still vibrating from the exhaustion of playing at peak level for an hour straight, but I do my best to try and keep steady as I step forward to shake the man's hand.

"I'm Al Simpson, and I'm an executive producer at Megaloud

Records, an affiliate of Geffen. Sit down, sit down, we should talk."

The four of us, still sweaty, grab drinks from the table in the middle and choose a seat as Al sinks his round body into a chair in front of us.

"Listen, I'll be honest. When I came out here, I thought you guys were going to be a bunch of wannabe rockstars who only covered other artists, but those original songs? Well, I mean, you heard the crowd. Phenomenal, especially the one at the end. Who wrote that?"

My stomach clenches hard as I raise my hand. "I did."

"What's your name again?"

"James Walton."

He presses his lips together and nods. "Genius. That melody? Broke my goddamn heart in the most metal way possible. You know all the best metal bands? It's not just about kick-ass music, it's about emotion. Escapism and relatability. And I think that song in particular has all of that."

I feel a slap on my shoulder followed by a tight squeeze as Dave grins from ear to ear. "Knew you were something special, kid."

"The sound you guys had tonight is a lot different than the demo you sent months back. What changed?"

Dave jerks his head at me. "New blood."

Al's eyebrows nearly disappear. "Oh, you replaced an original member?"

Nodding, I'm happy that he seems impressed.

"How long have you been part of the group then?"

"About six weeks."

"Six—" Al sits back in his chair. "Six weeks? And you guys played like that tonight after only six weeks?"

There's a grin on every face as I look around the room.

"How old are you, James?"

"Nineteen."

"Well, fuck me," Al says, pulling out a kerchief as he wipes at his sweaty forehead. "Well, listen, I don't normally do this, but I think you guys show a lot of promise. If this is how you sound after six weeks together, I can only imagine what you'll sound like when you get in a studio. What do you say you fellas come out to California and we get you some studio time and try to slap together an EP?"

Perhaps the world has lost its pull, or gravity no longer exists, because I'm not sure if my feet even hit the floor for the next five minutes. Between being tossed around by the guys and jumping up and down like a kid who just scored the best toy on Christmas morning, I'm floating. Al simply laughs at us, rightly assuming we've agreed. He holds out his business card to Dave, who's standing on top of the small table in the middle of the room, and tells us he'll see us in a few weeks.

"Holy shit!" I yell. "Holy fucking shit!"

My chest might actually explode. Or cave in. Or I'll simply die right here. As the others continue their sporadic happy dance around the room, each cracking open another beer and chugging it down, the cushions beneath me sink against my weight. Goosebumps sprout up and down my arms and back and my mother's face blazes so brightly in my mind's eye it's as if she's here with me.

If I hadn't promised her I'd graduate, if I hadn't moved here, if Noreen hadn't got me a job here, this never would've happened. This once-in-a-lifetime series of events never would have unfolded. Maybe it's all part of some grand design after all. A way for the universe to make it up to me. A way for my mother to make sure I capture my dream.

"So, Jamesey, we good to head out for San Fran next week?" Dave asks, sinking down next to me and handing me a beer.

"Yeah . . . yeah, I am. Sorry, I'm just a little stunned." I take a long sip. Will Rebecca come with us? I don't want to do this without her.

"You know, from the first moment I saw you," Dave continues, "I knew you had something. I didn't even have to hear you play. It's like I could see it in the way you held yourself. You were meant to be a star."

WHEN THE GUYS finally release me from their crushing grips, I quickly duck into the attached bathroom and shower off before changing. While I love performing, it's hard work and exhausting, and I want to be able to kiss Rebecca without grossing her out with my sweaty-ass hair.

With my new guitar in its case over my shoulder and my duffle bag full of clothes I haphazardly took from Noreen's house that awful night, I push through the crowd toward the pink beacon at the back. It's surreal to think that these people are all clapping me on the back, telling me how awesome we played, when outside of this world people view me as such a stain on society. When I approach Noreen and Rebecca, they're all nervous smiles and nearly bouncing out of their seats. Rebecca's on her feet first, before she throws her arms around my neck, her pink dress rustling with every movement. My arms wrap around her, still hardly daring to believe she's really here, and I squeeze. She feels thin and, as she pulls back, I'm sure she hasn't been eating. My chest aches. Maybe she's been suffering just as much as I have. Maybe more.

"You were incredible," she says. "I've never seen anything like it. The way you look on stage—just hypnotizing."

Of all the compliments I've gotten tonight, this is the one that matters the most. She releases me, but my fingers still grip her waist. I never want to let her go. Noreen smiles at us, and I'm reminded that she brought Rebecca here.

"You came," I say to her.

She shrugs. "Needed to give this one a lift. Also, I had to see that gift in action."

"Thank you," I say, pulling her into a hug. "Thank you for both. For everything. I—I'm sorry that I took off."

She pats my cheek. "So, what's the news? Did the record label guy come? Rebecca and I were trying to figure out who—"

I look between the two of them. "They want us in the studio in a few weeks to make a record."

Their response is shrill screaming, the two of them crushing me with their hugs.

"James," Noreen says. "That's—that's incredible. Your mom would be so proud of you. Not just for this . . . but everything."

I smile. "I know."

Turning to Rebecca, she's excited but there's doubt in her eyes. She's worried about something, and she's going to tell me. No more secrets.

"Want to get out of here?" I ask her.

Her face softens as she nods. "Let's go."

We say our goodbyes to Noreen, then head out into the parking lot toward my van, her hand clasped tightly in mine. I help her up into the seat, then duck around to put my bag and guitar into the back. When I finally settle on the bench seat next to her, she says, "Are you sure you don't want to stay and celebrate with your friends? It's big news."

I grab her hand and kiss the back of her knuckles. "There's nowhere I'd rather be right now than with you at our spot by the lake."

THE DRIVE IS QUIET. Maybe she isn't sure how to start, or she's waiting for me to say something. Or maybe she knows that I'm still jittery from The Shipwreck and can tell that simply having her near, holding her hand, is what is calming my heart. When we pull down the long stretch of trees, the moon reflects off the still lake like a mirror, the stars bright and shining.

I put the van into park and turn off the engine. The silence is broken only by our breathing. Maybe I should start. But what do I say? Where do I even begin—

"They're forcing me to marry him," she whispers.

Okay. I guess we're starting with that.

"It was always the plan. But it wasn't supposed to be until after college. Then when the acceptance never came . . ." she continues, her eyes shining as she looks up at me. "I need you to know, it was never what I wanted."

My grip tightens on her hand. "Then why didn't you just tell me?"

"Because he threatened me."

Rage seethes under my skin. "What?"

She sniffs. "He told me to keep what we were doing a secret. That if anyone found out, he'd find a way to get you arrested—ruin your life. I couldn't let that happen."

My lips press together as my chest tightens. "Becks, you don't—"

"But I had to. You deserve to have your dreams come true. I wasn't going to let my pathetic joke of a fiancé ruin that."

"But you deserve the chance to make your dreams come true too."

She throws her head back and laughs. "What dreams? Going to college? I only wanted to go to college to get away from my parents. It wasn't like I had this huge aspiration of being a lawyer or a doctor. It was just an opportunity to escape. And now that it's gone . . . there's just nothing."

My arms wrap around and pull her into me.

"It's hard to dream when all you've ever done is survive."

My fingers hook under her chin to tilt her face up to mine. "So you were willing to marry that piece of shit . . . for me?"

"You were the first person to see me. Really see me. All that I was hiding. I couldn't help falling for you and when the opportunity arose to be able to be with you, even if it was only for a short time, I jumped at it. You were leaving, you never had to find out, and I . . . I didn't know how you felt. Maybe I was too scared to know the truth. Because if you didn't love me, then it would break my heart. But if you did, and you gave up on your dream for me, it would still break my heart. When Eric told you everything, I found out that you hating me was even worse."

"I could never hate you."

"Hurting you like that . . ." She takes a deep shuddering breath. "It nearly killed me. I wanted to explain, but you were gone. Gone from your room, from school . . . it was like you never even existed.

"Then you left me those notes, and I knew I had to tell you. You poured your heart into that envelope so I needed to do the same, because you deserve to know that I love you, James Walton. That I have ever since we sat here and you played that song—the one I heard again tonight—I couldn't let you leave thinking you aren't deserving of love. Because you are. You're *the most* deserving person I've ever met."

I pull her face toward me and kiss her hard. Her hands rest over my heart and when I pull back, her mouth is flushed.

"You know I won't be able to give you the life you want."

"What life do you think I want?"

"You know," I stammer. Maybe I've been wrong about what she wants this whole time. "A house and nice things."

"I have those already and they're a living nightmare."

"But don't you want to get married and raise a family?"

She closes her eyes and shakes her head. "That's all they've ever wanted of me. Told me all God wanted me to be was a wife and a mother. And sure, marriage might not be so bad with the right person but I don't—I don't want kids."

"You don't?"

She shakes her head. "It's horrible, I know . . . but, I can't stand little kids. I don't—they're whiny and selfish and . . . I'm terrified that I'll end up just like my own mother. That I'll somehow pass it on." She takes a deep breath. "I sound like a terrible person."

"No! No, you don't." I smile down at her.

"Is that—do you—?"

I've never really thought about it much. But when I did, I always imagined what I would have wanted growing up. Happy, healthy parents who would love me unconditionally. Not like all the shit foster parents I had, and even though my mom loved me, she was so sick she couldn't really do much. "I definitely don't want kids now, but I think if I ever did . . . I might like being a foster parent to teens who need a good home."

She smiles. "That sounds like something I'd like as well."

Her lips press against mine, their softness like silk petals. "I just want you, James," she whispers. "I just want you. To be with you, to be loved by you."

"Then run away with me."

The tears finally spill down her cheeks but she smiles. "Really?"

"Come to San Francisco with me. We could leave tomorrow. We could leave and never look back."

Her head shakes. "But they'll come after us, they'll call the police."

"You're over eighteen. You're an adult, and as for getting me arrested, they can't arrest me if we're gone."

“But you’re about to go and record an album, be a rockstar. You don’t want some silly girl hanging off you.”

“Becks,” I say sternly, “you’re the only one I want. The only one I’ll ever want. I love you.” More tears fall, but her face is bright, and she smiles wide. “Always with the waterworks.”

She laughs. “Then yes. I love you. I’ll run away with you.”

CHAPTER 40

In Your Eyes

REBECCA

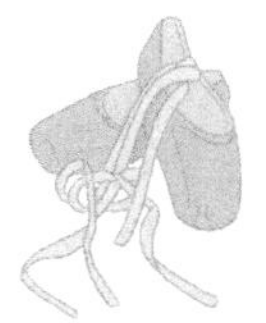

That smile. That sweet, sexy, smug smile turns my knees to jelly. Throwing my arms around his neck, our lips meet in a clash of teeth and tongues and I feel lighter than I've ever felt before. The weight of the guilt I've been carrying falls off as his hands skim over my body.

"James," I whisper against his jaw as his mouth chases mine. "I want you."

"I want you too," he says.

Maybe he's too worked up to understand what I mean. "No, James . . . I want you. All of you."

He stops to look in my eyes. "I—oh."

Those dark eyes turn black and sparkle like onyx. I push up onto my knees, then hop over the bench seat into the back of the van, kicking off my heels as I do. He turns to watch me as I take off the hideous pink headband and pull the pins out of my hair, letting the curls fall into my face and over my shoulders.

The next moment he's hopping over the bench too, his lighter in hand.

"Hold on," he says. "I've got some—here they are."

He pulls out a small box of tealight candles and puts a few on the makeshift shelves on the inner van wall to light them. The flickering orange light causes his eyes to burn like coal.

"I wish I could say it's a shame that dress has to come off, but—"

"It's hideous."

"—it's hideous."

"Tear it off me, then."

"Don't tempt me, angel. I'll do it."

I turn my back to him, pulling my hair over my one shoulder to expose the zipper on my back. Noreen bought me something to eat at the pub so now it's a bit tight, the metal teeth straining against the fabric with every breath. Waiting for him to unzip me, I jump at the feel of his lips on my exposed neck. Shivers tremble like a wave from my shoulders all the way down to my toes. His touch is pure love—my soul knows it.

I inhale sharply as his lips trail down my neck, the zipper coming apart and the fabric falling slowly from my shoulders as he pushes it down. There's a gentle suction just below my ear and a whimper escapes my throat. My head drops back to rest on his chest while his hands work on pulling down the dress until my torso is bare except for my bra.

"Becks," he says, voice rumbling through me, "you have no idea what you do to me." His lips latch onto my collarbone and my hand finds its way into his hair behind me. It's so soft. How I've missed the feel of it. The feel of him. I can't live without it anymore. Maybe I'll never have to.

"Show me," I whisper in his ear.

From over my shoulder he kisses me, fingers holding me in place as he undoes my bra.

I'm not nervous about him seeing me naked. He's seen me almost completely naked a dozen times now, whether by accident or by choice, but I *am* nervous. Who wouldn't be nervous about their first time?

"Okay?" he asks.

"Yes." I exhale slowly, then I pull the bra down and off of me, letting it drop somewhere to my left. The taffeta rustles as I turn around, chest bare. James's eyes are hazy and his face is flushed. A smile pulls at the side of my lips. The way he looks at me makes me feel so undeniably beautiful.

My fingertips find the hem of his shirt and he inhales sharply at my touch on his stomach. I want his skin against mine. It's never been everything before, there was always a shirt or boxers or something between us. Pulling the fabric over his head, his hair tumbles back down as his eyes dart over my face. My nipples pebble as his hand glides along my shoulder to behind my neck, then he pulls me forward in a gentle kiss. A little moan squeaks its way out between our lips and as our chests touch, I relax and sink against his body.

His other hand skims its way up over my arm, my shoulder, to twist into the curls of my hair. Blindly, my hands trace their way down his chest, over the lean muscles of his stomach to the waistband of his jeans. My fingers fumble with his belt, and he smiles against my mouth.

"Need a hand?"

I giggle. "Maybe."

For a second I watch as he unbuckles his belt, the button of his fly, pulls down the zipper—then I'm twirling the noisy dress in my hands so I can unzip it.

His hand captures mine. "Becks, it's okay, I can do that."

The backs of his fingers brush against my ribcage, the metal from his rings causing me to shiver.

"Are you cold?"

I shake my head. "No—your rings . . ."

"Shit," he says looking down at them, "I forgot, I'll take them off—"

"No," I say, gripping his wrist, "I like them."

Grinning wide, in one swift movement, he grabs me around the waist and tips me back on the mattress. His face is obscured by a mound of pink taffeta and tulle, and I giggle at the way he mutters, trying to search for the best way to pull it off me.

"Good lord, Becks, how do you even walk in this thing?"

I laugh again, but it fizzles out as I feel his fingers find the skin of my thighs.

"Ha!" he says triumphantly. "There you are. Not so funny now."

His head disappears under the tulle as he pulls the skirt and bodice down and I can't help but laugh at the sight. The giggles continue to pour out of me, a hand coming up to cover my mouth. The next moment, he emerges victorious, tossing the taffeta dress noisily aside, and he hovers low over top of me. Heat from his skin scorches my veins as he grips my wrist in his hand and pulls it away from my face.

"Don't hide from me," he says softly, seriously. "Don't silence yourself. The sound of your laughter is my favorite song." My eyes flutter closed as he kisses below my ear. "Every sound"—a kiss to my collarbone—"every face you make when I touch you" —a kiss between my breasts—"I want to see and hear them all."

His calloused thumbs brush over my hardened nipples, and I gasp with abandon. The wet heat growing between my legs makes me squirm and I'm aching—longing to be with him.

"Take—take yours off . . ." I stammer.

He never fully leaves me, but pulls away just a moment to kick off his jeans and socks and sneakers. Then it's just us, separated only by the thin cotton of our underwear on the mattress in the back of his van that smells like smoke and leather. His weight settles between my legs, and I feel his erection press against me. With wide eyes, my gaze meets him, and he seems to understand my concern.

"Are you sure you want to do this?" he asks breathlessly.

I nod. "Yes, more than anything."

"I'll do my best to go slow, okay? I don't want to hurt you."

"I know," I whisper, pushing the hair back and away from his face, "I trust you." My index finger traces the lines of his tattoos, and he sucks in a sharp breath. He gathers my hands in one of his and holds them tight. At my confusion, he smirks. "Any more of that and we might not get to the finish line the way we want."

Without thinking, my hips buck up to chase the feeling of him against me, and he groans before gripping my chin and devouring my mouth. I keep up with him, desperately trying to make sure he knows how much he means to me—how he saved me.

Fingers trail their way down my body, beneath the cotton of my panties, and he touches me exactly where I crave it. His mouth is on my breast, sucking my nipple and swirling his tongue torturously, as his fingers slide and circle over the sensitive flesh between my legs.

"James," I gasp.

"Goddamn, that is the sexiest sound I've ever heard," he says, mumbling into my chest. "Make it again for me." His mouth captures my other breast and I gasp again, my back arching up toward him. I realize only now that he's freed my hands, but all I can do is grip the sheets underneath me. That euphoric feeling is building inside of me, and while I want to touch him, I can't focus on anything else. It's so good, so all-consuming, so sinful.

His finger slides inside of me, and I moan loudly as my hips rock against his hand.

"You getting all worked up, angel?" he says, grinning.

My heart is frantic—pounding so hard, my pulse throbbing in my ears, my chest, between my legs.

"When you're close, tell me. I want to fucking hear you say it."

His finger and thumb work in tandem and the world falls away.

"James . . . oh my—I—I'm coming!"

I'm completely lost in my own selfish pleasure—vulnerable, all control gone. Nothing beats this, except for the look in his eyes as mine open. His kiss leaves me breathless, and my head is swimming.

"Lift your hips for me," he whispers.

I follow his instructions instinctively. The air cools my overheated skin as he tenderly rubs his thumb along the inside of my thigh.

With the little strength I have, I push myself up, wrapping my arm around his neck to hold him to me, but my hands are shaking.

"Shh," James whispers, "it's okay."

"It's not fair," I whine.

He blinks. "What's not fair?"

I brush the tip of my nose against his. "That I'm naked and you're not."

He grins and kisses me quickly. "Don't worry, we're not done yet." He turns away to grab something from the shelf, and when I realize it's a condom, my muscles tense. It's going to happen. Now. I'm ready for it, but also terrified. What if God really won't forgive me for this? This ultimate sinful act. But then I realize I don't believe in a vengeful God anymore. I believe in one that wants love and happiness for his creations and I feel more loved and more happy right now than I ever have.

James's boxers are gone, and I watch as he rolls a condom down his length. He sits on the mattress, his back against the upholstered interior, and reaches for my hands, guiding my knee over his legs so I straddle him. I can feel him, feel his hard length standing up against my wet sex.

He takes a deep breath. “Are you sure?”

I nod. “Yes. Yes, I’m sure.”

Brushing the hair away from my face, he holds me tenderly and kisses my face. “I love you, Rebecca.”

“I love you, James.”

CHAPTER 41

Somebody to Love

JAMES

I'm like a walnut that's been cracked open. All of my rough edges are laid out for her and she still wants them—wants me. Gently, I kiss her, then groan as her hips rock against mine. A sharp tremble shoots through my body as her wetness slides against my cock. My one hand moves to grip her hip, my fingers pressing a little roughly into her flesh, and the other holds her face, my fingers tangling in her hair. Breathe, just breathe.

"We can stop if you need to. If it's too much, just tell me." I might die, but I'll stop.

"Okay," she says, and her voice is surprisingly steady as she wraps her arms around my neck.

Taking a deep breath, I slowly let it out. "We can do it like this, that way you can go as slow as you need to."

She swallows and her green eyes capture mine. "Will you help me?"

"Yeah, here—"

I let go of her face to reach around and grab the base of my cock. I tip her forward just a little to line myself up at her entrance. My eyes close of their own volition as I rub my tip back and forth a few times, allowing her wetness to coat me.

"There," I say in a strangled voice. "Just—just sit down . . . slowly . . ."

The tight heat of her body pushes down over me and I fight against every nerve and fiber not to blow. My head falls forward, our foreheads touching as we both try and acclimate to the sensations. Less than an inch inside of her and she's gasping. Her face is pinched and her nails are digging into my skin.

I rub my fingers up and down her back. "Slow," I whisper, "you have to relax."

She nods, the ability to speak seemingly lost. I try to distract her and kiss along her jaw, my fingers on her hip release their tight grip to trace gentle circles on her skin. She slides down a little more, and I'm trying so hard not to explode.

"Fuck, fuck, *fuck*—"

"Are you okay?" she asks.

I laugh a little. "Trust me, I've never been better."

She smiles, but then winces as she sinks a little deeper into my lap.

I brush her hair away from her face and kiss her. Inch by inch as our bodies fit together, her breath hitching any time she moves and delirium washes over me. A feverish desperation to move inside her.

"Christ, you're so fucking tight," I mumble.

"Do me a favor?" she asks, her voice strained.

I nod. "Anything."

"Just . . . can you just go all in, all at once?"

I pull back to look into her face. "Are you sure? It'll hurt."

Her eyes are glassy already. "Yeah, but only for a moment."

"Okay," I say. Gripping her hips tightly, I plant my feet on the van floor and thrust up surely. All of me inside all of her.

She doesn't make a sound, but her eyes shut tightly, two tears spilling from the corners.

My heart aches. "I'm sorry," I say, wiping away the tears and covering her face in gentle kisses.

She shakes her head. "No, it's fine. Just—" She takes a very long deep breath then lifts herself up, sliding along my cock, before slowly sinking back down.

"Jesus *Christ*," I grind out. "You feel so good."

She moves again, up and down, up and down. I'm spiralling, the desire to just throw her down and fuck her bubbling underneath the surface of this calm demeanor I'm somehow managing to pull off. But I want her to feel good too, especially after all the pain to get here.

"Touch yourself," I whisper in her ear.

Her eyes turn to scan my face. "What?"

I grasp her hand from my shoulder and bring it to my mouth. Putting three of her fingers to my lips, I suck them inside and swirl my tongue around them. She inhales a sharp breath as I remove her now wet fingers and guide them down between us.

"Touch yourself," I say again, nearly choking on the words. "Make yourself feel good."

She hesitates for a moment, but then I feel the back of her hand against my abdomen and watch with fascination as her eyes flutter closed—her fingers circling her clit. After a few moments, I overtake her slow rhythm, thrusting my hips up to bottom out inside of her.

Nothing, no girl, no one has ever been like this. Then she does something I never would have expected in a hundred years. She reaches her free hand down to grasp my wrist from where it rests on her hip and brings it up to her neck.

"Oh, holy fuck—"

The tiniest of smiles graces her lips as she wraps my fingers gently around her throat.

"Fuck me, James," she says, her voice deeper than I've ever heard it before. "I belong to you."

My resolve finally snaps. I spin over on the mattress, pinning Rebecca underneath me. Her legs wrap around my waist as I thrust into her. I don't squeeze her throat, just keep it there to assure her that she's safe, that I accept what she's chosen to give me. That I'll protect her at all costs because she loves and trusts me. Her hands grip my forearms, and her eyes roll back. Her walls clench and spasm, then quicker than I want to admit, I'm coming so hard that my vision blurs—little white lights popping in my eyes.

Her hand rests on mine over her throat, the sound of her satisfied breath brings me back to reality. I tuck my face into the crook of her neck while my racing heart slows and my breathing evens out. Her soft hands gently glide up and down my tired arms that by now are slick with sweat again.

"I'm sorry, are you okay?" I ask, pulling out of her. Terrified that maybe I crossed a line too early, that maybe I hurt her, or maybe she didn't enjoy it as much as I thought.

"No—James, I'm fine," she says, nuzzling into my chest.

I lift her chin to look into her eyes. "Are you sure?"

She nods and smiles. "Yeah, that was . . . amazing."

"You're an absolute dream, Becks," I say. "I'm never letting you go."

She giggles, a content smile settling on her face.

I discard the condom into the little trash bag hanging on the shelf and grab the blanket to pull over us as we lay down together. Even the happiness I felt earlier tonight when speaking to Al about the record doesn't compare to the emotions that gurgle up inside of me at the sight of Rebecca wrapped up in my arms.

"James?" Her voice is so small and sleepy.

"Yeah?"

"You said . . . that night, that you broke all your rules for me. What did you mean?"

I bite into my bottom lip. She was honest with me, surely I

can do the same for her. *No more secrets.* "When my mom was dying, I decided I would do whatever it took to become a professional musician. After I promised her I would graduate and Noreen took me in, I knew moving here might change me, somehow steer me away from that dream. So I wrote down five rules for myself. I thought that if I followed them, I wouldn't wander too far off the path I'd worked so hard for."

Her eyebrows furrow. "What are they?"

"I had five. Always be myself and never apologize for it."

She frowns. "You broke that rule . . . for me?"

"You wanted us to be a secret. I thought you were ashamed to be with me, but I was too crazy about you to break it off so . . . I went along with it even though I hated hiding."

"You know that's not true, right?" she pleads, eyes wide and shining.

I nod. "Yeah, I know now."

"I'm scared to know the rest . . ."

"The next wasn't much to do with you. It was to never rely on anyone else. Noreen . . . she's done so much for me, and never wanted anything in return."

"That's because she loves you."

My face heats and my eyes prickle as I press my lips together. My aunt loves me too. How broken am I to not even think of that as a possibility?

I clear my throat. "The third rule was never run away from a fight."

She sighs. "That's such a boy thing to say."

I smile. "Both fights I walked away from were with your charming fiancé."

"I really wish you had broken his face."

Kissing her forehead, I stall.

"What was the next one?"

I run a hand down my face. "No virgins. No serious relationships."

"Oh."

"Yeah, I really kind of blew it on that one. But I don't regret it one bit."

She smiles again, a hint of trepidation in her voice. "And the last one?"

"Music before everything else."

"But . . . you didn't." She pauses. "You didn't give up music because of me."

I shake my head. "No, but ever since you came into my life . . . it wasn't music that I woke up thinking about. It was you. It wasn't playing guitar that I stayed up all night dreaming about. It was trying to figure out when I could kiss you again. Then, when Dave mentioned moving out west . . ." I swallow hard. "I was ready to give up on going to San Francisco for you. I would've stayed here to protect you. Do you have any idea the amount of times I wanted to ditch rehearsals because it was during the only time all week I got to see you?"

Her eyes soften.

"I wanted my cake and to be able to eat it too. I wanted the life of a rockstar *and* I wanted you. When I realized I might not be able to have both, if you wouldn't come with me . . . I would have chosen you."

"You don't have to choose," she whispers, placing her warm little hand on my cheek. "I'm coming with you. You're stuck with me."

My mom told me once when we were on the verge of being evicted from our apartment that home isn't where you live, it's where you love.

Rebecca Briar is my home.

CHAPTER 42

Walking on Sunshine

REBECCA

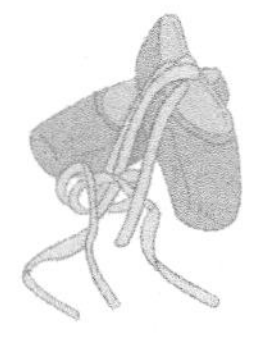

I wake up to birds chirping, the sound of soft breathing and the warmth of his skin against mine. Eyes blinking away the sleep, I take in my surroundings. James's eyes are closed, his dark curls falling over his face, so I push them back. He looks so peaceful that for a long while I just watch him—the slow steady rise and fall of his chest and the way his face twitches every so often like he's dreaming. Maybe he's dreaming of me.

The candles have burnt out, and the first light of morning is peeking its way through the trees but it's still fairly dark. As I snuggle closer to James, my body is sore. The dull ache of bruises forming on my collarbone and my hips reminds me of how I got them. How having sex with James was nothing like how people told me it would be. I expected more pain, more awkwardness, more anxiety. But it wasn't like that at all. Sure, there was some momentary pain, but there was nothing awkward about it. It was everything I hoped it would be.

A groan brings my focus back to his face, his arms pulling me tighter against him.

"James?" I whisper.

Chocolate brown eyes flicker open in the low morning light, then they widen.

"Becks?" he asks, his voice like a croak.

I kiss him gently on the corner of his mouth. "Morning."

He pulls me tighter. "I thought maybe I was having the best dream, but you're really here."

"I'm really here."

It's strange to say it out loud. That we're finally together and he's going to take me away from here. We'll finally be free and together.

"We should get dressed," James says, making no move to do anything of the sort.

"Can we just stay here forever?" I ask wistfully.

He grins wide. "No can do, angel. I've got a record to make."

My blissful state of mind starts to darken as I realize upon waking that I never went home. The sun has only just risen above the horizon when we get back into the front seat of the van. I'm wearing a clean pair of James's boxers and a T-shirt with an eagle on the front after deciding I never want to wear that stupid taffeta prom dress again. But my knee starts to bounce knowing surely Eric and my parents are looking for me by now.

"There's a few things I need to do," he says, grabbing my hand. "I've got to stop at Dave's place to grab my stuff and get the address of the house we're renting in San Fran. Then we can stop by The Shipwreck on our way out of town."

"What for?" I ask.

"My final pay."

My cheeks heat. I hate having no money. No way to contribute. Hate that at least for a little while until I can find a job, James will be financially responsible for everything.

"I wish I could help out in some way . . ."

He kisses my hand. "I know you do. But it's okay, we'll figure everything out."

"James," I say, needing him to know the imminent danger of my situation—of Eric's lingering threat. "We need to be careful. I never went home, they'll be looking for me."

Surprisingly, James doesn't seem as concerned as he should be. "You haven't done anything illegal," he says. "You're eighteen, and while they might not like it, you're not obligated to come home or tell them where you've gone."

"I know, but—"

"It'll be okay."

I want to believe him, but as James drives down the quiet streets, there's an eerie feeling lingering in the air, and an uncomfortable shiver spreads over my skin. He doesn't know this community like I do. And he definitely doesn't know Holy Grace.

He turns down streets I've never seen before, even after living here for ten years. It's the side of town I was told to stay away from, told it was dirty and dangerous. But as I look around, it's neither of those things. In fact, it's bright and beautiful—even if there isn't a church in sight. Then two short, high-pitched wails make me jump in my seat. James's grip on my hand tightens as the blue and red flashing lights reflect off the rearview mirrors.

"Fuck," James mutters. "Don't worry, it'll be fine. Becks, hand me the cards from the glove compartment."

My hand reaches forward, trembling as James slows and pulls over on the side of the road. I hand him the cards and sit back in my seat, ensuring the seat belt is fastened. Something painful jumps up into my throat when I hear the slamming of police car doors behind us.

"Don't panic," James whispers, taking the cards from me. "And don't say anything outside of what they ask you. We haven't done anything wrong."

A blinding light hits me right in the face as the police officer shines his flashlight through the window. James rolls his down as I spot the other officer on my side.

"Problem, officer?" James asks.

The officer on James's side of the van lowers his flashlight. "We're investigating some damage done to the Holy Grace Evangelical Church early this morning."

I think I've stopped breathing. That's my church. What could've happened?

The officer tilts his head then points the flashlight down at the pentagram on James's T-shirt. "You wouldn't happen to know anything about that, would you?"

James purses his lips and shakes his head. "Nope, sorry."

"You sure about that?" He looks around James at me in the passenger seat. Do they think he did the damage to the church? The officer's eyes travel up and down over my bare legs, taking in my makeshift attire before frowning.

"Yeah, I'm pretty positive about that," James replies.

"How old are you?" he asks me, shining the light in my face for a second.

"I'm eighteen."

"Got any ID?"

My knee starts to bounce. "No, sir."

The officer glances at the other one through the window and they share a look. What do they think? That James kidnapped me? That he's some kind of deviant? My stomach rolls. Isn't that exactly the rumor I let spread around the school after the party? That James tried to take advantage of me and Eric saved me? Bile rises up my throat and I press the back of my hand to my mouth to keep it down.

"You kids been drinking?"

We both shake our heads. "No, sir."

He stares at us for a very long, tense moment. "Sit tight."

Jerking his head at the other officer, we both watch as they meet behind the van and talk about something in hushed voices.

"James, what do we do?"

His eyes shift to me, but he tries not to move his body. "Just keep calm, it'll be all right."

What damage was done to the church? And do they really think James was involved? That's ridiculous right? But . . . what if Eric . . . What if this is his threat coming to fruition? Will these cops try and pin whatever happened on James? I know half of them are in his father's pocket. Would they even need proof to lock him away? They'd make an example out of him. Another story for the pretentious parents of my town to frighten their children with.

I gasp. "James, I think—"

"Shh, he's coming back," James whispers.

The one officer returns to us while the other gets in the cruiser.

"Going to need you to follow us to the station," he says.

James tenses. "Why?"

The officer jerks his chin at me. "Got to verify her age. Can't be too careful."

Verify my—how do they plan on doing that? Will they call my parents? Oh God, if they do, we'll never get out of here.

"We'll lead the way," the officer says. "You just stay on our tail."

James's grip tightens on the steering wheel. "Sure."

He takes another long look between us and heads back to the cruiser.

"Fuck," James mutters as he starts the engine and waits for the cruiser to pull out in front of us, lights flashing.

"James"—I grip his hand tightly—"what are we going to do? What if they call my parents?"

He shakes his head. "I don't think they will. But . . . I don't know . . . I don't know . . ."

"What if they try to blame you for whatever damage was done to the church? What if this was all Eric?"

"But we were nowhere near the church. Witnesses can attest to that."

I'm not so sure, and I don't dare say anything more, but I'm sweating profusely. I say a silent prayer to God, asking him to make something happen. Anything to distract these two officers so that they just take off in the other direction, tell us we can head on our way, but nothing happens and soon we're pulling into the lot of the police station on the far side of town.

"It'll be all right, Becks," James says. "Come on."

I slide over the seat and hop down. The morning air is still cool, and I wrap my arms around myself as we head inside the doors to keep from shaking. We enter the station and pass a front desk where an older woman is sitting and eating a Danish. She glances up at us and stops, the pastry only inches from her mouth. My heart sinks. I recognize her sallow face from our congregation. She knows me and she knows my parents. She's also very aware I'm about to get married, and not to the boy next to me. She frowns as she takes in James, an obvious sneer pulling grotesquely on her face as she sees us holding hands. I want to tell her to shove it. That I love him and that if everyone stopped judging him at first glance they'd all realize that he is better than any of them.

The officers lead us through a gate and toward a desk near the back. Thankfully, it doesn't seem like we're under arrest as we're not taken past the hallway covered by bars where I see one man being led in handcuffs. No, instead we're taken to a desk covered in old styrofoam coffee cups and papers piled everywhere. The officer who pulled us over gestures to the two chairs across from the desk and we sit down.

"Okay," he says, sinking into the leather seat. "What's your name, darlin'?"

I glance at James and he nods ever so slightly. "It's Briar, Rebecca Briar."

The officer stares at me. "Briar? You Richard Briar's girl?"

Oh no, he's definitely going to call my dad. But I can't lie about this. Maybe if I just tell the truth it'll all be okay. Maybe they'll check their computer and when they confirm I'm over eighteen they won't call him.

"Yes."

He looks at James then back at me. "He knows you've been out all night?"

I shake my head. "No, sir."

Grumbling something, he asks for my birthday, address and where I was born before turning to James. "I take it, since it's your van, you have some ID?"

James nods and passes over his driver's license. He writes down the information but doesn't give James back the card. Instead, he calls over the secretary from the front desk.

"Delores, run these names through the system will you? Verify their ages and addresses."

Delores takes another long, sneering look at both of us, as though she knows exactly what we were doing only hours earlier. Maybe we can get out of here before she can let anyone know where I am.

"Right, well, while we're waiting on that, where were you last night? What was it?" He glances at his notes. "Walton?"

"I was playing with my band at The Shipwreck over on Woolbury."

He nods. "And witnesses can confirm this?"

I can tell it's taking all of James's restraint not to be sarcastic. "Yes, several dozen, since I was the one on stage."

Grumbling something he writes another note on his paper. "And after?"

"After The Shipwreck, I spent the night with my girlfriend."

My face flushes, heat searing my skin as I cringe at this man knowing what we were up to, why I'm dressed the way I am. I'm even sure he can somehow smell it on us, like a bloodhound.

"Was Mr. Walton ever out of your sight?" he asks me.

I shake my head. "No, we've been together since we left the pub."

"Are you sure?" he presses. "You didn't make a quick detour past Holy Grace?"

"I wouldn't go near that place with a ten-foot pole," I say sternly. "Not if I have any choice in the matter."

The officer blinks, surprised at my tone and attitude. "Not a fan?"

Oh no, this was the wrong thing to say. Will he think because of my aggressive reaction to the church that we were actually involved? What if they think it was me? I suppose it's better than thinking it was James.

"I'm not a fan of a church that believes in only valuing women for what they can do for men," James says calmly.

Once again, the officer glances at the images on James's shirt. Why did he have to wear one with a pentagram on it today of all days?

"So," the officer continues, "because you don't agree with the church do you think it's okay to vandalize the building?"

James narrows his eyes as mine open wide. "Vandalize?" I ask.

"Yeah. Seems someone thought it would be a good idea to spray paint some very obscene imagery on the front of the building." He sits back in his chair and looks again at James's shirt. I start to realize why he's grilling him about this. "Someone called to say they'd seen a black van fleeing the scene."

Wait . . . maybe this wasn't Eric. Was this Jeremiah?

"Lots of black vans out there." James shrugs. "And to be honest, I couldn't be bothered. I had better things to do last night."

I swear there's probably heat waves coming off of my face right now and my ears are burning, but James simply squeezes my hand again. At least the officer looks uncomfortable enough that he doesn't say any more. My mind is racing. Why would Jeremiah vandalize our church? What could he possibly gain from it?

Delores returns with something on printer paper and hands it to Officer Jerkface. He looks it over then up at us a few times before sighing and handing James back his ID. We both exhale at the same time.

"Right well, looks like everything checks out. You're free to go."

I nearly sob with relief as my grip tightens in James's hand. I stand up, feeling lighter than air, ready to get out of here and step into the sunlight.

"Rebecca?"

James and I whirl around toward the front entrance. In walks the last person on Earth I want to see right now—other than my parents.

Pastor Campbell.

CHAPTER 43

A Lesson in Violence

JAMES

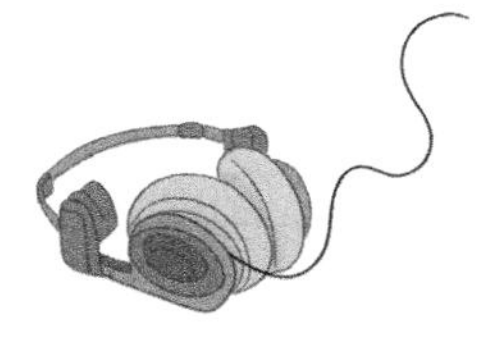

My eyes roam over the tall paunchy man. Who the fuck is this guy? It's not her dad, but the way she freezes next to me tells me she's just as afraid of him as she is of her father.

"I—I . . ." she whispers.

I grip her hand harder to let her know I'm still here. That I'm not letting go.

The man walks toward us from across the room like he's familiar with the place, the people. He wears an expression of concern, but there's anger burning behind his eyes.

"Rebecca," he says, slightly out of breath when he reaches us, "where have you been?"

Officer Douchebag looks between us as if he isn't quite sure how much he should say, or if he should interfere.

"It's—it's none of your . . . none of your business where I've been," Rebecca says, her voice trembling. But I'm so proud of her.

"Your parents have been worried sick, looking for you all night. When Eric told us you disappeared—"

Eric. That piece of shit. He vandalized the church to try and make it look like I did it. That's why they were out looking for us. Because of Eric fucking Corbley.

The man's eyes fall on me. I'm sure for a moment that he'll do the usual head to toe sweep, make his assumptions about me, about us. But he doesn't. Rather, the blood drains from his face and he looks like he's seen a ghost, his mouth slowly dropping open with surprise, or distaste, or . . . something.

"Pastor Campbell," Rebecca continues, "I'm eighteen years old, an adult, I can do what I want and . . ."

Is this the priest of her church? Fuck. He seems to collect himself, turning his attention back to her with a scowl.

"Whether you're an adult is irrelevant. You've disobeyed and dishonored your parents, sinned in the eyes of the Lord, and"—his eyes shift to me again, to our entwined hands—"I can only pray that you haven't dishonored yourself."

Rebecca's face flushes scarlet, her eyes brimming with tears again. I won't stand by while this fucking asshole makes her feel like garbage.

There's some commotion and murmurings that scatter throughout the room as another officer enters. This one is older, and dressed to the nines and from the way the other officers straighten up, he must be the one in charge. "All right, what's going on here?" he asks, then notices Pastor Campbell and his expression changes. They know each other. "Jet? What are you doing here?"

Jet? Jet . . . *Jet*!

Swallowing down the sudden bile that's risen in my throat, my body begins to shake.

"Your . . . your name is Jet?"

I can feel Rebecca's eyes on me, can feel the gears in her head clicking together quicker than my own can comprehend it all. "James—"

"It's Jethro. Jet's just an old nickname from school," he says, shrugging it off as if it isn't exactly the confirmation that I want to hear. All I can see is the mental image of my young, beautiful mother being wrestled into the dirt by this rapist to take what wasn't his. I can see the tear marks on the pages of her journal where she cried after he brutalized her in the worst possible way.

I drop Rebecca's hand and clench my fingers tightly into a ball. "Good enough for me."

Crack.

My fist collides with his face, then it's just a sea of red and rage and revenge. From somewhere in the distance I can hear Rebecca screaming, crying, pleading but I can't stop myself. This is the bastard that raped my mom. That made her run away from home. Made her so desperate and depressed she turned to drugs to numb the pain that *he* caused her.

He made her so sick from addiction that I had to grow up abused and beaten in foster home after foster home. Had to watch my once beautiful, smart and hopeful mother cough until she couldn't breathe. Cough until I wanted to slam my head through the wall. Cough until she fucking *died.*

My throat is hoarse and my fists are numb as hands grab me—someone finally pulling me away. Then I'm being tackled to the floor and handcuffed. The noise around me is deafening. Officers shouting, Jet gurgling, Rebecca crying, all over top of the blood pounding in my ears and the frantic beat of my heart.

Everything is a blur. I hear someone reading me my Miranda rights. Pointless, because they can get fucked if they think I'll say anything without a lawyer present. But as I'm hauled to my feet and pushed through the station toward that hallway covered with bars, I realize what I've done. My eyes search for hers across the room and my heart cracks. She's crying because she knows I've ruined it all.

I ruined our chance at a happy ending.

CHAPTER 44

The Sound of Silence

REBECCA

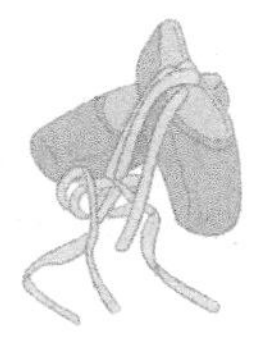

There won't be a happy ending for us after all. Not as I watch James being wrestled to the ground, then hauled off in handcuffs.

My body is trembling but not with fear. With anger—from despair. My whole life has been a lie. I was brought up to believe that our church was our moral compass. That they were the guiding light, the only correct path on the way to salvation. That the head of our church had a direct connection with God.

But that's not what I see here. This quivering, blubbering, bleeding mess on the floor before me—a rapist getting what he deserves because he's spent the last twenty years thinking he got away with it. How he ruined Dora Walton's life in one night. How her control and dignity were ripped away and dragged through the dirt by this man who dared speak to me about the precious gift of my virtue.

He looks up at me with one eye and reaches out a shaking hand. Does he really think I'll help him? Does he really believe I don't know? That I couldn't tell he recognized Dora's face in James when he finally got a good look at him? I saw the fear in his eyes—I'll never forget it.

Someone wraps me in a blanket as I watch Pastor Campbell being taken away on a stretcher. There's blood splatter on my legs and a small pool of it at my feet. Time seems to stop now, as though it knows I dread its relentless marching on. I wish it would simply rewind. That James and I had never left the lake. But life isn't fair that way.

Terror hits me hard when my parents walk through the front of the police station. Delores must have called them, as the officers were too busy dealing with James. They push their way over to me wearing their practiced expressions of concern and love—their stage masks—and I expect a brilliant performance from them now.

"Rebecca, oh thank Heavens, you're all right!" my mother says, swooping down to wrap me in her arms.

"Where is that son of a bitch?" my father says, whirling around at the other officers. "Where is that heathen who brainwashed my daughter?"

Another officer comes over when he hears the commotion. "Mr. Briar, don't worry, he's been placed under arrest for the assault of Pastor Campbell."

My mother lets me go and stands. "Assault?"

"He attacked the Pastor out of nowhere. He's on his way to the hospital now."

She takes a wobbling step backward and presses the back of her hand to her forehead as though she might faint. Unbelievable.

"Don't worry," the officer continues, "there's plenty we can charge him with."

"What about the coercion of my daughter?" my father adds.

"Dad!" I say, but no one hears me.

My dad's face turns purple with rage. "I called you folks about that boy months ago! That I was sure he would tempt our young citizens to join his Satanic cult. Now look at what's happened! My own daughter, seduced by that evil wretch!"

"He's not evil, Dad!" I yell, jumping to my feet. "And he's not in a cult!" I turn to the officer. "Please, sir, he hasn't done anything wrong. He's a good person. What he did to Jet—I mean, Pastor Campbell is—"

"Absolutely barbaric!" my mother cuts in. "To think if it hadn't happened here, he could have been killed!"

"No!" I sob. "Why isn't anyone listening to me?"

My father glares at me and a chill spreads through every nerve in my body. He turns his back to me and pulls the officer aside, but I can still hear him, even over the crocodile tears my mother sheds while she holds me tight enough to bruise.

"Listen Andrew, she's been through a lot lately. With the stress of graduating and exams, plus a fight with her fiancé—it's been too much for her. We're getting her some help."

"Fiancé?" the officer named Andrew asks, looking past my father at me.

"That's right, she's engaged to Eric Corbley, Michael Corbley's son."

"Oh."

The officer shrinks back. Understanding dawns on his face, and I feel the fight whoosh out of me so fiercely I drop to my knees. No one in this town will do anything to go against Mr. Corbley. Not if they want to keep their jobs. He's too powerful, too well connected, has pushed money into every important person's pocket in the county. Tears rush down my face. If a Corbley has anything to say about this, James may never see the light of day.

Over the grip of my father I start to try and kick my way free—I can't give up. "Please!" I plead with the officer. "Eric and I broke up. I can't marry him. And James . . . he's done nothing wrong. Pastor Campbell is evil!"

But the officer looks back at my father and they nod to each other and even though I could scream and yell and thrash, it won't do any good.

And to think James and I were so close to freedom.

IF I WERE to open the door and roll out of the car, would I be uninjured enough to make a run for it? Staring at the door handle, my fingers itch with the desire to pull it, but I wouldn't get far. I'm too tired, too weak to get far enough that it would make a difference. Besides, it won't help James.

My parents haven't spoken a word the entire drive home, but I can feel the energy in the air. They're simply waiting. Like predators stalking their prey, they're waiting until they're sure no one will hear, no one will see, before they show me exactly how furious they are. But it hardly matters. Nothing could be worse than what's already happened.

My father turns off the engine as we pull into the driveway. "Get in the house, Rebecca."

I blink. He sounds surprisingly calm, and somehow that's even more terrifying.

"Your mother and I will be in shortly."

I don't say anything. Simply get out of the car and walk to the front door dressed in James's boxers and T-shirt. Once I'm inside, the air smells stale, putrid, as if something died. Maybe it's because my life here is over. I won't do what they want. Not anymore.

Making my way up the silent carpeted stairs, my hand rests on the doorknob as I take a deep breath. Less than twelve hours have passed since I thought I'd never have to come back here. Everything is such a mess. I turn the handle and walk in. Heading straight for my dresser I grab some underwear and bras, a few shirts that I know fit loosely and the only pair of pants I own that

I can do up properly. I toss them on the bed, turn to the closet to grab my dance bag and freeze.

Hanging up on the open door of my closet is a wedding dress. High-collared, long-sleeved, in the most blinding white satin I've ever seen.

It begins in my toes—like it's boiling me alive, the pain and anger climbing viciously up my body.

"You wicked little bitch!"

I whirl around and barely have a chance to register that my mother is in my room before the sting of her slap shoots across my face.

"Ungrateful Godless whore!" she screams as my hair is yanked to the side. Toppling over, my ribs hit the side of my bed, and I fall to the floor. My scalp stings and my face burns.

"You spread your legs for that devil boy, didn't you? *Didn't you?*"

The shrill sound of her scream pierces my eardrums but James has taught me how to deal with the noise. To know my own heart and mind and to see that what my mother and father are doing is wrong. This isn't God's will, it's evil.

"Yes, I did. And I'd do it again!"

Another slap, but this time it doesn't hurt. My skin is still numb from the first one. My eyes blur, but I don't cry.

"How can you turn your back on Jesus? After everything we've done for you, this is how you repay us?"

"After everything you've—" I stumble over the words, so unbelievable it's hard to make them make sense. "After everything . . . You've been torturing me! My entire life, you've made me believe I was sinful and never good enough."

"You are sinful! Look at you. Look at what you've done!"

My face contorts with anger. How can she see her own daughter with such disdain? "I'm a good person, Mom! I'm smart and beautiful and worthy of love—"

"You think that boy loves you?" she laughs. "Rebecca, if that's what you think, you're even stupider than I thought."

I push past her to the closet and rip the wedding dress off the hanger. It's heavy in my arms, another way to torture me, I'm sure. To stuff me into a wedding dress that's so heavy I could never run away. I grab the seam at the side.

"What are you doing?" she shrieks, eyes wide.

But I pull with all my might, the sound of tearing satin and popping stitches like a drug that gives me strength to go on. My mother pulls on the other side, a vicious tug of war of beads and lace. I tear and tear until arms wrap around my middle, and I'm torn away, thrown onto the bed.

When I look up, my father is standing over me, his face a terrifying image of fury. I try to make myself as small as possible as he walks toward me.

"So this is how you honor your parents?" he says, looking down at me. "This is how you show your faith in God?"

My fists clench so hard they crack.

"Your mother and I find you a Godly husband to take care of you and you run off with a degenerate satanist?"

"I don't—"

He crouches down in front of me and rips my hair back to force my eyes to look at him. "What did you say?"

"I said," I bite out, "I don't *want it*!"

His fist clenches in my hair, but I try to not wince from the pain as my mother scrambles over the tattered pieces of the wedding dress.

"I won't marry him," I spit out. "You'll have to gag me and drag me kicking and screaming down that aisle!"

He releases me. "If that's what it takes." Standing, he begins to back away.

"Why?" I whisper.

His eyes narrow. "It's what God wants."

My head shakes and maybe it was the slaps to the face or just that my brain is finally functioning properly, but it seems to all click into place. "It's because of the money."

I know I've got it when his nostrils flare and his eye twitches. "What?"

Pushing myself up off the bed, I do my best to stand up straight. "Is that what all this has been about? The incessant phone calls that suddenly stopped when the Corbleys came for dinner. You're selling me into marriage to settle your debt, aren't you?"

The room is silent.

"Where did the money go, dad?"

He straightens and lifts his chin. "To Holy Grace."

"You—" I can taste blood in my mouth. "You gave two-hundred and fifty thousand dollars to the church? Why?"

"Because we are at war!" he shouts. "Now more than ever. The proof of the devil's work is clear as day in that boy from next door. It's spreading through this country like a virus. These satanists with their rock music and anarchy—it has to be stopped! We need to protect our congregation."

"That's why you hid my acceptance letters, isn't it? To make me believe I had no other choice and God had no other plan for me. To ensure this happens now." I turn to my mother. "And you've known this all along. That I'm just an object. Just a commodity to be traded. To be starved, bullied, squeezed and paraded around like a doll." Tears finally spring free. "Did either of you ever really love me?"

"All of this has been out of love for you," my mother says, her tone shrill, defensive.

My lips press together to keep from trembling. "No, this isn't love. I know what true love is, and this is the furthest thing from it."

My dad takes a step toward me, his pristine hair falling over his forehead. "You'll marry Eric and that's the end of it. We're lucky he even still wants you."

He turns and heads for the door, but I'm hot on his heels. Caution thrown to the wind. "Two hundred and fifty thousand dollars, and you had to go running to Michael Corbley to bail you out. Where is your God now? Because from where I'm standing, he abandoned you too!"

He spins, his hand hitting my face with the force of a baseball bat, and I fall as the world goes black.

CHAPTER 45

For Whom the Bell Tolls

JAMES

Fuck!

Fuck, fuck, fucking fuck.

I never thought I'd be here. Swore I wouldn't end up like this and spend my life behind bars. But after the best night of my life, how can I be so surprised? The universe is about balance. It gives out the best—it also gives out the worst.

Regret is like a bad sunburn. Like itchy, painful blisters on the skin. I shouldn't have hit him, but something primal in me snapped. I'm grateful it happened here, because if it had been anywhere else, I don't think there would have been enough people to make me stop.

Dave, Joel and Keith will never forgive me, I know it. My dream was handed to me on a silver platter and I spit on it. Gambled it away for the satisfaction of seeing that bastard's face turn into mulch. But even with all of that, the thing that worries me the most is Rebecca. Where will she go? What will she do now? What if her parents find her? They will be furious. What if they send her away? Do to her like my grandparents did to my mother?

"Walton?"

I look up through the bars of the holding cell as an officer unlocks the door.

"You get to use the phone to find representation."

Nodding silently, I get to my feet and follow the officer to the payphones. There's only one person I can call. I've never prayed before, but I pray now—pray that she's there and that she can help.

"Hello?"

"Noreen?"

"James? What's going on?"

My face scrunches to keep my emotions in check. "Is Rebecca okay?"

"Is she not with you?"

So much has happened, I don't even know where to start. "Noreen . . . I need your help. I fucked up. Bad. I'm going to need a lawyer."

TIME SEEMS to move differently when you're alone and panicking. It feels like years have passed before finally an officer comes to the holding cell.

"Walton, your lawyer's here."

I stand and hold out my hands for the officer to cuff me before following him to a small room with a table and chairs. Noreen is sitting next to a well-dressed man I've never met. She jumps out of her seat and runs around the table to hug me. I press my face into her shoulder, unable to hug her but wanting her to know how much I love her.

"James . . ." she says, patting my cheek. "Why did you have to do something so foolish?"

I look at the floor, ashamed. It *was* foolish. Perhaps, somewhere deep down, I tried to sabotage my own happiness.

"Where's Rebecca? Is she okay?"

Noreen's eyes fill with tears. "No, I don't think so."

Panic and fear freeze the blood in my veins.

"I heard shouting from next door. I tried going over there but they wouldn't answer the door. I called the police and they told me they'd send someone out to investigate but no one ever came. I'm going to try and speak to someone before I leave, but I'm worried about her too."

"Mr. Walton," the lawyer says, "have a seat, please."

I sit down in the hard metal chair and place my shaking, bloody hands on the table. I need to concentrate, but all I can think about is Rebecca in danger.

"I'm Rick Thompson, and I'll be representing you tomorrow at the bail hearing," he says. "I'm afraid it doesn't look particularly promising."

My stomach clenches painfully.

"They're charging you with aggravated assault, assault with a deadly weapon—"

"He didn't have a weapon!" Noreen shouts.

"Rings are technically considered a weapon under the deadly weapon umbrella," he continues, looking up at me apologetically. I'm not sure why he does—I'm the one who ruined my own life. "Assault causing bodily harm, vandalism," he continues as my head drops into my hands.

"Vandalism?" Noreen asks, looking up at me perplexed.

The lawyer reads through the file. "Apparently, they're claiming you're responsible for the pentagrams spray painted on Holy Grace Evangelical Church."

I close my eyes. "I didn't do that. I'm almost positive Eric Corbley did and is trying to get me to take the fall for it. That's why they pulled me over in the first place."

Noreen buries her face in her hands looking defeated.

"Anyway," the lawyer continues, "there's more, but those are the most pressing."

"Fuck . . ."

"The one good thing is that you have no priors. Other than some involvement with children's aid services which aren't relevant, you haven't been in much trouble, which we can use to our advantage."

A small spring of hope opens up in my chest. "Okay, good."

His face falls. "The bad news is that they're going to want to make an example out of you. You attacked a well-respected member of the community. This wasn't just a bar fight gone bad. You openly attacked a pastor without cause."

"Trust me," I mutter. "I had cause."

"Well, then, let's hear it," he says, folding his hands together.

I look at Noreen, who peeks up at me from behind her fingers. "Pastor Campbell," I spit, "is Jet."

Her eyes narrow as though she doesn't quite understand my meaning, then widen. "Oh my God!"

The lawyer looks between us.

Noreen turns to him. "We recently discovered through some old journals that my sister, James's mother, was raped by a man named Jet. We didn't know who he was—"

"Until this morning," I finish.

She reaches forward and grabs my hands. "Oh, James . . ."

"When did this happen?" the lawyer asks, writing some things down in his notebook.

I shake my head. "It was twenty years ago."

He frowns. "Unfortunately, Iowa has a ten-year statute of limitations on sexual assault, but it could help to explain to the judge why you attacked unprovoked."

I lean back in my chair. "Let's be honest here, Mr. Thompson. I'm fucked, aren't I?"

He sighs and looks back up at me. "Yeah, you're fucked."

CHAPTER 46

Don't Stop Believin'

REBECCA

My head feels like it's been crushed by a bowling ball. In fact, it hurts so much that I have trouble distinguishing what is up and down. But I think I'm on my bed. The ground beneath me is soft and . . . Yes, it definitely smells like my room.

Opening one eye, the room blurs and distorts as I grasp at my head. I hiss through my teeth as my fingers touch the tender flesh of my temple where the skin is jagged and rough. What happened? The last thing I remember, I was wrapped up in James's arms and was happier than I've ever been in my life. But now . . .

My brain is flooded with images of police sirens and Delores's glare and James swinging his fist. The blood on my legs from Pastor Campbell . . .

I push myself to sit up in the bed, my head throbbing angrily, but I'm definitely at home, the pink of my bedroom walls overly bright after so much time in the dark. I swing my legs over the side of the bed and notice the blood is gone. Worse than that, I'm no longer wearing James's T-shirt and boxers. I'm in flannel pajamas and—

Who redressed me? My stomach twists violently at the thought of my mother of all people taking my clothes off and finding the marks from James's love all over my body.

Standing on wobbly legs, I head for the door, but it's locked. My heart begins to quicken as I shuffle into my bathroom and try the other door into the hall, but it's locked too.

"No, please," I whisper.

I turn and gasp at the sight of myself in the mirror. My cheeks are swollen from the slaps my mother dished out, but what my father did is much worse. My right eye is nearly black and there's an angry red trail from my temple to my cheekbone. It looks like it was bleeding, the open skin blistered and angry, but someone has cleaned it up. Panic sweeps through me and I hobble as quickly as I can to the window, pulling open the curtains, but the window is boarded up making it impossible to escape.

I'm trapped, after all. After everything. After being so close to true freedom. And boarding up the window is the cruelest yet. It was what led me to James, but now that's gone too, and so is he. Trying to take in air is an impossible task, and I clutch at my chest and heave. I grab at something, anything to keep me from falling over. Somehow, I make it back to the bed and collapse onto it. Curling up with my knees to my chest, I try to calm myself but it's no use.

Everything is hopeless.

When I wake up, there's another bowl of oatmeal by my bedroom door. It's the only way I've been able to keep track of time since the fight with my parents. It's been three days. At least . . . I think it has. The boards over my window make it difficult to discern the time of day and my alarm clock is gone. I wonder if confusion is their intention. That I might just lose my mind here, become complacent and do as they wish. I won't though. Not after everything.

My head is still tender, but the bruising on my face is getting better. They removed the painkillers from my bathroom as well, like they knew I might resort to swallowing the whole bottle. I wouldn't though. Not now. Not when James needs me.

It's like being on a roller coaster. One moment I'm flying high and the next I'm plummeting so hard and so fast that I'm pitched forward into darkness, nearly spewing my guts over the carpet. I think of James. He must be in a cell somewhere. If he wasn't, he would have come for me—I know he would have. The thought of never seeing him again does make me feel sick and I rush to the bathroom to vomit, yellow bile from my empty stomach splashing into the toilet water.

"Rebecca."

I press the back of my hand to my mouth and look at the closed door. No one has spoken to me for as long as I've been trapped here, but the phone has been ringing off the hook and a few times the doorbell has rung followed by hushed conversations at the bottom of the stairs.

"Rebecca, get dressed and eat your breakfast. We're expecting company."

I hear my mother's heels retreating down the stairs and frown. Company? Who on Earth are they inviting inside their house when they have their daughter locked upstairs? Do they really think if they open that door that I won't try and run out of here? Maybe this is my chance.

I walk back to my closet and pull out a plaid pinafore dress that has pockets. I pull on a black long sleeve shirt then the dress over top. It's almost loose on me. No surprise there, all I've been given to eat the past few days has been the daily small bowl of oatmeal. I tuck a few extra pairs of underwear in my pockets in case the opportunity to run comes up. Then I lift my mattress where I hid the envelope of notes from James, but they're gone. My eyes sting and my face burns. Those beautiful words he wrote to me are gone. What if I'm never able to hear him say them in person? Footsteps on the stairs force me to blink and swallow back my despair.

Right now, I need to figure out what to do.

When the door handle jiggles, I ready myself. Maybe if I can just surprise them, I can get past the door and out of the house. Surely adrenaline could take me far enough I could try and hide. Maybe I could find my way to The Shipwreck and somehow get ahold of James's bandmates or call Noreen from there.

But when my bedroom door clicks and swings open, I freeze.

"Pastor Campbell?"

He enters my room with a slight limp. His face is bruised and torn up worse than mine, and a surge of pride ripples through me at what James managed to accomplish in only a few short seconds.

"Hello, Rebecca."

The door closes behind him and I hear the telltale sound of a lock clicking back into place. He points to my desk chair.

"May I sit?"

My mouth hangs open, unable to believe he's really here. Maybe this is just some bizarre head injury induced daydream. But no, I can smell him. That sickly sweet scent of lilies permeates the air and itches my nose.

He doesn't wait for my answer and sits down at my desk anyway, turning the chair to face me as I stand by the bed.

"Your parents called me over to try to talk sense into you, Rebecca," he says, rubbing those short, dry hands together. It makes my skin crawl. "To try and save your soul."

My jaw is so tense it takes a tremendous effort to unhinge it to speak. "I have no interest in talking to you."

He shakes his head. "I think you should at least consider

listening to me. Your parents are ready to send you to Mercy Christian Home for Girls. In fact, I believe your father is on the phone with them right now."

My breath halts in my chest, icy fingers like the touch of death squeezing my throat.

The black van. The same one that came for Dora. The one I've dreaded my whole life until James came along.

He sees my terror and smiling, he continues. "I know that's not what you want, and I know it's hard to listen to reason when you think you love someone. But it's not real."

His tone is softer than I've ever heard it. Rather than in those ridiculous pre-marriage counseling sessions where he lectured me on the qualities of being a good wife, here it sounds as if he actually cares. It makes me want to throw up again.

"You see," he continues, "that's exactly what they do. They pull you in with thoughts of liberation and choice, but that's not what God wants for you. God wants you here, with your family. He wants you happy in a loving marriage—something you worked so hard for. Eric—he's such a wonderful and forgiving young man. He still loves you, even though you've debased yourself with your recent behavior.

"These thoughts and desires you've developed for the Walton boy are the natural sins of a woman. You were not strong enough to resist it, but you can still find your way back to God by being strong now. By being an obedient daughter, an attentive wife and eventually . . . a loving mother. You were tricked Rebecca. That's what these Satan cultists do. They lure girls like you to pull them away from good men like Eric. Away from our church. Away from God."

My fingernails are digging so hard into the palms of my hands that I think I draw blood. From what he says, it doesn't seem like he knows about Eric and Jeremiah. If he did, he might not be so sure about me becoming a mother.

"Don't let one bad decision ruin your life."

He finishes his speech with a sympathetic smile, speaking to me like I still have any respect for him.

"Is that what you tell yourself at night?" I ask quietly.

His eyes narrow, smile faltering. "What did you say?"

"I asked," I speak slowly, "is that what you tell yourself at night? That one bad decision shouldn't ruin your life? Do you think that's what Dora Walton whispered into the darkness when she got into bed?"

He turns ghostly pale, even the marks and bruising on his face seem to drain of color at the mention of her name.

"How—"

"How do I know you raped Dora Walton?" I ask, stepping forward. "Because she died and her son had to move in with his aunt in order to graduate. He moved into the same room she used to cry herself to sleep in at night after Jet, the popular boy she liked so much, ground her face into the dirt and raped her. Where she wrote in her journal that she wanted to die after what you did to her."

He blinks at me, his face stricken and sweaty.

"So tell me, Pastor, what exactly are you doing to atone for your sins? Doesn't the bible say to stone rapists, Deuteronomy 22:23?"

Visibly flinching, he shakes his head and frowns. Anger returning the blood to his face, he stands and points at me. "No one will believe such lies from a Godless slut!"

"I promise you right now," I say, my voice shaking with anger, "I will ensure everyone knows what you did to her. How you tore that family apart. I will scream it at every sermon, at every church picnic. Every time I go to the grocery store I will pin up copies of her journal entries where she cried over the pages as she begged for death because she felt her life wasn't worthy of saving after you violated her. I will make it known that Pastor

Jethro Campbell is a dirty, disgusting rapist with no regard for God's design for the treatment of the human body."

His eyes dart over my face, his breathing hoarse.

"Unless," I say, pausing as a desperate plan comes to me. The image of Pastor Campbell entering the station, how he moved around the place like he owned it. How Police Chief Miller was his friend and called him his childhood nickname. "You convince the police to drop the charges against James Walton."

He scoffs. "You—you can't be serious! Look what he did to me!"

"You deserve far worse, since no one's throwing stones at you. Well, not *yet*, at least."

Teeth sneering and face twitching, he glances at the covered window. Does he remember Dora lived there? Is he remembering her? Has he thought about her once since that night?

"I can't just—What do you want me to do?"

"You'll get the charges dropped. No record, he'll go free. He'll leave town and I'll go willingly to the altar with Eric Corbley. I'll never speak a word about what you did to Dora, and I'll never disobey any of the expectations that are set out for me again. I'll be good. And you can repent for just a small fraction of the damage you did."

For a long time he stands, looking at the boarded-up window, his jaw tensing. I wonder what he's thinking. Does he actually feel bad? After what feels like hours, he turns back to me, eyes red and face stiff.

"Fine. I'll make it happen. But you've given me your word now, Rebecca. Deuteronomy 23:21. If you make a vow to the Lord your God, do not be slow to pay it, for the Lord your God will certainly demand it of you and you will be guilty of sin."

I nod.

He moves across the room, unsteadier than when he entered,

and knocks to be let out. I want him out of here. I want him gone so I can bury my face in my pillow and cry until I can't anymore.

"How did she die?"

"What?"

"Dora," he says. "How did she die?"

I press my lips together. This isn't my story to tell, but I want him to know. I want him to know how hard he made her life. "After what you did—after she was blamed for what happened, she ran away and turned to drugs to cope with it. Using drugs gave her a virus and . . . it's that virus that killed her four months ago."

He sighs. "I . . ."

"Is that what God wanted for her?" I ask. "Was that God's plan?"

"I will not cause pain without allowing something new to be born, Isaiah 66:9," he whispers. The door clicks open and he rests his short, clammy hand on the doorknob. "I'll make sure her son is free. God is forgiving."

But he doesn't say any more, he just leaves, the door relocking behind him. I'm left wondering if he genuinely feels guilt—if it's festered in him for decades—or if simply being confronted with it now has made him scared for his immortal soul. Whatever the reason is, I sit down on the edge of my bed, pulling my hand from my pocket where my fingers were crossed so hard they're cramping and for the first time in a long time, I pray.

After everything that's happened, I still believe. After everything they've done to me, I should reject the idea of God. But that's not the case. I just reject *their* version of God. The kind of God that doesn't see the worth in a woman simply because her body was touched by a man. The kind of God that doesn't value the happiness of his creations.

I don't believe in that anymore.

God brought James into my life to show me what true happiness and love really is, so that when I was strong enough I could fight for it.

I'll fight for it now.

Because James gave me the strength and love I needed. Because James is who finally showed me that a good God does exist.

CHAPTER 47

Hallowed Be Thy Name

JAMES

"I went to The Shipwreck and told John what happened," Noreen says through the phone from the other side of plated glass. "He gave me your final pay, which I was going to use for bail, but . . ."

I rub my chin, the stubble growing there longer than it's ever been. Maybe in a year I'll actually have a beard that isn't patchy as shit. "Yeah, well . . . we both know how that went."

She frowns and drops her head, defeated. "I'll just save it for you, then. Along with your guitars and—"

"What's the point, Noreen?" I ask harsher than I mean to. "It's over! I'll be locked up for years and it's not like they have a record studio next to the cell block."

Tears spill down her face. "Do you want me to call them? Dave and the others, I mean. To tell them what happened?"

I shake my head. "Not yet, just—we were supposed to leave on Friday and I . . . give me another day. I suppose I'm still hoping for a miracle."

If I tell them, it will mean it's really over.

She offers a half-hearted smile. "Okay."

I twist the phone cord around my finger. "Have you . . . Do you know if she's okay?"

Aside from agonizing over my dashed dreams of being a rockstar, all I've thought about for days is Rebecca. If she's okay. If she's in danger. If someone's hurt her. If somehow they'll force her to marry Eric against her will. The thoughts turn my stomach as I sit here trapped behind this plate glass with chains around my ankles and wrists thinking about it.

She shakes her head. "They boarded up the window. I tried calling and rang the doorbell a few times, but they just—they wouldn't tell me anything. They basically told me to fuck off. But I'm sure she's up there. I can see the lights turning on and off through the window sometimes."

I rest my head in my hands, my heart aching. "She would've been better off if she never met me."

"Hey!" Noreen chastises into the phone, her finger jabbing the glass. "You were the best thing to happen to her. It may not seem like it, James, but you saved her."

I scoff and drag my hand down my face. "Hardly."

"You did. That poor girl was starving, and you fed her. She was being tortured, and you helped her find relief when you could. You showed her what real love is. Not the twisted, fucked-up version she grew up believing."

"But what if they hurt her?"

Noreen shakes her head. "She'll fight back. She's strong. You helped her be strong."

THANK FUCK I'm used to sleeping in the van, because if I'm going to have to sleep on an inch-thick mattress on a metal slab for the next few years, at least I'm prepared for it. I desperately wish I had a pad of paper and a pen. To occupy myself, I've been composing—my fingers strumming invisible strings as the sounds dance around in my head.

I like to imagine Becks dancing to the beat. Her feet making some complicated little routine during a riff, or her spinning like a top to the bass beat. What I would give to see her dance again.

"Walton?"

Officer Jerkwad is back. "What now?"

He unlocks the cell door and holds it open. "You're out."

I sit up. "You're transferring me?"

He shakes his head. "No, dipshit, you're out. Charges were dropped."

Eyes darting around, I stuff my finger in my ear, sure I haven't heard him right. "Wait . . . what?"

The officer rolls his eyes and steps back. "You must have a guardian angel or something, kid, because you've just been granted a miracle."

Blonde hair and green eyes burn bright in my mind's eye. I do have a guardian angel and her name is Rebecca.

"Oh and kid?" the officer calls.

I turn. "Yeah?"

"Leave and never come back. Understand?"

"I have no intention to." But not before I get my girl.

CHAPTER 48

Tiny Dancer

REBECCA

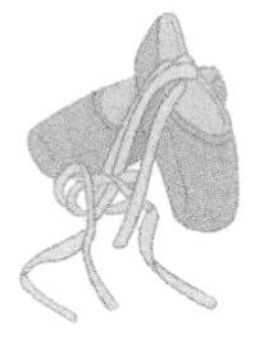

My mother enters my room late in the morning. Or at least, I think it's the morning. She carries the repaired wedding dress in her arms and hangs it back up on my closet door. I stare at it and she stares at me.

She's waiting for me to say something. Maybe she's waiting for me to try and tear it apart again. But it won't help me at this point. I sigh. "It's beautiful, Mom. Your best work. I'm sorry I didn't see that before."

Breathing deeply, her shoulders relax and she smiles. Crossing the room, she wraps her arms around me and hugs me softly. Delicately. It's so very unlike her that I'm taken by surprise, not sure how to hug her back.

"Sweetheart, I'm so glad you've decided to come back to us. We only want what's best for you. You know that, right?"

Somehow I don't think locking me up and knocking me unconscious was what's best for me, but I nod and smile at her. "Yes, I know. I'm sorry."

"Oh, Rebecca," she simpers. "Sex? Violence? Satan worshipers? How did it get this far?"

"I wasn't strong enough to resist the devil's temptation. Please forgive me?" It's all bullshit, I know, but she's eating it up. Maybe she'll actually let me out of here.

She caresses the same cheek she slapped. "We've got a long way to go for forgiveness, but I think you're finally back on the right path." She stands and smooths her wrinkle-free skirt. "Right, now, go get yourself cleaned up and dressed, then I can come back in and help you cover those bruises with some makeup."

She walks toward the door.

"Wait," I say, tensing and glancing at the wedding dress. No, it can't be today. It can't be. "Where are we going?"

"Your graduation ceremony. Everyone will be expecting you to be there and I'm not about to let people in on what happened on the weekend. What would people say? It's an embarrassment for Holy Grace. We've already had enough trouble figuring out what to say to the congregation. The Corbleys would be so embarrassed. No, you'll go to the ceremony as expected, get your diploma and come right home or suffer the consequences. It will be your chance to show your father and I that you really mean it when you say you want forgiveness."

My eyebrows lift, causing my bruises to throb. It's been almost a week? It feels like longer. I should have asked for proof that James was freed. How can I possibly trust them all after what happened? What if he's rotting away in that cell? If he's out, will he try to come for me?

Once she's gone, I shower and pull something my mom would approve of out of the closet. It's not like it matters anyway, I'll be wearing a graduation gown, but I don't want to chance making them mad. I don't want them to send me away to that awful place in that awful van. At least this hell is familiar.

I sit at my desk and look in the mirror. What would the old Rebecca say if I told her how different her life would be by graduation? She wouldn't believe any of it, surely. I pin back the front of my hair and wince as the back of my hand touches the blister at my temple. I reach toward my music box for a hair barrette. The top lifts and the little ballerina begins to spin to her sad song.

Beautiful, graceful, delicate . . . trapped. I wrap my fist around the bottom of her pointed legs, the music starts to skip, her loop desperate to continue on, but I pull her up sharply and the room is quiet.

"There's a whole world outside of this little box," I whisper. "I'd hate for you to never see it."

The door clicks and I quickly stuff the little ballerina into my pocket and slam the music box closed. My mother enters with a basket of makeup and immediately sets to work covering the bruises and blisters, either not caring when I cringe away from her touch or not noticing. I'm not sure which it is—I'm not sure which is worse.

HALF AN HOUR LATER, we're leaving the house, my parents on either side of me as they walk me toward the car. I can't stop from looking at Noreen's house—searching for him. But the van isn't there and I nearly trip over my own two feet. Maybe Pastor Campbell lied to me. If he did, he'll regret it. I'll make sure of it. I wasn't lying when I said I would make sure everyone knows what he did, no matter the consequences for myself. Even if that means being sent away.

The ride to the school is silent with not even the radio to ease the tension in the vehicle. My father hasn't said one word, but I can see him glance at me in the rearview mirror every so often. I can't believe he racked up a quarter of a million dollars in debt for the church. I nearly scoff as I think about the amount of sermons I've attended stressing the importance of "planting the seed" by handing over part of the household income, but this? This is madness.

We pull into the parking lot and the ignition is turned off. My parents make no move to get out of the car. They simply sit and wait, so I wait with them. Finally, there's a knock on the window and I look up to see Eric's face. *Oh no.*

The doors unlock, and Eric pulls my door open for me. "Hi, Becca."

I want to scream in his face. I want to bite into the hand he offers me. To shout that I know what he's hiding. That would distract everyone enough that maybe I could get away. But even with how much I hate him, I won't do that. I'm not a bad person. I need to behave. Throwing a tantrum right now won't help me. "Hi."

"Eric will make sure you stay where you're supposed to be," my dad finally says. "Remember, Rebecca, this is your one chance to prove you're worthy of our forgiveness."

He can shove his forgiveness, but I can't possibly say that. I simply nod and take Eric's arm to be led toward the growing group of seniors being fitted with gowns and caps.

"You look nice," Eric offers.

I close my eyes, feeling beaten. "Thank you. So do you."

"Listen, Becca," he says, stopping us before heading into the crowd. "Can we just . . . start over? I know you don't love me, but I think you could. I can try to be more attentive. You can even keep dancing after the wedding. Would you like that?"

Months ago, I would've been thrilled at the idea that Eric would allow me to keep doing what I love after we got married. But now, knowing what I know, I could never be happy with him. And even if I could still dance it wouldn't matter. My happiness is not boiled down to being able to dance or not. It's having the freedom to do as I wish without needing to ask for his permission.

"Maybe instead of keeping me here like a prisoner you could find your own way to be happy."

He stops and spins me around. "What are you talking about?"

"I know," I say. "I know about you and Jeremiah."

His face drains of color and for a split second his grip slips on my arm, but when I try to pull away, he grasps me even tighter. "You don't know what you're talking about," he snarls through gritted teeth.

"I know that this marriage will never make either of us happy. I get that you need this. Why you and your father want this so desperately that he's willing to pay a quarter of a million dollars for it to happen."

His lips part and his eyes grow wide. Did he not know about the money?

"You could be happy, Eric. Actually happy. I was . . . for a time. Don't you want to live without hiding who you really are?"

His gaze darts over my face, his shoulders rising and falling rapidly. We look at each other for what feels like forever until finally he whispers. "I can't."

"Yes, you can."

Shaking his head, he looks past me over my shoulder. "I'm terrified of what they'll do to me. What they'll do to him."

I turn my head and see that Eric is watching Jeremiah with his parents from across the parking lot.

He laughs sardonically. "Can you believe that moron thought spray painting pentagrams everywhere would distract everyone enough to keep him and me a secret? It's ridiculous."

I smile softly. "He loves you, and sometimes we do crazy things for the ones we love." I see the wetness in his eyes, the wobbling of his chin. "I know you're scared. So am I."

He looks at me for so long I wonder if he might actually let me go. He finally blinks, takes a deep breath then pulls me toward the stage. "Come on, let's get this over with."

The ceremony is a blur of black gowns and half-hearted applause. The bright noon sun over our heads causes everyone to pant and fan themselves with their programs and sweat like it's going out of style. Through it all, Eric never lets go of my arm. He must have been warned I'm a flight risk. How else am I to interpret the vice grip on my arm as anything other than to stop me from running?

If he let go, I could run, but I wouldn't get far. Not in this heat and not after only eating a small bowl of oatmeal every morning for the past week. I doubt I'd even make it much past the parking lot. And Eric is a track star. He'd catch me before I could even blink.

As the ceremony draws to a close, we begin to line up one by one to walk across the stage. I spot Mary ahead of me, whose face is crinkled with concern as her eyes roam over the makeup covering my battered face. "Are you okay?" she mouths as I pass.

I try to tilt my head toward Eric, to how he's gripping me like a trophy. Can she see the extent of the bruises on my face? I've probably sweated off all of the makeup by now. But this might be my only chance to get help. "Help me," I mouth.

Mrs. Henry is organizing the queue to climb the stairs. She takes one look at me and Eric and shoos him back a few people.

"Sorry Mr. Corbley but there's a few names between Briar and yours. Off you go."

I can feel his hesitation, the subtle pinch of my fingers as he lets go. But before he goes he yanks me toward him again. "Rebecca, I—"

He stops. His eyes dart frantically over my face and he swallows hard. As if I can see the words forming, he clenches his jaw, biting back what he wants to say then releases me. A sharp breath exits through his nose and he turns to get into his place in line.

Shaking the blood back into my fingertips, I wonder what he

wanted to say, but a cool breeze rushes over my hot skin and blows through my hair. From here I can see the bleachers and the track. I remember how James appeared beside me his first day of school, smoke puffing up around him like a cloud. How he told me if I were his I'd never be cold because he would've given me his jacket.

I remember watching the track meet and James coming to stand next to me. Just standing, his presence an all-consuming vortex that I got caught in like a riptide. How the barest touch of his fingers on my ankle burns even now. How many more have I had since that day? Have I appreciated them all? Savored the glory of all of his touches and words and looks. I'm sure I could've done better.

"Rebecca Amelie Briar."

My head snaps away from the field to the stage. It's my turn. I grip the railing and pull myself up the stairs onto the platform. Looking back over my shoulder I see Mary speaking to Mrs. Henry and pointing, her eyes latching onto mine. Is she telling her I need help? Would she even be able to help me at this point?

As I walk toward the principal holding my phony diploma in one hand, there's a crackle over the outdoor speakers of the school. Music begins to blare—the synth melody and sharp beats of *Runaway* by Bon Jovi rippling over the crowd. Without James in my life, I wouldn't even have known the name of the song. The spectators and students all turn to each other, wondering what's happening. The principal in front of me flushes purple and brushes past to the stairs, as the other teachers on the stage don't quite know whether or not they should follow.

I look out over the sea of confusion and my heart stutters when I see it.

A black van.

I look back at the school, the speakers still blaring the catchy tune, every lyric giving me the strength to run.

The crowd is chaotic now, everyone out of their seats and people chattering noisily over the music. Then I see Eric. His eyes hold mine for a long tense moment, then he jerks his head toward the parking lot mouthing a single word. "Run." He turns to Mary, engaging her in the discussion about the disruption as his hand behind his back waves me away. He's giving me an opportunity. My heart swells. I wish I could tell him he has that same chance. I wish I could thank him, tell him I understand, but this is my only opportunity and I'm going to take it.

Jumping off the stage, my feet hit the grass and I run. Promises be damned. I run and run and run, ignoring the shouts from behind me. Ignoring the way the music cuts out as I'm halfway across the parking lot. My graduation cap flies off my head and my hair blows out behind me.

"Rebecca!"

An angry voice shouts my name, but I don't look back. I can't. Not now, not ever. If Eric chose to chase me, I'd be caught by now. He's not following me. He's giving me this chance to get away and I hope God has heard my prayers and will reward me with this ultimate act of mercy. The ignition turns over. A smile spreads across my face and I don't feel the pain of the bruises, just a fire in my soul. I'm almost there, just don't trip, don't trip, *don't trip*!

My hand grabs the silver handle, and it wrenches open, James's smiling face beams down at me and I want to fall to my knees and thank God. He holds out his hand and grabs me around the wrist to pull me inside. Then he floors it. The tires squeal as he pulls wildly out into traffic and maybe it's the adrenaline or euphoria or stress but I bury my face in his shoulder and sob.

"Shh!" he says, petting the top of my head with one hand while he drives with the other. "I've got you now."

I can't even bring myself to look where we are, the fear of someone grabbing me and pulling me back to that nightmare still present even though I'm surrounded by the familiar smell of him. Of leather and the woods and smoke.

It must be an hour later when I stop shaking, and James eases up on the gas.

"Angel, it's okay. No one's following us."

The van stops and he pries me off of him and his now soaked shirt. As he grasps my face, I look into his eyes. Those dark chocolate brown pools that somehow shine with a light from within.

My fingers tangle in his shirt, barely daring to believe he's really here. "James?"

He chuckles warmly. "Yeah, Becks, it's me."

I crush our lips together—a feverish desperation behind this kiss. My hands are everywhere, and so are his. Like we're both checking to make sure we made it out in one piece. His thumb brushes along my cheekbone and I wince.

He pulls back, head tilting as he takes in the caked-on makeup, the dark bruises just visible underneath. Tears well in his eyes and he inhales a sharp breath. "I'll never let anyone hurt you ever again. Never." James leans forward to place the most delicate kiss to my cheek before pulling back and looking me over. "Are you okay?"

I nod. "I will be."

"Good."

I tell him about Pastor Campbell. How my parents asked him to come and convince me to return back into the fold, to obey or suffer the consequences. How I promised if he was set free, I'd do whatever was asked of me.

"You lied?" James asks, startled. "You lied for me?"

"Sometimes a lie is necessary. But I may have had my fingers crossed in my pocket."

He grins and kisses me again. "Come on, the guys are already on the road. If we're lucky, we can catch up with them in

Nebraska for dinner. I've got some clothes in the back and some turkey sandwiches in the cooler."

My stomach growls and I laugh. "That sounds like the best thing I've heard all week."

I pull off the graduation gown and while tossing it over the bench seat, I feel something poke me from my pocket. Slipping my hand inside, my fingers clasp around plastic and tulle. My chest swells as I stare down at the little ballerina from my music box—her pretty painted face shining in the sunlight. I reach forward and loop her through one of the chains hanging around the rearview mirror where she sways happily.

James grins at the sight of it then grabs my hand and kisses my knuckles before I head back to change and eat. As we drive west, I can't help but stare at him—stare at this beautiful dark devil with the heart of a saint, the lips of a sinner, who showed me the path to my salvation.

And I'll never look back.

SIX MONTHS LATER

Epilogue

JAMES

The quiet doesn't bother me anymore.

Rebecca has been the calm to my storm. Whenever things get too noisy and crowded in my head, she's there to clear it all away—make me see the clear skies ahead. Things haven't been easy over the past six months, but they've been an adventure. And Rebecca and I have each other, together with the members of Carnal Sins, who weren't as reluctant as I had thought they might be at the idea of my girlfriend moving in with us when we first set out.

In fact, it was a massive relief to watch sweet, ballerina Rebecca fit in so well with a bunch of rough metalhead musicians. The guys have all taken her under their wing like a little sister. She's never mentioned it, but from the way she interacts with them all, I think she likes having older makeshift brothers. For fuck's sake, she even attempted to make a cake for Dave's birthday two weeks ago.

Rolling over in bed, I squint against the sunlight filtering in through the blinds, my hand landing on the empty space next to me. Her smell lingers, but her warmth is gone. It must be well after noon by now. She must have left hours ago to get to class, and while I always prefer to wake up to her mess of blonde hair tickling my chin, her absence reminds me to appreciate the time we do get with one another.

"Walton!" Joel yells from the hall. "Get your ass to the kitchen, pronto."

Rolling over to the side of the bed, I stretch my limbs and back, my muscles still sore from the two hour gig we played downtown last night, then I crack every knuckle like bubble wrap.

I pull on a pair of jeans and a T-shirt before heading toward the kitchen and straight for the coffee pot.

"Nice of you to join us," Keith says, grinning as I sit down at the kitchen bar.

I sip the burning coffee and sigh as my shoulder pops. "I wasn't aware that I was needed anywhere until nine o'clock tonight."

"Thought you might want to read this," Dave says, slapping down the *East Bay Chronicle* on the counter in front of me.

I take a look at the headline. "Cary Grant died? Bummer. *North by Northwest* was an awesome movie."

Dave rolls his eyes. "No, dipshit." He flips through the paper to the entertainment section. "Here."

When I look down, my picture is staring back at me, my hair whipped back like I just tossed my head, the guitar Noreen gave me slung low on my hips, the strap cutting across my chest. My heart begins to pound against my ribs as I read the title of an article about us: "Thrash Metal's Newest Stars."

"Holy shit, is this real?" I ask, grabbing the paper.

"Looks that way," Joel says, grinning like a loon.

Carnal Sins has been tearing up the Bay Area Metal Scene after arriving from the midwest six months ago. Impressing a Megaloud producer at a bar in Iowa, the four members (Dave Noblar, Keith Prentiss, Joel Thanger and James Walton) traveled west to record an EP. With the way Al Simpson has been speaking publicly about Megaloud's new dream team, expectations have been sky high, and when their EP dropped this past Tuesday, this metalhead reporter was worried they simply couldn't live up to the hype.

My stomach flips. Would the guys beat my ass if I threw up on the newspaper?

Well, I'm here to tell you that Carnal Sins is the greatest thing to hit thrash metal since the Big Four (Metallica, Slayer, Anthrax and Megadeath).

"Holy shit!" I yell, looking up at the guys' ecstatic faces before continuing to read.

Their sound is unique while also staying true to the fundamental sounds of metal music. Somehow, they pay homage to the greats that came before them, while defining their own path in the music industry. I was lucky enough to see them play live last night in Albany Hill and was completely blown away by the caliber of their performance. Their stamina was impressive, playing for a solid two hours, without breaks and with the kind of camaraderie you'd expect from a band who's been playing together for years.

Imagine my surprise to find out that lead guitarist (Walton), whose girlfriend (Becks Briar) graces the album cover, was only added to the group less than eight months ago. Two things I know for sure—First, I can't wait to have Carnal Sins's full-length debut album in my hands this spring, and second, Miss Briar better damn well be on that album cover as well or it'll break my heart.

The paper drops from my hands as I try to make sense of everything I just read. Being compared to the best and most well-known metal bands in the world? "It's . . . unbelievable."

"It's real," Dave says, "It's unbelievable but it's real."

A dozen emotions burst forth at once, and I'm not sure what to do first. I think of my mom and how proud she'd be. How I want to call Noreen and tell her about the show last night, and send her a copy of the article. But most of all, I want to show Rebecca.

"Listen," Keith says, leaning toward me, "I guess I owe you a beer. You were right. Putting Becks on the album cover was the best idea you had. And based on this? It seems like she's going to have a fan base all on her own."

I smirk. Keith grew up with parents a lot like Rebecca's and was worried that such a scandalous image might wreak havoc on her conscience. "It's all good, man. I know you were just looking out for her."

"Looks like you'll have to keep her close, or someone might try and steal her away from you," Joel teases.

I shake my head. "I'm not worried about it."

"Not at all?"

"Nope." I look up at them all and grin widely. "Because when they credit her on our debut album she'll be Becks Walton."

Epilogue

BECKS

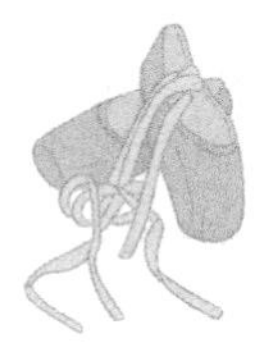

"Any plans for tonight, Becks?" Isabella asks me as we pack up our notebooks and pens and stuff them into our bags. Our history of fashion class is done for today and other than the exams over the next week, I have officially finished my first semester at community college.

We head for the doors. "James is taking me out to dinner. We haven't seen much of each other lately with him getting home so late and me either working at the shop or being in class."

"Oooh." She wiggles her eyebrows suggestively. "Big date night? I'm so jealous. Which restaurant? Maybe I'll go there myself and spy on you two through the bushes like the paparazzi."

I roll my eyes. "Please, we're hardly celebrities."

"I think that's about to change," she says with a smirk, pausing long enough to hold out a clipped newspaper article.

"What's this?"

She shrugs with a mischievous grin. "Just getting my daily gossip fix this morning, and who did I see on the front page of the entertainment section of the *East Bay Chronicle*?"

My heart flutters wildly as I snatch the article out of her

hands, my eyes focusing on the unbelievably sexy photo of James on stage at the show last night. I nearly start salivating at the sight of him, but first, I need to read the article.

Eyes flying over the words, the smile on my face grows wider and wider until I'm squealing, crying, and shimmying around the atrium. "I can't believe this!"

"People are going to start recognizing you on the street, in restaurants, at work, everywhere!"

"Sure they'll recognize James, but me? No way," I say, skimming over the article again as we continue walking.

Isabella frowns. "Are you forgetting that positively scandalous picture of you on the album cover? Everyone's going to know who you are. Especially now this article has referred to you by name."

Heat pricks at my cheeks as I think about the photo they used for the EP album cover. "I don't look like that all the time. That was the work of a very skilled makeup artist and hairstylist . . . Plus, it wasn't even all my own hair!"

She stops and points to me. "Ah ha! I knew that wasn't all natural."

"Anyway, if we do start to get recognized, I'm sure it'll be slow. Gradual. Not overnight."

"Oh my God," Isabella squeals, "I'm friends with celebrities!"

I giggle at her enthusiasm, but more than that, I feel like skipping. James and the guys have been working so hard and have been so nervous about whether they could possibly live up to everything Al has been saying about them. Their dreams are finally coming true. They're going to be rockstars.

And beyond that, they've all helped me realize what I want to be. That's what I'm doing here at Stoneman Community College. After a lifetime of never being able to choose what I wanted, all the way down to the very clothes I wore, I wanted a way to take control. When I got the job at the clothing store I realized just how fun it is to dress myself. Then when I saw the fashion courses at the college I knew that's what I wanted to do. I can only imagine what my parents would say about my choice of major.

It's not the big fancy college experience I thought I wanted a year ago—it's better. Because I'm paying for it myself and James has been nothing but supportive. It's been hard, sure. Especially with working at the clothing store full-time and taking classes at night and on weekends, but I know it'll all be worth it. And they even have a drop-in ballet class on Wednesdays. Plus, Isabella helped me set up a fundraiser, selling scarves we've made with leftover fabric. Giving all of the profit in James's mother's name to the local AIDS crisis center.

Sometimes the gravity of what I left behind pulls me back. Nightmares of being abducted by men in white uniforms or the end times often plague my nights. The shame and guilt that was indoctrinated into me for eighteen years resurfaces like an old wound splitting back open. Sometimes I know to expect it and sometimes it hits me out of nowhere. But James is always there to remind me that I'm safe and I'm loved. That I'm not ruined.

Isabella and I push through the double doors out into the setting sunlight, and just like he said he would, James is waiting for me, the black van parked along the curb, while he leans against it like he owns the place.

"There's lover boy," Isabella chimes in. "Seriously, Becks, there's no way girls aren't going to be throwing their panties at him on stage."

I choke back my laugh, thinking about how the only panties James had in his pocket last night were mine. I turn and squeeze my friend tightly. "I'll see you next week. Call me if you want to get together at the house to study?"

"Do you think Dave will be there?"

"Probably, I—" I stop and take in my friend's flushed cheeks and how she avoids my eyes. "Wait . . . do you *like* Dave?"

She shrugs. "I mean, he's a hot rocker dude. Who wouldn't?" The way her skin flames would indicate that there's a lot more going on there than she's admitting, but before I can ask her more questions she's backing away. "I'll talk to you soon. Have fun tonight."

I shake my head and break out into a run toward James. He grins that smug smile and scoops me up, spinning me around and peppering my face with kisses before setting me back down on my feet.

"Hey, angel." His fingers press into the skin of my waist. It's taken some time to get used to this new curvier, healthier body. For a while, I was sure it would make James regret bringing me along with him. But the way he's looking at me now—like he's ready to devour every inch of me, his eyes dark and burning in the setting sunlight, confirms he's as in love with me as he was six months ago. Maybe more.

"Hi."

"Ready to eat all the spaghetti and meatballs and garlic bread you can manage?" he asks.

My eyes close at the thought of eating bread. Of eating pasta with no one around who cares or criticizes. Fingers twirling in his hair, I nod. "Definitely. But first, I think congratulations are in order."

His head tilts. "For what?"

"For a certain glowing article in the *East Bay Chronicle*."

Sighing, he closes his eyes for a moment. "Let me guess . . . Isabella found it and showed you?"

I nod. He pulls away and opens the van door. "I wanted it to be a surprise. I was going to tell you tonight over dinner."

"I can act surprised," I offer as I jump up into the front seat.

He climbs in and shuts the door, but doesn't start the engine, his fingers instead beginning to tap on the steering wheel. He's nervous.

"James, are you okay?"

He turns to me and grabs my hand. "After today, after that article . . . everything might change. And to be honest, I'm a bit freaked out."

My chest tightens. "That's totally understandable. It's a huge deal. Life changing. Anything like that is scary." I know first hand how one thing can completely change your life.

"You know that no matter what happens, I want you with me, right?"

Tears prick at the backs of my eyes. "Of course I do."

He nods, his own cheeks flushed like he's trying to hold back his tears too. He takes a deep breath in and exhales. "Listen, umm . . . before we go—there's something . . . I know it's not the most romantic—" He stops, then reaches into his coat pocket to pull out a small black box.

With wide eyes, I watch as he pulls back the lid of the box to reveal a solitaire diamond set on a gold band.

"I know it's not much, and I know we're still young, so it doesn't have to be now. It could be in a month, a year, a decade . . . or, hell, we could drive to Vegas next week when we're both off and Elvis can do the honors. The point is, I want to marry you, Becks. I want you to take my name so that it doesn't hurt so much every time someone says the one your parents gave you. I want us to decide together how to live our lives without anyone else telling us what to do and who to be. Just you and me."

A joyous sob rips from my throat as the tears finally break free to spill down my cheeks in a rush. My heart is so full, my soul ablaze. "Yes!"

"You will?" he asks, eyebrows raised like he's surprised.

"Yes, yes, of course I'll marry you!"

His hand reaches behind my neck and pulls me in. Our lips

are desperate to translate all we're feeling in this moment to one another through their touch. When I'm breathless and dizzy, we pull away, our foreheads pressed together as the last rays of sun dip below the horizon.

"Are you sure, Becks? Are you positive you want this? Want me?" he whispers, thumb brushing along my heated cheek. Even after so much together, he still has a hard time believing he deserves to be loved.

"Yes."

He pulls back, eyes meeting mine. "How can you be sure?"

"Because loving you is like discovering the most amazing song, and even after hearing it a thousand times, it will always be my favorite."

THE END

Want More?

Thank you for reading *A Song of Sin and Salvation.* Want access to the bonus chapter? Scan the QR code below to sign up for my newsletter and download more of Rebecca and James. If you enjoyed the book a review would be very much appreciated as it helps other readers discover the story. For updates on future new releases or other works by L.H. Blake, please sign up for my newsletter via my website www.lhblake.com.

Praise for Where the Lights Lead

Have you ever read a book that had you completely hooked and invested in the story after only reading the prologue? Well that was this book for me.

KAYLIE H.

There are not enough stars for me [to] rate how good this book is. I actually cried when it ended and I didn't have any more to read.

Amazing characters, amazing plot, wondrous magic that stole my breath away.

DANA B.

I absolutely LOVED it! This book has some of the best character development and character relationships I've ever read! When I tell you I SCREAMED at the plot twist! I am not okay! Need book 2 already!

TAYLOR C.

Where the Lights Lead

A forgotten past, a spark between souls, and a light that calls from the dark.

Will Reed wants to break through the emotional fog after a terrible car accident. When Elora Green crashes into his life, he's sure she's the one he's been waiting for. Especially, since their meeting surfaces supernatural abilities. But with the abilities, comes enemies.

A hooded stranger with similar powers tries to kill them. Will and Elora must work together to survive and figure out what the stranger wants. Memories begin to flicker to life from the depths of their subconscious. Whatever lies there, it's something to kill for—something to die for.

Book 1 in The Elements Series, Where the Lights Lead is out now with the follow up book set to release fall of 2023. Available at retailers now!

Acknowledgments

Rebecca and James's story is so special to me. When the inspiration for these characters struck me, I was like a woman possessed. I had to get their story out into the world as fast as I could and I hope you love them as much as I do.

Phil, thank you so much for loving me no matter what. Your love of metal music and guitar knowledge finally paid off. I will admit that the image of you playing your red electric guitar when we first met has lived rent free in my head since that day and may have inspired some of this story. And to my three beautiful boys, I hope you grow up to be kind and respectful young men who always stand up against injustice and fight for freedom and choice.

A big thank you to my parents. Special shout out to my dad who drove a 1975 Chevy Vandurra like James. He outfitted the interior like a camper van by himself as a young carpenter. He and my mom used to go camping all the time and there are baby pictures of myself tagging along for the ride. The epilogue proposal is also inspired by my parents. My dad, who, on their way to an Italian restaurant, popped the question to my mother in the front seat. They've been married now for 42 years and their love for each other inspires me everyday.

A huge thank you to music artist Ethel Cain. Her album "Preacher's Daughter" was on repeat for the entirety of the writing process of this book. It's a hauntingly beautiful album about being the perfect daughter, the perfect Christian, the perfect American. Her messages ring very close to a lot of Rebecca's story and I highly recommend giving it a listen.

To Sam at Ink and Laurel. Thank you for putting up with my indecisiveness over the cover design. You brought my vision to life, even if I changed my mind and we needed to start from scratch again. I couldn't be happier with how it turned out. It's so beautiful it makes me cry.

To Theo Scott who did the beautiful bedroom scene art, you are so ridiculously talented. I can't wait to watch your art grow and develop. If anyone is interested in more of their art you can find them on Instagram @218s.art.

Maxi Weismantel did the art for the Carnal Sins album cover and I am obsessed. I wish you could illustrate every page of this book. If you would like to see her other art, her Instagram handle is @max.wise.art.

To my editor, Britt, you made the process of editing a joy. Your knowledge and expertise really made me feel like I was in such capable hands. Your suggestions and enthusiasm for this story gave me so much confidence and I can't wait to work on more projects together.

Beta readers, y'all are the real MVPs. You read the messy, unedited vision of this story and helped sort through it until it came out polished. Thank you to Joleen J, Lacy P, Annie A, Prissy, Jenny G, Anik, Natalie E, and Brandy N.

A huge thank you to Rachel for her sensitivity reading and insight. Your suggestions were so valuable and I hope helped the story feel more authentic.

Letizia F thank you for your infectious enthusiasm, your

hilarious memes and your love for this book. I'm so happy to have met you and become such good friends. Your insights, music knowledge and guitar suggestions made this feel so much more authentic.

To WH Lockwood. Not only is your writing so inspiring but knowing you has given me the courage to push myself in my craft. To challenge the way I write and try new things. Your insights into this book helped improve it greatly and I'm forever thankful. I wish you didn't live on the other side of the world.

Becky Q. Another amazing woman who lives way too far away. I couldn't think of a better person to share my protagonist's name. You are a ray of sunshine and your expertise and vibrant enthusiasm for this book always puts a smile on my face. I'm so glad to know you. Your talent is insane and the world is not ready for Rebecca Quinn.

Letizia L. Girl, I love you. From day one you were there to cheer me on while writing this book. To push me through when the story got too emotionally taxing. When I had to rearrange a million things and, gasp, cut whole chapters, you were there to keep me from losing my mind. You're always the voice of reason and my biggest cheerleader. And you do so much for me outside of writing too. You're an amazing friend and I'm still trying to figure out what I did right in this life to have you fall into it so effortlessly.

Finally, to the reader. Thank you so much for taking a chance on this book. I sincerely hope you enjoyed this story. If any of you grew up in a situation like Rebecca, I hope you are happy now. I hope you are loved and I hope you know that you are not to blame for the bad behaviors of men. And if you grew up in a situation like James, where maybe you felt like you were unwanted, worthless or struggling. I hope you know that you deserve love because you are worthy.

Thank you for supporting indie authors as we work so hard to provide entertaining stories that may otherwise have never been told. Please feel free to leave an honest review on your preferred platform.

About the Author

L.H. Blake is a loving wife and mother to three beautiful boys, as well as her dog Lucy. She is a full time high school teacher living in rural Ontario, Canada. An avid reader and creative writer since childhood, Blake has always loved fantasy and romance stories. This is her second full length published novel and plans to release two more this year. Outside of books, Blake has been involved in the arts her whole life with passions for dance, musical theater, crafting, embroidery and backyard astronomy. Visit L.H. Blake's website: www.lhblake.com

instagram.com/lhblake.author

tiktok.com/@lhblake.author

Printed in Great Britain
by Amazon